*I ho, enjoy this book*

# settlement

*anne Stormont*

# ANNE STORMONT

Rowan Russell Books

Copyright © 2018 Anne Stormont

The moral rights of the author have been asserted.

Published in 2018 by Rowan Russell Publishing
United Kingdom

All Rights reserved. No part of this publication may be reproduced, distributed, or transmitted, in any form or by any means, including photocopying, recording, or other electronic or mechanical methods without the prior written consent of the publisher, except in the case of brief quotations embodied in critical reviews and certain other non-commercial uses permitted by copyright law.

This is a work of fiction. Locations are mainly real but some are imagined. All the characters are fictitious.

Cover design and formatting by J D Smith Design
Editing by John Hudspith Editing Services

Published by Rowan Russell Publishing

Printed by Lightning Source

All enquiries to rowanrussellbooks@gmail.com

First printing, 2018

ISBN 978-0-9929303-6-3

**Also by Anne Stormont**

Change of Life

Displacement

## Acknowledgements

Thank you to all family members and friends who continue to offer encouragement and support to me and my writing – you know who you are.

Special thanks to: Margaret Bainbridge, Val McIntyre, Jan Hendry, Carole Hodgson-McAlpine, Debbie Smith and Maggie Christensen for offering their helpful opinions on early versions of the book's cover. And to Iain Stormont for ruthless proof-reading,

I'd also like to thank both my wonderful editor John Hudspith who accepts nothing but the best, and my talented book designer Jane Dixon-Smith who has ensured that the book looks good both inside and out.

# Chapter One

*Jack*

It's not the way I would have chosen to die, but I'm glad it's nearly over. The pain from the beatings has gone way beyond what I can bear. This hasn't stopped my captor having one last go. But now, at last, he's pointing a gun at me.

Or rather he's waving it about. I tell him to get on with it, but he says he doesn't want it to be quick and he doesn't want me to know when he's going to do it. It might be now, but then again it might not.

I'm not sure how long he's had me here. I've tried to keep track, but the periods of unconsciousness after the beatings haven't helped.

And, as to where I am, I guess I'm not that far from the Edinburgh street where I was taken, but I have little hope of rescue. Bridget's the only person who'll notice I'm missing and she'll put that down to my fickle nature. And even if the alarm is raised, my phone's been disposed of, so there's no chance of using its signal to locate me.

I take refuge in thoughts of Rachel, as I've done throughout my time of captivity. I try to relive the good times, and I tell her I still love her. I try not to dwell on the fact it's over between us but I do apologise to her for making such a stupid hash of things.

I first met Rachel Campbell when I hauled her from a river one January night about a year-and-a-half ago. I'd only recently arrived on the Scottish island of Skye. Newly retired from the police following a heart attack, I'd bought a house to renovate and use as a holiday place, or maybe move into permanently if I didn't miss life in Edinburgh too much.

Rachel's croft house is close to mine, and the river that nearly claimed her life runs alongside it. She'd got into difficulties while rescuing one of her sheep from the fast-flowing water. She'd lost her grip and I got to her just in time.

I'd never met anyone like her before. Yes, my ex-wife and the other women I'd been with during and since my marriage were all strong, independent, high-achievers – as Rachel was. But Rachel was no city-dwelling, suit-wearing, promotion-seeking professional working in policing, politics or PR. She was a crofter, a writer and artist. She was small, with wild red hair, and jeans and wellies were her outfit of choice. And she bore the worst bereavement of all – the death of her son – with the most amazing courage. She was also the most honest and direct person I'd ever known.

I admit I was an idiot, thinking it was all going to be straightforward and happy ever after, and then reacting badly when it wasn't. I didn't read the situation correctly – so much for all my years as a Detective Inspector. I was also dishonest, didn't have the guts to explain what was wrong when she asked me. But then, I'm sure if you were to ask my ex-wife or any of my ex-lovers, long term relationships never were my strong point. I may be fifty-eight, but I guess I'm no wiser than an eighteen-year-old when it comes to women.

Our relationship developed slowly. When I first knew her, she'd been sad and a bit lost. Not only had she recently lost her mother, but she was also still grieving the death of her soldier son killed in action a couple of years earlier. But over the months that followed she seemed to find her way again. Going to spend the summer with her brother in the Middle East was a turning point and she came back changed; a new, noticeably different woman.

It was after she got back that we became lovers. It was wonderful at first, but like I say I got things wrong. Rachel continued to change. She moved on and flourished, and all she wanted from me was love and support. But I failed her.

I've never loved anyone the way I love Rachel and the one thing I dreaded was hurting her. But I did it anyway.

We both had baggage. The difference was Rachel dealt with hers and moved on. I didn't.

And now that my past has caught up with me, my biggest regret is I probably won't get the chance to tell her how I really feel.

I want to say all the things I should have said to her before she left. Things like how much I will always love and admire her, how proud I am of her. I want to tell her she was right about me, and not to waste a minute grieving for me when I'm gone.

## *Rachel*

When I heard what had happened to Jack it was like hearing about the death of my son all over again. Although, when Finlay died, there'd been no uncertainty. He was definitely gone, blown up by an IED while serving as a Royal Marine Commando in Afghanistan. But with Jack no-one seemed sure at first. He'd been shot, that much was certain, and he was on his way to hospital with terrible injuries.

I'd only got back a few days before. I'd been away for three months working in Israel and Palestine, and I'd expected Jack to be at home on Skye when I returned. He hadn't told me he'd taken a job with the Historic Crimes Unit in Edinburgh. But then that wasn't surprising as he'd broken off contact while I'd been away.

And now it seemed he'd been shot by some notorious

criminal from his past. I struggled to process it all, struggled not to faint, struggled not to throw up. I was devastated. I loved him so much. I couldn't lose him as well.

I wanted to go to him right away. But it was night time. He was in Edinburgh and I was hundreds of miles away on Skye. I was persuaded to wait until morning.

I went to bed but I didn't sleep. My body was flooded with adrenalin and anxiety, my head still full of questions, confusion ... and Jack Baxter.

What was it that was troubling him so much during the months leading up to me leaving? Why wouldn't he talk to me about it? And why would anyone want to kill him?

Was what had happened to him down to me? Had he taken the job in Edinburgh because he believed things really were over between us?

Why had it gone so wrong?

Why could he not support my return to the Middle East? Couldn't he see how important my work is to me? Why couldn't he trust me?

And when I couldn't bear the circling questions any longer, I tried to focus on the things I was certain of. Things like not only had he saved my life, but he'd helped make it so much better. Things like how much I loved him and wanted to be with him. And that although my work on the croft, on the children's books, and on this new Israel-Palestine project meant a lot to me, without Jack there'd be no joy in any of it.

I was also certain that I should have tried harder to put things right.

And I was distraught that now it seemed I wasn't going to get the chance.

# Chapter Two

*Four Months Earlier*

*Rachel*

I was up early on the morning of the wedding because wedding or not, all the usual jobs on the croft still had to be done. I watched the dawn break over the loch as the hens bustled out of the coop and squabbled over their breakfast. Then, accompanied by my sheepdog, Bonnie, I fed the sheep and checked the pregnant ewes.

I was impatient to get all the jobs done and to get on with the exciting part of the day. It felt like a turning point – a turning point towards better things.

But, I didn't realise at the time that it was also when the cracks in my relationship with Jack would start to appear, or rather it was when they began to appear more obvious.

No, all I felt on that April morning, as I looked up at the pink-streaked sky, was happy and hopeful.

And, once back indoors, as I stood at the living-room window with my coffee, looking at the view of sea, mountains and cliffs, I felt love and gratitude along with my earlier feelings of hope and happiness.

Even though it had now been six years, I was still grateful to be back on Skye, and loved living in the house where I grew up. I'd returned after my divorce in 2008. And despite having spent the previous thirty years living in Edinburgh, my roots here on the island remained deep.

I felt a profound and proud love as I thought of my daughter Sophie and a fierce, almost overwhelming, love for my beautiful, four-month-old granddaughter, Miriam. And I was so glad and grateful that with Sophie and Steven now living here, the croft would remain in the family in the future.

I also felt an aching love for my darling son, Finlay. It was nearly two-and-a-half years since his death at the age of twenty-four. I now accepted I'd never get over the loss, but I was thankful that we'd at least been able to lay him to rest here on the island.

And then there was my love for Jack.

All the wedding guests were seated. I glanced around, smiled at my best friend, Morag, and her husband, Alasdair, and many of the other guests who looked my way. And I had to admit the community hall looked very pretty, quite transformed from its usual basic functionality. As well as Jack and me, there'd been a whole team of friends and neighbours who'd worked most of the previous evening to get it ready.

And now, with the scent of roses and freesias filling the air, the April sun streaming in through the big window at the front of the hall, and the sound of the piper preparing to play, the wedding was about to start.

I don't know why I felt nervous. Sophie and Steven loved each other and it was wonderful to see my daughter so happy. It was wonderful to see her at all. I felt a pang as I remembered our estrangement but I pushed it away. We were reconciled and that was all that mattered.

Miriam, who was nestled asleep in my arms, didn't stir when the piper began playing and we all stood up.

As Sophie walked down the aisle accompanied by her father, I let out a little gasp. She looked so beautiful. My brother Jonathan, standing behind me, squeezed my shoulder. I glanced round at him, and as I did so I saw that his friend, Eitan, was looking at me. He smiled. I turned to the front again, flustered, feeling more like a fifteen-year-old girl than a fifty-five year-old grandmother. And I sensed Jack standing beside me, watching.

Of course, I'd been expecting Jonathan and his wife – Deb – and their teenage children – Gideon and Mari – to come from Israel for the wedding.

But what I hadn't expected was Jonathan's call a few days earlier to say Eitan was coming with them and would it be okay if he came to the wedding. I said it was fine, said it would be good to see him again. And it was. It was very good. Eitan Barak, talented artist, large, loud, infuriating and opinionated charmer, and the man who, at the end of my visit to Israel the previous year, had suggested we get married.

Miriam stirred in my arms and I stroked her soft little face as she yawned, displaying pink, toothless gums. I smelled her gorgeous, rose-scented baby breath. She opened her eyes and looked at me and, as the music of the pipes died away and her parents joined hands in front of the registrar, my granddaughter giggled. The delightful sound made everyone laugh and I relaxed as the ceremony got underway.

After the signing of the register, we all moved outside. The spring sunshine and unusually light breeze meant it was pleasant enough to do so. Across the single track road in front of the hall was a large expanse of grass where we all assembled. Skye was in full show-off mode. Guests unfamiliar with the island exclaimed at the view over a sparkling Loch Dunvegan and onwards to the Western Isles and the hills of Harris.

I noticed one guy, standing away from the main group of guests. He caught my eye as he was dressed casually in jeans and a waterproof jacket and I didn't remember him from the ceremony. He wasn't looking at the view but seemed to be staring directly at me. He raised a camera to his eye and I saw him press the button as Jack appeared beside me.

"Do you want me to tell him to get lost?" Jack said.

"No, no, it's fine. He's probably a tourist – you know what some of them are like. They think Skye's one big theme park and us locals are acting a part."

"If you're sure."

"Once a policeman, always a policeman," I said, smiling at him.

I turned to watch my daughter as she stood with her new husband, her arm linked through his as they posed for photographs. Both of them laughing as they tried to follow the official photographer's instructions.

Sophie looked so lovely, the cream silk of her wedding dress complementing her red hair and fair complexion perfectly.

But it was more than the dress, more than the hair and the make-up, Sophie's loveliness came from within. My previously troubled, angry, and rather lonely daughter was happy at last. And that made me feel a level of contentment I had almost given up on ever feeling again. I shifted Miriam to my other hip and turned so she could see her parents. "Your mummy and daddy look very happy," I said to her.

"They do, don't they," said Peter, who'd appeared at my side.

I turned to my ex-husband. "Steven's right for her, isn't he?" I looked away, tears in my eyes.

"Hey," Peter said, putting his hand under my chin and turning me to look at him. "No more crying. You did enough of that during the ceremony."

I almost managed a smile.

"She's going to be fine and so are you and her." Peter put his arm round my shoulder. "She never really blamed you for the divorce or for Finlay. It was anger – anger and grief – that made her behave the way she did."

"I know. I know, and I'll always be grateful for your help with that, for bringing her up here so we could talk about everything …" I was crying again. "Sorry," I said. "I promised myself I wouldn't cry, but …"

Peter pulled me closer to his side. I leant my head on his

shoulder as he stroked my hair. "Today was always going to be emotional," he said. "I feel it too – Fin's absence. I actually went to his grave this morning, had a chat."

I looked up at him. "Did you?"

"Yes, a bit of a catch-up and to let him know he'd be especially missed today. But I realised as I chatted to him, he *is* here in a way, isn't he? He's always with us – his parents, his sister, his niece." He moved slightly to stroke Miriam's face. "And we'll all make sure this young lady knows all about her uncle too."

"Sorry to interrupt," Jack said, as he walked up to us. "But Miriam's presence is required for the photographs. Then it'll be you two next." He stretched out his arms. "I'll take her," he said. "Let you two finish your conversation." And, as he nestled the baby in one arm, he raised his other hand to stroke the tears from my face. "Here," he said, reaching into his pocket and producing a white cotton handkerchief. "Take this and get ready for your photo call."

And as I watched Jack walk away with Miriam, more tears came. I dabbed them away with his handkerchief.

"I'm pleased for you, you know," Peter said. "Pleased things are right with Sophie and that she'll be up here on Skye with you, and pleased you've got Jack."

"I wouldn't say I've *got* Jack exactly. We've only known each other for a year and a bit and we've only been ... been close for a few months."

"So you're not thinking of moving in together, settling down on a more permanent basis?"

"What? No! No, not all. We're nowhere near anything like that." I knew I'd snapped at Peter. My level of annoyance at what he'd said surprised even me.

Peter put up his hands. "Okay, okay. Sorry, I didn't meant to—"

But we were saved from having to continue the conversation when our names were called. We were needed for the photo shoot.

# Chapter Three

*Rachel*

Photos over, we all moved inside for celebratory drinks and a chance to mingle during the pre-dinner lull. Morag, Alasdair and their team of volunteer guests had done a great job of moving the chairs so they were now in place around the tables.

After I'd checked with the caterers that all was in order for the meal and the bar, I noticed Lana waving and walking towards me. It was good to see her. Lana Edwards had been my literary agent for many years, but she was also a good friend and I was touched she'd come all the way from Glasgow to be at the wedding.

"Congratulations!" she said, as she hugged me. "Or whatever you say to the mother of the bride."

"Oh, I'm happy to accept congratulations," I said. I looked round the room. "This all feels like quite an achievement."

"Come on," Lana said. "Let's get a glass of bubbly."

"Slainte mhath," I said, using the Gaelic toast for good health as we clinked glasses. "I'm surprised you haven't got yourself a drink already. Not like you to be so slow."

"I got waylaid by a handsome man," Lana said.

"Oh, you did, did you?" I smiled at her. "Don't you think Sophie and Steven's friends are a bit too young for you?"

"No, I don't actually," Lana said. "But no, it wasn't one of the young guys. It was your brother's rather lovely friend, Eitan. I must say I do understand what you saw in him. He is very attractive. I certainly would." She wiggled her eyebrows suggestively.

"Stop!" I said, laughing. "You're terrible. You've only recently got over Mark. And besides, my life's complicated enough without you hooking up with my brother's best friend."

"I didn't need to get over Mark. I dumped *him*, remember. He got far too serious which was a shame. I thought he was a keeper, but once he mentioned marriage that was it. Anyway that's in the past. Eitan's the present – and what a lovely present." Lana grinned at me.

I knew Lana was just being Lana, knew she was only having a bit of fun, but talking about Eitan like that made me uncomfortable.

"You're something else," I said, trying to hide my discomfort.

But she knew me well. "Oh, come on, lighten up. I'm joking. Anyway what would it be to you if I did make a move on the guy? Eitan asked you to stay in Israel, but you chose Jack."

I held up a hand. "Eh, for the record, I didn't choose Jack over Eitan. I chose Scotland over Israel. Jack and I were no more than friends at that stage."

"If you say so. And you've no regrets? No regrets now you've seen Eitan again?"

"No, of course not."

"And Jack's okay, is he? About Eitan being here?"

"He's fine," I said. "Or at least he's trying to be."

"Can't be easy for him seeing you being all hospitable and friendly to the guy you were in a relationship with before him."

"It wasn't a relationship. It was—"

"Sex – exactly – good sex, the first sex you'd had in ages—"

"Okay, enough," I said. "Eitan's here as a family friend, come to experience some Scottish hospitality. After the wedding I'll wave them all off on their Scottish holiday. The rest – Eitan and me – that's in the past. Okay?"

"Okay."

"Now, can we leave it?"

Lana looked thoughtful. "Hmm, I can leave it. But will you be able to?"

"Able to what?"

"Will you be able to leave it – with Eitan – when you're back in Israel in a few weeks' time?"

I put my hands to my face as a rush of excitement flowed through me. "You mean—"

"Yes," Lana beamed at me. "The publishers have confirmed. Your proposal has the go ahead and they're fine with the dates you suggested. I would have messaged you, but I wanted to tell you in person."

"Oh, Lana, I can't believe it. That is so good."

"Isn't it? Well done, you. I knew you'd be right for this project of theirs. I've got the paperwork with me. I thought I'd call in tomorrow before I set off for home, get your signature, if that's okay."

"Of course it is."

We didn't get a chance to discuss the good news any further as the best man announced that we should all make our way to our tables as the speeches were about to begin.

"To be continued," Lana said, as she walked away. I watched her as she approached Morag. Next thing I knew, Morag was shifting place cards around and Lana was taking a seat opposite Eitan at the table he was sharing with my brother and his family. She winked at me as she sat down.

# Chapter Four

*Rachel*

Sophie had finished feeding Miriam and was settling her for a nap in her buggy behind the top table as I approached. We both stood for a moment looking at the already drowsy baby.

"Happy?" I said, looking at my daughter.

"More than I can believe." Sophie hugged me and I held her close.

The last twelve months had been as eventful for Sophie as they'd been for me. She'd met Steven through her work as a BBC researcher in Glasgow, when her team was preparing a documentary on injured Afghanistan veterans returning to Scotland. Steven, like Finlay, had been involved in an IED explosion. He'd survived, but he'd lost both legs below the knee. Falling in love with this ex-commando and getting pregnant by him hadn't been part of Sophie's plan.

Peter was already at the top table when I took my seat beside him. His notes for his speech lay on the table in front of him. "How are you holding up?" he asked.

"I'm fine. Sophie's happy, so I am. But I'll be glad when this bit's over." I nodded towards his notes.

"Yes, me too – I hope I can hold it together."

But he'd no need to worry. Peter, a Q.C., whose natural habitat was the courtroom, was in his element as he addressed the guests. Traditionally, the father of the bride says good things about his daughter and expresses how glad he is with her choice of husband before proposing a toast to the couple. But Sophie had wanted a bit more than that and Peter had already shared with me the gist of what his speech would contain.

So I was as prepared as I could be for what followed. Peter began by paying tribute to Steven, not only for his bravery as a Marine, but also for his fortitude in recovering from the terrible injuries he'd sustained. Peter also paid tribute to Steven's former comrades who'd joined us at the wedding.

All of this was hard enough to listen to. But then Peter went on to talk about Finlay. He spoke of the special bond between Sophie and her brother, and then, with a hand on my shoulder he spoke a bit about what his loss had meant to us and how much we missed him, not only on this special day but every day. When he proposed a toast to Finlay and to other absent friends, I gave up all hope of not ruining my make-up and let my tears fall.

The rest of his speech was much lighter in tone and included a surprise slideshow of photos from Sophie's childhood. There was a lot of laughter and the happy mood was compounded by Steven's and the best man's speeches which followed.

During the meal, the relaxed atmosphere continued. I was sitting between my new son-in-law and Peter, and being at the top table gave me a good view of the room. The guests were all seated at circular tables and it was lovely to see my local friends chatting with guests from further afield. Or rather it was mostly lovely.

I told myself it wasn't jealousy that I felt as the meal came to an end and I watched Lana put her hand on Eitan's arm and gaze into his eyes as she flirted with him. But I did wish she'd stop it. It wasn't that I thought it would be making Eitan uncomfortable, quite the reverse, and that's what I didn't like.

Perhaps Eitan sensed me watching. He looked over at me, and raised his glass. I gave a small nod of acknowledgement, then found myself glancing at Jack who was seated at the same table.

It was ridiculous, I know, but I hoped he hadn't seen. I needn't have worried. He appeared to be deep in conversation with Carla.

Peter followed my gaze. "Well done, Jack," he said. "He seems to be coping."

"Coping? You mean Carla might be hard work?" I couldn't keep the sarcasm out of my voice. This was the closest Peter had ever come to criticising the woman he left me for.

"No, that's not what I meant." Peter's tone was good-humoured, but he gave me one of, what I used to call, his 'courtroom' looks. "It's simply that I can't see them having a lot in common and Carla can be quite—"

"Overbearing, opinionated, insensitive." I looked at my ex-husband and knew he could see I was teasing him. I no longer felt any bitterness about his final betrayal. Carla hadn't been his first infidelity, but she had been the most serious and she was the one who ended our marriage. A twenty-nine-year marriage I'd struggled to hold on to and tried very hard to save.

"I was going to say full-on and enthusiastic. She loves to talk about the Arts and culture."

I'd only ever heard Carla talk about herself, her expensive holidays, shopping habits and money. But all I said was, "And you thought Jack wouldn't be up to such lofty topics?"

"No, all I meant was I can't see them having much to chat about."

"Oh, I'm sure as a former policeman, Jack can talk to just about anyone. He's met all sorts and he can be very charming."

Peter nodded, finished the wine in his glass. "Like I said, he seems like a good guy. I only commented out of relief."

"Relief?"

"Carla wasn't all that keen on coming to the wedding. She didn't think it would be her sort of thing, said she wouldn't know anyone. She would have preferred it if Sophie had gone for a big Edinburgh wedding and the guest list had included all our friends. I had to do a lot of persuading. She didn't fancy Skye as a destination."

"Not her usual sort of holiday island, I'm sure. And I can see that this is a much smaller affair, with a lower class of guest than her ideal. But it's what Sophie and Steven wanted and Carla's always made such a big thing of getting along with Sophie, I'm surprised she wouldn't want to be here to reinforce that point ... to me at any rate."

"Whatever, I'm grateful to Jack for making an effort to make her feel included." And with that Peter excused himself to go in search of some more wine.

I looked over again at Jack. He was laughing at something Carla had said. I was sure he was merely being polite, but it was good to see him looking so laid-back. And I found myself wondering if maybe I'd been mistaken thinking there'd been something troubling him over the last couple of months.

Certainly, when I'd recently asked him about it, he'd assured me there was nothing wrong and said that I wasn't to worry. I tried not to. But I couldn't deny that I'd felt shut out, that I'd sensed a disconnection beginning between us.

Steven's voice interrupted my thoughts. "I wanted to thank you, Rachel," he said as he returned from chatting to some of the guests and sat down beside me. "It's all ... perfect."

"You're welcome," I said. "But it wasn't only me who made today happen. It was Morag and Alasdair and Jack and lots of other folks too."

"I know and I'm grateful to them all. But I wasn't only talking about the wedding. I meant thanks for giving us this chance – me and Sophie – handing over some of the running of the croft, offering us the land to build our house on, letting us live with you in the meantime. We – *I* won't let you down."

"I'm sure you won't," I said. "I'm delighted you both accepted."

"Who wouldn't want to live and work in such a beautiful place?" Steven paused. "To be honest, your offer ... it ... it saved me."

"Saved you?"

"Yeah, don't get me wrong, the military recovery centre I was sent to was great, but none of their suggestions as to what sort of work I could do filled me with enthusiasm. But this chance you've given me to do challenging and useful work, it's more than I ever hoped for." He cleared his throat before continuing. "And you've given me Sophie. It's all perfect."

I'd only known Steven for a short time, but I already loved him. Loved him for the good man he was, but also for how much he loved my daughter. He'd helped her heal, helped her come to terms with the fact her father and I had divorced, and helped her move on with grieving for her beloved younger brother. And by doing so he'd made it possible for Sophie and me to mend our relationship. He'd given me more than I'd ever be able to give him.

"It's me who's grateful ... grateful Sophie has you. And, as for the croft," I said, "you're doing me a favour. It'll be good to hand over some of the hard work, especially some of those all-nighters and early mornings during lambing."

"Don't listen to her," said Sophie, slipping her arm through Steven's as she too came back from speaking to some of the guests and sat down beside us. "She's been pretty hopeless at delegating so far."

"Guilty," I said. "But I'm going to have to get better at it."

"Oh, why's that?" Sophie said.

"I'm going to be busy with other things," I said. "I've not only got the new children's book coming out, but Lana's just confirmed that the non-fiction book has got the green light. So I'll be going back to Israel to do the research."

"Oh, Mum, that's great news. I know how much this project means to you." Sophie hugged me.

"Wow, congratulations," Steven said. "You must be excited."

"I am. I can't wait to get started."

"When will you be going? How long will you be away?" Sophie said

"Most likely early May, and for about three months probably."

"And you trust us to look after things here?" Steven asked.

"Yes, I do," I replied. "You've already learned a lot in a short time. It'll be good for you to have full responsibility and there are plenty people you can call on if you need to."

Steven stood up as, behind us, Miriam stirred in her buggy and let out a little cry. "I'll see to this young lady," he said, picking her up.

"And Jack?" Sophie said, as we watched Steven walk off down the hall with his little daughter in his arms.

"What about Jack?" I said, unable to keep the defensiveness out of my voice.

"Have you told him ... that you're definitely going?"

"Not yet," I said. "Please don't say anything to him. He should hear it from me."

"Of course, but he'll be okay about it, won't he?"

"Yeah, why wouldn't he be?" I said, trying and failing to sound convincing, as I recalled Jack's lukewarm response when I'd first mentioned the possibility.

"Sounds like you're not too sure."

I sighed. "No, I'm not actually."

Sophie looked at me and shook her head. "Sorry, ignore me. It's none of my business. I didn't mean to upset you."

"You haven't upset me," I said. "But I suspect Jack won't be happy about me going back ... and I ... I ..."

"You value your independence too much to let whether Jack minds or not influence your decision?"

"Yes," I said. "Yes, I think I do. I love the croft, I love Skye and I love Jack. But—"

"But you're not ready to settle down?"

"No, I don't believe I am."

# Chapter Five

*Rachel*

I'd hoped to get a chance to talk to Jack after the meal and before the dancing got started. I wasn't planning to tell him about the confirmation of the book. That would be better done in private. But I did want to thank him for everything he'd done to make the wedding go smoothly, and apart from that I wanted to spend some time with him.

It wasn't to be. Jack was busy with a few others moving the tables to the edges of the hall in order to clear a space for the ceilidh. And I was sidetracked helping Sophie get Miriam organised before handing her over to Morag for the evening.

Sophie was cradling a sleeping Miriam when Morag joined us in the community hall's small back room.

Morag beamed at my daughter. "All set?"

"We sure are," Sophie said, fastening Miriam into her buggy. "Put her into her cot when you get to Mum's and she should be fine." Sophie crossed her fingers.

"Don't worry," said Morag. "Even if she does wake, we'll cope."

"Thanks again for doing this – you and Alasdair – Steven and I really appreciate it."

"It's no bother and you need to enjoy the party without being distracted by this wee one," Morag said, tucking a blanket around Miriam. Then she looked at me and winked. "And we couldn't have your mum leaving early. She's got lots of dancing to do."

"Thanks Morag," I said. "I owe you."

"You enjoy yourself," she said, giving me a hug. "That's all the payback I need."

After we'd said our goodbyes to Morag and Alasdair, the band leader announced that the dancing was about to start and that the bride and groom should make their way to the floor for the first dance. I joined the circle of guests that surrounded Sophie and Steven.

Steven, his collar-length blond hair tucked behind his ears, his kilt swinging as he waltzed, only had eyes for Sophie. And so assured was he, it was difficult to believe he was wearing prosthetics. He grinned as his friends clapped and whistled as he danced past them.

I thought again of Finlay, but I didn't have time to dwell on the poignancy of his absence as Steven's father swept me off to join in the dance.

The first waltz was as staid and controlled as the dancing got. And after a Dashing White Sergeant partnered by my brother Jonathan and a slightly bewildered Deb, followed by an incredibly energetic Eightsome Reel with Peter, I was desperate for a seat and a cold drink.

Eitan appeared beside me as I arrived at the table where I'd left my bag. He was carrying a tray of drinks. "I got you these," he said, once we were sitting down. He put a glass of iced water and a glass of white wine on the table in front of me.

"How did you—"

"I guessed you would be thirsty and I saw you drank white wine at dinner, so ..." He pointed again at the glasses as he sat down beside me.

"Thank you," I said before taking a long drink of water.

"I tried your Scottish dancing at Mari's bat-mitzvah last year, but I'd forgotten how it is very ... what do you say ... very—"

"Energetic?" I asked, laughing.

"Yes, energetic. I'm sorry my English is not so good. I have not spoken it much since we met in Israel. I need to practise."

Eitan ran his finger along the back of my hand and up towards my wrist as he spoke. "I need to spend time with you again, I think." He grinned at me, his dark eyes full of suggestive mischief." And I must tell you how beautiful you look. Your dress is perfect in its style for your small neat shape – and the colour – it goes so well with that amazing red hair, which I'm pleased to see you haven't cut."

Flustered, I turned from his gaze. I pulled my hand away, glanced down at my dark red shift dress, and touched my hair. And embarrassed though I was, I did have to smile at his artistic appraisal. I picked up my wine glass. "Cheers," I said.

As I took several large sips of wine, I glanced back at him. He was still looking at me, still smiling. "Cheers," he said, raising his own glass. "A fine whisky. It was your friend Lana's suggestion."

"Oh, right. That's good," I said. "She's nice, isn't she, Lana?" I was aware how stilted and nervous I sounded, and I blushed as I remembered exactly how comfortable I'd once been with this man.

"Yes, Lana is very nice. But now I would like to enjoy your company for a little while, if that is all right with you?"

"Yes, okay." I glanced around the room.

"Ah, you are looking for Jack. You don't think he would approve of me and you catching up?"

"No, no. It's not that. It's none of his ..." I took a breath. "He won't mind. I just wondered where he was, wanted to make sure ..." I spotted him dancing with Sophie.

"Jack has had an interesting life, chasing the bad guys. I liked talking to him at dinner. And he's comfortable with women too. He certainly seemed to impress Carla and Lana."

Part of me would have loved to know what the conversation between Jack and Eitan had involved, but there was another part of me that didn't. So all I said was, "You seem to have made quite an impression on Lana yourself."

Eitan nodded and smiled his big, easy, smile. "Yes, I thought so." He took another mouthful of whisky.

"Why are you here, Eitan?"

He laughed and stretched his arms towards me in an unconvincing gesture of innocence. "I needed a holiday, needed to ... to refill my ideas, my imagination."

"But why Scotland? Why now?"

"Why not? You and Jonathan, you have told me a lot about your country, about its beauty and its history. I wanted to see for myself. So, when Jonathan told me about the wedding and his trip home with his family, I thought it would be a good time to come. I'd have expert guides and I'd get to see you. Perfect!" Eitan shrugged, as if bewildered at having to explain something so obvious. He sat back, completely at ease, looking at me. "Aren't you pleased to see me?"

"Yes, of course I am."

"Good, that is good." He put his hand on mine again, his expression more serious now. "Jonathan told me some time ago you might be coming back to Israel to work on a book."

"Yes, that's right."

"But would that not be a threat?"

"A threat?"

"To your relationship with Jack."

"It's got nothing to do with Jack. It's up to me what I do," I said, feeling even more sure than when I'd said the same to Sophie.

"So, when the book is approved, you will come to Jerusalem?"

"It *has* been approved. And so, yes, I'll be returning to Israel very soon."

"I'm glad to hear it." Eitan's voice was quieter now and he took both my hands in his, his gaze intense.

"Sorry to butt in, but I wondered if you'd like to dance." Jack's voice made me jump. I turned to look at him, pulling my hands free of Eitan's, and feeling my face reddening.

I wondered how long he'd been there watching, waiting to speak. I felt defensive even though I told myself I'd done nothing wrong. "Eh, right," I said. I looked at Eitan who remained completely relaxed, and then back at Jack.

"It's a St Bernard's Waltz, if that helps you decide," Jack said. He seemed unperturbed.

"Sorry, yes, I'd love to dance." I turned to Eitan as I stood up. "Excuse me," I said.

Eitan picked up his glass, "Have a good time," he said.

Jack looked very handsome in his Baxter tartan kilt, and he smelled wonderful too. It felt good to be in his arms at last.

"Enjoying yourself?" he said, as we spun round.

"Yes, very much."

"Me too," he said, pulling me closer.

When the waltz had ended and we were walking off the dance floor, I looked up at him and said, "Thanks, Jack."

"For what?"

"For everything you've done to make today a success. It's been great."

He stopped walking and turned me to face him, his hands on my shoulders, his expression serious, almost sad. "It's all I want, Rachel ... to be with you, to make you happy."

I put my hand to his face, looked into his lovely brown eyes, and resisted the temptation to run my hand through his dark, silver-streaked hair. "I want to be with you too, Jack. But—"

"The trouble is—"

"What? What's wrong?" I stepped back from him. That uneasy feeling was back and now I knew I wasn't imagining it. Something wasn't right with him.

"I ... oh, nothing ... forget it ... not now, not today." He started to walk away.

"Wait," I said.

He turned back to face me. "Don't look so worried. It's nothing, really, it isn't." He gave me a quick kiss, then looked over my shoulder. "Your brother's approaching, looks like he wants the next dance. Go on, have fun."

All I could do was watch him as he walked away.

In the end, I was on the dance floor for most of the rest of the evening and I did have fun. I concentrated on getting the steps right and being in the moment, determined that the day would remain a happy one.

The ceilidh caller did a great job of shouting out the dance steps and the non-Scottish guests tried, not always successfully, to keep up. The dancing finished with a Strip the Willow and Lana did a brilliant job of pushing and pulling Eitan to where he needed to be, much to everyone else's amusement. Eitan of course was unfazed and laughed as much as anyone at his confusion.

The dancing was punctuated by the usual ceilidh mix of songs, music and recitations and it was especially lovely to have some of the guests from far away contributing. Steven's father did a superb rendition of the Robert Burns poem, *A Man's a Man for a' That* which was met with enthusiastic applause. And Jonathan and I, accompanied by a couple of my neighbours on fiddle and guitar, did a short set of Gaelic songs which the company also seemed to enjoy.

And then, all too soon, it was over. The guests encircled Sophie and Steven and sang *Auld Lang Syne,* before waving them off to Portree and a night in the town's poshest hotel.

Most of the off-island guests were staying locally in various holiday cottages and B&Bs scattered around Halladale. So we all left more or less together. We flicked on our torches as we set off, some heading south, and the rest of us north, along the township's dark, single-track road. Jack and I walked with Lana. Eitan and Jonathan and his family followed behind us.

We got to Lana's B&B first. She wished everyone goodnight and then, as Jack and Jonathan's group set off walking again, she hugged me and said, "Thanks for inviting me. I had a great time, and thanks for the introduction to the gorgeous Eitan."

"You're incorrigible," I said, as I hugged her back. "And I'm sorry I haven't the space to put you up."

"I told you it's fine," Lana said. "Now go and catch your man up and I'll see you in the morning."

Jack was waiting for me a few yards along the track. He slipped his arm through mine and we walked on. "Jonathan's gang said to say goodnight and they'll see you tomorrow," he said. "I think all that Scottish dancing has exhausted them."

"I know how they feel," I said. "I'm shattered."

"But happy? At how it all went?"

"Oh, yes, very happy."

"Good." Jack put his arm round my shoulder and kissed the top of my head.

As we passed Morag's house, I looked along the driveway towards her holiday cottage – the cottage where Jonathan and his family and Eitan, were staying. It felt weird to have Eitan so close by and I was aware that Jack's glance had followed mine.

When we arrived at Burnside cottage, the light above my front door flicked on. I glanced up at Jack. "You could stay here tonight," I said. "We'd have the place to ourselves."

"Probably best not. We're both tired and you've got Miriam to look after too."

I knew these were excuses. But I'd no idea what the real reason was. "Right," I said, my voice quiet, stifled by disappointment and sadness.

"Come here," he said. He put his arms around me and held me close. Our kiss was as loving and passionate as it had ever been, but then he stepped back and stroked my face, looking at me intently. "I love you, Rachel. Please don't ever doubt that."

And with that he turned and disappeared into the darkness.

# Chapter Six

*Rachel*

I didn't sleep well and it was nothing to do with the baby. In fact I was glad she woke early and I had an excuse to get up.

Bonnie greeted us when we went into the kitchen, and I let her out into the garden. Miriam and I followed her outside as I needed to let the hens out. I managed to feed them one-handed as my granddaughter wriggled in my arms. She seemed to enjoy watching them as they flapped, squawked and pecked.

Back indoors, I watched Bonnie from the window as I waited for Miriam's bottle to warm in the microwave. Thoughts of Jack and Eitan, of the past and the future, darted through my mind. But then Bonnie's barking to be let in for her breakfast, and Miriam's equal impatience to be fed, brought me back to what needed to be done in the present.

But once I was settled on the living-room sofa, Miriam in my lap enjoying her bottle, my thoughts were free to roam again. I glanced at the mantelpiece, at the family photos, at the photo of my mother. I wished she'd lived to see me and Sophie reconciled, to see Sophie so happy, and to meet her great-granddaughter. She'd arrived in Scotland as a child refugee before the Second World War – one of hundreds of Jewish children saved by the Kindertransport out of Germany. But her parents and her sister didn't escape and they later died in Auschwitz. So the rift between me and my daughter had particularly pained her.

Mum hadn't been the easiest of people. She was strong and stoical and expected everyone else to be too. She said what she thought, even if it wasn't what you wanted to hear. But she'd been such a source of strength too. She'd supported me through the divorce and Finlay's death, and I missed her. But I caught myself on the edge of this dangerous emotional territory and immediately turned my attention back to my granddaughter.

When Miriam had finished her bottle, I walked to the window with her. I rubbed her back as I watched high white clouds chasing across the morning sky. A buzzard circled the croft's lower field and I could hear the distant bleating of the ewes. I looked out over the loch and down towards the Cuillin mountain range. And as always Skye's ancient landscape worked its magic and I felt at peace.

I'd got Miriam down for a nap and was making my own breakfast when Lana arrived.

"Sorry to be so early," she said as she sat at the kitchen table. "But it's a long drive back to Glasgow and I don't want to be too late setting off. And yes, please, I'll join you with the tea and toast. I told the folks at the B&B I'd be breakfasting with you."

"Yes, ma'am," I said smiling.

"Yeah, cheeky cow, I know. But that's why you love me."

As we ate breakfast, we talked a bit about the wedding and had a bit of a catch-up more generally.

Then we got down to business.

"Here's the contract," Lana said, laying some papers on the table as I poured her a second cup of tea. "I've emailed you a copy for reference but it's all standard stuff. You leave in a month's time. Communicado will organise flights etc., and you'll need to confirm that you'll be staying mainly with your brother."

After I'd read through it all and signed in the appropriate places, I handed it back to Lana. "Thank you," I said. "It's down to you I got this."

"Not at all, I was simply doing my job."

"It was more than that. It was you who came up with the idea and approached them in the first place."

"And it was your pitch that nailed it." Lana put all the paperwork back in her briefcase. "So, are you excited?"

"Yeah, but a bit apprehensive too."

"You'll be great. Communicado Press don't just pick anybody, you know. They liked what you said about your first impressions of Israel and Palestine, especially the emphasis you put on personal stories and listening to people whose views you don't agree with. You're perfect for their Peace Talks series."

"Don't get me wrong, I'm thrilled to have been commissioned," I said. "Challenging prejudices, promoting peace, of course it's something I want to be involved in."

"Which is exactly why I suggested you."

"But what if I can't deliver? I mean two of the books – the one on Iraq and the one on Afghanistan – they've been nominated for awards."

Lana frowned. "That's a good thing, surely?"

"Well, yes, for the authors it's great, but for me, it sets the bar very high. And as for other books in the series, they've been put together by some talented folk – a professor, a war artist, a couple of BBC foreign correspondents, an award-winning poet—"

"So you're part of a high quality group."

"Exactly, that's why it's a bit daunting. I feel like a bit of an impostor. I mean, I'm only a humble jobbing illustrator and author of children's books."

Lana looked even more serious now. "You're a talented writer and artist, an experienced professional with transferrable skills, and you have an agent and a publisher who believe in you. You can do this."

"Sorry," I said. "I didn't mean to sound negative or ungrateful. I'm definitely up for this and I'll give it my best."

Lana grinned. "That's my girl." She sat back, looking at me.

"What?" I said.

"I admire you. Not only for your professional skills, and not only for the way you picked yourself up after ... after everything ... which is amazing enough, but also for going off to Israel last year and doing so much more than simply being a tourist. You're one of the bravest and strongest people I know."

"I'm not sure bravery or strength came into it. I picked myself up because there was no other choice. And I went to Israel because I wanted to. It was part pilgrimage and part quest. I went in honour of Mum, to find out more about what it means to be Jewish, to explore what my brother loves so much about the country."

"Whatever, I think you're great." Lana glanced at her watch. "And now I really must go."

I walked her to her car. "I'll be in touch soon," she said. "Communicado are putting together some contacts for you and as well as the travel arrangements, they'll want to liaise about appointments for meetings and so on."

"A lot to organise in a short time," I said.

"And speaking of a short time, you better get on with the finishing touches on the children's book before you go."

"Will do," I said.

"You're doing the right thing, you know," Lana said as we hugged. "Getting out there, doing something new, not just settling."

And, as I watched Lana drive off down the track, I hoped she was right.

# Chapter Seven

*Rachel*

Sophie and Steven arrived not long after Lana left. They looked happy and relaxed and said that they and Miriam would be going back into Portree for lunch. They were meeting up with Steven's parents and some of their friends before they all began their journeys home. And Steven, despite my protests that I was happy to do it, insisted he'd do the late afternoon check on the sheep when they got back. He promised he'd fetch me if he had any concerns. So I accepted his offer and said I'd go and do the morning check and feed.

I was in the porch pulling on my wellies when Bonnie started barking. I looked up to see Jonathan and Eitan approaching.

I zipped up my bodywarmer, grabbed my crook and headed outside.

"A cup of coffee not on offer then," Jonathan said, laughing as he approached. He turned to Eitan."The sheep wait for no men."

"As it should be," Eitan said, looking at me and giving a little bow of his head.

"Sorry," I said. "I do need to get on, but you're very welcome to go in and help yourselves."

"I'm only teasing," Jonathan said. "We've been out for a walk. Deb was with us, but she's gone back to drag our two lazy kids out of bed. And I need to get back too."

"Oh ... so?" I said, slightly distracted as I watched Bonnie enjoying being made a fuss of by Eitan.

"Yeah, we're taking the kids into Portree for lunch and then I plan to inflict a walk around town on them, with compulsory commentary from me on all the places that meant something when I was growing up."

"Your poor, poor children," I said.

"I don't know what you mean," Jonathan said with mock indignation. "Anyway, I came to ask you if you'd like to join us for dinner later, at the holiday cottage, Jack too, if he wants."

Of course I wanted to go, to spend precious time with my family. But Eitan and Jack together like that, I wasn't sure how that would be. "Thanks, but I don't—"

But Jonathan wasn't going to be put off with any feeble excuses I came up with. "It'll save you cooking, give the newly-weds time alone, and I can pick your brains for sightseeing ideas for the next few days. Besides, it's Deb who'll be cooking, so you know it's bound to be great."

"Okay, okay," I laughed. "Thanks. I'll come for dinner. And I'll ask Jack if he's free." I glanced at Eitan as I spoke, but he still seemed absorbed in fussing over a delighted Bonnie.

"Now, I really must go. I'll see you both later."

"Great," Jonathan said. "See you around six."

A little while later, as I crossed the track that led to the common grazing, Bonnie started barking and running in circles, her tail wagging. She was looking back towards the house. I set down the wheelbarrow with its sack of feed and saw Eitan jogging towards us.

He waved and I waited for him to catch up. "I thought I would join you," he said, indicating with his arm that we should move on.

"Join me checking the sheep?" I asked as we started walking.

"Yes, I know nothing of these animals. I thought I might learn from you."

I looked at him. "Really?"

He laughed. "No." He caught my arm. I stopped, set down the wheelbarrow once more.

"So, why then?" I said, turning to face him.

"I do not want to go walking with Jonathan and the family in Portree. It will be good for them to have family time without me. And I *am* interested in your farm. But mainly I wanted to have you to myself for a while."

"I see." We started walking again, my thoughts all over the place. I knew I needed to get a grip, act like a grown-up. Eitan and me were never a couple. Yes, we'd been to bed together when I'd been in Israel. Yes, part of me would always love him for how he'd made me feel alive again. He was a great lover and a great guy. He was my brother's best friend and I liked to think we'd always be friends too.

So why was I having this fluttering and flustered reaction to seeing him again? I told myself it was because it had been a surprise. I hadn't had time to get used to the idea he was coming to Scotland. But now he was here, it was time I acted like a friend and made him feel welcome. I would calm down and enjoy his company.

Eitan's voice broke into my thoughts. "But if you'd rather be alone—"

"No, no, not at all. I'm happy to have you come along. But there's one thing I should make clear."

"Oh, what's that?"

"It's not a farm. It's a croft, much smaller than a farm, and much more complicated to explain. There's a humorous definition that crofts are small pieces of Scottish rural land bordered by legislation."

"Right," Eitan said, looking puzzled. "I will try to remember." I waited beside him as he paused for a moment to take in the view. I could see him taking a deep breath as he did so. "The smell," he said. "It is very different here to how it is at home."

"It is," I said, my attention drawn to the familiar scents of damp earth and sea. And at this time of year there was also the coconut and almond smell of the gorse which was in bright yellow flower all around us.

We reached the common grazing and I explained to him how this part of the land was shared by the whole township of Halladale, and that crofts were for small scale, subsistence food production.

Eitan helped me distribute the feed to the younger ewes. They wouldn't be lambing this time round, so were still free to roam on the grazing. I also introduced him to my two veteran tups, Jason, the four-horned Jacob's sheep, and Hector, the black Hebridean.

"They are handsome," Eitan said, as we watched them eating. "They look like they will make good lambs for you."

"Ah, I'm afraid their fathering time is over. To keep the flock strong you need to bring in fresh breeding stock regularly. I used a couple of neighbouring crofters' rams this year."

Eitan rubbed Hector's back. "Poor guys," he said. "No sex for you. Outrageous, that's no way to live." He looked at me and I knew what he was thinking.

I didn't go there. Instead I said, "I should probably sell them on, but I'm quite fond of them. They're such characters. In fact Jason's the main character in my next book."

"A fine choice of subject. What will it be called?"

"*Jason Jumps Over the Moon*."

Eitan's laughter showed how much he liked the title. "Wonderful," he said.

I was ridiculously pleased that this opinionated, assertive, unsettling man approved. He hadn't seemed particularly interested in the details of my job as a children's author and illustrator before, so I was touched that, as we walked back over to the field behind the house, he asked me more about my series of books.

So I told him about how I'd gone from illustrating children's books written by others to being both author and illustrator of my own series. I told him about my main characters, Shona and Fergus, who'd been based on Sophie and Finlay as children, and that they lived on a croft where they and the animals such as Seamus the sheep and Henrietta the highland cow had all sorts of adventures.

"I see," Eitan said, looking more bemused than impressed.

"Hmm, I'm not sure you do," I said, laughing. "Anyway, the Jason book will be the sixth and last in the series. And I need to get it all done before I come to Israel as it's due for publication at the end of the year."

Eitan nodded. "I would like it very much if I could see the books," he said.

"Oh, right," I said, again feeling pleased at his interest.

Eitan also seemed interested in what was involved in looking after the pregnant ewes. He watched me closely as I checked the bellies of some of the mothers-to-be in the large holding pen, and I told him I didn't think it would be long before lambing started. He also helped me fetch and distribute their feed.

Then, as we washed our hands at the outside tap, I found myself asking Eitan if he'd like to join me for lunch.

# Chapter Eight

*Rachel*

I was glad I'd defrosted some of my homemade bread, and that I also had a nice big chunk of locally made cheese. This along with some of Morag's chutney would make what I hoped would be an acceptable meal for my guest.

While I put the food out onto the kitchen table, Eitan occupied himself looking at the photos and sketches I had on the kitchen wall. "Who is Poppy?" he asked, pointing to a brightly coloured crayon drawing.

I told him she was Jack's granddaughter. "She drew it last year when they were both staying here at the cottage with me."

Eitan raised an eyebrow. "Jack lived here with you? I didn't know you'd been so committed."

"Oh, no, it wasn't like that. Jack was still fixing up his house and he had to look after Poppy. Her mother was pregnant and there were problems. It's a long story, but it was here or a caravan, and the weather was awful."

Eitan was smiling. "Rachel, it is fine. I was teasing. I was simply interested in the artist. I can see it is a child's drawing, but it is very good."

"She was only six when she did it. It's of her and me and Jason and Hector – the two rams you met earlier."

"I guessed that. And she has written a lovely message saying she loves you. It is charming."

"Yes," I said, my voice tense. I hoped it didn't betray how awkward and exposed I felt. Having Eitan here on the croft, in my kitchen, looking at my things, it all seemed so surreal. Once again I told myself to relax, to be as relaxed as he was, to enjoy his company.

He was a good man who'd made me very welcome when I'd visited his country. The least I could do was make him feel equally welcome now he was in my home. I smiled at him and pointed to the table. "Please, come and sit down. Let's eat."

"Thank you," Eitan said, as he piled his plate with bread and cheese, "for letting me go with you as you worked. I found it very interesting."

"You did? You found the sheep interesting?"

"Not the sheep, Rachel. You, I find *you* interesting. I enjoyed watching you, watching you doing what you're good at, what you enjoy." He looked around the kitchen. "I can see why it means a lot to you – the croft and this beautiful island."

"It's home," I said.

"But I fear you are too comfortable here, that in the end you will settle for this."

"I *am* settled," I said. "This is the place I choose to come back to. But it's not some sort of hideout. After all, I'm coming back to Israel, working on a book that excites me, working for … I don't know … maybe not peace, but at least some better understanding between people. That's not settling, not in the way you mean." I stopped to draw breath, surprised at how sure of myself I sounded.

Eitan looked at me, his smile growing broader, and his stare more intense.

"What is it?" I asked when the need to know what he was thinking got too much.

"What do you mean?" he asked.

"Your smile. That look. What are you thinking?"

"I'm thinking this is the real Rachel. This is her! There is the fire and the passion. There is the artist, the writer, the woman of courage, the woman with something to say."

"Yes," I said, delighted at his words but trying to appear cool and calm. "I'm definitely not someone who's retiring from the world."

Eitan gave a small nod of acknowledgement. "Tell me more about this new book, the one that is bringing you back to Israel. Jonathan has told me a little bit, but I'd like to hear it from you."

So, trying to hide my nervousness at how he might react, I began to describe my new project. "The publishers are a Scottish company called Communicado. They do fiction and non-fiction and they're all about personal stories – about dialogue and conciliation – between cultures, races, religions – about lessening the fear of the other. For me it's about gentle protest and people showing respect and compassion, in order to make small changes for the better." I paused, knowing from previous conversations that he had strong political views and might not agree with my rationale.

But all he said was, "And what form will your book take?"

"It'll contain both words and pictures – some sketches, some photos and it'll be part of a series called Peace Talks. I'll use my own contacts and some provided by the publisher. The publisher will take care of all the permissions and everything. The plan is that ordinary people doing extraordinary things on all sides will speak for themselves. I'll outline the context and make notes and sketches recording and reflecting what they say."

"Where else in the world have they done books?"

"All over," I said. "Afghanistan, Iraq, Syria, but not only from places where there is war or widespread violent conflict. There's one that was done in the US, one in Australia, Germany, Spain and there are ones proposed for the UK and for France." I reached for my tablet. "I can show you their website," I said, bringing up the site before handing him the tablet.

As he studied the site, he gave no hint of what he was thinking. Eventually he spoke. "Impressive," he said. I see they have a YouTube channel. And some of their authors have done video talks to share their ideas on the excellent TED website too."

*Settlement*

"Yes," I said, pleased that he was impressed. "They do a lot of social media stuff. Apparently, I'll be working with a professional photographer who'll be filming and doing still shots too – all for sharing on the web at a later date. There's even talk of the BBC doing a Communicado documentary at some point."

"It all sounds excellent – the series and your part in it." Eitan said. "And I hope you will let me help in any way you need."

"I'd like that," I said, smiling with relief that he seemed to approve and pleased that he wanted to be involved. But I also realised how exposed I'd felt talking to him like this, about something that meant so much.

"That's enough about me," I said. "Tell me what you're working on at the moment."

He began by telling me about a landscape commission he was working on for a private client. It was a cityscape of Jerusalem, the old city skyline. "Not exactly exciting," he said. "But the money it will earn me allows me to follow the less commercial but more interesting concepts."

"Oh? Like what?"

"There's something Deb is involved in. In fact she said she was going to tell you about it later as it could be something for your book. Anyway, she suggested me as the ...what do you call it ... an artist who helps with publicity and develops a project?"

"Artist-in-residence," I said.

"That's it," Eitan said. "The project is called *My Jerusalem*. It was started by another teacher at Deb's school, an Art teacher. You know the school where Deb teaches, where Gideon and Mari attend? It takes students from all backgrounds, Jews, Muslims, Christians, whatever."

I nodded.

"The teacher asked her students to draw what Jerusalem meant to them. They could interpret it any way they wanted and she was amazed at what came back. There were ordinary landscapes, yes, but there was much more. Some impressionistic, some abstract, even some surrealism, but all of it saying something. She had the idea to extend it to other schools. She got Deb and some of the other teachers to help her and next thing it's on television and in the newspapers. Now it's spreading, beyond the schools and even beyond Jerusalem to other cities and towns. And it has sponsors and trustees from across the political spectrum as well as from an Arts charity and a couple of private philanthropists."

"It sounds amazing. What's your role exactly?"

"I help people get started. I go one day to a factory, the next to a hospital or an office or a school. I listen to the people's ideas and I show them how to draw, sometimes at the basic level, and I help them do exhibitions and booklets with the finished pictures, connect with the press and so on, and do the social media stuff."

"And people can express their idea of Jerusalem, or wherever, any way they like, regardless of the politics?"

"Yes, they can."

"You don't have a problem with that?"

"Me? No, of course not." Eitan looked puzzled. Then he smiled and shook his head. "You think I would not support a project that gives people who disagree with me a voice." He paused before giving me a knowing look. "That is why you looked so scared as you began to tell me about your book. You thought I would not approve?"

"I ... yes, I know you have strong views and—"

"Ah, Rachel, I remember well our political discussions, our disagreements. But they were good, were they not? I enjoyed them. I like a good debate and I would never deny another person the right to take part."

"Yes, I know, sorry."

Eitan shrugged. "It's okay. The point of the project isn't to score points. It's simply a way – a peaceful way – of letting people show their point of view. There is no judgement. I think that is why the sponsors are comfortable with it. And even the politicians tolerate it. It shows them in a good light, they appear open-minded and relaxed, and as the people taking part aren't activists or revolutionaries, there is little political risk."

"But it does get people thinking and talking ... maybe even listening to people they wouldn't normally listen to?"

"Exactly."

"It sounds perfect for inclusion in the book," I said, already excited at the possibility of working with him.

# Chapter Nine

*Rachel*

After lunch we moved through to the living-room and I let Eitan have his moment looking out the back window. It was something all first-time visitors to the house did. Momentarily stunned by the view over Loch Snizort, their gaze would go from the mountains of Harris lying far out to the north-west in the Minch, then along the sharpness of the Trotternish ridge, and south to the jagged tops of the Cuillin Mountains.

Eitan took his time, looking, and looking again. "Beautiful," he said eventually, turning to me. "You grew up with this?"

"Yes."

"You are fortunate. The light here, it is different to what I'm used to, and it is always changing. I can see how it would make an artist out of you. If I was you I would be always painting."

I smiled. "You don't give up, do you?" I said. But I knew he was right. I should make more time for painting.

"Never." Eitan turned from the window and looked round the room. "Now, tell me about this painting," he said, as he walked over to look more closely at a framed picture hanging on the wall near the fireplace. "You did this?"

"No," I said, as I went to join him in looking at the watercolour. It was a picture of a small red-roofed house in a pretty flower-filled garden. "I found it rolled up amongst my mother's things … last year, after she died. The signature is Simon Weitzman, her father's name. I can't be sure, of course, but I believe it was painted by my grandfather. Perhaps it's my mother's childhood home ... her home before her family got her out of Germany."

"But you didn't know of the painting until after she died?"

"She kept the few belongings she'd brought with her from Germany, but Jonathan and I didn't know any of them existed while she was alive. She rarely spoke about her heritage or about being a Jew. I think she saw being Jewish as being vulnerable."

"Yes, Jonathan has told me she didn't approve of him coming to live in Israel."

"She certainly didn't. That's partly why I left it so long before visiting him."

We both stood for a moment, looking at the picture. As we did so, Eitan said, "Perhaps you get your artistic talent from your grandfather."

"I like to think so."

Eitan put a hand on my shoulder and when I turned to look at him, he moved his hand to my face. "It is so good to see you," he said softly. He moved his face closer to mine. The slightly rough skin of his thumb on my cheek, the scent of sandalwood, the muted tone of his normally loud voice, it would have been so easy to give in. I gently removed his hand from my face and took a step back. Eitan inclined his head, a small smile at one corner of his mouth, acknowledging the rebuff.

"Perhaps I should go now," he said.

But that was the last thing I wanted. "No need to rush away," I said. "Why don't you come through to my work room? I can show you my books, like I promised."

"I would like that."

Eitan laughed his hearty laugh as he read through the full set of my picture books. And after he'd looked over the proofs for the new one he declared it was his favourite. "And I can tell everyone I have met Jason, the hero," he said. "I should have got his ... his ..." He mimed a writing action.

"His autograph," I said, laughing.

Then Eitan spotted my easel tucked away in the corner, the water-colour I'd done of Burnside the previous autumn still on it. The painting showed my house in the foreground, with the river at one side, and the rowan tree, its branches loaded with red berries, at the other. Orange crocosmia covered the ground and red rosehips filled the hedgerow. And Ben Halla filled the background. Eitan went over for a closer look.

He also noticed one of my old portfolio folders propped against the wall behind the easel. It was one from my student days.

"May I look?" he asked, pointing to the folder.

I nodded.

He laid the portfolio on my desk and untied the top. It had been so long since I'd looked at my Art school stuff, I'd forgotten most of what was in there. I stood beside him as he looked through it all.

"Some of these landscapes, they are very good. This one, it reminds me of the painting I did of Masada. It has lots of drama and it is done in oil."

I knew the Masada painting. It was a stunning picture of the ancient desert fortress in southern Israel and it hung on the wall of my brother's living-room. I didn't think my painting was anywhere near as good. "It's nice of you to say so, but—"

"I'm not being nice. You know that is not my way. I mean it. It is very good. It is strong and it is brave. Where is this place? And when did you paint it?"

"It's Salisbury Crags in Edinburgh, and I must have been about twenty when I did it, when I was at Art school in the city. I haven't done any oil or large scale landscape work since my student days."

"What? You haven't painted any of this?" Eitan indicated the view from the window.

I shook my head. I could see my watercolour of Burnside didn't count.

"You should, Rachel. You should be the brave girl you were and let the fire burn." And again he stroked my face, but this time he followed up with a kiss, a brief, soft pass over my lips.

"Hello! Rachel? Anybody home?" Jack's voice made me jump. And then he was there, standing in the doorway looking from me to Eitan. "Sorry," he said. "Didn't mean to intrude."

"You're not," I said, unsure if he'd seen the kiss and trying not to sound defensive.

"It is fine," Eitan said. "I am leaving now." He took hold of my hands. "Thank you for the tour and lunch and for showing me your work. I have enjoyed it." He kissed me on the cheek. "And I look forward to talking more and to seeing you at dinner this evening."

I raised my eyebrows at Eitan. I knew he was being provocative.

Jack's face gave little away, but I knew him well enough to see the slight tightening at the corner of his mouth. He stood aside to let us pass and I saw Eitan out.

"Dinner this evening?" Jack said when I came back. "You and him?"

# Chapter Ten

*Jack*

I heard the jealousy in my voice as I spoke, and I'm sure Rachel heard it too.

She put her hand on my arm. "Jonathan's invited us to join them for dinner at the cottage. Deb's cooking. It should be good."

"I don't know—"

"It would be a chance for you to get to know Jonathan and the others a bit better." She stood in front of me, put her hands on my arms and looked up at me. "Please come."

Part of me yearned to kiss her, to take her to bed right then, in the middle of the afternoon, to go back to how it had been before. I missed that. I missed her. And that was the moment when I should have told her, the moment when I should have been honest about what was wrong and, for once in my life, put some effort into maintaining a relationship. But I didn't. Instead, I shrugged, turned away to look out the window and got lost in my own thoughts.

It had been weeks since we'd been together properly. Yes, there had been a lot going on. As well as Rachel's usual croft work and the push to get her new children's book finished, there were all the wedding preparations too. And, since January, she'd also had Sophie, Steven and Miriam living with her while their house was being built.

But these things weren't the real problem. After all, Rachel being busy with work and family was normal, and if we wanted some private time together, we had my place for that.

The real problem lay in the stuff I wasn't telling her.

And on top of that there was the difficulty I was having with the possibility of her going back to Israel. Not only had she spent a lot of time on the bloody book proposal, but she was so taken up with the whole concept, I was finding it hard to compete.

I understood what she was hoping to do and I admired her enthusiasm and commitment. Rachel's quiet but passionate determination was one of the reasons I loved her. I so wanted to be supportive and generous. But I was jealous and I was afraid, afraid I might lose her to the other more worthy, more exciting things going on in her life. And deep down, I hoped the project wouldn't happen.

So, much as I yearned for her, I was also holding back, protecting my fragile ego. I knew I was being petty and pathetic, but acknowledging it didn't mean I was able to change it.

However, my ridiculous insecurities weren't the whole story either.

The reasons for me stalling with Rachel were only partly to do with her and what she might do in the future. It was also down to stuff in my past. Stuff I so far hadn't been able to share with her. And on top of that, I had propositions to consider from both my ex-wife Ailsa and my ex-lover Bridget.

It was Rachel who broke the silence. "What's wrong, Jack?" she said. She spoke so gently, her concern so obvious, that I felt ashamed. "It's more than Eitan, isn't it? I know you keep denying it, but you've seem troubled for a while now."

I knew it was the perfect opportunity to open up, to tell her all of it. But I wasn't brave enough. I hated feeling vulnerable and it put me on the defensive.

"Not this again," I said. "Will you please stop asking? It's like you want there to be something wrong."

I wasn't proud of how hurt Rachel looked at my response. "Sorry," she said. "But I'm concerned about you ... about us ... especially after ... after—"

"After what?"

"Last night ... after last night, Jack. You didn't want to come back here. You didn't want to sleep with me. It's been ages since we ... since we ..." She looked away.

I couldn't stand seeing her upset, couldn't stand that it was because of me. "Come here," I said, taking her in my arms. I stroked her hair as she leant against me. "I'm sorry," I said. "Sorry I snapped at you. You didn't deserve it. But there is nothing wrong."

She stepped back slightly and looked up at me. "I'm not losing you then?"

"What? No, no, of course not," I said. I pulled her to me again, overwhelmed by guilt at having caused her pain. "You've had a lot on lately, and I didn't want to be in the way. And last night – last night we were both tired."

Her eyes looked into mine. "I love you, Jack," she said, her voice a whisper.

"I love you too," I said.

Our kiss was tentative, slow and gentle, as if testing how things were between us.

As the kiss ended, I stroked the side of her face. "Things will settle down," I said. "We can make more time for us. Maybe we could go away next month – go on our first proper holiday."

"That's a nice idea," she said, her smile somewhat apprehensive. "But it can't be next month or the two after that. Maybe when I get back?"

"Back?" I said, but I knew what was coming.

"Yes," she said. "It's all confirmed. The publishers have commissioned the book. I'm going back to Israel at the beginning of May." Her smile was more certain now.

"When did you find out?"

"Lana told me yesterday and I signed the contract this morning."

"Right," I said. I knew in the fast-disappearing, reasonable and objective part of my mind that I should keep calm, but the more primitive, defensive, easily rattled part had quickly taken over. "And you didn't want to discuss it first with – with anybody?"

"No, not really. It's my work, my decision. It's nobody else's business." She put her hand on my arm. "Please, Jack – please try to be happy for me. Everyone else is."

"Everyone else?"

"Sophie and Steven were delighted. And Jonathan, he's excited. He rang me last night to congratulate me after Eitan told him. And when I called Morag she—"

"Eitan knows? You told him already?"

"I told him when we—"

"And, I'll bet *he's* glad for you. That why he was here? You two planning to work together?"

"We may—"

"So I'm the last to know."

"It's nothing to do with being first or last. I wanted to tell you face-to-face and in private because I guessed you'd find it difficult, and I'd hope we'd—"

"You got that right."

She put her hands up. "Stop," she said. "Stop interrupting me. Let me speak. The book, the research, the travelling – the whole thing – it's what I want to do. I've never been more excited about anything. It's such a great opportunity."

"I'll bet it is," I said. I could hear the scorn in my voice, feel the fear at the root of it in my gut.

"What's that supposed to mean?"

"It's about him, isn't it? Yes, there's the work, but you'll get to see him, be with him. Three months is a long time and you've got history."

"Enough! That's enough."

It was the first time I'd seen or heard Rachel so angry.

"I'd guessed you wouldn't be keen on me going. I stupidly thought it was because you didn't get what it meant to me or, even more stupidly, that it was because you'd miss me. But your lack of trust – I didn't anticipate that and it's ... it's completely unfair and totally unjustified." She turned away from me.

I put my hand on her shoulder. "Rachel, I'm sorry. Please—"

Rachel shrugged my hand away."Leave it, Jack," she said, still with her back to me. "And it's fine about dinner. It's probably best you don't join us." She walked over to sit at her drawing board, still not looking at me. "See yourself out," she said.

# Chapter Eleven

*Jack*

Rachel texted me next morning to say she'd decided to join her brother and the others on their tour of the Highlands, and that she'd be gone for about a week. So even if I'd known how to begin to put things right, I was going to have to wait.

And while I waited, I asked myself the same question over and over.

Why, instead of telling Rachel what was really on my mind, did I have to go and say all those stupid things?

I suppose it was partly down to pride, that and being useless at relationships.

My way of coping with the real-life demands in my marriage to Ailsa had been to adopt the ostrich position. I had affairs as a sort of distraction. Then, after the divorce I became addicted to the buzz of initial attraction that each new affair offered. As soon as things got complicated or more serious than I'd like, I moved on. I liked things simple.

That's why me and my most recent ex, Bridget, lasted so long. She'd made no demands, didn't want to leave her husband and basically wanted good uncomplicated sex.

But with Rachel it was different. She was different. I loved her more than I'd ever loved anyone and I wanted it all. I wanted a long-term, together forever whatever, sort of relationship. And I'd fallen at the first hurdle.

After several sleepless nights, when the demons from my past continued to taunt me, I decided to follow Rachel's example and get away.

I went down to Edinburgh for a week, surprised my daughter, Maddie, by turning up for Easter. I was close to my daughter. She was my only child and although I'd have been proud of her whatever she did, I was especially pleased that she'd decided on a career in the police. I got on well, too, with my son-in-law, Brian, also a police officer. And I always enjoyed being with my grandchildren.

Eight-month-old William was now able to sit without support and was even trying to crawl. He laughed a lot and liked it when I lay on the floor and let him clamber over me. And seven-year-old Poppy was her usual happy and energetic self. Her latest passions seemed to be horse-riding and ballet. Spending time with the kids did help. When I was with them, I followed their lead and tried to stay in the moment. It was at least a partial respite.

As for Maddie, she was suspicious as to why I'd turned up at short notice and she'd commented on my low mood when the children weren't around to distract me. She guessed it was to do with Rachel, but for once, she accepted my unwillingness to discuss it.

By the time I got back to Skye lambing had started. So I told myself Rachel was understandably busy, and it wasn't that she was avoiding me. It didn't work.

And there was another unrelated torture – this one caused by the feelings of guilt and shame which had taken up more or less permanent residence in my head.

I tried to distract myself. I began sorting through the hundreds of photos I'd taken since my move to Skye over a year before. There were some landscape shots, but mostly they were of the night sky, and they needed to be moved from camera to computer and to be sorted into folders. But I was too easily sabotaged and distracted by my thoughts to be able to concentrate.

I thought about going for a walk or doing some work in the garden. Both were things I normally enjoyed and would have undoubtedly helped my mood. But I couldn't get up enough enthusiasm to head out, especially as I knew I'd have to come back to what felt like a very empty house now there seemed to be no prospect of Rachel visiting.

Even everyday tasks such as shaving or tidying up were becoming too much of an effort and I only did the minimum.

In the end, it was Alasdair who encouraged me to at least make a start on sorting things out. Alasdair Nicholson, married for over thirty years to Rachel's oldest and dearest friend and neighbour, Morag, was a retired Geography teacher and still active crofter. He was also an astute and compassionate man whose friendship I valued.

It was about a week after I got back from Maddie's, and after I'd already twice declined his suggestion of an evening visit to the pub, that he took action.

I was sitting in the kitchen, having just finished breakfast, when I heard a shout from the hallway. I'd got used to the Skye way of knocking and entering other people's houses, so I wasn't too surprised when Alasdair appeared in the kitchen doorway.

"Ah, good, you're not busy," Alasdair said, pulling out a chair and sitting down opposite me. "The Landy's outside, sandwiches and flasks are made up. So get your gear. We're off on a trek."

I shook my head. "Good morning to you, too," I said. "I suppose it would be pointless to tell you I already have plans."

"And do you?"

"No, but—"

"So come on then you miserable sod. Look lively. You've spent quite enough time feeling sorry for yourself."

Once we were on the road, Alasdair surprised me by not pulling in at Sligachan. Instead he carried on driving south down the main road. I'd been sure we'd be heading for one of the still snow-covered peaks that make up the Cuillin ridge. I glanced at him as we passed the Slig turn off, but he tapped his finger to the side of his nose.

All became clear when he drove into the ferry terminal car park at Sconser.

"Would I be right in thinking you've never been to Raasay?" Alasdair said, as he parked the car.

"You'd be right," I said.

"High time then."

The crossing to Skye's small neighbouring island was short but impressive. Raasay sits between Skye and the mainland and it only took the ferry twenty-five minutes to cross the Sound. However, during that time we saw a pod of dolphins who breached and dived alongside the wash of the boat for several minutes. We also saw a sea eagle. Alasdair and I were seated outside at the bow end when it appeared, gliding and circling ahead of us. Its white tail along with its wingspan of barn door proportions made it unmistakeable. I managed to get what I hoped would be a couple of reasonable shots, including one of it swooping down towards the water, and another as it rose up with a fish gripped securely in its talons.

"That was a bonus," Alasdair said, still obviously impressed despite his many years as a keen birdwatcher.

"It's a beautiful creature," I said.

"Careful," Alasdair said, smiling. "You almost looked slightly less miserable there."

"Yeah, yeah," I said, turning away, hoping Alasdair wasn't about to enquire what was bothering me. I looked back at Skye disappearing behind us. It was a cold but bright day and the island was at its breathtaking best. The lower hills were covered in what the locals called lambing snow, and the jagged peaks of the Cuillin mountain range retained their own winter-long coating. A line of little, white croft houses straggled along high above the shore, and sheep grazed below them. I breathed deeply and wondered how I could even consider leaving such a beautiful place.

We disembarked at Suisinish pier and, shouldering our rucksacks, we set off. We began our walk by following the line of a disused railway which Alasdair explained had at one time been used to transport locally mined iron ore.

The way was steep at first as we passed the ruins of the mine workings. But it soon levelled out. We walked on through a pine forest, over stiles and across burns. We didn't talk much, preferring to concentrate on our walking and on taking in the landscape around us. We saw deer on the high ground, and I spotted what I think was a stoat running along the top of a crumbling dry-stone wall.

After another bout of steep climbing we crossed soft, peaty moorland, followed a path above a loch, and arrived at the base of Raasay's highest point, Dun Caan. Breathless, we zigzagged up the boggy path until we arrived at the summit of this conical, flat-topped hill.

"Time for lunch, I think," Alasdair said once we'd taken in the view – and what a view. From a lighthouse to the north of us, the panorama swung eastwards to the Torridon hills and the mountains of Kintail on the mainland, and then all the way round to the Skye Bridge, the Cuillin and the Trotternish Ridge. Again I breathed deeply, trying to focus only on this magnificent natural setting, and on the present.

We spread out a groundsheet and tucked into ham and cheese rolls, followed by slabs of Morag's cherry cake, all washed down with good strong tea. As we ate, we remarked on birds spotted and landmarks observed, and Alasdair told me more about Raasay's history.

However, this safe conversational territory wasn't to last. Alasdair's visit had a more serious purpose. It was as he poured the last of the tea from the flask that he hit me with it. "So, you and Rachel – things not going so well?"

"What? No! We're fine."

"Really?"

"Yes, really."

"Sorry. It was Morag. Thought there might be trouble. Told me I should ask you if things were okay."

"Ah, Morag," I said. I couldn't help smiling. I didn't doubt that Morag might have noticed a distance between Rachel and me, and I wouldn't have been surprised if Rachel had confided in her. But I knew Alasdair well enough by now to guess that his concern came from him and from his own observations.

"Yes, Morag," Alasdair said. "And there'll be hell to pay if I have to tell her I didn't mention anything."

"So, you have mentioned it. You're in the clear." I stood up and drank the last of my tea. "Here," I said as I handed the cup to Alasdair. "Time we were moving on."

We didn't say much as we made our way back downhill. I took a couple of shots of the beach we crossed. I also snapped the great view we got of Beinn Tianavaig, one of Skye's iconic peaks. An hour or so later we'd completed our circular route and were back at the village of Inverarish. We had a bit of time before the late afternoon ferry so Alasdair suggested we go to the Raasay House cafe.

"It's a great place," he said. "Part posh hotel and part hostel for the boots and fleece brigade."


"This was a good idea," I said, as we settled at a table by the window with our coffee. "Thanks for suggesting it."

"No problem," Alasdair said. "Like I said, I've been worried about you."

"*You* have. I thought it was Morag?"

Alasdair looked sheepish. "You got me there, detective. But yes, I have. I understand you don't want to talk about it, but maybe you should. And I'm happy to sign a confidentiality agreement."

I smiled and shook my head.

"I mean it. I can resist Morag's interrogation techniques. What's said on Raasay, stays on Raasay."

"Okay, okay. I'll talk," I said. "And, yes, you're right. I've got a lot on my mind. And, yes part of it is me and Rachel. That's if there still is a me and Rachel."

"Oh?"

I leaned forward, my elbows on the table, my forehead resting on my hands. I wanted the relief of saying what I feared out loud, but I was also reluctant to put it into words. Alasdair waited. Eventually I was able to look him in the eye. "I think I might lose her," I said.

Alasdair didn't look surprised. He nodded, waiting for me to continue.

"She's ... I don't know ... recently it feels like we're not as together as we were."

"She's had a lot on, the family moving in, the wedding."

"I don't think it's that. It's this bloody trip to the Middle East. It's distracting her."

"The trip's for work. It's not like she's running away from you. Besides, I'd have thought you'd be pleased for her. She seems very excited at the prospect."

"Doesn't she just," I said.

"What do you mean?"

"*He's* there and they'll be working together."

"He?" Alasdair asked. "Oh, *he*. Eitan you mean?"

"Yes, Eitan. I'm guessing he's the reason she's so excited."

"You jealous, Jack?"

"No! That is ... yes, I am."

"Don't you trust Rachel?"

"Yes, but—"

"Because you should. You should trust her. I don't know exactly what the relationship was between her and this guy. I don't need to. But Rachel is one of the most loyal and honest people you'll find. And it's you she loves."

"You can't know that. And even if she does, it doesn't stop her straying, does it?"

"It does actually. In Rachel's case it does. Apart from the fact she's incredibly loyal, she's been on the receiving end. Her ex-husband repeatedly cheated on her. She knows what that's like. It isn't in her to inflict that kind of hurt."

"And that's just it."

"What?"

"I think she's having second thoughts about me, about us. What her husband did, I'm guilty of the same. I wasn't faithful to my ex."

"You think *she* doesn't trust *you*?"

"No, I don't think she does." I hadn't fully realised this until I said it out loud. "I don't think she does. I suspect for her our relationship's run its course. And now she's distancing herself."

Alasdair sat back. He put his hands behind his head and looked up at the ceiling, as if weighing something up. When he looked back at me he said, "Do you mind if I tell you what I honestly think … even if you might not like it?"

I sat back too. "Go for it," I said.

"I think you and Rachel love each other very much, but neither of you are very good at maintaining a relationship. Rachel because she's got a bit damaged, and you because you've never done the long haul."

"Don't pull your punches, Alasdair. Give it to me straight."

Alasdair's smile was sardonic. "You said to go for it."

"Yes, I did, didn't I? So Rachel and me, you're saying it needs work."

"If you want there to be a you and Rachel in the long term, yes."

"Of course I do. I want to marry her. I even had the proposal all planned … until … until all this."

"I wouldn't go proposing yet. You need to finish the foundations first – make them good and strong."

"And how do I do that?"

"You need to be completely honest with her, and you need to let Rachel know she can talk to you, that she can say anything and you'll listen, and that you're prepared to compromise. She needs to know she can trust you and that you won't disappear at the first sign of trouble."

"Ah," I said, raising my eyebrows. "So that's all there is to it."

"I know," Alasdair said. "I'm not saying it's easy. Morag's my best friend, and I hope I'm hers, but we haven't stayed married all this time without a lot of effort and a lot of give and take from both of us."

"That's just it," I said. "That's the part I've never done, never been able to do."

"Aye, that first flush of romance – it's all very nice – but it's not enough. It's the daily rubbing along that's the hard part."

"Yeah, I know. You're right, of course." I sighed.

"Chin up, Jack. I have faith in you. I think you love Rachel enough to make it work. Take it slow and steady."

"And this going to Israel thing. What do I do about that?"

"No-brainer, Jack."

"What?"

"You do nothing. You give her space, you wish her well and you do nothing ... other than trust her."

# Chapter Twelve

*Jack*

I stared out of the window, processing what Alasdair had said, but he wasn't finished with me yet.

"You said Rachel was *part* of the problem. So what else has been troubling you?"

I came close to fobbing Alasdair off, but for one thing I knew he wouldn't accept that and more importantly I acknowledged that I needed to tell somebody. "Something I thought was over seems to have come back to haunt me."

"Oh no, not – what's her name – the woman you were with before Rachel – the one who turned up on Skye last year, at the same time as Rachel arrived home from Israel, caused bit of a stir. She's not back in your life, is she?"

"You mean Bridget? No, no it's nothing like that. No, it's an old case from nearly two years ago – one of the last cases I worked on before the heart attack – before I decided enough was enough and retired."

"In what way has it come back?"

"It's been a gradual thing. At first, back at the beginning of the year, I found I was thinking about it, reliving what happened. I didn't actively bring it to mind. I tried to stop it. But it's got worse and the guilt that's come with it – it's almost unbearable, if I'm honest." I felt the sweat starting as I talked.

"Good grief, Jack. What on earth? Why the guilt?"

"I ... I messed up." I paused, looked out of the window, tried to get my breathing under control, before turning back to face Alasdair. "Someone died because of me." I wiped at the sweat on my forehead and noticed my hand shaking as I did so. "My colleague – Mike – he was shot and killed because of me. "

"I see," Alasdair said, his voice was calm and he didn't appear to be shocked by what I'd said. "Do you want to tell me what happened?"

Again I paused. I'd never been any good at talking about myself, about my feelings or my doubts or any of that. But for some reason, with Alasdair, I was prepared to give it a try. "I was a Detective Inspector in Major Crimes, and Mike – Mike McRae, he was a Detective Sergeant. We were part of a team investigating organised crime in Edinburgh. There was a particular group in the north-east of the city – drugs, prostitution and money laundering was their thing. The head of the group was Harry Gray, a well known gangster in the city. I'd been on his case one way or another since I'd started in the CID. We were fairly sure he was responsible for at least three murders, but he was clever and we could never quite get him on anything. Anyway it was decided we needed to be more proactive, infiltrate the gang and catch Gray in the act next time something big was planned."

"So how did that work?"

"Like I said, we needed someone on the inside. But it had to be someone unknown to the Edinburgh criminal fraternity. So Mike was seconded from Aberdeen. He got a job as a barman in the city centre nightclub that Gray owned and used as his headquarters. I was Mike's handler. We ran a meticulous and thorough operation, played the long game over the best part of a year, and as Mike got in deeper, became part of Gray's inner circle, we built up a substantial file of useful stuff on him." I took some sips of coffee to ease the dryness in my throat. Meanwhile the sweating had got worse and I felt it slide down my back.

"You all right?" Alasdair asked.

"Sorry ... yes ... it's not easy ... but I'm okay."

Alasdair glanced at his watch. "Take your time. We don't need to be on our way for a while yet."

"Right," I said. "So, the night Mike was killed I was on surveillance, part of a team, outside the nightclub. We knew there was a big drug delivery and payment due. We didn't know exactly when the transaction would take place but we were certain it was due at some point that week. Our orders were to watch and listen and call for back-up if and when it was needed.

"Mike was inside, wearing a wire, so me and the team could hear what was happening. Mike had been summoned to the club office where it seemed Gray was serving champagne. From what we could hear there were several people there, including Gray's older son, Tommy.

"Tommy was someone else we desperately wanted to get our hands on. He was shaping up to be an even worse version of his old man.

"Anyway, we got the code word from Mike that this was it, the drugs had been delivered. I called for the tactical firearms unit and we waited. But then something spooked Gray and he pulled a gun on Mike."

"Why did he do that?"

"We don't know exactly. Don't know if Mike gave himself away somehow. We heard Gray say Mike was police. Mike let us know about the gun by asking Gray to put it down and we heard him being hit for his trouble. Then Gray told the others to run for it and I sent the rest of the team off in pursuit."

"And what did you do?"

"Gray spoke to me via Mike's wire. He'd guessed it would be me on the other end – like I said we had history. Told me I was to come in, no-one else, only me, unarmed. The firearms guys were still a couple of minutes away. So I decided I better do as Gray asked."

Alasdair looked shocked now. "That was either very brave or very foolish," he said.

"Yes, that was what the boss said to me afterwards – or words to that effect. It was against protocol, but at the time, in that moment, it felt like I had no choice. I had to try to save Mike. I figured if I waited Gray might shoot Mike and run."

"So what happened?"

"Gray had a hold of Mike, had a gun to his head. Gray's younger son, Danny, still a teenager, was there too. He looked absolutely terrified. I did the negotiating thing, told Gray it was over, told him armed police were on their way, that we had evidence and proof of his activities, but that if he co-operated now it would help his case. It looked for a minute like he'd do a deal, give himself up, let Mike go, but then the armed response guys burst in and Gray shot him." I had to pause again as anxiety circled round me like a snake preparing to constrict its prey.

Alasdair's expression had changed from shock to compassion. "Jack, if this is too difficult—"

"No, no," I said. "I want – I need to finish."

"If you're sure."

"It all got a bit chaotic. One of my armed colleagues shouted at Gray to drop the gun. Gray hesitated. Young Danny ran towards his father shouting don't shoot, and I managed to wrestle Gray to the floor before he was shot and wounded by one of the team. And that was it. It was over."

"It doesn't sound to me like you've got anything to feel guilty about," Alasdair said. "You didn't know Gray had suspicions about Mike. You didn't know Gray had a gun."

"I was Mike's handler. I was responsible for his safety. I shouldn't have accepted that we couldn't have armed back-up in situ because of budget constraints. I should have insisted – or at least got them there sooner."

"Hmm, you'd have needed psychic powers to have been any quicker and policy wasn't down to you. I doubt your insistence would have changed it."

"That was the view of the enquiry that took place afterwards," I said. "Officially I wasn't held to be in any way to blame. But it hasn't helped me not to blame myself."

"No, I can see that. And Gray, what happened to him?"

"He got life. The drugs consignment was seized – over half a million pounds worth. And a couple of others were caught and are also serving long sentences. But the rest evaded arrest including the older son, Tommy. He's still very much the subject of ongoing police interest."

"What about the younger boy? Danny was it?"

"Yeah, Danny. He was arrested and tried as an accessory. That was unavoidable, and he was advised to plead guilty, but I spoke up for him at trial, said I thought his involvement was minimal."

"That was very gracious of you."

"Yeah, well, I don't know – I had a feeling about him – that basically he was a good kid in a bad situation. And the judge seemed to agree – gave him a one year suspended sentence."

I sat back, exhausted.

Alasdair sat back too – gave me a minute before he spoke. Then he said, "Thank you, Jack, for telling me all that. It can't have been easy. As I said, I don't think you've got anything to feel guilty about, but I also know that what I think is no real help to you." He looked again at his watch. "Shall we head to the ferry?"

"Yeah, let's go," I said, glad that Alasdair could see I'd had enough talking.

Even once we were on the boat, Alasdair remained companionably quiet for the most part, something I appreciated. Any conversation we did have was about safe neutral topics, such as birds we spotted on the return crossing, good places to go walking, and the latest escapades of our grandchildren.

It wasn't until we were back in Halladale and I was about to get out of the car that he returned to what I'd told him earlier. "I meant what I said, Jack," he said. "No one will hear any of what you said about what's troubling you from me."

"Thanks," I said. "I haven't told anyone else what I told you ... and I've no idea why it's raised its head now."

"The mind's a tricky thing. But I do think you should get some help with the anxiety – maybe see the doctor. And maybe you should tell Rachel."

"I don't know," I said. "I—"

"No need to justify or explain. It's your decision. All I'm saying is give it some thought."

"I will," I said as I got out of the car. And as I did so I wondered what Alasdair's advice would be about Bridget. I hadn't been entirely honest when he mentioned her.

She wasn't exactly back in my life, but she was lurking in the wings.

And then there was my ex-wife's offer. What would Alasdair make of that?

# Chapter Thirteen

*Jack*

As for Alasdair's suggestions as to what I should do about the stuff I'd shared with him, I did give them *some* thought, but probably not as much as he would have liked.

Indeed, I'd already made up my mind not to take a couple of his pieces of advice as he drove off. Talking to Alasdair was one thing, but to a doctor – that wasn't for me. As for telling Rachel, I definitely didn't want to do that. I didn't want to upset her, but more than that I didn't want her to know I'd got somebody killed, that because of me someone else's son had lost their life. And besides, I dreaded her seeing me as weak. After all she'd coped with something much worse than I was going through.

But I did feel slightly better for having talked to Alasdair and I even managed to get something approaching a decent night's sleep for the first time in a while. These two things combined with an early morning phone call from Maddie helped me reach a decision.

My daughter had got in touch to confirm arrangements for her bank holiday weekend trip to Skye with her husband and the two children. I said how much I was looking forward to seeing them and I meant it. It was only when Maddie mentioned that Poppy was desperate to see Rachel, and to help with the lambs that the conversation got awkward.

"Ah, right," I said. "I can't promise. It's a busy time for Rachel. I'll see what I can do."

"Dad, are you okay?" Maddie asked.

"Yes, yes, I'm fine."

"You suddenly sound a bit flat. I know you don't want to talk about it, but are things still difficult between you and Rachel?"

I considered denying it. But I knew it would be pointless. "We're ... yes, we're still having a few problems, but—"

"Oh, Dad. For heaven's sake! Relationships need to be worked at you know."

"Yes, I—"

"Look, sorry I have to go. William's crying and Poppy's calling for me. Sort yourself out, Dad. Love you. See you soon."

So, spurred on by Maddie's challenge, my talk with Alasdair, and having slept for a few uninterrupted hours, I decided.

I didn't need professional help. I didn't need to share my troubles with Rachel. But I did need to stop dwelling on the past and to sort things out.

I began by having my first shave since the wedding followed by a long, hot shower. Then it was on to some overdue housework. I stripped the bed, put in a load of washing, did a bit of vacuuming. And, as I tidied up, I told myself this was more like it. I simply needed to get a grip. I needed to kick all this guilt and anxiety stuff into touch and get things back to how they were.

It was in this optimistic frame of mind that I set off in the late morning to see Rachel. My intentions were clear and straightforward. I felt good and I'd let her see I was fine. I'd put things right between us. And yes, deep down, I hoped she'd reconsider her plans to go away.

Sophie met me at the door of Burnside Cottage. She was putting Miriam into her buggy and was about to set off on a walk. "And about time too," she said, grinning at me. "You'll find Mum in the barn with Steven."

Rachel was in one of the lambing pens, helping a ewe give birth. I stood and watched her. She was talking to Steven about what she was doing. Both of them were so absorbed that they didn't realise I was there. Even in her work clothes and wellies, and with her auburn hair held back in a clip, Rachel still looked beautiful. Her expression was intense, and her small, strong hands soothed the ewe while she indicated to Steven what to do. And as I watched her work, I was overwhelmed once more with my feelings of love for her. I sighed.

Both Steven and Rachel looked up from the newly delivered lamb.

"Sorry," I said. "I … sorry, I can see you're busy." I turned to go.

"No, wait. Jack, wait, please." I was surprised by the urgency in Rachel's voice. I stopped, looked back from the doorway.

Steven waved in greeting. "Good job you came. She's been here since five o'clock this morning. Even had her breakfast here. Been trying to persuade her it's time she had a coffee break." He turned to Rachel. "Go on," he said. "I can take it from here."

In the kitchen at Burnside, I made the usual fuss of Bonnie while Rachel got the coffee. Me and the dog had bonded almost as soon as we met. Rachel and I'd made our first tentative moves towards friendship while out walking with her. And when Rachel had been away in Israel, Bonnie had even moved in with me.

Rachel laid the coffee mugs on the table. "I see you're as popular as ever with Bonnie," she said.

"Not so popular with you though," I said as we sat down, facing each other across the table.

Rachel's look of hurt and pain churned me up inside. "Jack, please—"

"No, no. I'm sorry," I said.

"Let's drink our coffee," she said.

And as we drank, we chatted amicably enough. I asked her how lambing was going and she asked me about how Maddie and the family were. But none of it was what I'd come to say.

Eventually I reached for her hand. "I truly am sorry," I said.

"What for exactly? What are you sorry for?"

"For being a dick basically."

She gave a little laugh.

"Feel free to argue against that," I said.

She withdrew her hand from mine. "No, it's about right. You went from loving and supportive to moody and distant but you denied anything was wrong."

"I ... I didn't want to admit I how I was feeling."

"And how *were* you feeling?"

"I don't know – resentful I suppose. It sounds pathetic now but I resented the fact that you had Sophie and Steven living with you, resented that you'd be going away. And ... and I was scared."

"Scared? Scared of what?"

"That you were moving on, that for you, it was over between us. You seemed so excited about the whole Israel thing ... and then when Eitan turned up ... I'm sorry I got it all wrong."

Rachel pushed her hair back from her face and leaned back in her chair. I wished I knew what she was thinking. Then it was if she'd made some sort of decision. "I know we need to talk," she said as she stood up. "And we will. But right now, I have to get back to the barn."

I stood up too. "I'd like to take you on a picnic," I said. "As soon as you've got a bit of spare time."

Rachel smiled, a smile that gave me hope. "I'd like that," she said. "Call me tomorrow."

# Chapter Fourteen

*Jack*

Two days later, I put the picnic things in the car and went to pick up Rachel and Bonnie. The cold easterly wind that had been blowing for the last week had dropped and the sun was shining. I allowed myself a little optimism as I stopped the car at Rachel's gate and waited for her to join me.

"Are you still happy to go to Waternish Point?" I asked when we reached the end of the Halladale track.

"Yes, that's why I brought these," she said, indicating the bunch of white flowers she was holding. "If it's all right with you, I'd like to stop at the cemetery."

"No problem," I said.

I'd not been to Finlay's grave before. It was in the churchyard at Trumpan, the village where our walk would start, and I offered to wait by the ruined church while Rachel paid her respects. But she surprised me by saying she'd like it if I went with her.

She placed two of the flowers on her parents' grave before turning to the adjacent plot where her son lay.

The headstone was simple – a slab of grey limestone inscribed with Finlay's name and dates and describing him as a beloved son, grandson, brother and friend. There was nothing to suggest the horrific way he died. After Rachel had laid down the flowers, I stepped away to let her have a private moment with her boy.

I looked around as I waited. Despite the spring sunshine the churchyard was bleak. It had its own history of bloody conflict. The first time we'd come on this walk, Rachel told me the story of the sixteenth-century clan massacre that took place in the church, of how one group of people set fire to the building with another group of people trapped inside. I glanced back at Rachel, crouched over her son's grave, bereft by another conflict five hundred years later. Man's inhumanity. I shook my head and turned my back on the ruins. I looked to the sky, tracked a couple of gannets flying out over the sea towards Ardmore Point, and took in a deep breath of the fresh salty air.

A movement at the edge of my vision made me turn back towards the graveyard. Rachel was now standing, shoulders hunched. I walked over to her and she turned to me as I approached. She was crying. She walked into my arms and I held her tight.

Eventually she looked up at me. "Sorry," she said, wiping at her tears.

"Don't be," I said, cupping her face in my hands. We looked at each other. I was thinking about kissing her when she moved away.

"I still miss him," she said, looking up at the sky as she hugged herself.

"Of course you do," I said, stepping behind her and putting a hand on her shoulder.

She leant against me. "I think I'm all back together again, but then it all cracks and crumbles."

"Does it help at all, having him buried here, close by?"

She nodded. "It does. We agreed it between us – me and Peter. He wanted the full military funeral at his church in Edinburgh. He wanted the speeches from the Lieutenant Colonel and the company Major. He wanted the religious solace. None of that meant anything to me, but I didn't have a problem with it if it helped Peter. And it gave Finlay's comrades and his old friends from school a chance to say …" she sighed, wiped at her cheek with her sleeve.

I squeezed her shoulder. "To say goodbye," I said.

Again she nodded. "But I wanted him here, laid to rest in the family plot beside my mum and dad, and Peter didn't have a problem with that. So we had a private burial here the day after the service."

The sun was suddenly obscured by a cloud and Rachel shivered.

"Come on," I said. "Let's get walking."

We collected our backpacks and Bonnie from the car and set off. We followed the track, passing by the ruined remains of two Iron-Age brochs. Rabbits scuttled across our path and little birds, disturbed by our steps, flew up out of the ferns and boulders. We paused occasionally to look at the view across the moor, but mostly we just kept walking, tramping over the rough ground and trying to avoid the marshiest bits of the peaty terrain.

Soon we were getting glimpses of the lighthouse at the top of the headland. We passed the rubble that was all that remained of long-deserted crofts. We crossed fences and fields and we stepping-stoned our way across a couple of burns until, eventually, we arrived at the Point. We stopped by the lighthouse, getting our breath back and looking out to sea. The cloud had mostly cleared and it was good to feel the sun on our faces.

Rachel took a small pair of binoculars from her backpack and scanned the shoreline. "Seals," she said, pointing at the rocks below the cliffs. She handed me the binoculars. It took me a moment to pick them out, but sure enough there they were, about eight of them, spread out like sunbathers.

To the west of us a ferry made its way across the Minch towards the Western Isles and to the east we could see the full length of the Trotternish Ridge with Duntulm castle at its head. It was the kind of view you would never tire of.

I spread out the groundsheet and we sat side by side, Bonnie beside us on the grass alert and sniffing the air. At first neither of us spoke as we took in the view, both of us momentarily lost in our own thoughts.

It was Rachel who broke the silence. "It's not only the missing him," she said.

I looked at her.

"Finlay," she said. "It's not just missing him that's so upsetting. It's the frustration, the sense of ... of waste." As her tears began to fall, I reached into my pocket. "Thank you," she said taking the cotton handkerchief I offered her. "I knew I could rely on you for one of these."

"I know it'll never go completely," I said. "The grief, I mean. But I thought it had got a little better for you – after the counselling – and with the time that's passed."

"Not better, no. It's been two years and eight months and it *has* changed, but it's no better."

"How has it changed?"

"I suppose the shock and the anger have gone, but ..."

I felt a small shudder go through her. "But what?" I asked.

"But so has the pride," she said, her anguish obvious in her voice.

I put an arm round her shoulders and she leant in towards me. "You don't mean you're no longer proud of Finlay, of his bravery?" I said.

"No, not that exactly. I *am* proud that he died saving his comrades, taking the ... the force of the blast like he did. But as time goes on it's less and less of a comfort ... if it ever really was. I don't get the point of it, of why he was in Afghanistan in the first place, why any of them were. Our troops have pulled out, the Americans are leaving soon, and in Helmand, where Finlay died, the Taliban are back in charge. What is there to be proud of? It all feels like a pointless waste."

"I don't know what to say," I said.

"There's nothing to say." Her voice was flat, devoid even of anger or sorrow. She looked up at me as I stroked her arm. "Right," she said. "I need a hot drink and some food. Let's have lunch."

This was a typical Rachel reaction. She didn't do self-pity.

"Good idea," I said, smiling at her. The smile she gave me in return gave me hope, and as I unpacked the picnic, and Rachel organised some water and biscuits for Bonnie, my optimism grew. This was more like it – spending time together, talking, touching. We needed to find the time to do more of this. And, stupidly, I thought I had the perfect answer. I hadn't forgotten Alasdair's advice that the time wasn't right, I just chose to ignore it. I'd ask her when we were finished eating.

I was about to hand her some foil-wrapped sandwiches when she put her hand on mine. "Thanks, for listening," she said. "And I'm sorry for breaking down like that. It's … it's hard sometimes, trying to keep it all together."

My mouth went dry as I looked into her beautiful eyes. I cleared my throat before I spoke. "I want to be that person, Rachel – the person you can share all the difficult stuff with."

She moved her hand to my face, her gaze intense. She smiled a small, wry smile. "Same here," she said. "I want to be the person you share your troubles with."

"You are," I said. And, despite being all too aware I was avoiding doing that very thing, I squared it with my conscience by telling myself I'd be fine now things were better with Rachel. And having witnessed how much she was still suffering from her grief, I was even more certain that my own troubles were trivial.

"I hope so," she said.

I put her hand to my lips and kissed it. "Okay, let's eat," I said.

As we ate we talked about all sorts of things, about family things, ordinary things, safe things.

We were onto our second cup of tea when Rachel said, "I know I mentioned it in passing on the day, but I want to say thank you properly, Jack."

"What for?"

"For everything you did at the wedding – before and during. It meant a lot to me and I appreciate it."

"Not at all," I said. "I hope it makes up for me being such a tit afterwards."

*Settlement*

She laughed. "Just about."

"How are the newly-weds?" I asked. "Are they settling into married life?"

"They're great – very happy. Although I'm sure they're impatient to get into their new house."

"What about you? You must be keen to have your place back to yourself?"

"It's fine," Rachel said. "I'm used to lodgers, remember."

"So you are." I smiled as I remembered living at Rachel's the previous year. It wasn't long after we'd met. I'd planned to live in a caravan while I renovated Dun Halla cottage, but when I had to look after my granddaughter, Poppy, while her mother was ill, Rachel insisted we both move in with her. It had been a happy time and our friendship had grown and strengthened.

"Besides," Rachel continued, "it's lovely having Miriam in the house and being able to help with looking after her."

"And, Steven and Sophie, they seem to like being crofters," I said.

"Yeah, Steven's got his experiences of school holidays on his uncle's farm. And it's amazing the stuff Sophie's remembered from holidays here with my parents," Rachel said. "My dad had both her and Finlay helping to deliver lambs when they were still at primary school."

"Really?" I said. "As young as that?"

"Yeah. Smaller hands – easier to – you know?" She made a gesture with her hands. "Get a stuck lamb out."

I laughed and made a face. "Please, I'm eating," I said.

She laughed too. I loved that she did. This was more like it, more like it had been at the beginning.

A little while later when we'd finished our lunch, and I was packing the groundsheet and other stuff away in my rucksack, Rachel said, "Seriously, though, Sophie and Steven are naturals on the croft. Steven's a fast learner. He's been great with the lambs. He's even talking about maybe reintroducing cows to the croft. He's got all sorts of plans for the future."

And that was my cue. I laid down my bag. "That's good," I said. "And speaking of the future, there's something I'd like to ask you."

"Oh?" Rachel said, pausing as she zipped up her jacket.

I stood facing her, took her hands in mine. "Yes," I said. "Now we've ... you know sorted things out—"

"But there's more—"

"No, let me finish. I need to ask you this. Now things are right between us again. Rachel, will you marry me?"

There was no discernible shock on Rachel's part and no hesitation before she answered. "No, Jack, I won't."

# Chapter Fifteen

*Jack*

"Right," I said, swinging the rucksack onto my shoulder. Disappointment, disbelief, shock – they were all there. "Thanks for giving it some thought." I couldn't keep the sarcastic edge out of my voice.

"Look, I'm sorry," Rachel said. "I know it's hurtful, and I'm touched that you asked me, but I can't marry you." She picked up her bag and began walking.

"Wait," I said, grabbing for her arm. "You don't even want time to think it over?"

She stopped, turned to me. "I don't need time to think it over. You, me, the future – I've been thinking of little else recently."

"But I thought ... you ... we ... now I've apologised and we're talking again ... you don't need to worry about us anymore. We have a future surely?"

"I ... yes, I hope so. I really do. But there's other stuff too."

"What other stuff?"

Rachel took a deep breath, as if she was about to answer me, but then she sighed, looked out to sea.

"Rachel?" I said. "What other stuff?"

She turned to me, raised her hands as if trying to pacify me. "Let's finish our walk. Then when we get back, I'll come to yours and we'll talk some more."

This was all too ominous. What was so important or so difficult that it had to wait till we were home? But it didn't look like I had a choice.

The walk back wasn't great. I don't remember what we saw or the small talk we engaged in to try to fill the awkwardness that once more filled the space between us.

It was around four when we got back. I dropped Rachel off at Burnside. She said she'd check on the lambs, grab a quick shower, and be at mine in an hour.

Somehow I filled the time. I told myself to keep calm. Whatever she told me, I would accept and I'd try to understand. I also beat myself up for rushing into the proposal, but then I told myself it was salvageable. I needed to be supportive and show Rachel I could be a good husband to her.

It began well enough.

For a moment I gazed at her as she stood there on the doorstep. She looked great in a dark green sweater and jeans. She'd left her hair down and it was all I could do not to take her in my arms there and then.

"I brought this," she said, holding up a bottle of red wine.

"I'm sorry," I said once we were sitting in the living-room with a glass of wine each. Rachel sat on one of the armchairs by the woodburner, her legs curled underneath her. I sat on the edge of the sofa. "Sorry I went rushing in with that stupid proposal."

"It wasn't stupid. It was—"

"Inappropriate, irrelevant, not the right time."

Rachel smiled. "I was going to say unexpected, but yes, probably those other things too."

"So what's going on? What's this other stuff that's troubling you?"

She laid her glass on the side table, rested her chin on her clasped hands for a moment as she thought. "I've come a long way – emotionally – since we met and a lot of that's down to you, Jack. You saved me – not just from the river – but from a very dark place. I'll always be grateful to you for that. And I've loved being your friend and lover. I don't want that to end."

"But?"

"But nothing. That's how it is. My life's gone from being completely uprooted to being back on solid ground again. It's great that things are sorted between Sophie and me. It's great that I made the trip to Israel, and that I've begun to properly live again. But lately I've realised, there's more I want to do – that I *need* to do."

"And this stuff you want to do, it doesn't involve me?"

"Not directly, no, I don't think it does."

"So, you've had your fun with me and now you're moving on." So much for calm and supportive – all I could hear in my voice was sneering and sarcasm.

"No! That's not how it is at all."

"No?"

Rachel ran her hands through her hair. "I love you, Jack. I want you in my life."

"Sure—"

"No, let me speak," she said. "I want you in my life, but I also want it to be *my* life, on *my* terms."

"Okay," I said. But I wasn't sure it *was* okay. And I wasn't even sure what she meant. Did she want me in her life or not? But I forced myself to keep quiet, to let her speak.

"When I got back from Israel last year and we got together, I thought I was ready to settle, that all I wanted was to be here on Skye and to be with you."

"But now?"

"But now, I see that's not enough. Israel helped, but my life's still in a bit of a stall."

"In what way?"

"When I came back to Skye after the divorce, my plan was to buy my own place, establish my career as a book author in my own right, as well as an illustrator of other people's work. But instead I ended up moving back into my parents' house, taking over the running of the croft when my father could no longer do it, helping to nurse him before he died, and then taking care of my mother."

"But you did become an author. Your Seamus books—"

"Yes, yes I know. And I'm proud of the Seamus books, but I want to do more, to do different stuff, extend myself."

"Being married to me wouldn't stop you doing that," I said.

"I know, but it's not only about my career. I've compromised for years on everything, first of all with Peter and then when I moved back to Skye. But now I don't have to be answerable to anyone and I like that. I intend to enjoy it for some time yet."

"Right," I said. It was all I could manage. I really was struggling to understand.

"I have this feeling, an irresistible urge that I need to do some good in the world, some good beyond here." Rachel stood up, walked to the window and looked out over the loch. "As I said, I'm troubled by this feeling that Finlay's death was pointless." She turned to face me. "War solves nothing."

It sounded like a challenge of some sort. I sensed I was required to respond. "Sometimes it does," I said. "The Second World War – Hitler had to be stopped. *You* know that."

"Yes, I do. But in the long term – we seem to end up back at square one – back at war – and more people like my mum having to flee their homeland and lose everything – including the people they love in the process."

"So what's the answer, what's *your* answer?"

She shook her head. "I don't have a definitive answer to such an enormous question. But I do know what *I'd* at least like to *try* to do." She came over and sat beside me on the sofa. She took my hands in hers. "This new book – it's about much more than me developing as a writer. I'm so excited by the prospect of returning to Israel and maybe doing my tiny bit for peace, and for fighting hatred. This new book – the whole project – it's about getting people talking – communicating with people they might not normally communicate with. It might actually do some good."

"I get that," I said. "I do." And I meant it. I could see this was something she needed to do, that whether I liked it or not, she was going away, going back to Israel. I had to accept that. "You'd be going with my blessing," I said.

She let go of my hands, sat back. "I'd go with or without your blessing."

"Sorry, this is hard."

"What is?"

"This working at relationships stuff."

"Have you only just realised?"

"Yeah, I don't think I've ever done it before. When I was married, or in any of my other relationships, I ignored any difficulties, hoped they'd sort themselves out or just go away."

Rachel's raised eyebrows hinted at her disbelief. "And when they didn't go away?"

"I distracted myself with other stuff, work and ... you know ... other things."

"Other women?"

"Yes, sometimes."

"Settlement cracks," she said.

"What?"

"Settlement cracks. I remember my dad talking about them when he built Burnside. You get a nice new home and you move in, but then as it all beds in, the settlement cracks appear in the plaster. And you have to chip those bits away and renew the plaster if you don't want the cracks to get worse."

She looked at me and gave a little laugh. "Don't worry, I can see you're baffled. Let's just say you'd ignore the cracks and then when they didn't go away, you'd move house."

"I see," I said.

"No, you don't," she said. "But never mind. I suppose I should be honoured that with our relationship you at least want to try to fix things."

I allowed myself to relax a bit, could feel my earlier irritation dissipating. "You're worth the effort," I said.

She looked as surprised as I was by the break in my voice as I spoke. She put her hand on my arm. "Don't look so sad," she said. "This was never going to be easy. You and me, with our ... our baggage, it was never going to be sailing off into the sunset, happy ever after. And besides, real life's not like that."

"But that's not a reason to give up, to not try to be happy."

"Of course not," she said. "All I'm saying is, it's not surprising that at this stage we're having to take stock."

"I suppose so."

"Look, Jack, thank you for the proposal. Thank you for being my friend and my lover. I don't want that to change. But if we got married, lived together day after day, it would all come down to whose turn it was to cook or hang out the washing. There'd be bickering, and trampling on each other's dreams. I've been there." She looked down at the floor. "I'm not going there again."

I put my hand under her chin and gently tilted her to head up so she was looking at me. I stroked her hair back from her face. "So what now?" I asked.

# Chapter Sixteen

*Jack*

"This," she said. And she put her arms round me and kissed me on the mouth.

I got over my surprise and returned her kiss. Then she took my hand and stood up. "Come on," she said. She led me out of the room and upstairs to the bedroom. "Now, we make love," she said, as she undid my shirt buttons. "Now is all that matters."

I let Rachel take the lead, let her kiss and caress me, watched her lovely face, enjoyed her gentle touch. And then it was my turn, my turn to demonstrate for the first time in weeks how much I fancied her, how much I loved her. And afterwards, as we lay together, limbs woven around each other, I wished our minds could communicate as well as our bodies.

"Thank you for that," I said, before kissing the top of her head.

"My pleasure," she said, and I could hear the smile in her voice. She moved so she was looking at me. "We're good together, like this, as we are now. So can we please focus on the present?"

"I'll try," I said. "I do love you, you know. And however you want to play it between us is fine by me."

She stroked my face. "I love you too, Jack, very much, but let's just keep it real, not expect too much."

"Whatever you say," I said.

"Good," she said. "And don't leave it so long next time – if something's up – can you please tell me, don't go all moody and broody?"

"Message received," I said.

"Promise? We promise to talk, listen and support each other?"

"I ... yes, yes, okay I promise," I said.

"It's the start of a commitment, Jack, not a marriage, not even living together, but a faithful, loving relationship with each other."

"Right," I said again. The fact I hadn't told her everything that had been troubling me recently niggled in the background. But I told myself it was fine, told myself that what had been said was enough, and that, really, Rachel didn't need to know the rest.

"God, you look terrified," she said.

"Yeah, well, like I said, I'm new at this ... this working at relationships stuff."

Rachel kissed me again. "Don't worry," she said. "Like I said, let's go one day at a time, enjoy these ... these moments ... and what we have now." Then she sat up. "Right, I hope you've got some food in because I'm starving."

I made us macaroni cheese, threw in some bacon and a bit of leek, and Rachel declared herself impressed as she devoured it. We were sitting at the table in the living-room. The evening sun shone in through the west-facing window and the logs crackled in the woodburner. It had been a while since I'd felt this relaxed and I smiled as I watched Rachel eat.

"What?" she said, catching me watching her.

"I was enjoying watching you eat. You certainly don't pick at your food."

"Lambing, walking and sex," she said. "Makes a girl hungry."

We were sitting on the sofa with our coffee, an easy silence between us as we watched the flames behind the stove's glass door, when I remembered. "I have a special request for you," I said.

She looked at me over her coffee mug. "Oh?"

"Maddie and the family are coming up next weekend, and I know it's close to you going away, but Poppy's been asking if she can help with the lambs like last year."

Rachel smiled. "Of course she can. I'd like that." She glanced at her watch and stood up. "But now I must go."

I got to my feet too. I was torn between wanting her to stay over and being relieved she wasn't. The last thing I wanted was for her to see how disturbed my nights were. But I also didn't want her to leave just yet.

She put her arms round me. "Sorry not to be staying," she said, before kissing me. "I'm going home to sleep. It's a bath, an early night and then up at about four-thirty for lambing duty for me."

"I see," I said.

Rachel smiled. "That your supportive face?" she said.

"Yeah, I take it, it needs some work."

She kissed me again. "You'll get there, Jack," she said. "You'll get there."

# Chapter Seventeen

*Jack*

It was around five the next morning when I finally gave up on getting any proper sleep. The nightmares and the flashbacks were the worst yet and had forced me awake several times during the night. I tried to distract myself from the tortures of the night by thinking about Rachel and whether we really did have a future. But I also recalled what she'd said about enjoying the here-and-now, about not looking too far ahead. And that's when the idea came to me.

A short time later I was dressed and on my way to Rachel's, complete with a flask of coffee and some rapidly cooling foil-wrapped toast.

She was on her knees in one of the pens when I got to the barn. She was talking to a ewe as I approached, her tone soothing, but also breathless.

"Hard at work," I said.

She jumped at the sound of my voice. "Jack! What a fright. What are you doing here?"

"Woke early and lay there thinking about you and your wise words. So, I decided to seize the day and bring you breakfast." I lifted the flask so she could see it.

"That's a kind thought," she said. "But it'll be a while yet before I can take a break."

"It'll keep," I said, putting the food and the flask down on a workbench at the side. "No Steven this morning?"

"No. He was up in the night with Miriam, so I told him I'd get this."

"So, this one, she's about to pop?"

"Yes, or rather she should be, but things seem to have got a bit stuck. I'm going to have to check it out." She reached into her pocket and pulled out a rubber glove. "Okay, mummy," she said, inserting her hand into the ewe's rear. "Let's see what's going on here."

I could only lean on the railing that edged the pen and watch as Rachel seemed to push, pull and twist. I wasn't used to feeling this helpless or useless, but this was way outside my area of expertise. And as I watched her at work, kneeling in the straw, dressed in her shepherd's uniform of wellies, old jeans and a not very clean fleece, I was again reminded of how much I loved this woman. Her hair had fallen free of its clip and she kept swiping it out of her eyes with her free hand. I climbed over the railing and crouched down beside her. "Allow me," I said, pulling her hair back from her face.

"Thanks," she said without looking up. "Lamb's stuck, one leg back."

I did my best to reclip all the strands on top of her head. I also did my best to ignore the delicious smell and sheen of those auburn curls and the creamy skin I'd revealed on the back of her neck. My daydreaming was interrupted as Rachel moved suddenly, almost falling backwards as a small, slimy white creature emerged from the ewe. And the previous heady scents were overlaid by something decidedly less pleasant.

Rachel pulled away the slimy bag that encased the lamb and grabbed some straw which she used to wipe its nostrils. I assumed this was to clear them of gunk. She stood up and let the lamb hang by its legs until finally it bleated. "Yes!" she said, turning at last to look at me, her smile triumphant. She placed the lamb beside its mother who promptly began sniffing and licking her new baby.

I was surprised to feel a bit emotional as I witnessed the birth and its aftermath. I had to clear my throat before I spoke. "That was pretty awesome," I said. "Well done, you."

"All in a day's work," Rachel said, as she peeled off the glove and dipped her hands in a bucket of disinfectant liquid. "But yes," she said, drying her hands on a bit of ragged towel, "a new life is always an awesome event."

I watched as she prepared a syringe and injected the ewe. "Just a precaution against infection after me having to intervene," she said.

I nodded as she put on fresh gloves. She explained this was to dispose of the afterbirth. "You don't have to stay," she said. "It was kind of you to bring breakfast and I *will* have it later, but this must be very boring for you."

"Not at all," I said. I hadn't expected to be so absorbed or moved by the lambing process. And I was also enjoying seeing this aspect of Rachel and her daily working life that I knew so little about. "I'd like to stay ... if that's okay with you."

"Right then," she said. "Take this." She handed me a tub of pellets. "It's high time this wee one had a bit of a suckle, and since Mum's not showing much interest, I need you to distract her while I have a go at getting her started."

"Okay," I said.

"Offer her the tub. Hold it up and let her eat." Rachel picked up the lamb, and as the ewe watched Rachel, Rachel watched me.

I shook the tub, rattled the pellets and then put them under the ewe's nose. She was soon facing me rather than the lamb and tucking in.

"You're a natural," Rachel said, smiling, as she tried to get the lamb to latch on to one of the ewe's teats. It wasn't long before the newborn was having its first drink and Rachel told me I could put the tub down and leave them to it.

Eventually having checked the other ewes and lambs who were also in the barn, Rachel was able to take a break and we sat together on a hay bale in the corner.

But as we had our coffee and toast, I was all too aware that in a week she'd be leaving for the Middle East. I fought to suppress the dread this realisation brought. I reminded myself about staying in the present, but it wasn't easy. "Won't you miss all this when you're away?" I said.

"Yes and no," she said. "I won't miss the early starts and the being out in the worst of the weather, but I'll miss the animals – the sheep, the hens, Bonnie."

"So you wouldn't want to give it up completely?"

"Not completely, no. But I never intended to be a crofter. It just happened. I came home after the divorce, then when dad died, I took over. Now though, with Steven and Sophie on board, it'll be easier to split my time. They'll gradually take over the day-to-day running, but I'd still want to be involved."

Right on cue, Steven arrived. "And your help will always be very welcome," he said. "Good morning both." He nodded at me and grinned as he said, "I hope you're not keeping the staff off their work."

"Hey, I'm still the boss for now," Rachel said, laughing. "And Jack was kind enough to bring me breakfast."

"Don't worry," I said. "I made sure she put in a full shift first."

Rachel got to her feet and showed Steven the newest arrival. Then she turned to me and said, "Thanks for coming over and for breakfast, but now I must get back to the house. I've got to at least think about what I'm going to pack and there are all the travel arrangements to confirm."

"I'll be in touch when the family arrive at the end of the week," I said, trying to keep my tone light. "But I'll leave you in peace until then."

"Thanks, I'd appreciate that." Her parting kiss and embrace were warm. "See you soon," she said, her voice soft and her smile loving.

I suppose I should have felt reassured. But I didn't. All I felt was the dead weight of dread.

# Chapter Eighteen

*Jack*

For the next few days, I did my best to distract myself from my disappointment at the failed marriage proposal, and my trepidation at Rachel's departure. I prepared for my weekend visitors and tried to keep my mind on how much I was looking forward to seeing them.

I also decided to get Bridget off my back. She was one distraction I could do without, so I called her. She picked up immediately.

"Jack, hi, this is a pleasant surprise."

"It can't be that much of surprise. You've been hassling me to get back to you."

"Not hassling, just keen to move on. I've had enough of hotel living. And if—"

"It's okay. You can move in – my flat – you can have it as long as you need it."

"Oh, that's great, Jack. Thank you. Like I said, it makes sense for both of us. This way the flat's not standing empty and I don't have to commit to a six-month let which I most likely won't need. And that's assuming I could find something in Edinburgh's overpriced and scarce rental market. It's ridiculous—"

"I said you can have it. It's fine. Take as long as you need."

"James has promised me a quick divorce – now that he's met the love of his life. So as soon as I get my financial settlement I'll be buying a place of my own. And—"

"You explained all that, Bridget. And I've agreed. You can move in any time. I take it you still have a key?"

"I do as it happens. I remained hopeful – you know – that you'd tire of your exile and of your little shepherdess, and come back to civilisation."

"Even if I did, you and me are over. I told—"

"Yes, yes, I know. Doesn't stop me hoping though. Anyway how is life in the back of the back of beyond? You and Rachel still in love?"

"I have to go, Bridget."

"Oh, right, but we haven't discussed rent and things."

"It's fine. I don't want rent. Now I must go."

I was relieved when the call ended. And not only because I'd finally dealt with Bridget's request. Speaking to her had unsettled me.

While I agreed with Bridget that it would be good to have someone living in the flat, I realised I should be selling it. If I was committed to life on Skye, there was no point in keeping it. After all I could stay with my daughter anytime I was in the city. But that was just it, I didn't know if I *was* committed to Skye. If things didn't work out with Rachel, then I couldn't see me staying on.

But I had two other more immediate dilemmas to sort out. And having resolved the Bridget dilemma, I decided to keep up the momentum. So I made two phone calls— one to a local guy on Skye, and one to my ex-wife.

It was around four p.m. on the Thursday, as I was finishing off my preparations for the arrival of the family the next day, when Alasdair dropped in unexpectedly. He said he'd been out for a walk and had dropped in on the off chance the kettle might be on. I made us both a coffee and we took our drinks outside to the bench at the back of the house.

"So," I said. "Did Morag send you? She got more concerns

about me?" I tried to keep my tone light, tried to seem relaxed. But I think it came out as forced.

"No," Alasdair said. He sipped his coffee, slow, deliberate, infuriating.

There was definitely an agenda. "Right," I said warily.

"Morag didn't send me. I'm here as your friend. And after our conversation the other day, I wanted to see how things were with you."

I looked at him and nodded. "Sorry, like I said, I'm not very good at meaningful conversations."

"But you did manage to have one – did you – with Rachel?"

"Yeah" I said, my increasing wariness obvious in my voice.

Alasdair raised an eyebrow, but his tone was kind when he spoke. "And how did it go?"

I gave him an edited version of what I'd said to Rachel and how she'd responded. I assured him things were better between us. I left out the marriage proposal and the fact I hadn't mentioned any of the Mike stuff to her. I hoped that would suffice.

"That's good," Alasdair said, but he looked suspicious. "And did she agree with me that you should get help with your flashback and anxiety problems?"

"Ah ..." I said, "I didn't actually tell her about any of that."

"Tell me to mind my own business, but why not?"

"Because I can't ... that is ... I don't want to worry her ... and I ... I just can't, okay?"

"Okay, okay, sorry – your decision. But have you at least considered professional help?"

"Considered it, yes. But decided against it. Thing is, I figure if I can keep myself busy it'll all settle back down."

"Hmm, and how do you plan to do that?"

"By working – I've had the offer of a job – or rather two jobs."

"Oh?"

"Yep, one's here on Skye," I said. "You know that photographer chap, Richard Macdonald, the one who runs the residential holidays for photographers?"

"Oh aye, he has a B&B in Uig. Morag follows him on Facebook, he has a page, if that's what you call it. She's shown me some of his photos. Takes folks out and about to all the wild places, helps them get good pictures."

"That's him. We met a while ago when we were both doing some night photography at Neist Point. We got chatting, ended up having a pint together. Anyway, he's offered me some work."

"Has he now?" Alasdair said.

"He's looking specifically for someone to lead night shoots – someone who can help clients with the technicalities of dark sky photography and who knows their way around the night sky."

"And you're that someone?" Alasdair smiled.

"Richard seems to think so. It wouldn't start until October when the nights get darker again. He's already getting enquiries and he's thinking of offering several two or three-night packages with one-to-one tuition during the winter months."

"And will you take it?"

"Yes, I think I will. After all, one of the things that attracted me to Skye was its dark skies and the chance to hone my own photography skills and night-sky knowledge."

"And this way you get paid while you do it."

"Yeah, although it's not about the money."

"No, I get that. And the other job – what does it involve?"

"Ah, well, if I go for it, that one involves me going to Edinburgh and going back to work for the police."

Alasdair raised his eyebrows and I couldn't quite decide if his expression was one of surprise or scepticism. He didn't say anything, merely indicated that I should continue.

"My ex-wife, Ailsa, she's an ACC – an Assistant Chief Constable – now and she's in charge of Major Crimes and Public Protection. Anyway, she also oversees the Historic Crimes Unit and she's been on at me for a while to do some work with them."

"You'd be going back to being a policeman?"

"No, I'd be there as a consultant, helping with unsolved cases – mainly ones where I was the lead investigating officer. It would be for three months, and, ideally, they'd like me to start next month."

"And you're giving this serious consideration, are you?"

"Yeah, I called her earlier, got more details. Truth is I miss it – the buzz, the camaraderie, the structure."

"I can relate to that certainly. Retirement takes some getting used to, but I can't say I've any regrets."

"Nor me, not really. It was the sensible thing to do after the heart attack and the surgery. But that doesn't mean I don't miss it and, as I said, I need something to occupy my mind – keep me from thinking about – you know – all that other stuff."

"But won't being back there make it worse? Won't it trigger more bad memories?"

"I don't think it will. I think it'll be good for me to be back catching criminals. I reckon it'll make me feel less useless, give me a chance to redress the balance."

"Hmm, I can sort of see how that might work," Alasdair said, making an admirable attempt to hide his scepticism. He looked at his watch. "But now I better go. I need to get organised. I'm off down to Edinburgh tomorrow – catch up weekend with an old friend from university days."

"Sounds good," I said, as we both stood up. "And thanks for calling round and for listening."

Alasdair smiled. "That's what friends are for," he said. "Oh, and I meant to say, I could check your flat for you when I'm in Edinburgh, if you like. I remember you saying your daughter goes in occasionally, but since the wee one was born it's been harder for her to fit it in."

"Thanks for the offer, but no need." And as I said this I realised I'd have to let – a most likely disapproving – Maddie know sooner rather than later about my new tenant.

"Okay, if you're sure," Alasdair said. "Don't know why you don't get a tenant in – make some money out of the place."

"I have done," I said. "There's someone moving in very soon." But, of course, I didn't mention that it was Bridget.

# Chapter Nineteen

*Jack*

It was mid-afternoon the next day when the family arrived. As soon as her father stopped the car, Poppy got out and jumped into my arms shouting, "Grandpa, Grandpa, we're here."

"Yes, you are," I said, as I hugged her. Then she was off running towards the house, saying that she needed to explore.

After we'd all greeted one another, Maddie went to get baby William out of his car seat and into the house, while I helped my son-in-law, Brian, unload the car of what seemed to me an incredible amount of stuff.

"Don't worry," Brian said, "we're not moving in. It's mostly William's stuff. Eight-month-olds can't travel light, apparently."

"So I see," I said, laughing, as we took the last of the luggage out of the boot. Maddie was on the doorstep with William in her arms and Poppy was dancing round her as Brian and I approached. I always enjoyed seeing them but this time, it felt especially good to have them there.

"Where's Rachel, Grandpa? I thought she'd be here," Poppy said, slipping her hand into mine as we all made our way indoors.

"She's at her own house. She'll most likely be working with the sheep." Of course I knew as I said it that this response wasn't acceptable.

"But I need to see Rachel now."

"I don't know if now would be a good time," I said. I sensed this too was an inadequate response.

It was no use looking for backing from Poppy's parents. Brian had already disappeared upstairs with some of the bags and Maddie had followed him, saying she needed to change William's nappy.

Poppy and I went into the living-room. I hoped to distract her with the colouring books I'd got for her. But I didn't even get as far as taking them out of the drawer.

"And the lambs," Poppy said. "I need to see the lambs. *And* I've got my books to get signed."

"Your books?"

"Yes, I've got them all with me, but only one is signed."

"Okay," I said, still unsure what she was on about.

Poppy sighed. "Right," she said, in a tone that could only be described as primary school teacher. "When Rachel gave me *Seamus the Sheep to the Rescue* at Christmas she signed it. But all her other books, which I already had, were at home. I said I wished they were signed too and Rachel said to bring them the next time I came to Skye and she'd sign them for me then. So—"

"So you've got them with you."

"Yes. Good, so now you understand, Grandpa. I need to see Rachel now."

"But, like I said to you, she'll be busy with—"

"No, she said she could see me today."

"When did she say that?" I said.

"I texted her when I was in the car coming here."

"How did you do that?"

"With Mummy's phone, of course."

"Of course," I said, laughing.

"There's nothing funny about it, Grandpa."

"Sorry, I wasn't laughing at *you*. I was laughing at me for being surprised at you using your mum's phone."

"I asked Mummy first."

"I'm sure you did," I said.

"Anyway, Rachel texted me back and said she'd see me when I got here."

"Well unless she's hiding, she's definitely not here," I said. "Did you check the cupboards?"

"She's not hiding! You are silly." Poppy giggled.

"Yes, he is, isn't he?" We both turned to see Rachel in the doorway.

"Rachel!" Poppy ran to her, causing Rachel to stagger a little as she was hugged tightly around her waist.

Rachel returned the hug. "Hello, sweetheart," she said. "It's so good to see you. How are you?"

I loved the warm smile and the soft tone of voice Rachel used whenever she was with my granddaughter. She and Poppy had established a rapport from their very first meeting and I loved that too.

"I'm fine thank you," Poppy said, still holding on to her. "Grandpa thought you'd be too busy to see me today. But he was wrong, wasn't he?"

Rachel smiled at me over the top of Poppy's head. "Yes, he was. I couldn't wait to see you after I got your text. So here I am."

"I'll go and get the books," Poppy said, finally letting go of Rachel. "I think Daddy's taken them upstairs in my bag."

"Sorry," I said, as Poppy ran off upstairs. "I'd no idea our arrangements were going to be overridden."

Rachel smiled and shook her head as she walked over to me. "You should know who's boss by now." She kissed me on the cheek. "I won't get too close," she said. "I've come straight from the barn."

I looked at her, standing in front of me, dressed in her work jeans and a faded cotton shirt, sleeves rolled up and hair all tousled, and thought that close was exactly what I wanted her to be. "Not a problem as far as I'm concerned," I said, as I ran my thumb along her jaw.

She caught hold of my hand, kissed it, and then leant her face against it as she looked into my eyes. But before she could say or do anything else Poppy was back.

"Here they are," Poppy said. She took the books over to the

table. "Grandpa have you got a pen Rachel could use please?"

"I certainly do," I said, picking one up from the coffee table and handing it to Rachel.

There were four books to sign and Rachel looked serious and thoughtful as she sat at the table, writing on the fly leaf of each one. As she was handing them back to Poppy, Maddie and Brian came into the room along with William who was now in his father's arms.

Poppy was exuberant."Look Mummy, look Daddy, Rachel signed my books."

While Poppy's parents examined the signed copies and then got chatting with Rachel, I went through to the kitchen to make everyone a cup of tea.

Maddie joined me while I waited for the kettle to boil. "Just need to heat this up," she said, waving a bottle of baby milk before putting it in the microwave. "Those were lovely comments that Rachel wrote in the books."

"I'm sure they were," I said.

"So did you sort things out? Did you talk to her?"

"Yes, we talked."

"And?"

"And things are better," I said.

Maddie raised an eyebrow. "Hmm, you don't look or sound convinced." The microwave pinged and Maddie removed the bottle. "Don't go giving up, Dad. And don't do anything stupid either."

While the rest of us drank our tea and Brian fed William, Poppy began working on the colouring book I'd got for her. The conversation was relaxed as we all caught up with each other's news. But the relaxing was over when we got on to how the lambing was going.

Poppy only needed to hear the word lamb and the colouring was set to one side immediately. "Rachel, can I see the lambs today?" she asked.

Rachel smiled at her. "I don't see why not."

So a little while later, Rachel, Poppy and I walked to Burnside together. We'd left Brian and William snoozing on the sofa and Maddie settling down to enjoy some reading and some rare peace and quiet.

It felt good as Poppy skipped along between us holding hands with us both. Then, once we got to the barn, the good feeling continued as I stood back and watched. I watched Rachel handling the lambs and explaining things to Poppy. I watched as she let Poppy bottle feed a triplet lamb whose mother couldn't quite cope with three babies. I was mesmerised as I looked at the wonder on Poppy's face and the tenderness on Rachel's. This was how it had been as I'd fallen in love with Rachel the year before. Maddie was right, I'd be a fool to screw up what we had.

When it was time for me and Poppy to go home, Rachel suggested that as the weather forecast was good, we all meet up for a walk the following afternoon. She also suggested that we all eat at Burnside afterwards.

"Sounds great," I said, "I'm sure my lot will be up for it. But are you sure about having us all back to yours to eat?"

"Yes, I wouldn't have asked otherwise."

"Okay then. Thank you. And thanks for what you've done for Poppy already – the books, the lambs – you've been great – especially when you've got such a lot on."

"It was a pleasure. I love spending time with Poppy. And the to-do list is almost complete." She counted the items off on her fingers as she recited her recent tasks. "Lambing's nearly finished, Steven and Sophie are ready to take over here with Alasdair on standby to help, the Jason book illustrations and text are with the editor, and I've even done most of my packing. So it wasn't a problem to take some time out." She smiled, but then put her hand on my arm as she looked at me. "What's wrong?"

I hadn't realised that the pain induced by her mention of packing had shown quite so clearly on my face. "Nothing ... really ... nothing's wrong ... I ... I'm not looking forward to your departure, that's all."

"I thought we'd sorted all that out. I thought you were okay with it, that you got it."

"I *am* okay with it," I lied. "It's just ... I'm going to miss you."

Rachel surprised me by kissing me on the lips, but before she had the chance to say anything, Poppy appeared beside us, having finished saying goodbye to each lamb individually. It was time to go.

# Chapter Twenty

*Jack*

The next day lived up to its forecast of good weather so, after lunch, Rachel and me and our families set off for a walk at Halladale beach. Steven carried Miriam in a sling, which allowed her to snuggle into her father's chest and she was soon asleep. Brian was also on baby-carrying duty and had William in a sturdy looking backpack, which allowed the wee lad to see roundabout him as we walked, or to drop off if he wanted to. Sophie and Maddie walked behind their husbands, chatting and laughing as they went. Rachel and I, with Poppy between us, walked at the back of the party and Bonnie ran in circles round us all, doing her sheepdog thing of keeping us together and making sure there were no stragglers.

It felt good. I felt good. I sighed.

Rachel glanced round at me. "Was that the sound of you relaxing?"

"I believe it was." I smiled at her.

"It's good, isn't it ... like this ... our families together ... us together?"

"Yes, it is."

"So, relax and enjoy it. It's enough isn't it?"

I nodded. It was enough for now. But I wanted so much more.

Poppy, who'd got slightly ahead of us, as she skipped along, stopped suddenly and swung round to face us. She grabbed my hand, "Can you, me and Rachel go and fly my kite tomorrow, like we did before?"

I hesitated. "I don't know if—"

"Oh, please, Grandpa. Please, Rachel."

"I think it's a very good idea," Rachel said. "I enjoyed it last time we did it, so count me in. What about you, Grandpa?"

"Great," I said, laughing. I'd got Poppy the kite the year before when she'd been staying with me and the three of us had a wonderful time flying it. Rachel and I were still just friends at the time, but seeing her as exhilarated as Poppy was by our time on the hill with the kite, tipped me further into love with her.

By now the track had led us to the machair, the grassy stretch at the top of the dunes, which sat above the beach. We headed down the sandy hill onto the shingle.

After she'd checked, in her matter-of-fact way, that Steven would be okay on the beach with his prosthetic legs and had been reassured that he would, Poppy ran after Bonnie and stood at the water's edge as she watched the collie chasing the waves. And, after a short time during which all of us adults did the standing and staring thing, the babies were handed to their mothers so that Brian, Steven and I could have a bit of a stone-skimming contest. Rachel watched the contest for a while. Then she stepped in and ended it. She did two sets of five leaps with her skimmers – the cue for much applause from Sophie, Maddie and Poppy, and much gawping and gasping from us men.

There were also allegations of sexism from the women – allegations which led to some chasing and attempts to push partners into the sea. Poppy laughed and clapped her hands as she watched the adults having fun, and Bonnie barked and circled us as she tried to get everyone back into some sort of orderly group.

On the walk back to Burnside, with the three of us again at the back of the group, Poppy ordered me to walk between Rachel and her and to hold hands with both of us.

"Yes, ma'am," I said, as I did as I was told.

Poppy laughed. "Oh, Grandpa, you're so funny. I do love you."

"I love you too," I said, squeezing her hand.

"And you love Rachel too, don't you, Grandpa?"

"Yes, yes I do," I said, glancing at Rachel. She was looking directly at me and held my gaze as I said, "I love her very much."

"Then why don't you marry her?" Poppy said.

In the heart-stopping moment after Poppy had spoken, I felt what I can only describe as a blush, probably my first in decades, creep over my face. I looked at the ground. "I don't think ... that is I've..."

Rachel stroked my arm with her free hand. She leaned round me to look at Poppy. "Grandpa did ask me," she said.

Poppy's eyes widened, as she let go of my hand. "Yes!" she said, jumping up and down. "You're getting married! That means I'll have three Grandmas. Grandma Ailsa, she was married to Grandpa before and she's mummy's mother. And then there's Grandma Grace, she's Daddy's mother, and then after you're married I'll have Grandma Rachel. That is so cool!" She skipped ahead of us then stopped to say, "Can I be a bridesmaid?"

I still seemed incapable of offering any sort of reply, didn't know where to start.

"No, sweetheart, I'm afraid you can't." Rachel went to Poppy. She guided her to a large boulder by the side of the track and helped her up, so they could sit side-by-side on top of it.

I stood close by, awkward, looking at the sea and the sky, wincing inwardly as Rachel explained.

"Grandpa asked me to marry him, but I said no."

"But why?" Poppy said. "You love each other so you *should* get married. That's what Mummy and Daddy did. That's what grown-ups do."

"You're right. It's what lots of grown-ups do. But not everyone wants to get married – even when they love someone very much. Some people like to keep things the way they are. They think getting married might spoil all the nice things, the good things they share – that it might mean they don't stay friends."

"You mean like my friend Coral's parents? She said they used to have lots of fights and arguments and they got divorced and now she lives with her mummy and sees her daddy on Saturdays and Sundays. She says they both love her, but don't like each other at all anymore."

"Yes, like that. I would hate it if Grandpa and me didn't like each other anymore."

"But that wouldn't happen. Not to you and Grandpa."

"I think it could. We've both been married before and we weren't very good at it."

"So you're not marrying Grandpa because you're scared?"

"Yes, I suppose I am a bit scared, but I also like how things are now."

"So, you love Grandpa and he loves you?

"Yes."

"And you're best friends and you always will be no matter what – like me and Coral?"

"I hope so."

"But you don't want to get married?"

"No."

"Okay then," Poppy said with a sigh as she slid down off the boulder. "But I'm still going to think about maybe calling you Grandma Rachel and then you'll still have to be my grandma, even if you and Grandpa fall out."

And with that Poppy dashed off along the track calling for her parents to wait for her as she ran.

As I watched her, my gut churning, my heart aching, I wished I could have even a tiny fraction of her resilience and positivity.

Rachel walked over to me. "Sorry, Jack – all that with Poppy, I know it's not what you wanted to hear, but I thought it was for the—"

"Best? Best to be honest? Yes, and you're always that, aren't you? No sugar-coating from you." I nearly choked as I spoke, trying so hard to keep the bile from spewing out, to keep the bitterness out of my voice. Some hope.

But Rachel didn't flinch – my strong, brave, beautiful Rachel. "Yes," she said. "I am. I can't be any other way." She took my hands in hers. "But I hope I'm not cruel. Not accepting your proposal, I know I hurt you and I'm so sorry."

I looked at her, at her lovely face marred by her stricken expression and my pain receded. And all I wanted at that moment was for Rachel not to look that way, not on my account.

I pulled her to me, kissed her hair and then my lips found hers. "I love you," I said when we finally drew apart.

Dinner preparations began as soon as we got back to Burnside. Steven and Sophie were in charge in the kitchen. And while they cooked, Rachel went to check on the sheep accompanied by Maddie and Poppy. This left me and Brian on baby duty. I was given the baby monitor and instructed to listen for Miriam waking up while Brian got on with feeding William.

I'd just brought Miriam downstairs when the sheep team got back and I was walking the floor, and talking to the wee one in what I hoped were soothing tones, when they came into the living-room.

"Guess what, Daddy," Poppy said, rushing over to sit beside her father on the sofa. "I got to check all the hens were safe in the coop for the night. And Mummy pushed the wheelbarrow with the ewes' food in it."

And as Poppy and Maddie told Brian and baby William what they'd been up to, I looked over at Rachel who was still standing in the doorway. I'll never forget the tender expression on her face as she watched me rocking her little granddaughter. "You're a natural," she said, her voice soft. And I can't be sure, but I thought I saw tears in her eyes.

But before I could reply she'd turned away and was gone again, saying she'd let Sophie know Miriam was awake and would take over from her in the kitchen. I wasn't sure if she was hiding the fact she was upset or was simply being her practical self.

Dinner was a tasty bolognaise with salad and garlic bread on the side followed by ice-cream for dessert. We all sat round the big table in Rachel's warm, comfortable kitchen. The babies were passed from lap to lap as we ate, and the conversation was easy with lots of anecdotes and laughter. Rachel seemed fine. She sat at the head of the table and appeared relaxed as she told tales of Sophie as a child, much to her daughter's good-natured embarrassment. I too shared some of Maddie's escapades, much to the delight of Poppy in particular. A couple of times I caught Rachel's eye and she smiled at me. I smiled back, of course, but I also couldn't help wishing.

# Chapter Twenty One

*Jack*

And I had the same yearning the following day when I watched Rachel flying the kite as she, Poppy and I stood at the top of Ben Halla.

The afternoon was fair but blustery, and felt more like March than May, but we were prepared in waterproofs and scarves. Ben Halla is only around 150 metres high, but the going is steep in places. However, Poppy coped well with the climb, as she had the previous year, sometimes holding my hand, or Rachel's, and sometimes striding out on her own.

At one point when Poppy was up ahead and waving back at us, Rachel said,"She's a great wee girl, isn't she?"

"I think so," I said.

"She sometimes reminds me of me when I was little."

"In what way?" I said.

"Oh, I don't know." Rachel smiled. "Her persistence, her frankness – that stubborn streak."

"Right," I said, smiling too.

"This is when you say you find that hard to believe," Rachel said.

"Oops, sorry. Yes, of course – because now you're compliant, tactful and open to persuasion."

There was a small gasp from Rachel and I had to defend myself as she went to punch me on the arm. "Sarcastic bastard," she said, laughing as I caught hold of her.

I laughed too as I looked down at her, caught in my embrace. This was more like it. "Violence *and* swearing," I said. "My sarcasm was justified, I think." I kissed her for a few delicious moments before a little giggle made us pull apart. We both looked to see Poppy standing there, arms folded around the kite and and a cheeky grin on her face. "Right," I said, "let's get moving," and we walked on arm-in-arm.

"But seriously," Rachel said a little while later. "I enjoy Poppy's visits very much. I love her like she's one of my own."

"I know you do, and she adores you too."

"We are so lucky to have our children and grandchildren" Rachel looked up at me.

"Yes we are."

"When I think how it was when Sophie ... when Sophie wasn't speaking to me ... that I could have lost her as well as Fin..." She looked away, wiping the back of her hand across her face."

"Hey," I said, stopping and turning her to face me. "Hey now." I saw a tear run down her face.

She let me hold her for a minute, before she pulled away. As we started walking again she said, "I don't know why I'm crying really. I mean it's great – Sophie's here – here because she wants to be and I've got Miriam too – and it's all good and I'm very, very grateful."

"Tears of gratitude?" I said.

"Yeah, that's probably it," she said, with a slightly embarrassed smile. Then she started running. "Last one to catch Poppy's a wise old know-all."

I won the title.

Poppy went first with the kite. I helped her get started and reminded her of the finer points for keeping it in the air. Fortunately the breeze was brisk enough and I was soon instructed to let go of both her and the kite string so she could do it herself. "Wow!" she shouted, laughing and staggering a little with the strength of the wind and the pull of the kite. "This is awesome."

Rachel and I got a brief go each before we had to return the kite to Poppy. It was while Poppy had her second go with it that Rachel walked a little bit away and turned in a complete circle, taking in the full 360 degree panorama from the hilltop. "I've loved this view forever," she said, as I joined her. "You can see it all – the mountains, the lochs, the whole glorious lot."

"Something else to be grateful for," I said. "Living in such a beautiful place."

"Indeed," she said. "I'm going to miss it while I'm away."

*"Then don't go,"* I wanted to say. *"Stay, here with me. Stay with the family you love so much. And we can have more days like this, more days and evenings like yesterday – all together as a family. Stay and be my wife."* But I didn't say any of it.

Rachel slipped her arm through mine. "And I'll miss you too," she said, leaning her head against my arm.

But again I couldn't say what I was thinking. I couldn't say how much I dreaded her going, how I feared I'd lose her to Eitan. The rational part of my brain where the fact she'd told me she loved me, loved her life on Skye, and that this trip was about work seemed to be in lock-down. And it seemed the more primal part of my brain had taken over. All I could feel were fear and dread and the awareness that the demons relating to Mike's death were also circling, biding their time until I had little else to fill my mind.

"Jack? Did you hear what I said?" Rachel was shaking my arm and looking up at me.

"What? Sorry, no."

"I said Sophie's doing me a farewell dinner tomorrow. You will join us, won't you?"

"No thanks," I said. I knew I couldn't face it, but Rachel's look of hurt and surprise prompted me to try to explain. "Thanks for the invitation, but it should be time for you and your family ... your last night at home for a while. Maybe you could call in at Dun Halla before you leave on Tuesday morning?"

Rachel looked at me for a moment before she replied. Her expression going from hurt to uncertain. She frowned a little as she spoke, "Okay," she said. "I want to get away early, but I'll see what I can do."

# Chapter Twenty Two

*Jack*

When I got back to the house with Poppy, Brian was cooking dinner. I played with Poppy and William, determined to make the most of our time together before they returned home the next day. I tried not to think about Rachel.

After dinner, having first got William settled, Brian put Poppy to bed, and then tactfully, but not entirely subtly, said he fancied a long soak in the bath followed by an early night.

Maddie so clearly had an agenda that I knew resistance was pointless. She began by telling me that Poppy had mentioned the conversation she'd had with me and Rachel about us getting married. And she finished by saying, "I can see you're not your usual self and I'm worried about you. So what exactly is going on with you, Dad?"

In the end I told her it all – the stuff I'd talked about with Alasdair, the subsequent discussion with Rachel – and yes, the proposal. I also told her about the job offers and about Bridget moving into the flat.

Her reactions were similar to Alasdair's. She was shocked when I told her about the flashbacks and the guilt and anxiety. She urged me to get professional help. "That kind of stress," she said, "it can't be good for your heart. You need to deal with it. It's nothing to be ashamed of. Lots of us in the police experience this sort of thing and there's help available."

As I'd suspected she didn't entirely approve of my new tenant. "It's good the flat won't be empty," she said. "But Bridget, Dad – really?"

"Why not Bridget?" I said. "At least I know her. She's not some random tenant. She'll look after the place, and she's says it's not for long."

"Just don't let it be a way for her to get her hooks into you again," Maddie said. "Don't be tempted because things aren't perfect with Rachel. I know you can sort that, especially after what I've seen the last few days. I can see you still love each other – a lot – and you're good together. You're going to have to be patient, that's all. Be supportive, don't go all needy, and give her the space she needs."

"I know you're right," I said. "But it's not easy."

"No, it isn't, but it's worth it. And I think you should give Mum's job offer serious consideration. It will give you something else to focus on while Rachel's away. And then you'll have the photography job to come back to. All sounds good to me."

I sighed.

"Hang in there, Dad," Maddie said. "You'll get through this. Get help with your mental health. Take the job. And believe in Rachel."

Not for the first time, I wondered how my daughter was so much wiser than I was. She made everything sound so reasonable – so possible.


Next morning, I tried to keep it light as I helped Brian and Maddie get all their stuff together. But Maddie knew me well. We were doing a last check of the spare rooms while Brian got the children into the car when she said, "Chin up, Dad. It's hard enough to say goodbye without you looking so miserable."

"Sorry," I said. "It's been good having you here and I'm going to miss you."

Maddie stroked my arm. "Oh, Dad, what am I going to do with you?"

I managed a smile. "Go on," I said, hugging her. "Get out of here."

After the family had gone, I did my best to keep busy. I tidied up the house and got the guest bed linen and towels all washed. I cut the grass and did a bit of weeding. Anything to keep my mind occupied and off the subject of Rachel. And it worked – up to a point.

That evening I dined on too many whiskies and a load of self-pity. I didn't go to bed until around two a.m. and lay awake and restless for what felt like hours. It was starting to get light when I eventually fell asleep. But it was a sleep once again filled with disturbing dreams of locked doors and screams for help.

"Jack, are you there?" A voice pulled me awake.

Rachel, it was Rachel calling from downstairs. I struggled to open my eyes. It hurt. I squinted at the clock – eight thirty. I got out of bed. That hurt too. My head ached, my mouth was dry and foul tasting. I stood there in my jeans. It seemed I'd only removed my socks and shirt before collapsing into bed.

The bedroom door opened and there she was. I didn't need to look in the mirror to know how bad I looked. Rachel's expression did the job. "You look rough," she said.

"Yeah, didn't sleep well."

"I came to say goodbye. You know, like I said I would."

So much for my plan of having fresh coffee and toast ready for a farewell breakfast. I sensed that wasn't going to happen. "Can I get you a coffee?" I asked, trying not to sound desperate. I grabbed yesterday's shirt and wrestled my way into it.

"No thanks. I'm fine," Rachel said. "But you're clearly not." She came over to me as I struggled with my shirt buttons. "Here, let me."

It was almost unbearable. Her fingers brushed against my chest as she took over the buttoning. Then there was the scent of her, her freckled skin, the sheen on her hair, and the sound of her voice, its gentle tone and her soft, Skye accent. I winced as the pain of her imminent departure hit me.

"Sorry," Rachel took a step back. "Did I hurt you?"

"No, no, it's nothing. I was just..." I stopped. Telling her what I was thinking was futile. She was leaving. "Got a bit of a headache that's all."

"Right ... I better ..." she turned to leave.

"Yes, right. I'll walk you to your car," I said, determined to prolong my pain until the last second. I followed her out, held open the car door for her. For a moment we stood there, looking at each other.

I struggled to find more to say, desperate to delay her departure, but at the same time wishing the agony was over.

She stepped towards me, put her hands to my face and kissed me. I overcame my surprise and held her tightly as I returned the kiss.

Then she looked into my eyes and whispered, "I'm sorry, Jack, but I have to go."

# Chapter Twenty Three

*Rachel*

The long drive to Glasgow gave me a chance to think. I was able to reflect on how well the wedding and the lambing had gone. I congratulated myself on the successful completion of the proofs for the children's books and although I was a bit sad to be saying goodbye to the series, there was the pre-Christmas launch to look forward to. And any sadness I felt at the children's books coming to an end, at least for now, was far outweighed by my excitement at the prospect of the new book project.

But then, inevitably came thoughts of Jack – infuriating, lovable, romantic Jack. Where we were heading, I had no idea. All I did know was I'd no regrets about what we'd had so far, and no regrets about turning down his proposal.

And as I drove, the memory of his touch, the sound of his voice, and of how our recent painful, but honest, exchanges had brought us close again, played over and over in my head. And then there was the memory of how he'd looked earlier when I'd gone to say goodbye. I'd almost abandoned all my plans. It had taken all my willpower to leave him. I'd meant it when I said I had to go. In the logical, rational part of my brain I knew it was right. I did have to go. But even now as I drove, even now as I looked forward to being back in Israel and working on this wonderful new project, I came close to turning the car round and heading back home to Jack.

With all this going on in my head, I was glad I'd arranged to stay at Lana's that night as, being alone in one of those functional but soulless airport hotels might have broken my resolve.

Lana suggested dinner at her local Italian restaurant. And as we ate and chatted, I was honest with her when she asked me how Jack was. I told her how things had been since the wedding and I even told her about my rejection of his proposal, but I also told her I didn't want to discuss it. And she accepted that. Instead we talked about the book and what awaited me in Israel, and this proved to be exactly what I needed to restore my excitement and anticipation of what lay ahead.

The long flight and the stress of passing through Israeli immigration did dampen my enthusiasm a little. But Jonathan's warm welcome when he met me at Tel Aviv airport, and his excited chatter on the drive to Jerusalem soon brought it back.

It was around seven in the evening when we got to Jonathan's apartment. And, as I'd done on my first visit almost exactly a year before, I paused for a moment when we got out of the car. I breathed in the warm air laden with the smell of pine resin, a scent I'd forever associate with Jerusalem, and I looked down the hill towards the lights of the ancient city. It did feel like a bit of a homecoming. I sighed and couldn't help smiling as I turned to my brother.

"Glad to be back?" Jonathan said, grinning back at me.

"Yes, I do believe I am."

The delicious smell of garlic, spices and roasting meat greeted us when we went into the flat and Deb appeared from the kitchen. "Rachel," she said, as I came down the few steps that led from the front door to the main living area. "Welcome back." She hugged me and then kissed me on both cheeks.

Jonathan took my bags through to my room and, after I'd had a big hug from Mari and a smile and a handshake from Gideon, Deb took me by the arm. "Come," she said, leading me to one of a pair of low, grey sofas. "You must be tired. Take a seat and I'll bring coffee."

"Thank you," I said, indeed beginning to feel the effects of almost twelve hours of travelling. "Coffee sounds good." And it was. It was Turkish, strong and black, and was accompanied by a hearty slice of beautifully moist apple cake. After this lovely snack, I was further revived by a shower and change of clothes. So by the time I got to the dinner table, I was feeling refreshed.

It was good to be back. Even without the underlying reason for my return, it was good to be back in my brother's home, back with him and Deb and my nephew and niece. It was good to be sitting round a table with them again. Even although it had only been a month since we'd all been together in Scotland, I hadn't seen nearly enough of them over the years.

"So, is this going to be an annual event?" Jonathan said, as we all tucked into a tasty lamb and aubergine casserole. "Auntie Rachel's May visit?"

"I don't know about that," I said. "But I'd definitely like to keep coming back, if you'll have me."

Jonathan shook his head and smiled. "I don't know. In the twenty years or so I've lived here you never came and now twice within a year."

"I know. Better late and all that," I said. "But there were Peter's objections and then when I was back living at Burnside, Mum didn't—"

"It's okay," Jonathan said. "No need to defend yourself. I was teasing. I know it was difficult."

"I do wish I'd come sooner. We didn't see enough of each other when the children were young. It was always up to you to come home. But it is what it is. And now I can put it right."

"So, we've been warned." Jonathan laughed.

Deb shook her head at him then turned to me. "It's lovely to have you here and you're welcome any time. That is what my husband is trying to say."

"Yeah, that's what I meant." Jonathan said, raising his eyebrows and grinning cheekily at Deb.

I envied the ease and closeness of my brother's relationship with his wife. Deb grew up in London, the daughter of Turkish Jews who'd settled in the UK when she was ten. Then at the age of twenty-five she'd emigrated to Israel. It was Eitan who'd introduced her to Jonathan and she was such a lovely person that I could see why my brother had fallen for her.

Jonathan picked up his wine glass. "And speaking of Mum, I think a toast to her memory is in order. She was a remarkable woman."

After we'd all raised our glasses, Deb said, "I wonder what she'd make of your new book project, Rachel?"

"I think she'd approve," Gideon said. We all turned to look at him. He didn't usually have much to say at the dinner table, his main aim, as a typical sixteen-year-old, being to devour his food as quickly as possible and then get back to his phone or some other screen-based activity.

"What makes you think that?" Deb asked.

"Aunt Rachel's book, it is all about working for peace, for getting people to see past the politics and to accept we are all human, we have that in common before everything else. I think Gran would like that very much." Gideon sat back, gave a little shrug.

"Spot on," Jonathan said, looking approvingly at his son.

"Thanks, Gideon," I said. "That was a lovely thing to say. And I'm touched you've taken the trouble to find out what I'm here to do."

Gideon shrugged again, and a smile almost made it past his teenage diffidence. "Dad told me about it. It's good you'll be using your artwork too – and it will not all be writing."

"Our boy's becoming quite an expert photographer," Deb said. "He's got some great photos from Sophie's wedding and from our travels in Scotland. You must show them to Aunt Rachel, Gideon."

This was the cue for another shrug.

"I'd love to see them," I said. "Perhaps you could take some photos when I visit your school – some that I could use in the book?"

Gideon looked at me. "You would want me to do that?" Now he was blushing.

"Yes. I would. My publisher has organised a professional photographer to go with me on most of my visits. But for this particular one, having some photos taken by one of the students would be good too – whether to refer to when I'm doing the sketches, or for possible inclusion in the book.

"Cool," Gideon said. "I'll need time out of class, of course, if I'm to help you." He looked at his mother.

"I'll see what I can do," Deb said, laughing. She looked at me. "For once my son approves of me being a teacher at his school."

"It has its uses occasionally," Gideon said.

"And while we're bragging about our children's talents," Jonathan said. "Mari too has been busy. She has done a very fine painting of the view from Burnside cottage which you must see."

Mari rolled her eyes. "Abba," she said, using the Hebrew word for dad, "you are so embarrassing! It's just a painting – not very fine."

"Aunt Rachel will be the judge of that," Jonathan said, smiling at her.

Mari looked back at him, her expression one of exasperation mixed with affection.

And as we ate the rest of our meal, the conversation moved from topic to topic. We caught up with each other's news, talked a bit about my timetable. It was very pleasant and relaxing – so relaxing that I couldn't help yawning as I finished my dessert.

"Bored already?" Jonathan laughed as I tried to hide my fatigue.

"Sorry," I said. "I guess it's the long journey catching up with me."

I didn't argue when Jonathan and Deb refused my offer of help with the clearing up. And neither did I argue with their suggestion that I have an early night.

By the time I woke the next morning, Jonathan had already left for his shift at the hospital and Deb and the children were gone too. I took my time showering and dressing, glad I'd kept my first day free to acclimatise and prepare. I helped myself to some breakfast and ate it sitting on the balcony. I checked my phone as I sipped my second cup of coffee. I'd texted Sophie, Morag and Jack the night before to let them know I'd arrived. There were replies from Sophie and Morag, but nothing from Jack. I wondered for a moment what his lack of acknowledgement might mean, but then I forced it out of my mind.

After breakfast, as I'd done on the first morning of my previous visit, I went out for a walk. I walked down the hill from the flat to the main road. Everything was as I remembered it. I passed the row of shops with the little art gallery at the far end, and, after about another ten minutes, arrived at the Ramat Dania park. I made my way up the park's steep path and sat on the bench at the top.

Surrounded by olive and fig trees, I watched the tiny humming birds darting in and out of the purple flowers on the bougainvillea bushes. I breathed in the smell of the foliage mixed with the aroma of the falafels from the nearby food van. I listened to the birdsong and the incomprehensible conversations of the passers-by. And I gradually took in the fact that I was back in this ancient and exotic city in this beautiful, but conflicted, land. I also reflected on the fact that this time I had a job to do and I hoped I'd do it justice.

# Chapter Twenty Four

*Rachel*

After lunch back at the flat, my earlier slight apprehension about the work that lay ahead changed to anticipation as I set up an office space in my bedroom and re-read all the information I had about the people and institutions I'd be engaging with. I sent some emails and made a couple of calls confirming my arrival and also confirming some planned meetings and visits. The enthusiastic and prompt replies I received to my emails, and the positivity and warmth from the people I phoned all served to further heighten my excitement and impatience to get started.

I lay down on the bed for a siesta, but my brain was buzzing and I couldn't sleep, so as soon as I heard someone coming in through the front door, I got up. It was Gideon back from school. I offered to make us a coffee in exchange for him showing me some of his photographs and we were soon sitting out on the balcony together.

"I have hundreds of shots on my camera and on disk but I've printed some of the best ones," Gideon said, as he handed me a folder. "Jack suggested it. He said I should start a ... a what's the word, like you artists have for examples of your work—"

"A portfolio," I said.

"Yes, a portfolio."

"And it was Jack's suggestion?"

"Yes, at the wedding, he said he'd noticed me taking lots of pictures. He asked to see them."

"Right, and what did he think?"

"He said they were good. He liked them." Gideon smiled, and again there was that mix of diffidence and embarrassment. "He said I have a good camera and he gave me some ideas how to improve my shots, and told me about other lenses I could get, and he said if I was serious about my photography I should start editing and picking out my best ones, make a … portfolio."

I was surprised Jack hadn't told me about the conversation, but I was touched that he'd shown such an interest in my nephew's efforts and that he'd shared his expertise and been so encouraging. Such a strong spasm of yearning went through me as I thought of Jack, that it took a big effort to return my focus to the folder of photos.

There was no doubt Gideon had talent. "These are very good," I said, as I slowly turned the pages. There were some black and white, and some colour prints. There were some great informal shots of Sophie and Steven and the wedding guests. There were a couple of sweet ones of baby Miriam. There was even a not bad one of me. It was a head and shoulders shot, I was looking to the side and laughing. I'd no idea the picture was being taken and I looked happy and relaxed.

"Jack liked that one," Gideon said. "It's him that you were talking to when I took the photo. He asked me to email him the j-peg – which I did."

"Oh," I said. I turned the page, didn't look up, moved my thoughts on.

As well as the portrait stuff there were several good landscape shots, some taken on Skye and some from around Loch Ness and the other places Gideon and the rest of us had visited after the wedding. And then there were pictures taken at home in Jerusalem, and in other parts of Israel.

"You have an artist's eye. There's no doubt about that," I said when I got to the end of the collection. "Thank you for sharing them with me. And if you don't mind, I'd like to have copies of a couple of them myself."

"I don't mind at all. Thank you for looking. It's good you like them ... with you being an artist ... it means ... it means maybe I do have some talent. Abba doesn't think it's what I should study."

"No?"

"He doesn't take it seriously, doesn't see it as leading to a good job. He says I should keep it as a hobby."

"Your father is being a responsible parent. Life as any sort of artist is precarious." Gideon and I turned to see it was Eitan who'd joined our conversation.

"Hmm, that is what you *would* say, taking Abba's side." Gideon got to his feet as he spoke, grinning at Eitan as he did so. "But thanks for your support, Aunt Rachel. Now I must go. I have homework to do."

I stood to greet Eitan as Gideon left us. Eitan kissed me on both cheeks. "You look well," he said, holding me at arm's length and looking me up and down. "I knew being back here would suit you."

I laughed. "I only arrived yesterday."

"Ah, but this country – it will instantly invigorate you." Eitan smiled at me. "Your face," he said, stroking my cheek. "It is already not so white."

I stepped away, trying to appear calm, trying to look as if the touch of his hand had no effect on me. "I didn't know you were coming over," I said. "And, come to think of it, how did you get in?"

"I still have a key – from the days I used to babysit. Deb called me earlier to invite me for dinner. I had a client to see in the area so when we had finished our meeting, it made sense to come straight here. There was no answer to my knock – so I let myself in."

"Ah, sorry," I said. "We were out here, as you can see, didn't hear you."

I suggested a cold drink for us both and headed for the kitchen. I needed time to calm myself down. As had been clear at the wedding, there was no denying Eitan's presence still did things to me. I still found him attractive, tempting, dangerous. I still liked being with him.

When I returned to the balcony, Eitan was sitting at the table, looking through Gideon's portfolio.

"These are good," he said, as I sat down opposite him. "This one especially." He turned the folder so I could see. Before I even looked, I could tell by his smile which one it was. "I will ask for a print of it, I think."

"No ... really? Why? A photo of me ..." The thought of Jack and Eitan both having the same picture of me was too weird.

"Yes a photo of you – to remember you when you go. That is unless I can persuade you to stay ..." He reached across the table, took hold of my hand.

I pulled my hand away. "What? No! That's not—"

"Rachel, Rachel, please. I am sorry." Eitan sat back, his smile kind, his gaze as open and honest as ever. "I am teasing you. I would like this picture of you, yes. And I know you're not here to stay. Your heart – it belongs elsewhere. I know that."

All I could do was nod and smile. I knew I needed to calm down around Eitan, to treat him as the good and trusted friend he was, especially as I'd be spending some of my time working with him. It wasn't going to be easy.

"Hallo," a voice called from inside. Deb was home.

I tried to hide my relief. Eitan's grin told me I wasn't successful. I stood up, picked up our empty glasses. "I'll go and see if Deb needs a hand with dinner," I said.

Eitan gave a little bow of his head and picked up Gideon's portfolio once more.

Mari joined Deb and me in the kitchen. She proved to be a much more able sous-chef than I was. I did my best to help, but as it was another traditional Turkish recipe passed down from Deb's mother, I mostly watched. Mari chopped and ground the garlic, cumin and oregano that would be added to the meat to make the kofte meatballs, and Deb worked on the stock for the rice pilaf.

I chatted to Mari about school and the subjects she was studying. "I don't really have a favourite," she said when I asked her. "I enjoy Science and Maths, and most of the other subjects too – but Art is my passion. I don't think of it as a school subject."

I'd been impressed with my niece's drawings and paintings on my previous visit and it was good to hear she was keener than ever. "I'd love to see what you've done since last year," I said.

"I'm more into sculpture now," she said. "Most of what I've done is in the studio at school but I have some pieces at home which I can show you. And you can see the rest when you visit the school."

I smiled at her. There was none of her brother's diffidence, no embarrassment. She seemed older than her almost fourteen years, confident and happy in her skin. "Thank you," I said. "I'd like that."

Jonathan arrived home as we were serving up and we were soon all sitting round the table enjoying the meal, and the food lived up to the promise of its delicious aroma.

Everyone shared how their day had been – apart from Gideon that is. He was his usual quiet and apparently uninterested self. I was going to say something about him showing me his photos and how good I thought they were, but I stopped myself. I realised he'd hate being the centre of attention at the dinner table. And, as I looked at him, it prompted a memory of Finlay at the same age, same shy reticence, same dread of the spotlight, and I knew he'd agree with me. Teenage Finlay, my darling boy, for a moment I could see him, standing smiling at me – it was a breathtaking memory.

"Rachel, are you okay?" Jonathan's voice pushed its way into my thoughts. "Eitan asked you a question."

It took me a moment to remember where I was. "Yes, yes sorry. I'm fine," I said. I was aware of Eitan looking at me. I turned to him. His expression was sympathetic and I guessed he knew where my thoughts had taken me. "Sorry, what did you say?"

"I asked if everything was in place for your visit to the school tomorrow," he said.

"Yes, I think so. I'm going in with Deb."

"Everything is ready for you," Deb said. "Some of the students have put a presentation together on the *My Jerusalem* project and they're excited to meet you and eager to answer your questions."

"I'm excited too," I said.

"I will meet you there," Eitan said. "I too am looking forward to it and to being interviewed by you."

"I thought we could do the interview after lunch," I said.

"Excellent," Eitan said. "And I know the perfect place where we can go."

When we'd all finished eating, I insisted that I do the clearing up. And Eitan insisted he would help me. The family put up no resistance and left us to it. Jonathan and Deb both said they had work to do and disappeared into their shared study. And Mari and Gideon went off to their rooms.

"Gideon – he continues to remind you of your son," Eitan said, as he put the last of the dishes into the washer and I finished wiping the worktops.

"I … yes … that is …" I paused, looked down at the floor, unsure whether I could trust myself to speak without emotion getting the better of me. And I recalled a similar conversation Eitan and I had during my visit the year before. Eitan was nothing if not perceptive. He could certainly read me.

"Come," Eitan held out his hand towards me.

Without thinking about it I took hold of his hand, allowed him to lead me to the balcony.

"It is still very painful for you, I think," Eitan said once we were sitting down.

"Yes it is. It's been over two years since Finlay died, but yes, it's still painful. I think it always will be. People say you move on but I don't think you do. The grief's there all the time. It's part of who I am now. Most of the time I cope with it. But earlier …"

"You looked at Gideon and you saw Finlay?"

"Yes." I closed my eyes for a moment as I sighed. "There isn't a strong physical resemblance. Fin had my colouring. He was red-haired like me not dark like Gideon. But it's in Gideon's behaviour, his mannerisms and attitudes – even more than before – he is so like Fin."

"When my brother Amnon died, I saw him everywhere, in every other young man I passed on the street or saw in a shop. It's not surprising you are seeing your son in your nephew. And it's not about physical appearance."

"I guess not," I said, recalling Eitan had lost his soldier brother more than forty years before – aged only nineteen and also in a military conflict.

"I was like you are whenever I saw our cousin. He didn't look like Amnon but he was almost the same age, had the same attitudes and approaches to life. Then our cousin got older and the similarities ceased, which in some ways was a blessing."

I could only nod.

Eitan stood up, held out his arms towards me. "Come," he said.

I went to him, walked into his arms, allowed myself to be enveloped in a strong hug.

"It is good you came back, Rachel," Eitan said, as he released me. He put his hands on my shoulders. "And I do not mean only from my personal point-of-view. It is good you are here to do this work. This work for peace, for better understanding – it will help you with the loss of your son. Perhaps make meaning out of something that seems meaningless."

"I hope so," I said. I smiled at him. "And thank you."

"For what?"

"For understanding, for getting how it is with Finlay, and me being here to do what I've come to do. You're a very dear friend."

Now it was Eitan's turn to nod, his expression briefly thoughtful and a little sad, but then his smile returned. "As you are to me, my very dear Rachel. And I'll do whatever I can to help you with your work here, drive you, accompany you, whatever you need, just call." He glanced at his watch. "But now I must go. I too have work to do this evening."

I said I'd see him out and he called out his thanks and goodbyes to Jonathan and the family as we went. "Goodnight, Eitan," I said as I opened the front door. "And I meant it, thank you for your support."

He looked at me, his expression sad and thoughtful once more. He put his hands either side of my face. "Ah, Rachel," he said. "I wish ..." Then he kissed me briefly but very tenderly on the mouth and left.

# Chapter Twenty Five

*Rachel*

After Eitan left, I was glad to be distracted by Mari. She began, at my insistence, by showing me her Burnside painting which, as I said to her was indeed impressive. But she moved on quickly to show me the sculptures she'd told me about earlier.

"These are some of the first ones I did," Mari said, pointing at the three items on her desk. "They are all clay, but at school I have other pieces made from other materials. I will show them to you when you come to school tomorrow."

"Right," I said, bending down to get a closer look. There was a duck, not fired or painted, but its proportions were good and the features well-defined.

"That was the first one worth keeping," Mari said. "And this one," she picked up a coloured and glazed penguin, "was my first satisfactory ceramic clay, all hollowed out and fired and finished. He's not perfect but I am proud of him."

"So you should be," I said smiling at my niece.

"I know there is a lot to learn. I've only done a little bit of carving with wood and stone and I'm working on a metal ... a metal ... what do you call it?" She flapped her hands as she tried to find the word. "When you put things together piece by piece?"

"Assembly?" I said. "You're assembling a metal sculpture?"

"Yes, that's it," she said. "It's working with rods and wires and recycled materials. I won't get to try casting with metal until I go to Art school. But I can wait."

"Art school? That's what you want to do?"

"Yes it is. Even if Abba doesn't approve."

"Doesn't he?"

"I haven't told him yet. But he doesn't approve of Gideon wanting to be photographer. He doesn't see Art as a proper job."

"I'm sure that's not true. It's like he said to Gideon. It can be difficult to make a living as an artist. He wouldn't want you to struggle. He'd want you to be aware of the possible problems."

"Yes and he'd believe I'd give up on it. He'd say I've got plenty time and that I will change my mind many times before I need to decide, but I know it's what I want to do."

"I admire your determination," I said. I had a feeling Mari would win her father round. And I hoped she'd never lose that self-belief. I smiled as I remembered Jonathan telling me how she'd insisted on delaying her bat-mitvah by a year. She said that girls should be the same as boys. Boys had their bar-mitvah rite of passage at thirteen rather than at twelve as it was for girls. She believed the sexes should be equal and that thirteen was the more appropriate age, as it was the start of the teens.

"Why are you smiling?" Mari asked. "Do you think I am not serious?"

"Oh, I know you're serious. I'm smiling because I love your positive attitude." I hugged her. "You follow your dreams, sweetheart, wherever they may take you."

"Thank you, Aunt Rachel." Mari picked up the third little sculpture. "I'd like you to have this," she said, handing me a ceramic sheep. I know it's not perfect, but I think it looks a bit like Jason."

I laughed. The sheep was painted white with brown spots – as a Jacob sheep should be. "It's got the right markings," I said. "And I'm impressed that you did the four horns."

"That was tricky, for sure," Mari said. "And they're not quite right."

"He looks perfect to me," I said. "But are you sure you want me to have him?"

"Yes. I made him for you when I got home from Skye, after you told me about your new story book. Gideon had a photo of the real Jason and I used that to help me."

"I don't know what I did to deserve all your hard work."

Mari shrugged. "I know that sometimes you are sad and you miss Finlay very much. I wanted to give you something to cheer you up." She spoke gently and I saw she had tears in her eyes. And by now so did I.

All I could do was hold her tightly, quite unable to speak.

And then later, as I lay in bed, my niece's kind-hearted action was just one of the things going round and round in my mind. I thought about Sophie, my own strong-minded daughter. I thought about Gideon, about Finlay, about what it was to be a parent. I thought about Eitan and about how well he understood me and how he made me feel.

And then there was Jack. Still no reply to the text I'd sent to say I'd arrived safely. I recalled how terrible he'd looked when we said goodbye. Did he still not get why I had to come back here in spite of what he'd said about being okay with it? Why couldn't he see things like Eitan did? And why did I miss him so much already?

Bloody Jack! This book was important to me and I was determined I wasn't going to let his attitude spoil this trip. I struggled to push thoughts of him out of my head. Eventually I fell asleep.

Next morning, any tiredness from my bad night quickly dispelled when I got to the school. After introducing me to the head teacher, Deb took me on a tour. I already knew that the school educated both Arab and Jewish children together and that it followed the principles of the Waldorf system. That is it took a holistic approach to learning and gave equal value to the intellectual, practical and artistic aspects of learning. But nothing could have prepared me for seeing it in action.

The building itself was beautiful, managing to be both light and cool. The school took children from kindergarten right through to the end of high school and in every space and in every classroom there was a buzz of purposeful activity. The classes were all bilingual in both Hebrew and Arabic and Deb told me the children were from diverse backgrounds, ethnicities and traditions – and from various religions and none. Some were the children or grandchildren of immigrants, others from families who'd lived in the area for many generations.

Soon it was time to go the school's main assembly area. As we were going in, a young woman came up to me and introduced herself as Sylvia Newman. I recognised the name. She was the photographer who the publishers had engaged to do the stills and videos and to obtain the necessary permissions for their possible use. We'd exchanged emails before I left the UK confirming dates and venues, but it was good to meet her face to face.

Her accent and use of English gave away her American origins and she explained she'd immigrated five years before.

She assured me she wouldn't get in the way and that if she was doing her job properly, I should forget she was there most of the time. One person who wasn't likely to be unaware of her presence though was Gideon. He appeared beside me while Sylvia was introducing herself. By the time I explained who he was, and that he too would be taking photos at some of the planned events, he was obviously smitten. When Sylvia invited him to take his place alongside her at the side of the hall and then showed an interest in the camera he was using, his face was crimson.

I felt like a guest of honour having been presented with a bunch of flowers and then shown to a seat in the front row. Eitan joined us and sat beside me. Deb explained that those sitting in the rows of seats behind me were representatives from the staff, parents, and from all the year groups of pupils.

The presentation itself was enchanting. It was a mixture of on-screen video and slideshow along with live presentations. Pupils of all ages contributed and most of it was done in English for my benefit. Each item began with a lead pupil welcoming me personally with a 'Hello Rachel'. They told the twenty-year history of the school, about other similar schools in Israel and beyond, and about the philosophy behind them. They shared what the school meant to the pupils, staff and parents. Eitan and Deb also spoke. They explained about the *My Jerusalem* project and how it had started at the school and grown from there.

The presentation ended with a song from the school choir. It was sung in a mixture of languages, including English, and the lyrics were on the themes of unity and understanding.

And then it was my turn to speak. Normally I'd have struggled with any kind of public speaking. But the ethos and atmosphere around me was so inspiring, I managed to find the words to express my appreciation and gratitude. I also spoke a bit about the book and how fitting a starting point the school was. And then without meaning to, and to my utter surprise, I shared Finlay's story and how I wanted to promote peace in his memory. And I did so without succumbing to tears.

Deb squeezed my hand as I returned to my seat, and Eitan gave me a hug during the applause that followed.

My morning finished with a visit to the school's gallery space to see some of the many drawings, paintings and photos the members of the school community had created as their personal representations of Jerusalem and what it meant to them. Some had gone for the famous, more obvious landmarks like the Wailing Wall or the golden-domed Al-Aqsa mosque. But others had gone for the more personal or even quirky.

I was fascinated by the pictures of families – babies, children, parents and grandparents with their houses behind them – ordinary people at home in extraordinary circumstances. I liked, too, the pictures of the streets, synagogues, mosques and churches where participants lived and worshipped, the pictures of workplaces, shops and cafes showing so many aspects of the everyday life that Jerusalem provided. I was also taken by the portrait photos and paintings of individuals, captioned to explain why this one person encapsulated Jerusalem for the artist or photographer. They included pictures of orthodox Jews, of Imams, Rabbis and church Ministers, as well as soldiers on patrol and people going about their daily business in markets and on the streets. There was even a doctor in scrubs standing outside what I recognised as the Hadassah hospital, a place of healing and treatment open to all ethnicities and cultures, and the place where Jonathan worked as a paediatrician.

The images that made some of the deepest impressions on me were the ones showing how conflicted a place Jerusalem was. There were several pictures of the separation wall and of its checkpoints and the young soldiers who manned them. And there were others, drawings mainly, but also a few photos too of contributors' relatives and friends who lived in East Jerusalem. They were shown on their daily walk to school and work walking past hostile looking soldiers. And some of these pictures also showed them walking through clouds of tear gas.

But the picture that quietly said it all to me was one of an elderly couple standing side by side, the woman holding a key and the man holding a black and white photo of a house. The caption explained they were Palestinians, a brother and sister, and that the house in the photo had been forcibly taken from their family in 1948 during the establishment of Israel as an independent state. According to the caption, they still apparently hoped it would one day be returned to them. It was poignant and to the point.

Before I left for lunch with Eitan, I said goodbye to Sylvia who assured me she had some good photos and clips of the morning and of the exhibition which she'd send to me later. She also praised Gideon, who was still close by as we talked, for his photographic expertise. This caused much mirth amongst his classmates and I rescued him from his obvious mix of pride and embarrassment by getting him to show me to the school's Art studio. Mari joined us and, as promised, she showed me the rest of her sculptures.

"These are amazing, Mari," I said as I looked at her collection of clay animals – sheep, goats and a fierce looking alligator. There was also the beginning of a stone sculpture which was already recognisable as a lion.

"It's my first attempt to work with stone," Mari said, as I ran my hand over the lion's mane. "I know I've got a lot to learn."

"You've made an excellent start," I said, smiling at her. "Is this yours too?" I asked, pointing to an assembled metal structure further along the bench.

"Yes, it's not finished but it's my favourite piece so far. It's an olive tree. Doing the leaves and the olives was tricky." Mari smiled, obviously pleased with what she'd created.

I took a quick picture of it on my phone and made a mental note to ask Gideon to take a proper photo of it for me. "The branches seem weighed down and the tree itself seems twisted," I said, as I looked at the tree more closely.

Mari's expression became serious. "Many Palestinians have lost their rights and access to their olive fields. The fields are now surrounded by Israeli settlers. The farmers have to apply for a special permit to harvest the olives in autumn. They don't always get permission. Sometimes the trees are poisoned, or even chopped down."

"Really? That's terrible," I said.

"Yes, it is," said Mari. "My sculpture is meant to be ... what is the word? It mocks the olive branch as a symbol of peace." She looked at me, frowning.

"Ironic?" I said.

"Yes, that's it, ironic. I know it won't change things on its own, but it lets me show how I feel."

I felt humble as I looked at my niece. Not yet fourteen, but so committed, so aware of politics and injustice and so talented too. "Come here," I said and I hugged her close.

As I released her she looked at me and said, "You're not crying, are you? I haven't upset you, have I?"

"No, not all," I said. "You've made me very proud and you've given me hope."

# Chapter Twenty Six

*Rachel*

Lunch with Eitan was as enjoyable as I'd expected it to be. He took me to a small restaurant on a street corner in the Old City. We sat at a shaded outside table. The hummus and tahini Eitan ordered for us was the most deliciously fresh and tasty I'd ever had. The pitta bread that accompanied the dips was freshly baked and the tomato salad was slathered in an intensely flavoured olive oil.

Eitan smiled at me as I wiped my chin with my napkin. "You are enjoying the food," he said.

"Mmm," I said, smiling back at him, my mouth too full to reply properly.

"It's all made here every day. It is one of my favourite places to come when I am working in the city."

"It's delicious, thank you," I said.

We did the formal interview for the book while we had our coffee. I asked Eitan about his involvement with *My Jerusalem* and about how his residency with the venture was going. I wasn't surprised that he was an excellent interviewee.

"I can take you to meet some of the people who've taken part," Eitan said as I switched off my voice recorder.

"If you're sure you've got the time," I said.

"Of course. It is, as I said, part of my job to let people know about the project." He leaned forward, put his hand on mine.

"And it is good to share my project with yours. They go well together I think."

I couldn't help laughing. He truly was impossible. I looked across the table at him, at this big, loud, egotistical, but kind and uncomplicated man, and smiled at him as I moved my hand to take hold of his.

"Why do you laugh at me?" he said, feigning a hurt expression which made me laugh more.

"I'm not laughing *at* you," I said. "I'm laughing because you make me happy. You're funny and nice and I like being with you."

For once Eitan seemed to have nothing to say. He regained his voice as he drove me back to Jonathan's and we chatted more about how the morning had gone.

"So, I will see you on Monday for the tour," he said as we pulled up at the apartment block.

"I'm looking forward to it," I said. I'd been surprised when he'd agreed to take the tourist tour of the city's separation wall with me. It had almost been a dare on my part when I'd emailed him about it.

"I look forward to it too. I will be interested to hear your opinion."

"I'm sure you will. And thanks for everything today." I kissed him on the cheek and turned to get out of the car.

But before I could open the door, he put his hand on my shoulder. I turned back to look at him. He stroked both sides of my face before he spoke. "Ah, Rachel," he said, his voice husky.

"What?" I said, my own voice no more than a whisper.

He let go of me. "Go," he said. "It is best that you go. I will see you on Monday."

"Right," I said as I stepped out of the car. Eitan accelerated away almost before I closed the car door. My heartbeat had also accelerated, and as I watched the car disappear down the hill, I realised that of the several emotions I was experiencing, disappointment seemed to be the strongest one.

I managed to put Eitan out of my mind over the weekend. School finished early on Fridays, so Deb, Gideon and Mari were already home when I got in. And I hadn't been back in the flat for long when Jonathan called to say he'd be taking us all out for Friday night dinner and to be ready to leave around five.

We had a magical family evening. We went to Mari and Gideon's favourite pizzeria to eat and Jonathan had to listen to all of us recount how the school visit had gone. It was wonderful to be part of the enthusiastic chat and to share in the family banter. It was wonderful, too, to listen to the voice of the muezzin at a nearby mosque. His chant carried on the warm, pine-scented air as he called the Muslim faithful to prayer as their Sabbath came to an end. The a little while later, as the Jewish Shabbat began, we paused on our way home to watch the big Mediterranean sun as it set over the Mount of Olives.

Saturday was busy for the family as they crammed all the usual weekend activities into this part of the world's one-day weekend.

I kept out of everyone's way as much as I could and got on with sorting through the many photos and video clips of Friday morning that Sylvia had emailed to me. She was obviously talented and I could already see that making selections from such excellent material was going to be difficult. Gideon, too, shared the pictures he'd taken. Among them were several shots of Mari's tree – all taken from different angles. Each shot was different and perfectly judged, and I was once more impressed by his skills.

As well as sifting through the visual stuff, I also worked through the notes I'd taken on the visit, writing down my first thoughts and impressions.

And besides going for a walk in the relative cool of the early morning, I spent most of Sunday working too. I sat out on the balcony and did some preliminary sketches based both on my own impressions and on some of the photos. I noted down some thoughts about how I might structure the finished book and how

I might balance the text and picture content. I also considered how the video clips might be used to support the project.

I didn't think about Eitan and I didn't think about Jack – or at least I tried not to.

On the Sunday evening I did find myself sending another text to Jack. When I still got no reply, I told myself it was probably due to the mobile signal on Skye which was sometimes so poor that texts could be delayed for days. I made the same excuse when I tried to call him and his phone went straight to voicemail. So then I emailed him and when there was still no reply on Monday morning, I told myself that broadband could also be unreliable on the island. This was, of course, ignoring the fact that corresponding with Morag and Sophie had not met with these difficulties.

But missing Jack – and I missed him sooner and more deeply than I thought I would – didn't make me any less enthusiastic about the job I'd come to Israel to do. And, on Monday morning, as I waited for the tour bus with Eitan and Sylvia, I felt motivated and excited. Yes, my positivity was strengthened by Eitan's presence but it was more than that. At that precise moment I knew it was where I was meant to be.

Our tour party was made up of a mixture of American and British tourists and the tour was run by a company called Perspective on Palestine. We'd assembled at the meeting point outside one of Jerusalem's hotels. It wasn't yet nine a.m. but even in the shade it was already very hot.

"I will not speak and I will pretend to be a tourist for the duration," Eitan said, as we waited. "I am here to observe and to accompany you and I will not distract you."

"Okay," I said, smiling at him, not sure he would succeed in blending in or in keeping quiet, but touched that he wanted to try.

Sylvia, too, said that she'd keep in the background and that I should concentrate on forming my own impressions.

The tour guide welcomed us aboard the cool of the air-conditioned bus, and told us that the tour was designed to go beyond the normal tourist destinations and to show the real Jerusalem, the complete picture not normally shown to tourists. She explained that we would see the separation barrier and cross over into the West Bank. She told us we would visit Palestinian villages and that we would hear both the Israeli and the Palestinian perspective on the need for and the effects of the wall.

I'd done a West Bank tour the previous year with Deb, but the focus had been on the territory beyond the barrier rather than on the barrier itself. So I was particularly interested to hear more about its history as we drove alongside.

Our guide explained that the term West Bank referred to the Palestinian territories which are situated on the west side of the river Jordan, and that it includes the eastern part of Jerusalem.

We were told that construction of the barrier which is intended to separate the West Bank from the rest of Israel had begun over a decade before and wasn't yet complete. It had been built after a wave of Palestinian suicide bombings carried out in Israeli territory. The Israeli government decided a security barrier was needed to prevent further attacks.

But the guide also pointed out that the Palestinians viewed the building of the barrier as an act of apartheid. And, although the International Court of Justice had declared it illegal, its construction proceeded. When it was eventually finished, the wall would be two hundred and eighty miles long. Its official title was the Separation Barrier and the fencing – and it was mainly fencing rather than actual wall – was eight metres high in places. And despite its stated aim of preventing Palestinians from entering Israel, it was a fact that thousands of Palestinians crossed to the Israeli side every day in order to look for or get to work.

And the barrier had strayed significantly from the official border and now eighty-five percent of it was on Palestinian land. This, along with the more than two hundred illegal Israeli settlements built so far, meant an Israeli controlled area the size of Chicago had been established on Palestinian territory. As a

*Settlement*

result many Palestinians lost their land, livelihoods and homes.

I glanced at Eitan as we listened to all these statistics, but his face gave nothing away.

Once we'd crossed to the other side, we stopped in the Palestinian village of Daaba. We left the bus and walked.

We were shown the homes and school that had been damaged when dynamite was used to clear the way for the barrier. Later we were shown the gate through which Palestinians with permits, like those Mari had told me about, were allowed to go once a year to harvest their olives.

Another village we visited had the barrier running right through it. A couple of families who lived on the Palestinian side were now cut off from their fellow villagers and could not be visited by them. And, for those Palestinian villagers on the Israeli side, although they were therefore technically part of Jerusalem, they received no civic services such as rubbish collection, while their Israeli neighbours did. The guide told us it was easy to spot which were Palestinian houses and which were Israeli settler homes by looking at the house roof. The Palestinian houses all had water collection tanks on their roofs; the settlers' homes did not. This was because the Israeli authorities daily turned off the water supply to the Palestinian homes – sometimes for hours at a time. Meanwhile the larger settler homes had enough water for their private outdoor swimming pools.

I could feel my anger building as I listened to all of this. And I could only guess how much angrier and more frustrated those on the receiving end of this treatment must feel. Again I looked for a reaction from Eitan, but although he appeared to be listening intently, he remained impassive. Other fellow passengers weren't so restrained. The most common utterance being, 'I didn't know!'

The last place we visited was Bethlehem and my outrage increased. I hadn't managed to fit in a visit there the previous year and had been looking forward to seeing it this time. And, even though I knew it was on the West Bank, I had assumed that as a world famous religious site, this little town would be doing all right, reaping the rewards of many tourist dollars. I was wrong. It was a rundown and desolate place. It was almost completely isolated by the barrier and by the surrounding Israeli settlements. Its economy had been devastated by this stranglehold, and the town was even cut off from its own agricultural land and its churches. It was so sad to see what should have been an iconic world heritage site reduced to this pathetic level.

Overall I was left feeling indignant and infuriated by what I'd seen. And my feeling from my first visit to the area was stronger than ever. I wasn't sure how much protection the barrier actually offered, but I felt what it did do was impose division, cause suspicion and foster dangerous resentment.

# Chapter Twenty Seven

*Rachel*

It was just after twelve o'clock when we got back to the drop-off point. It was sweltering and, even in the relative cool of the minibus, I could feel the sweat running down my back. I was cross with myself for having forgotten to bring either a hat or a bottle of water. I felt exhausted and I had the beginnings of a headache. This and the need for a bit of time to calm down and process all I'd heard on the tour, meant I didn't say much as Eitan drove us back to the flat.

When I invited Eitan to join me for lunch, it was out of a sense of gratitude for his willingness to accompany me on the tour and for driving me. But what I really wanted was to be on my own. I wanted to lie down on my bed, blinds drawn and ceiling fan on. I hoped I seemed glad about it when he accepted my invitation.

It didn't take me long to assemble some bread, cheese, salad and fruit. I also filled a jug with pre-chilled water from the fridge and added ice-cubes and some slices of lemon and lime.

According to the wall-mounted thermometer, it was forty-one degrees on the balcony, so we ate indoors with the curtains drawn and the air-conditioning on. But it still felt stifling.

"You are very quiet," Eitan said as we began eating, or rather as he began eating. I didn't feel hungry. All I wanted was to gulp down the cold water.

I drained my glass and then refilled it as I replied. "Sorry," I said. "This morning – it was full on – a lot to take in."

"And what did you think of what you saw and heard?" he asked.

"It made me angry," I said.

"You saw injustice?"

"Yes."

"Then it is not surprising you are angry."

"But?"

"But nothing. Injustice is unfair, not right, unacceptable. If you think that's what you saw, then it is understandable you are upset."

"If I think that's what I saw? Are you patronising me?" My head was pounding. I hadn't had a migraine for ages, but the pain I was feeling had all the makings of one.

"I am not. I am respecting your opinion." Eitan spoke calmly, his usual unflappable self.

"So what is your opinion of what we saw? You didn't see injustice? You don't feel angry?" I tried to be as calm as Eitan, but my irritation wasn't helped by the throbbing pain spreading across my scalp, now being accompanied by the beginnings of nausea.

"I was upset by some of the things we saw and yes, some of it appears unjust. But there are reasons for much of it, good reasons."

"Good? I saw nothing that was—" I put my hand to my mouth, pushed my chair back and ran. I just made it to the bathroom, but with no time to close the door, before I threw up.

When it was over, I sat on the bathroom floor, my back against the wall. I didn't have the energy to stand up. I heard footsteps in the hallway and Eitan appeared in the bathroom doorway.

"Hey," he said, as he bent over me. "Come." He scooped me up into his arms and carried me down the hall to my bedroom. Once I was lying back against the pillows, Eitan switched on the fan and brought a glass of iced water. He supported my head and held the glass to my lips. "Little bits," he said as I drank the icy cold liquid. "Just little bits."

I nodded.

After a few more sips, he put the glass down. He then produced a cold, wet cloth and bathed my face and neck with it. It felt good. I closed my eyes. The last thing I was aware of before I fell asleep was Eitan singing softly as he stroked my hair.

I don't know exactly how long I was asleep for, but I'd only been awake for a short time when Deb knocked and put her head round the door.

"Come in," I said, as I sat up.

"How are you?" said Deb. "Eitan told me what happened." She put a fresh glass of iced water on the bedside table and sat down on the end of the bed.

"A bit headachy still, but nothing like earlier. I've got tablets in my handbag." I moved to get up but the pain of moving made me wince.

"Stay where you are," Deb said. "I'll get your bag."

"I haven't had a migraine like this for ages," I said, before swallowing a couple of pills. "It came on very suddenly."

"Jonathan said he will check you over when he gets home," Deb said.

"How does he know—?"

"Eitan texted both of us to let us know you were ill. He said he'd stay with you until one of us got back. He's been checking on you every now and then while you were sleeping."

"Is he still here?"

"Yes. He's about to leave but he'd like to see you before he goes – if that's okay with you."

I put my hands to my face and groaned. "I'm so embarrassed – getting ill like that in front of him. What must he think?"

"I'm sure there's no need to be embarrassed on his account. He's concerned for you. He cares about you. He cares about you a lot." Deb raised her eyebrows in a meaningful look.

"I know," I said. But I felt too weak to pursue exactly what the look meant. "Tell him it's fine to look in before he goes."

"I'm sorry," I said as soon as Eitan came into the room. Again I tried to get up, but all I succeeded in doing was making the room spin.

Eitan came over to me. He put his hands on my shoulders and pushed me gently down and back against the pillows. "You shouldn't try to move," he said. He sat on the edge of the bed. "Lie still." He stroked my face. "It is I who am sorry. I should not have upset you. I saw you were tired. I should have left you alone."

"You didn't upset me," I said. "Not enough to make me sick anyway." I managed a smile. "I think it was simply a bit too hot out there for me today."

"I should have seen that. I should have taken better care of you."

"It's not your job to take care of me."

"Ah, Rachel," he said, as he took hold of my hand and put it to his lips. "I would like it if you let me take care of you."

"I – I don't need—"

"Shh," he said, releasing my hand and standing up. "You should rest and I must go. I will call you tomorrow."

After Eitan left, I lay in the half dark, not sure what I was feeling. Physically I just felt exhausted, but emotionally I was all over the place. I could feel tears running down my face and down my neck. The optimism of the morning, the feeling of being in the right place, of being where I was meant to be, had gone. Eitan had unsettled me. Israel had unsettled me. Suddenly I felt homesick. I missed Sophie, I missed Miriam and yes, I missed Jack.

I must have fallen asleep again because when Jonathan knocked on the door he woke me from a dream. A dream in which I was lost.

"Your temperature's slightly high and your pulse is a little elevated," Jonathan said, when he'd finished checking me over. "But your blood pressure's okay. A bit of heatstroke and dehydration is most likely the cause of your trouble."

"I thought it was a migraine," I said.

"It could have been that too, brought on by you overheating. You'll have to be more careful. Stay in the shade, wear a hat, keep drinking."

"Yes, doctor," I said.

"I mean it. It was intensely hot today – exceptional even for here – and it's set to remain so for the next couple of days."

"I've learned my lesson," I said.

"Good." My brother smiled at me. "I'm interested to hear what you thought about the tour, but not now. Now you need to—"

"Rest!" I said. "Yes, I know, so go away and leave me in peace."

# Chapter Twenty Eight

*Rachel*

Fortunately I had no visits or meetings planned for the following few days. So I was able to take things easy and recover. On the day after the tour I slept until lunchtime and didn't do any work at all.

But by the next day I felt much better and I was able to begin to make sense of my thoughts and feelings about what I'd seen on the West Bank. And complex though those thoughts and feelings were, they were easier to work through than the ones I was having about Eitan.

He was infuriating at times, but he was also warm, kind, uncomplicated and very sexy. I was fairly sure that with the smallest signal from me, we'd end up in bed together. I'd no regrets about having had sex with him when we'd gone away for a few days together during my previous visit. It would be easy to give in, to have good, no strings sex with this always interesting, challenging and captivating man.

He texted a couple of times to check how I was, but we didn't speak until the end of the week, four days after our West Bank tour. And by then I was not only fully recovered, but I'd also reached a few decisions about how I wanted the rest of my time in Israel to go.

The first decision was to hire a car. It was all very well being driven everywhere, but unlike my previous trip which had been a holiday, this time I was there to work and being dependent on others didn't feel professional somehow.

My second decision was about my feelings for Eitan and how I'd like our relationship to be.

So when Eitan phoned on the Friday afternoon to invite me to dinner at his place the next day, I was happy to accept. He also suggested I stay over afterwards and I agreed to that too.

But there was one more decision I needed to make – and that was what to do about Jack. I'd still heard nothing from him and I needed to hear his voice.

So after Friday night dinner with Jonathan and the family, I went to my bedroom and called Jack's landline and, for the first time in ten days, I spoke to him.

He sounded distracted when he answered, his tone impatient. "Yes? Who is this?"

"It's me, Rachel."

"Oh, Rachel."

"Didn't you see it was me? On the ID?"

"What? No. I just got in, heard the phone as I came in the door, didn't take time to look who it was."

"Sorry if this isn't a good time."

"Good a time as any."

"Okay. Right. Didn't you get my messages?"

"Yes ... yes I did, thanks."

"But you didn't feel like responding ... or maybe even acknowledging you'd got them ... any of them?"

He didn't even try to repress a sigh. "I should have acknowledged them. But, no, I didn't feel like responding."

"Oh, right, I see." I hadn't seen that coming. "Are you okay?"

"Yes."

"You sound a bit ... a bit flat."

"It's been a busy day ... a busy few days."

"Right." I waited for him to elaborate. I was desperate for him to elaborate. But there was only silence. "I've been busy too. Overdid it a bit at first, made myself ill, but I'm getting lots of interesting stuff for the—"

"You were ill? What happened? Are you all right now?" Jack's concern made him the most animated he'd been so far.

"A bit of heatstroke combined with a migraine. I'm fine now. Eitan looked after me ... that is he was here in the flat ... when I became unwell ... and then Jonathan did his doctor thing."

"Right ... well ... as long as you're okay."

"I am."

"Okay. Look I have to go. Stuff to do. And, Rachel?"

"Yes?"

"Maybe it's best if we ... if we leave things for now. You get on with your stuff and I'll get on with mine. I don't know about you, but I could do without the distraction right now."

"What? No, Jack, no ... that's not what I—"

"It's for the best ... really it is."

"But we can't leave it like this. We need to at least talk. I can't—"

"Look, you chose to go half way round the world to get on with what's important to you. And I've decided to do the same thing here. There's nothing to talk about. So please, can we let things be for now?"

"If you're sure that's what you want, then—"

"It is ... now, sorry, I must go."

"Please, Jack don't do this." But a glance at my phone screen told me he'd ended the call.

"Bye then," I said, feeling tears ready to spill. I flung the phone down and collapsed onto the bed.

There was a knock at the open door and I looked up to see Deb standing there. "There's coffee if you – oh no, Rachel, what's wrong?" She grabbed a box of tissues off the chest of drawers and sat down beside me on the bed.

"Oh, Deb," I said.

She put her arms round me and let me cry. "Here," she said, handing me a tissue when I eventually stopped. "Do you want to talk about it?"

"Jack," I said. "It's bloody Jack."

"Look, come through to the living room. Don't worry, the kids are in their rooms allegedly doing homework and Jonathan's gone back to the hospital to check on a patient who had surgery earlier." Deb picked up the tissue box. "I'll take this with us and you can have a coffee and tell me what's happened."

Once we were settled on the sofa, Deb said, "So you spoke to him at last?"

"Yes – sort of." I told Deb about the conversation, about how stilted and awkward it was, about how he didn't want to keep in touch. "So it seems I'm now a distraction from some more important business." A sob escaped.

Deb stroked my arm. "I'm sure that's not true. Maybe you caught him at a bad moment. You said he'd just got home. Maybe he was tired."

"It was more than that. Besides, being tired doesn't explain why he's made no contact since I got here." I looked up at the ceiling and sighed and a new tear found its way down my cheek. Deb handed me more tissues. "He sounded so ... so cold."

"Hmm," Deb said, frowning slightly.

"What? What does hmm mean?" I asked.

"Jack loves you. It's obvious. Jonathan and I, we both saw it when were with you for the wedding."

"So why doesn't he want to talk to me? I'm going to be here for three months and he doesn't want to talk to me."

"How did he feel about you being away for three months? Was he supportive?"

"Yes ... or no, not at first, not after I turned down his proposal, but then after we talked—"

"His proposal?"

"Ah," I said. "Yes, Jack asked me to marry him."

"And you turned him down?"

I told Deb the whole story. I told her about Jack's mad, romantic proposal and my reasons for not accepting. "But after we talked, he seemed to get where I was coming from, he seemed to accept it and to support my coming here."

"It sounds to me like Jack is missing you as much as you're missing him. It sounds like he's hurting, maybe scared he's going to lose you and he's trying to protect himself. Maybe the only way he can cope is to maintain a bit of distance?"

I sighed and shook my head. "Whatever it is that's wrong with him, the way he's behaving it's hurtful and it's bloody infuriating!"

Deb laughed. "That's my girl," she said. "Don't get sad, get angry." She stood up and picked up our cups of cold coffee. "I think we should swap these for something stronger."

We took our whiskies out onto the balcony. Deb lit the candle that sat in the middle of the little circular table and we sat and looked out over the city.

"It seems to me you and Jack have got a lot of thinking to do. Perhaps it's good you have some time apart?"

"Yeah, maybe you're right," I said. "No, actually you *are* right. I'm bloody well going to get on and enjoy this project. And I'm not going to worry about bloody Jack until I get home."

Deb raised her glass. "To not worrying about bloody Jack," she said, grinning.

And I meant what I said about trying not to think about him, but I knew it wasn't going to be easy. I couldn't stop loving him. I couldn't stop missing him. However, I also knew there was nothing I could do about any of it while I was away.

So, before I went to sleep that night, I resolved to focus on what I'd come to do. I wasn't going to let anyone or anything make me lose focus on my reasons for doing the book in the first place. I was in Israel to create something positive, something that could help people everywhere get along better, something in honour of my son. And that's what I was going to do.

# Chapter Twenty Nine

*Rachel*

I hadn't visited Eitan's home on my first trip so I was curious to see what it was like. It was around four p.m. the following afternoon when I set off, and aided by the sat-nav and Jonathan's directions, it took me about forty minutes to drive there. As I drove I thought about the text I'd received before I left. A text from Jack – and all it said was *Remember, whatever happens, I love you*. But thinking about it didn't help me understand why he'd say that, especially after what he'd said the previous day. Was it a farewell, a warning, an attempt to ease his conscience? I had no idea – but whatever it was, now wasn't the time to ask. I'd arrived at Eitan's.

The house sat alone at the end of a curved driveway, at the top of a gently sloping road. It was a long low L-shape, with white walls, red roof tiles and lots of glass, and there was a terrace which looked like it probably went all the way around. When I got out of the car, I could see that both house and terrace were surrounded by mature looking gardens. There were plenty of shade-giving trees and I could smell the lavender which lined the top of the driveway.

I was getting my overnight bag out of the car when Eitan came out to meet me."Rachel," he called. "You found me!"

"Yes," I said laughing, as he walked towards me, arms outstretched. "Don't sound so surprised."

He kissed me on both cheeks and then he stood back, his hands still on my shoulders, and looked at me. "You look much better than you did the last time I saw you."

"I feel a lot better," I said.

"I am glad. Now, please, give me your bag and follow me."

As we stepped into the house there was an open door straight ahead and through it I glimpsed what I took to be the living-room. We went past it and turned left into a corridor that I assumed ran the length of the long part of the L-shape.

Eitan stopped at the first doorway on our left. "The guest room," he said, opening the door and indicating I should go in ahead of him. "The ensuite is in there," he said, pointing across the room. "And here is the air-conditioning control." He put my bag down on the white bedcover and went over to the far side of the room. He pushed the closed curtains aside to reveal a long, folding glass door that ran the length of the wall. You have access from here to the terrace and garden," he said, before closing the curtains again. "You can have the drapes and the door open in the early morning when this part of the house is in the shade. I hope you will be comfortable here."

"I'm sure I shall," I said, looking around. The walls were white as were the marble floor tiles. Indeed the only colour in the room was provided by the purple agapanthus flowers that sat in a clear glass vase on a white chest of drawers, and by an oil painting that hung on the wall opposite the bed. It was an abstract picture made up mainly of great swirls of red, ochre and white.

Eitan saw me looking at it. "Good isn't it?" he said.

"Yes, it's very ... powerful."

"It was painted by my friend, Magda," he said. "Now, she is a woman who is not afraid to express herself."

I got the implication right away but I could only smile and shake my head when I saw Eitan's mischievous expression. "A *good* friend, is she, this Magda?"

"Definitely, she is a *very* good friend." Eitan grinned. "But now, please, you must be in need of some refreshment."

I followed him back along the corridor to his sleek, high-tech, chrome and stainless steel kitchen. And after a delicious glass of home-made lemonade and a shared plate of ice-cold slices of water melon, Eitan showed me the rest of the house.

He explained that it had been designed to his specification by an architect friend and that he'd done much of the building himself. The other two bedrooms, including his own, were further down the corridor and were just as neat and functional. There was also a wet-room which had the biggest shower head I have ever seen and was even more of a chrome and marble palace than the kitchen.

He told me he generated all his own electricity from solar panels, so running the air-conditioning was not expensive. This meant the house was always at a comfortable temperature and this was most evident in his studio.

The studio was situated on the end of the other leg of the L. It was a large space and was remarkably cool considering it too had not only a wall of glass but a skylight in the ceiling. The glass was shielded by electronically controlled, slatted shutters but for the moment they were open and the light flooded in. It too was white-walled but that's where the similarity to the other rooms ended. Three easels, each bearing a large, work-in-progress canvas were placed around the room. There were finished paintings everywhere – both hung on and leaning against the walls. In one corner there was a stack of blank canvases and in another there was a desk with lap-top and a pile of sketchbooks sitting on it. One wall was taken up with shelves which were laden with box-files and large hard-covered Art books. And a paint-spattered workbench covered in brushes, tubes and pots of paint, jars, rags and palettes took up most of another wall. The room was crammed with colour and texture. There was a full-on sensuousness to it. It buzzed with life, and overflowed with the possibility of creativity, much like Eitan himself.

He seemed pleased at my enthusiastic reaction to his workspace and told me take my time looking at the paintings while he went to get on with dinner preparations. He also suggested I take a walk round the garden and then go and relax in the living-room until the meal was ready.

The paintings were worth taking my time over. I recognised a few of the landscapes as places I'd visited in Israel the year before. I examined the colours, inhaled the oily trace, and ran my fingers over their textured surfaces. There was a beautiful one of the Sea of Galilee, all blues and greens, but smoother to the touch, and with a degree of calmness not present in most of the others.

The garden was delightful. It had been carefully planned with its cultivated areas placed so they flowed like a stream along the creamy-coloured, pebble-covered ground. There were clusters of low-growing alpine plants, and areas of fragrant herbs such as rosemary, lemon thyme and tarragon. There were circles of lupins and lilies and clumps of cyclamen. And at the edges, young trees – olive, lemon, orange and fig according to the descriptions on their labels – with headily scented lavender bushes nestling close by.

After taking some photos on my phone, I sat for a moment on a shaded bench. The air was laden with fragrance and with the birdsong of the tiny, brightly-coloured birds that flitted in and out of the foliage. It was a moment of feeling truly present and at peace. I closed my eyes and whispered my son's name. I'm not religious and I don't believe in ghosts, but in that moment I felt that Finlay was with me.

And when the moment passed I went back indoors. The feeling of wellbeing stayed with me as I sat on one of the two large sofas in Eitan's living-room. My resolve and conviction about what I'd come to Israel to do was stronger than ever. Whatever it took, I was now most definitely committed.

I felt restless with possibility and purpose. I got to my feet. The glass doors were open and folded back now that the day was cooling and, for a few minutes, I stood looking out over the garden. I wasn't used to feeling so motivated – or so good – good *about* myself and good *within* myself.

After I'd browsed Eitan's bookshelves and admired the glass-topped dining table which was set ready for dinner, I went to take a closer look at the paintings hanging on the walls of this room.

I recognised one landscape immediately.

"You remember that view?" Eitan said, coming up behind me.

"The Dead Sea," I said, still staring at it, remembering more than the view. "It's a great painting ... very vivid ... the colours are amazing ... it's like you could put your hand in the water."

"You inspired it. I returned there after our visit last year. You were so much in my head. I wanted to see again what we saw together, to be where we were. I needed to put it in a painting."

I was aware of him looking at me. I could guess what he was thinking. I could feel my neck and face flushing. I glanced up at him. "Eitan, please, I—"

"No, please, do not worry," he said. He put his hands on my shoulders and turned me to face him, then he took my hands in his. "You made it clear, when you agreed to come here to my house that you were coming as a friend only. I respect that, but it does not mean I do not wish for more."

We stood there, looking at each other. My thoughts flitted back to the night we'd spent together at the guesthouse in Ein Gedi during our Dead Sea trip. My mind again flirted with the possibility of some uncomplicated sex. Except for me it wouldn't be uncomplicated.

"Do not look so afraid," Eitan said. He let go of one of my hands and stroked my face. "I am thankful to know you. I am happy to have been inspired by you to paint this picture. And I am very pleased to have you here in my home. Okay?"

"Okay," I said.

"Good. Now, let's eat."

We began with tabbouleh – a tomato, mint and parsley salad, dressed in olive oil and with a sprinkling of bulgur wheat grains mixed through it. The flavours were so much richer, sharper and stronger than I was used to and suggested a level of freshness I rarely experienced at home. Even the bread had zest. Eitan smiled as he watched me tearing off another piece of bread and wiping my plate clean of olive oil and tomato juices. "I can tell you are enjoying it."

"Mmm," I said, as I grabbed my napkin and wiped olive oil from my chin. "It's incredible."

The main course was a chicken casserole with couscous, and again the flavours were intense and delicious. The wine was excellent too. And, as I ate, I found myself thinking that if Eitan was trying to find a way to my heart, he was going the right way about it. Jack with all his moodiness and baggage seemed very far away, whereas across the table from me sat a man to whom the term *what you see is what you get* definitely applied. He was a man who didn't promise fidelity, but who did promise honesty, a stimulating artistic challenge, and the excitement of intellectual and political debate at a level I hadn't experienced before. He was also an excellent lover.

"You are hidden in your thoughts," Eitan said as he put my empty plate on top of his.

"Sorry, I don't mean to be rude. I seem to have a lot to think about."

"Don't be sorry," he said as he stood up. "But perhaps over dessert you might share some of those thoughts with me?"

"It's a deal," I said, smiling at him and blushing slightly as I thought I probably wouldn't be sharing *all* my most recent thoughts.

"Lemon semolina cake," Eitan said when he returned from the kitchen with a tray.

"Wow," I said. "I was impressed with your cooking skills, but you're a baker too."

"Ah, I cannot claim to have baked this. It was actually Magda – the friend I told you about."

"Oh, you mean your *good* friend, the artist? She baked it?"

"She did. I told her about you and I told you she would be

coming to dinner. And she said she'd like to bake us a cake."

"That was kind of her."

Eitan passed me a slice of the cake. "She also said she would like to meet you."

"Right. So would that be possible?"

"It would. She could join us tomorrow morning for coffee before you leave – if you would like."

"Yes, I'd like that very much."

"I think you will have a lot to talk about."

"Yes, Art and baking at least," I said. "And you, of course."

"Oh not only those," Eitan said, smiling. "Magda is a settler."

I looked at him, puzzled.

"A settler. She lives in one of the settlements on the West Bank, one of the settlements that was described to us on our tour as illegal."

"Okay," I said. "That will be interesting."

"So you would still like to meet her?"

"Definitely," I said.

"Good, I will let her know. But first I shall make coffee."

# Chapter Thirty

*Rachel*

"So, tell me, what is your opinion about what we saw on the West Bank?" Eitan said a little while later as we settled on the sofa with our coffee.

I had to smile at his complete inability to do small talk, but any amusement I felt at his directness soon vanished as I thought back to the tour. "Like I started to say on Monday, I felt shock, anger, frustration," I said.

"Why shock? You went to the West Bank last year with Deb. You knew what to expect, no?"

"I thought I did, but it seems to me now that I only saw relatively positive aspects on my first visit. Or perhaps the situation has deteriorated."

"In what way?"

"Deb and I stayed in Beit Sahour at the Arab Women's Guesthouse. The town was lovely. We were pleasantly surprised. And yet it's very near Bethlehem and what you and I saw there was horrible – all that destruction. Hana Aker who runs the guesthouse told us of some of the difficulties and we heard more at a talk in Hebron about what daily life is like. And ... and there was an elderly Bedouin man who told us about the water shortages. But..."

"But what? What was so shocking this time?" There was something in Eitan's tone and expression that suggested I should have known what to expect, and even that I was over-reacting.

"What was so shocking was *seeing* it for myself. Hana and the others spoke with such a ... such a quiet dignity. It was almost like they'd accepted things, were resigned to it all. But *seeing* it all – the size of the settlements, the water situation, the contempt of the soldiers, the plight of the farmers, that was shocking, that was what made me angry."

"And how do you interpret what you saw?"

"What do you mean?"

"You say you are shocked and angry. That is the reaction of many non-Israelis. What is it that offends you?"

"It's everything about it – the illegality of it, the stealing of land, the threat to life and to the very existence of the Palestinian people. Doesn't it offend you?"

"It does not offend me no."

"But how? How can it not?"

"Because I see the reason for it."

"What possible reason could there be for treating people in that way?"

"When they pose a threat, when they bomb us, when they want to take our country away from us – we must defend ourselves – those are the reasons."

"But wouldn't it be better to talk, to try to understand their point of view, to come to a peaceful solution where both sets of people could share this country?"

"Ah, Rachel, that is of course what you would suggest." Eitan smiled, but there was a touch of condescension in his expression.

"What do you mean?" I asked.

"I mean you have a very British point-of-view. The Brits are always like the sensible adults telling off the naughty children. It is patronising and it is hypocritical. It is also none of your business."

Part of me knew this was classic Eitan, knew it wasn't personal, but part of me was angry. "How dare you?" I said. I stood up. If I hadn't been over the alcohol limit for driving, I'd have left right then, not because I couldn't take being offended, but because I knew I was in danger of losing my temper.

Instead, knowing I was stuck there, I took a deep breath, began pacing, and tried to keep calm. I really did want to understand where Eitan – an intelligent, creative, empathetic artist – a good man in so many ways – was coming from. "It is you who is being patronising."

"Oh, how—"

I stopped pacing and turned to face him, raising my hand to silence him as I did so. "No, let me finish. Don't use my nationality to dismiss me. I know us Brits are far from perfect, I know there's plenty in our own history, and currently, that we should be ashamed of. I know it was Britain who made possible much of what's happening here today when it handed Palestine over to allow the foundation of the state of Israel. Yes, it provided a much-needed home for Jewish people. And yes, Israel has a right to exist – but it has proved to be at a terrible cost to some of the people who were already living here before its foundation.

"*But* I'm not speaking as British," I continued. "I'm speaking as a human being. And I'm speaking about the plight of fellow human beings who are being ill-treated. So it is very much my business."

Eitan gave a sort of half nod, not quite a bow of submission, but enough to let me hope I might have got through to him.

He leaned forward, thoughtful, hands clasped under his chin. Then he sat back and looked at me, hands open. "Of course, you are right. You speak as a humanitarian on a humanitarian issue. And I see it that way too."

"You do?" I sat down on the other sofa.

"I do. I do believe we have a right to defend ourselves – but the political situation is complex. The humanitarian one is not. I do not like that people lose their homes. I do not like that they lose their jobs and their communities. I saw how the Palestinians suffer and like you I did not like it."

"And were you shocked or angry like me?"

"I admit I was shocked at the extent of the difficulties. And I was angry at the situation and sad for those who suffer."

"But not enough for you to want to change it?"

Eitan hit the arm of the sofa. "Don't presume!"

"Sorry, I—"

"No, I am sorry. I should not have shouted. But this is the problem. Everyone makes judgements but nobody listens. Please, don't presume."

"So you would like things to change?"

"Yes, I would. I would like us all, Israelis and Palestinians, to live here as one nation. It would be better for everyone – Jews and Arabs. I would like there not to be a wall. I would like it if everyone could get on with their lives in peace, raise their families, live on their own bit of the land. I would like everyone to be treated with respect. And I do see how the way we are acting in the occupied areas can be seen as bullying – and worse." Eitan sighed and shook his head, his expression anguished. "But there is so much at stake. I am afraid if we let our guard down we will lose our country."

I moved back to sit beside him. "I understand that," I said. "I suppose it comes down to communication, honest communication that builds up trust and allows everyone to see some common humanitarian ground."

"But for that we must first have peace and an absence of threat."

"Yes, and somebody has to make the first move."

"You think it should be Israel?"

"Israel is in a position of strength."

"Yes, but it is only after much struggle and sacrifice by the Jewish people. There has been the struggle to survive persecution, to survive attempted annihilation, and to establish a homeland. And through all that there has been the determination to never be the victims again. It's what my brother died for, what so many of us died for."

I thought of my mother, of how she'd lost her entire family

in the Holocaust and of how she'd come to equate being Jewish with being a victim and being vulnerable. "I know. I get that. I really do. And I know, too, that sometimes wars have to be fought against very real enemies of humanity."

But then it was Finlay who came to mind. Finlay, who'd believed he and his comrades were sent to protect the people of Afghanistan. "But sometimes – most times – conflict, war, aggression – they're not the answer. Sometimes, we need to talk and more than that, we need to listen. We need to take the barriers down. We need to show each other some respect." I sat back, feeling exhausted. I closed my eyes, felt some tears escape.

I felt Eitan's hand on mine. "Oh my dear Rachel," he said.

I opened my eyes and turned to look at him. His expression was tender. "Sorry," I said.

"Why do you apologise? You should not be sorry for feeling things so passionately." He moved his hand to my face, "You are a good person. But the world it is not so good. And this makes you sad."

I took hold of his hand, moved it from my face. "I don't know about being a good person and I'm done with being sad. Now I'm angry and ... and I'm frustrated that I can't see things changing."

"Your anger is good. You are using it to drive your work."

"But am I kidding myself?"

"What do you mean?"

"I'm here to create a book, a book promoting peace, a book in memory of my son. But it's not going to change anything, is it?"

"You cannot know that. You cannot know what conversations or actions will come from a person reading your book or engaging with the wider project. But you ... you are taking action ... you are personally taking a position, an action for peace."

"The politicians aren't going to be influenced though, are they? And they're the people who have the power."

"Not all the power. We, as individuals, we have personal power. Our actions can change things one step at a time, but it takes courage and it takes – what is the word?" Eitan flapped his fingers and frowned as he thought. "When your mind is set on a particular action?"

"Determination?" I said.

"Yes, determination and courage – such as you have – they matter. Person to person communication can build something honest. Ordinary people can and do put pressure on politicians and systems. If the people of this country, or anywhere else, are to have true peace, then they need to talk, to connect, to build trust and respect for each other. That is the true starting point. Anything else is meaningless theory, meaningless political chatter, with often deadly motives."

"I doubt that this book will change the world, but, like you say, I would hope it would be a starting point, a starting point for the sort of conversations you're talking about. And I want the book to share the work of people like you and the *My Jerusalem* project, and all the other projects and initiatives I'm going to be visiting. "

"I agree. I love my country, love that we Jews have our homeland, but in its present condition it is doomed. A solution is needed that is fair to all Israelis and Palestinians and where we can live together without walls and checkpoints and threats. And so far no politicians, our own, or those in the UK or USA have come close to getting it right."

I was on my feet again, pacing, my mind buzzing with thoughts. "And it's not only here, there's ethnic and racial conflict almost everywhere. At its worst, lives are being ruined or even sacrificed for often spurious agendas and political gain. And at best, the smoke and mirrors of politics, and of vested interests, leaves people feeling frustrated, unsafe and powerless." I paused in my pacing, stood at the open doors, looking out into the now dark garden.

Eitan came to stand behind me. He put his hand on my shoulder. "Indeed," he said, and I could feel his breath on my neck as we looked out into the darkness.

I turned to face him. This time it was me who took his hands in mine. I looked up at him. "Wouldn't it be great if this country set a good example of how different tribes, nationalities and races could live positively together for the good of everybody?"

"It would." His smile was broad. "Imagine if we could let go of the past, build a new way of living and a new legacy."

"It sounds so simple, but in reality it's daunting."

Eitan put his hands on either side of my face. "But not impossible. It needs the will to do it and it needs people like you – you Rachel – to act to make a difference."

And as I looked at him, looked into his eyes, I knew he understood. He may not let me off with sloppy thinking or sentimentality but he understood me, why I was there, what I hoped to achieve.

I realised, too, that I loved this man, loved his uncomplicated and unconditional acceptance of me as a person, and his willingness both to argue with me but also to listen to my views.

So the kiss was inevitable. It was also passionate. And it was more than gratitude and the platonic love of a friend that led me into Eitan's embrace. I was still attracted to him. Being enveloped in his muscular embrace, smelling the musky scent of his skin, feeling the building urgency of his kisses – it would have been so easy to give in, give myself up to the straightforward pleasure of making love with him.

But I couldn't do it. Because there was Jack – yes, bloody Jack. He was there in my head – and in my heart – and I couldn't do it. I put my hands on Eitan's chest as his lips moved to my neck. "No," I said, taking a step back. "I'm sorry, I can't."

Eitan looked at me, frowning. "You were enjoying it, were you not?"

"Yes, I was and I *am* attracted to you – tempted. That's the trouble."

"It should not trouble you. You know I do not equate sex with commitment. It would simply be for our enjoyment – as it was once before."

"Yes, I know, but it *would* trouble me." I bit my lip, anxious not to offend him. "For me ... for me it *is* about commitment."

Eitan's smile was kind, his voice gentle. "Come, don't look so scared," he said and he took me by the hand and led me back to the sofa. "Jack is a lucky man." He put his arm around me and I let him pull me in close beside him.

"Hmm, I don't think he sees it that way at the moment," I said.

"What do you mean?"

So I told him. I told Eitan all about Jack's proposal and my reasons for rejecting it. And I told him how things had been between us since.

"Why are you so scared to commit?" Eitan asked when I had finished.

I laughed as I replied. "You're a fine one to talk!"

"Yes, I am. I do what I want to do. I don't analyse my relationships. I enjoy them for what they are. You should not let your past history or Jack's make you scared to follow your heart. If you love Jack and he loves you, and you both want an exclusive and committed relationship, then what is the problem?"

"You make it sound so simple. But it's not – not for me. I don't think I want to be married again. Like I said, marriage is no guarantee of a happy ending."

"Nothing in this life is guaranteed. But if Jack is willing to take the risk of commitment, willing to be faithful to you, and you love him as much as you seem to do – then I say, to hell with the risk. Enjoy what you have while you have it."

"But that's just it, I don't know what we have anymore especially after – after what he said to me yesterday – and then there was a text from him earlier. And now I'm more confused than ever."

"Tell me."

So I did.

When I'd finished, Eitan said, "I think that Jack – I think he is finding it difficult to be apart from you – but he is trying to support you too. And I guess he thinks that by leaving you alone it makes it easier for you and for him."

"And the text – what does that mean?"

"That he loves you whatever happens."

"As simple as that?" I said.

"Yes, as simple as that."

"And what should I do?"

"Do? Do nothing. Respect his wishes and remember that he loves you. Then you will talk when you go home."

"Hmm," I said.

Eitan moved away slightly so he could see my face. "Hmm? What is this hmm?"

I looked at him, at his quizzical grin. "How did you get so wise?" I said smiling back at him.

# Chapter Thirty One

*Rachel*

I slept well that night at Eitan's. At first I'd lain and thought about Jack, wished he understood me the way Eitan did, wished he could be as open with me. I considered trying to get him on the phone, but I sensed that even if he did answer, any conversation we had would be pointless. So I decided to take Eitan's advice and to wait until I got back to Skye before having it out with Jack. And having made that decision, it wasn't long before I was asleep.

It was after breakfast the next morning that Magda arrived. She wasn't what I'd imagined. She was older for a start – in her early sixties I guessed – but still a striking looking woman. She was tall, with olive skin and her hair hung in a long silver plait. Her smile as she shook my hand was warm and she spoke English with an eastern European accent.

After he'd introduced us, Eitan suggested we all go out to the garden. He directed us to a table on a shaded part of the terrace and poured us all a glass of freshly made lemonade.

"Lacheim," Eitan said, raising his glass as he spoke the Hebrew toast to life. "To life in all its preciousness."

Magda and I also raised our glasses and joined in the toast. "I am so glad you agreed to meet me," Magda said, smiling at me. "When Eitan told me about you and why you are in Israel, I did not think you would."

"Oh?" I said, wondering if I'd ever get used to Israeli directness. "Of course I wanted to. You're a friend of Eitan's – that alone made me want to meet you, but also seeing your wonderful painting – the one Eitan has – I was very keen to meet the painter."

"You are very kind. It means a lot to have another artist compliment my work. But I thought you would not approve of me because of where I live."

"What? No! It's not a question of me approving or not. But I *am* interested to know why you have chosen to live in one of the … the settlements … to live on the West Bank."

"It is all right, you can say it," Magda said.

"Say what?"

"That I am an illegal settler, living on land said to be Palestinian."

"Okay," I said. "So tell me, why do you live where you do?"

"It surprises you, no? It surprises you that I, an artist and presumably therefore, an intelligent and sensitive woman, am comfortable living on so-called stolen land."

I glanced at Eitan, was aware of him watching Magda and me, of his eyes moving from one to the other as we spoke. It wasn't like him to be so quiet, but he was obviously enjoying being a spectator.

"Yes, I suppose it does. But I'd like to try to understand why you've chosen to do so."

Magda's smile was broad and warm. She looked from me to Eitan. Eitan raised his hands and tilted his head in a sort of I told you so gesture.

"What?" I said. "Am I missing some joke here?"

"Not at all," Eitan said.

"No joke," Magda said. "It's simply that Eitan explained about the book you're here to work on and he told me you'd want to hear my story, maybe use some of it in the book, and I did not believe him. So many people from outside Israel – and yes, some Israelis too – they don't want to hear, they only want to judge."

*Settlement*

"Well, Eitan was right. I'd very much like to hear your story." I took my phone out of my pocket. "And do you mind if I record what you say?"

"No, I suppose not."

"Don't worry," I said. "I won't be reproducing it all word for word. The book will be mainly pictures but I will need to add some explanatory text. Nothing will be put in the book without your permission."

"Right. So what would you like me to tell you?"

"Tell me about your early life, about your work as an artist, about anything you think is worth telling – and then I'd like to know what prompted you to go and live as a settler."

"Okay, I'll do my best."

"Please, go ahead," I said as I switched on the voice recorder.

"My parents were Polish Jews. They met as teenagers in Auschwitz. They were the only members of their families to survive that place. I was born in Poland, but at the end of the 1950s my parents and my brother and sister and me, we emigrated to Israel. We settled in a kibbutz, my parents worked hard to help build the young nation. My father also managed to get himself an education, became a successful architect. My mother died when she was thirty-eight years old, respiratory problems that were a legacy of her time in the concentration camp. I was only twelve, my siblings younger. She lived just long enough to see the beautiful house Father designed and had built for us. My father gave us a good life. He even paid for me to do my Art degree in London."

Magda continued to tell her story with occasional prompts from me and Eitan. She recounted how she'd met the love of her life when she was a post-grad in Paris. He was French and he too was an artist. He followed her home to Israel at the end of their studies but he couldn't settle. And within a year he'd gone back to France. He did ask her to go with him but she couldn't bear to leave Israel so he left without her. He left her despite knowing she was pregnant. She never saw him again and she raised their son alone. She said it had not been easy, but she earned enough as an Art teacher to keep them both and she continued to work on her painting whenever she could. She'd gradually built her reputation, met Eitan along the way, and got to the point where she could stop teaching and earn her living as an artist.

It was at that point that Eitan suggested we break for coffee. And while he was making it I asked Magda if I could do a sketch of her.

"It feels strange," she said as I began to draw. "I'm not used to being the subject."

"Nor me," I said. "I much prefer to be doing the drawing."

"So, tell me about your work," Magda said, as I sketched.

I was in the middle of telling Magda about my children's books when Eitan came back outside with our coffee. "She is also a fine painter, but she needs to do more of it," he said, as he laid the tray on the table.

"Not all artists have to paint, Eitan," Magda said. "There are many ways to be creative and to express yourself."

"Thank you, Magda," I said. "I've tried telling him that too. I used to paint when I was younger and I've done a couple of paintings in the last year, but nothing on a grand scale, not like you or Eitan."

"Exactly," Eitan said. "That is my point."

"What is?" I asked.

"You need to let go, to express yourself on a much bigger canvas."

Magda laughed as she looked at me. "Don't even try to argue with him. He is impossibly opinionated and always right."

I finished my sketch of Magda between sips of coffee and when our break was over she continued telling me her story. She finished by telling me that although she still had a home in West Jerusalem – a house Eitan described as beautiful and complete with its own studio – she had for the last three years lived in a small rented apartment on what she described as reclaimed land on the West Bank. She said the move was something she'd felt compelled to do and that she also believed it was right.

This was my cue to begin questioning her. But for a moment I hesitated. I found that against all my expectations, I liked Magda and I didn't want to offend or upset her. But those were my feelings on a personal level. I was there to do a job. If my book was to going to achieve its aims then I, as the author, had to present the opinions and experiences of those on all sides.

Eitan noticed my hesitation. "Go on," he said. "Magda can take it. She is tougher than me."

"So why did you move?" I asked. "Why did you become a settler?"

"I wanted to ensure my – *our* – country keeps hold of its land. It scared me when some territory was designated Palestinian. I feared it was the start of us losing everything. I felt as other settlers do that we have to maintain a presence throughout our country. Then whatever happens, whether there is ever a two state or a one state solution to this country's problems, and whether we choose the solution or whether it is imposed, we will not lose ground."

"But the land the settlers have taken, it is land that was internationally agreed, would be Palestinian. And even without the settlements, that barrier – it has destroyed homes and villages—"

"Yes, it has. But the Palestinians, by their own actions have shown that they do not deserve to keep their land, and they have not proved to be trustworthy neighbours. Without the wall they were free to attack us. Putting the wall up has made us safer."

"But hundreds of Palestinians cross over at the checkpoints every day to get to work."

"Yes, precisely, at the *checkpoints* they are checked. There are virtually no attacks now."

"But you've gone the other way. You've crossed over to live in amongst people you describe as hostile."

"We cannot merely hope for the best. Like I said, there is too much at stake to trust politicians – ours or anyone else's. If they got the chance, the Palestinians would push us out of this country completely," Magda said, echoing what Eitan had said the night before.

"So instead you push them out first?"

"Exactly, we would be mad not to. There has been too much sacrifice on our part already. We are done being victims."

"What has been sacrificed exactly?"

"You mean apart from the Holocaust? Apart from the soldiers killed in the wars we've had to fight against our aggressive neighbours?"

"Yes, apart from those. I'm not belittling those sacrifices. But I'm talking about more recently. It doesn't seem like it's Israel that's making sacrifices. It seems to me it's Palestine that is paying the ultimate cost."

Magda paused and gave a little smile. "Look, I get it. You're British. You live in a peaceful and long-established country. I don't expect you to truly understand the legacy of the Holocaust and the threat we Jews still feel to our very existence, or what it is to personally lose loved ones in wars or terrorist attacks."

I was aware of Eitan flinching at Magda's last remark. "Magda, no, I must ask you to stop." He looked from Magda to me. "Rachel, Magda, I am sorry. Rachel, I did not feel it was for me to tell the whole of *your* story to Magda."

Magda looked as stricken as Eitan."I'm sorry. What have I—"

"No, no, both of you, it's all right," I said. "Thank you, Eitan. I do have some personal reasons for doing the book, but can we leave that to one side for now. What I want is to learn, to understand how people on both sides view the conflict here. And, yes, Magda, I get what you say about me being British. I know it probably seems like it's none of my business, that it's not my fight."

I felt sweat on my forehead and the back of my neck, felt its dampening effect in the small of my back. The day was heating up. The table was now only in partial shade. I knew I should probably move inside. But stating my reasons, saying out loud, yet again, what was driving me – the explicitness of it reinforced my own motivation. So I kept talking.

"But I reckon it's everyone's business," I continued. "It should be all of humanity's business to try to understand each other better, to see our similarities and to value our differences, and ultimately to see there's more that unites than divides us. And if we can't or won't have these conversations on a personal level, then we are going to have to rely on our politicians and governments to take actions on our behalf. And they're not making a very good job of it. By commissioning this series of books and other resources, by letting people in areas of conflict show and tell their stories, my publishers hope to get people talking. And you're right, I don't understand your position – not yet, that's why I'm asking questions."

"We should move inside," Eitan said. "Air-conditioning and more cold drinks are needed." He stood up. "Come, you two can continue the conversation and I shall organise us some lunch."

"I did not mean to offend you," Magda said after we'd gone inside. Eitan went straight to the kitchen while Magda and I enjoyed the comfort of the shady and pleasantly cool living-room. "To accuse you of being incapable of understanding was unfair of me. I was being defensive."

"You didn't offend me. We are talking about difficult things. I appreciate you taking the time to talk to me at all. I'm grateful. I need to hear from both sides."

Magda nodded. "And I appreciate getting to tell my story." She looked down at her clasped hands before going on. "My brother, he was killed ... in the Yom Kippur war ... 1973 ... same war as Eitan's brother ... at the same age ... both of them nineteen. It's how Eitan and I met."

"I see. I am so sorry. I—"

"Thank you. It was a terrible loss. It's partly why I feel so strongly, so protective of my country. And there's everything my parents endured."

"Yes," I said. "I can see what's motivated you. But I must admit it's hard to be sympathetic when I see how the Palestinians are treated."

"It is unfortunate, but I see no alternative."

"So you wouldn't contemplate a country that is united, one state including Israelis and Palestinians as equals?"

"Now you sound like my son. It is idealistic, unrealistic and naive to think that such diverse peoples with such a diverse history could ever coexist in one state."

I actually gave a little laugh at this, prompting Magda to ask why.

"I was thinking about the history of the United Kingdom. Before it existed, it would have been hard to believe it would ever work either. And we're a far from perfect example of a one-state solution for diverse nations and mixed races peacefully sharing a small space. Historically Scotland and England fought many bloody battles over territory and nationhood. There are still Scots who feel a sense of injustice and would like Scotland to leave the union, but nowadays those feelings are expressed in a lawful and peaceful manner. And more recently there were years of violence and many deaths in Ireland before a fragile peace was achieved there. But surely the very fact that it *has* been achieved should give hope that the seemingly intractable tribal violence and distrust here can be resolved. Political will and mutual respect can go a long way."

"Wow!" Eitan said. "That was quite a speech." I hadn't noticed him coming back into the room. He was standing by the table, now all set for lunch, and smiling at me.

"Yes," Magda said, also smiling. "Exactly what I was thinking."

"Hmm, I'm not sure myself where it came from. But you two are very good for me. You're making me think, examine my assumptions. I'm finding I'm saying things aloud that I didn't realise I believed, or even knew."

"Excellent!" Eitan's laugh was typically loud and hearty. "Now, please, come and sit. Lunch is ready."

Lunch was simple but very tasty. There was hummus and tahini, falafels and salad and a fresh loaf of poppy seed encrusted bread to go with it. The conversation continued as we ate.

"You mentioned your son," I said to Magda as we ate. "Does he not support your move to the West Bank?"

"He doesn't. He is completely against what the settlers are doing." Magda paused, took a sip of water. "Sorry, it is painful to me to speak about it."

"Please, if you'd rather not, please don't answer," I said. I reached out to pause the recording.

"No, it is all right. I want you to have the full story. There is sometimes a cost to living by your principles."

I looked at Eitan. But he just shrugged. I turned back to Magda. "If you're sure—"

"I am," Magda said. "At first we talked about it, but now ... now he will not speak to me, will not see me."

"That must be hard," I said.

"It is ... especially as I'm not allowed to see my grandchildren." Again Magda paused. "But, that is how it has to be for now. I must take my stand, and my son must take his. We both love this country – but we see things very differently. It is my hope that one day we can start talking again."

It was at this point I stopped recording.

Over coffee, Magda showed me some family photos she had on her phone. There were pictures of her son and his wife, and of her two little grandsons. My heart ached for her over her separation from them, especially as I was reminded of the period of estrangement that had existed between Sophie and me. It also reminded me of how big political questions are often reflected in our personal interactions.

"So, Rachel, what is *your* story? What exactly has led to this book of yours? Why do you care so much about peace in this mad country?" Magda asked, as Eitan began clearing the table. "All I know from Eitan is that you're the sister of his friend Jonathan and that your mother was Jewish. I also know this is your second visit to Israel and that you made quite an impression on Eitan when you met last year."

Eitan paused, plates in hand. "She most certainly did," he said. "And yes, Magda you should hear Rachel's story. As I said earlier, I did not feel it was my place to tell it to you. So please, take a more comfortable seat and talk. I will be in the kitchen."

We did as we were told and moved back to the sofas. And I told Magda my story. I told her more of the details about my mother, about her experience of the Holocaust, and about my brother and his decision to live in Israel. I told her about my working life – the croft and the children's books. I shared with her that I was divorced and that I had a daughter and a granddaughter. I also shared that I had experienced a period of estrangement from Sophie, but that it was over and we were now closer than we'd ever been. And then I told her about Finlay and about his death.

Magda listened mostly in silence. She nodded sympathetically at times or said *I see*. But when I told her about Finlay she gasped and got to her feet. She came over to sit beside me, rummaging in her handbag as she did so. She produced a tissue for my inevitable tears and handed it to me. "My dear," she said, taking my hands in hers. "I am so sorry, so sad for your loss."

I closed my eyes for a moment, willing the emotion to subside, trying to regain a professional demeanour. When I opened my eyes, Magda was looking at me. Her expression was kind. I sensed her compassion. "Thank you," I said, indicating the tissue before drying my tears.

"I can see now why peace matters to you," she said. "We both want some sort of settlement."

# Chapter Thirty Two

*Rachel*

Magda left a little while before I did and, having exchanged contact details, we promised to keep in touch with each other. I was grateful to Eitan for setting up our meeting. It had clarified so much for me and given me an insight into yet another point of view. And I was also grateful to Magda for her honesty and openness about what motivated her.

So before I left I thanked Eitan for introducing me to her as well as for all the great food and attentive hospitality. "It was lovely to see your beautiful home," I said, as we stood at my car. "Thanks again for inviting me."

"Thank *you* for coming," he said. He kissed me lightly on both cheeks. "I'm glad we were able to spend more time together, even if it was not quite in the way I had hoped." Then he kissed me on the lips and said, "You are a most fascinating woman, Rachel."

I drove off feeling bemused, confused and yes, flattered, by Eitan's evident and persistent attraction to me. And it had me wondering – wondering what if? What if I did go to bed with him? It wasn't such a big deal, was it – sex with a man I cared deeply for?

But I didn't have time to dwell on such thoughts. I needed to process and edit all the material I'd gleaned from the weekend as far as the book was concerned. I was two weeks in to my twelve-week visit and I had a lot of work to do.

I soon got into a daily routine. My visits and interviews were carried out mostly in the mornings and I enjoyed driving myself around the city and getting to know my way around. Afternoons usually included a siesta followed by working on sketches, going through photographs, and making notes. I'd persuaded Deb and Jonathan to let me cook dinner once a week and I enjoyed the challenge of getting what I needed from the markets and supermarkets. I also insisted on doing some of the household chores as a way of thanking them for having me to stay for such an extended period. I got floor sweeping and ironing, activities which let me think through my latest material as I performed them.

Weeks two and three were filled with Jerusalem visits.

I revisited the beautiful, golden-domed, Dome of the Rock mosque and in order to refresh my memory, I also took the guided tour again. Next, I toured the equally historical and beautiful Hurva synagogue in the Jewish Quarter of the Old City. It was once a ruin but had now been completely rebuilt. And I completed my visits to sites of worship by also revisiting the Church of the Holy Sepulchre, also in the Old City, and variously believed to be built on the site of Jesus' crucifixion and of his tomb.

On these visits I didn't take photos or do drawings and I didn't talk to worshippers, pilgrims or visitors. I simply went to observe and to contemplate. And after each visit I wrote down my reflections on what I'd seen. The publishers had arranged for Sylvia to go to each place of worship at a later date. And she'd liaise with the relevant authorities as to what she could photograph.

I wasn't religious myself, and I wasn't sure how I'd use my observations in the book. But I recognised that what these religious sites represented was important when it came to encouraging mutual respect and understanding between the humans who identified with them.

And it was in a similar contemplative mood that I went back to visit Yad Vashem, the Holocaust Remembrance Centre. I found it as hard a place to visit as I had the year before. But with the establishment of the state of Israel and the events of the Holocaust so inextricably linked, it was vital to do so. Again, pictures were out of the question and I simply wrote down my impressions afterwards.

But, after the sad solemnity of the Remembrance Centre, accompanying Deb one evening to sing with and talk to members of a choir she belonged to proved uplifting. The choir was made up of Jewish and Arab women and, I was delighted to discover, included Sylvia among its members. They'd been meeting every fortnight for a few years and they sang mainly in Arabic and Hebrew, but in other languages as well. They sang traditional songs, modern songs and had even had a couple written especially for them. And everything they sang was on the theme of peace.

I was made so welcome that I realised Deb and Sylvia had already done a fair bit of PR on my behalf. I did a short talk on the book and the women had lots of questions for me – as I did for them. They didn't mind Sylvia taking some photos of them and several were happy to provide me with quotes on what this multi-cultural, multi-faith choir meant to them. They sang a medley of haunting and beautiful songs for me and I didn't need to speak the language of the lyrics to get the sentiments behind them.

And then I was also required, and it was made clear it was non-negotiable, to sing a couple of traditional Scottish songs for them. I chose The Silver Tassie and The Flowers of the Forest which were both in keeping with the choir's spirit of a yearning for peace and reflected on the human cost of war. When I'd finished singing, there was applause followed by demands that I teach them the songs. I did my best to deliver. It was one of the most life-affirming and enjoyable evenings I'd ever experienced.

I spoke more with Deb about the choir the following week

when the two of us were travelling to see Hana. We were on a minibus, having decided to use the same tour company we'd used the previous year. It was the simplest and safest way for us to get to the West Bank and the Arab Women's Guesthouse.

We crossed through the checkpoint manned by young conscript soldiers with automatic rifles over their soldiers, and seeing them, reminded me of some of the conversations I'd had with the choir members.

"Several of them expressed concerns about their children going into the military, about doing national service and possibly having to fire weapons and be put in combat situations," I said.

"Yes, it's something we talk about a lot," Deb said. She sighed. "You'll understand only too well why it concerns us so much."

"Of course. But with Finlay – with what happened, I was at least able to tell myself that joining the Marines was something he'd chosen. It wasn't much comfort – but it helped a little."

Deb squeezed my hand. "I don't mind admitting I'm already dreading Gideon's call up. It's still two years away, I know, and I keep hoping the situation will change before he or Mari have to be involved."

"That song the choir sang, the one written during the First World War – *I didn't raise my boy to be a soldier* – that said it all."

"God, you were amazing when they sang it – I wasn't at all sure they should, but you were so ... so graceful about it."

"Maybe more people need to hear it," I said.

"Yes, but would they listen?"


It was good to be back in Beit Sahour and back at the guesthouse again and it was great to see Hana. As on our previous visit, she was waiting to greet Deb and me along with our fellow passengers, as we alighted from the tour bus. Hana was expecting me and not simply as a returning tourist. She and I had bonded during a middle of the night heart-to-heart conversation the year before. She'd proved to be an excellent listener when I opened up to her about all the difficulties I'd been experiencing in my personal life. And it was she who had first opened my eyes and my heart to the plight of the Palestinians.

So, when I was thinking about who and what to include in the book, Hana had been an obvious choice. This small, elderly Palestinian woman in her long, traditional dress and hijab was no stereotypical little old lady. She worked hard offering hospitality to women tourists from all over the world. And she shared her experience of life on the West Bank with her guests.

Hana had sacrificed her marriage and the chance to live in the UK where her ex-husband was an academic and activist for the Palestinian cause, in order to live and work for justice in her homeland. Her family had been forced off their farm, their home demolished and their land confiscated by the Israeli state. But she'd remained stoic and quietly dignified. And in that respect she reminded me of my mother.

After dinner on the day of our arrival, Hana invited Deb and me to have coffee with her in her private living-room. It was wonderful to talk with her again. She was interested to know more about my visit to Deb's school and asked Deb lots of questions about how the school worked. She also wanted news of both our families and she insisted on seeing all the photos I had of Miriam on my phone.

And the next morning when I conducted the formal book-related interview with Hana, she was supportive and enthusiastic about the project. "You are doing what I try to do," she said. "You are making a gentle protest through your work and through respectful conversation. And that way you hope to make the world a little bit better."

"Oh, Hana," I said. "What a wonderful thing to say and such a lovely way of saying it. Yes, that's exactly what I'm trying to do."

I went on to tell her about the tour Eitan and I had taken and she said she'd heard of such tours. She concurred with the impressions I'd formed of the daily and increasing injustices faced by the Palestinians.

I completed my official time with Hana by taking a few

photos and doing a sketch of her sitting in the guesthouse's pretty garden. And as I did so, birdsong and the scent from the stone containers overflowing with bellflowers and anemones filled the air. It all seemed so quiet and normal as we sat there, but I did wonder how much longer all this would remain untouched.

After lunch, Deb and I had another West Bank location to visit. This particular visit had been organised by the publishers and they'd arranged for a car and driver to collect us from, and return us to, the guesthouse. They'd also arranged for Sylvia to join us.

We were going to the rundown and battle-scarred town of Ramallah and we were going to see a skatepark. I hadn't been sure what to expect, but Deb and I were both left speechless and emotional as we watched around thirty Palestinian youngsters, obviously enjoying the thrills of skateboarding.

Our host and guide at the skatepark was a young volunteer in his twenties. He explained the park had been built with money raised by a UK based charity. A charity that had been started by a young British man named Jamie. Jamie had come to the area as a volunteer teacher of English a few years before and he'd brought his skateboard with him. He soon found that crowds of children and young people would gather to watch him on his board. They'd never seen anything like it and thought his twirling and jumping were down to some sort of trickery.

Jamie realised that although more than half the Palestinians living in the occupied territories were under twenty-one, there were very few constructive opportunities and activities available to them. This led to his idea to provide them with the chance to skateboard. And now the charity he set up had built parks all over the West Bank. At a basic level they were providing skateboarding lessons. But it was more than that. Skateboarding gave these young people the much-needed opportunity to participate in an inclusive, stress-relieving and confidence-building sport. It wasn't competitive, and it didn't discriminate according to age, gender or race.

At first we simply observed the youngsters' enthusiasm and enjoyment. Sylvia took lots of photos and did some filming while I sketched, and Deb took pictures and notes of her own saying she wanted to share what she'd seen with her students.

And later, as I spoke to some of the young people, I hardly needed our guide to interpret their responses about what skateboarding meant to them. It was obvious in their eyes and body language. It was changing their lives. Somehow it gave them hope.

# Chapter Thirty Three

*Rachel*

Over the weeks that followed, I continued to meet with and talk to various groups and individuals who were working for some sort of constructive and fair settlement for all the people of Israel-Palestine. Most of these encounters had been set up by the publishing company, but some were also arranged by Deb and Jonathan. Eitan also organised visits for me to some of the other places involved in the *My Jerusalem* project.

And Sylvia went just about everywhere with me, and the more time I spent working with her, the more I came to value and respect not only her abilities as a photographer, but also her quiet, unobtrusive professionalism.

She was with me when I went to the pretty port city of Haifa and there, sitting in the beautiful Baha'i Gardens, I met with two artists who lived and worked in the city. Both were women, both were Israelis, but until that day they hadn't met. One, Salma, was Arab and the other, Esther, was Jewish. They talked to me – but more importantly – they talked to each other – about their work, their lives, their hopes and their dreams. The two of them concentrated mainly on women as the subject of their art and this was obvious from the samples of their work that each had brought. They spoke of how they valued both diversity and harmony. It was a privilege to listen to them and to observe their dignity and mutual respect.

I also interviewed political activists, such as the group who voluntarily took it in turns to stand watch at West Bank checkpoints to see that the human rights of those Palestinians making the crossing were observed.

I spoke to groups of Israeli conscientious objectors about what their stand against national service had cost them including, in some cases, time in military jails.

I listened again, as I had on my first visit to Israel, to ex-soldiers from *Breaking the Silence*. This organization was made up of Israeli veterans who had served in the Israeli Defence Force and who aimed to raise awareness amongst the public about the reality of everyday life in the Occupied Territories. They spoke with humility about incidents against Palestinians that they were now ashamed to have been involved in.

I met with some Israeli mothers who had organised themselves into a protest group against not only the conscription of their children into the military, but also against the kind of intimidating behaviour they'd be expected to engage in against the Palestinians.

I talked to academics, artists, writers and musicians. I spoke to people on both sides and heard differing views about the politics and daily realities of life in Israel-Palestine.

Amongst the Palestinians there were some who were resigned or in despair, there were some like Hana who accepted all the difficulties but maintained an amazing resilience and optimism, and there were some who were frustrated and angry.

Amongst the Israelis there seemed to be a majority who either supported and approved of how things were and saw no problems with Israel's colonisation of Palestinian territory, or who maintained a state of happy ignorance of the realities of the situation and were happy with the status quo. But there were some Israelis who wanted a more peaceful, fairer, all inclusive single nation where everyone's rights were respected and equal. And they were prepared to work towards it, to state their case openly even if it damaged their reputation, their career, or even threatened their safety.

And it was the children, teenagers and young adults to whom I spoke that gave me the most hope for a more peaceful, better future for the country. Armed and primed with knowledge gained from global social media, they were generally well-informed, more democratically minded, and quite simply more humane than the older generations.

And in between all the spells of hard work, I had more informal conversations with my brother and his family, and yes, with Eitan about their lives in, and hopes for, their country.

I was touched by how engaged my brother was with what I was attempting to do. "We set this whole sorry mess up," he said when we were talking one evening. It was after dinner and we were sitting out on the balcony at the flat. We were discussing the origins of the state of Israel and the seventy years of conflict that had ensued.

"How do you mean?" I asked.

"We – the British – during the thirty year Mandate up to 1948 – it was our policies that set up the conflict between the communities here and resulted in two million refugees being trapped in Gaza for the last seventy years."

"I wanted to visit Gaza – but the publishers wouldn't hear of it," I said.

"Quite right too," Jonathan said. "East Jerusalem and the West Bank are risky enough, but Gaza is a whole other level."

"Yes, but I can't help feeling it will be a significant part that's missing, when it comes to raising awareness of the Palestinian plight."

"At least you're doing something. I don't see the British government trying to help resolve the situation in this infuriating country."

"So why do you stay if you find it so infuriating?"

"I don't know. I suppose it's like staying in a sometimes difficult marriage. I love Israel – even though I sometimes wonder why I stay. And I love that we have a homeland ... but sometimes it just makes me so angry ... and so sad that it seems to be so broken ..."

"Oh Jonny," I reached out and put my hand on his.

He managed to smile. "But I love what you're doing, Rache. I love that you're doing something so positive."

"I don't know how effective it'll be, but if governments won't act for peace and justice, then it's down to us as individuals to take a personal initiative – no matter how small – to try to improve things."

"I'm proud of you," Jonathan said. "I wish I had half your courage."

"Don't be daft," I said. "It's me who's proud of you. Look at the work *you* do – working where you do treating anyone who needs it." On my first trip to Israel I'd visited the Hadassah hospital where Jonathan worked. I'd been impressed by the facilities – but even more so by the hospital's philosophy of accepting all patients regardless of race or religion.

"Yeah, well, it sometimes doesn't feel like much – not against the backdrop of all the continuing injustice."

"But that's just it," I said. "What you do *does* make a difference. It makes a positive difference to the children you treat and to their families and it's a great example of fair and indiscriminate action. You and me – and others like us – we can't change the world on our own – but we can try to improve a small part of it."

Jonathan grinned at me and shook his head.

"What?" I asked.

"You're becoming quite the motivational speaker."

Throughout the weeks, I kept in touch with home too. I made regular phone calls to Morag and apart from dodging her questions about Eitan, it was good to talk to her and catch up on island gossip. Lana and I spoke regularly too, partly so I could keep her up to date with the work side of things but also to chat as friends. And I spoke to Sophie regularly, including some Skype calls so I could see Miriam.

But there was nothing from Jack. I tried not to think about him but it was difficult not to. My brain would call up unbidden images of him at random moments. I'd remember his laugh, or the sound of his voice and his Edinburgh accent. My breath would catch when I recalled some of our most tender moments like when I watched him cradling my little granddaughter. At other times I'd remember his touch.

Neither Sophie nor Morag mentioned him much. I think Sophie sensed quite quickly I didn't want to talk about him. However, Morag did say at one point that he was away in Edinburgh. She didn't go into any details and seemed to assume I knew this fact. I said something non-committal that I hoped implied I did indeed know.

But, in truth, I knew nothing of Jack's precise whereabouts, knew nothing of what he was currently doing, and worst of all I knew nothing of what he was feeling towards me. All I did know was I loved him, I missed him and I'd work hard at putting things right between us when I got home.

# Chapter Thirty Four

*Jack*

Not only did I mess up saying goodbye to Rachel before she left, but in a mood of self-pity, embarrassment and shame, I ignored her messages and calls. Then about ten days after she left, I unwittingly picked up when she called my house phone. Instead of being interested and supportive like any normal and loving partner, I let my petty selfishness win. And I felt jealousy rather than gratitude when I heard that Eitan had taken care of her when she was ill. So, in a particularly stupid act, I told her I thought it was best if we didn't keep in contact while she was away. What I didn't tell her was that I missed her so much it hurt, that I was increasingly tormented by ghosts from my past, and that I'd decided to go and live and work in Edinburgh.

I'd contacted my ex-wife earlier on the same day as Rachel's call, and I told her I wanted to accept her job offer. Not only did I need to get away from constant reminders of Rachel, but I knew that without some sort of major distraction, my dark thoughts and anxieties would only increase.

But besides those negative reasons, I also decided to take the job because, as I'd said to Alasdair, there were aspects of my working life that I missed. And, having made the decision I was keen to get started.

So when Ailsa asked me when I'd be available, I said that I could be down for the beginning of the next week.

"Excellent," Ailsa said. "Especially now that there's been a development."

"Oh, what's that?" I asked.

"Harry Gray – he's got cancer and it's terminal."

"Can't say I'm sorry to hear that," I said.

"No, can't say I blame you. And there's more."

"Oh, what?"

"He's made an appeal on medical grounds for compassionate release to a hospice."

It took me a few seconds to process what Ailsa had said.

"Jack?" she said. "You still there?"

"Yes, still here, sorry, don't quite know how to respond to that. He's got a nerve is probably the politest reaction I can come up with. He won't get it, will he?"

"He might. The Justice Secretary is considering it. It's all strictly confidential at the moment, but your old friend Bridget Barstow is preparing a press release as we speak. However, whichever way it goes, Harry's dying and with him gone—"

"Son Tommy will step up."

"Indeed. And all the signs are he'll be even more ruthless and deadly than Gray senior. So now—"

"So now's the time to stop him."

"Exactly. And if anyone knows the Grays and how they operate – it's you."

By the time the call ended I was more convinced than ever I was doing the right thing. Helping to nail Tommy Gray would go some way to atoning for Mike's death and might help me deal with the guilt.

But my demons weren't finished with me just yet.

The next day dawned still and dull. The loch's surface was flat and grey and the oppressive atmosphere seemed to have invaded the house. I had planned to tidy the place and get it ready for my absence but instead found myself brooding about Rachel. So I abandoned my half-hearted attempt at housekeeping and spent the rest of the morning working in the garden. But she was still in my head and when the urge to communicate with her became unbearable I sent her a text – telling her I loved her whatever happened. It was spontaneous and it was heartfelt but I regretted it the minute I sent it. What would she think when she read it? Probably that I was a manipulative, inconsistent fool.

At lunchtime I phoned Bridget to let her know that I'd be joining her at the flat and explained a bit about the work I'd be doing. She sounded both surprised and pleased. I sensed she wanted to talk more, but having ascertained that sharing the flat wouldn't be a problem, I kept it short and to the point.

After lunch I decided to see Alasdair. I wanted to let him know my plans and to ask him to keep an eye on Dunhalla while I was away. But he wasn't in. Morag told me he'd gone to help Steven with something sheep related and then he'd be heading into Portree. She said I might still catch him if I was quick and they'd most likely be in the barn.

When I got to Burnside, there was no sign of Alasdair's car, but I decided to check the barn just in case. There was nobody there. Then, as I turned to come out of the barn, there was a loud bang. And that was it. Fear and anxiety overwhelmed me and I fell to my knees, struggling to breathe.

I felt a hand on my shoulder. A voice said, "Jack, Jack, are you all right?"

I looked up, still fighting to breathe, a cold sweat trickling down my back. Steven was kneeling beside me. "Breathe, Jack," he said. "Breathe slowly – in for five through your nose – and out for five through your mouth. Focus only on that." He began counting and I listened to his voice as I tried to get my breath under control.

Gradually the nauseating dizziness and disorientation subsided and I found myself sitting alongside Steven on a hay bale. "Thanks," I said, staring at the ground. "Sorry you had to see that."

"It's me who should say sorry. I'm taking down the old lean-to and I dropped one of the corrugated iron sheets from the roof."

"Why are you sorry about that?" I said, turning to look him.

"The bang it made – it most likely triggered your panic attack."

"Panic attack? No, no I got a bit breathless – that's all. It was—"

"Jack, I know a panic attack when I see one," Steven said. "I should do. I suffered enough of them myself."

"Ah," I said.

"How long?"

"A few months."

"Getting any help?"

"No."

"You should."

"Uh huh."

"So what's causing it? Traumatic incident to do with work by any chance?"

"A shooting – a colleague was shot dead during an operation we were on together – and it was – it was my fault." I paused, took a moment to get a grip before going on to tell Steven the whole story. "But it doesn't make any sense," I said when I'd finished. "I mean, why now? It happened almost two years ago."

"It makes perfect sense. It's how post-traumatic stress works. You think you've got away with it – that you've come through whatever it was unscathed – but eventually it comes out."

"PTSD? You think that's what this is? But I'm—"

"I'm not a therapist. But that's how it was with me. After the ... the incident where I lost my legs, it was awful. But all the operations, the physical rehabilitation process, and getting my head round what I'd lost ... it was ... it was something to concentrate on. But when that phase ended, it was like my mind didn't have all that to concentrate on anymore so it went off on its own."

"So, what happened?"

"Over the top anxiety, depression, and then there was the guilt – that was the worst part – the sense of survivors' guilt – it was overwhelming."

"But you ... you're all right now?"

"I am now, yes. Still find sudden loud noises challenging, but I got help – counselling – and Sophie – she's been great."

"She knows?"

"Of course she does. I told her I was a mess when we met." Steven paused. He frowned slightly as he looked at me. "Have you told Rachel what's been happening to you?"

"No, the only person I've talked to about it is Alasdair."

Steven nodded but he couldn't hide his surprise. "Right," he said. "Maybe you should tell her. I'm sure she'd—"

"Rachel has enough to deal with without worrying about me," I said, probably more forcefully than was justified. "And I'd appreciate it if you kept this ... this episode to yourself."

Steven put up his hands. "Sorry, none of my business – and neither is what I'm about to say now. But you really should get professional help, Jack. This sort of thing – it doesn't go away on its own. "

"Yeah, that's what Alasdair said." I stood up."Actually it was him I was looking for," I said, hoping to change the subject.

"Ah, right," Steven said, also getting to his feet. "He was here but he left a wee while ago. He was heading into Portree."

"I'll catch him later. I wanted to let him know I'm going down to Edinburgh next week."

"Off to see the family?" Steven said, as we left the barn and started walking up the path.

"Not exactly." I told Steven about the job, told him I'd likely be away for most of the summer.

"I see," he said when I'd finished. We were by now at the door of Burnside cottage. "Do you want to come in, have a coffee?"

"No, no I'm fine," I said. "I won't take up any more of your time and I need to get on." But the truth was I couldn't bear to go into Burnside knowing Rachel wasn't there.

"I hope the work goes well, Jack, honestly I do. But don't be fooled about the PTSD."

"What do you mean?"

"Like I said, it's fine when your mind's occupied with other things. But it waits, it bides its time. It's like – since the shooting – you had to focus on recovering from your heart attack, then you had the move up here and the house to work on and so on. But now things have gone quiet, it's making itself known."

"That's one of the reasons I've taken this job."

"I do hope it helps, Jack. But I still think you should consider consulting a counsellor."

"I'll think about it," I said. But I wasn't sure I meant it.

# Chapter Thirty Five

*Jack*

Alasdair called round later that evening. "Morag tells me you were looking for me earlier," he said, as he came in. He put the bag he was carrying on the kitchen table. "So I've come bearing beer."

"In that case you better come through," I said, smiling at him.

"You've been keeping a low profile since Rachel left," Alasdair said once we were seated in the living room, beers in hand. "How have you been?"

"Okay," I said.

Alasdair nodded and sipped his beer.

"I've decided to take up the job offer in Edinburgh and I'm hoping you'll keep an eye on this place while I'm away."

Alasdair raised an eyebrow but didn't say anything. I could see I was expected to continue.

"It seems like the right decision," I said. "Timing's good too. The reason's confidential at the moment – but it seems there's about to be a bit of a push on to finally get Tommy Gray – the son of the bastard that shot my colleague."

"I see." Alasdair nodded, but he looked sceptical.

"What?" I said

"Like I said before, I wonder if it's a good idea – you know – in view of how you've been suffering of late. To go back and be so close to it—"

"But that's exactly why I think it's a good idea. Not only will the work in general give me something constructive to concentrate on, it's also a chance to bring the whole Gray thing to a satisfactory end."

"Hmm, if you say so."

"I do."

"But haven't you got someone living in your flat at the moment?"

"Not a problem," I said. "The tenant's an old friend, quite happy to share, especially as it will reduce their rent." I felt uncomfortable giving Alasdair this edited version of the identity of my prospective flatmate, but I couldn't face having to defend the arrangement if I told him the whole truth. I was relieved when he didn't seem to notice any evasiveness on my part.

"But you'll come back, won't you?" he said. "You've got the photography job lined up and Rachel will be home."

"This stint is for twelve weeks, so, yeah, I'll be back in the short-term at least, and I must admit I'm keen to do the photography work. But long-term – I'm not so sure anymore."

Alasdair's expression had changed from sceptical to concerned. "But what about Rachel? I thought you'd sorted things out. She'll not want to leave Skye. She's—"

"No, no – please," I said, raising my hands to stop him saying any more. "Please, can we steer clear of Rachel?" This was way too painful. I couldn't face telling him how I'd messed up. "Things between Rachel and me, they're ... they're complicated. She's away getting on with her life and I need to do the same."

"When you put it like that," Alasdair said, "maybe going to Edinburgh *is* a good thing. The time away might well let you complete unfinished business and it may also help clarify what you want for the future."

"I was hoping you'd see it like that," I said.

"Really? Does it matter what I think?"

"Yeah, crazy, I know. You may just be an old, tweed-jacketed, retired Geography teacher, but for some reason I value your opinion."

Alasdair smiled. "Okay then. If that's the case, here's more opinion. Yes, going to Edinburgh and doing what you have to do could be a positive move. But I think you'd be mad to move away from Skye permanently, and downright stupid to give up on Rachel."

"I suppose I asked for that," I said, smiling back as Alasdair grinned at me. And for the first time in what seemed like ages I actually felt myself relax.

I remained relaxed for the rest of the evening as we continued drinking our beers and chatting. It felt good to have a friend like Alasdair, it felt good to have made my decision, and it felt good to have a sense of purpose once more.

I even slept relatively well and was up early the next morning to finish my packing and other preparations before setting off for Edinburgh.

It was as I was putting my bags in the car that Morag appeared.

"Good Morning, Jack," she said. "I hear you're leaving us for a while." There was a slight edge to her voice and she seemed nervous.

"That's right," I said, as I closed the boot. "Have you come to see me off?"

"Not exactly," she said. "It's just ... that is ... I wanted to say ... I—"

"Do you want to come inside, tell me what it is over a cup of tea?"

"No, no, it's fine ... I'm fine. Alasdair told me about this police job you've got in Edinburgh and I wish you all the best with it. I know there are things you told him in confidence and I don't know the whole story. But he did tell me that he sensed things between you and Rachel aren't good and you might leave Skye for good. And that's why I decided I had to speak to you."

"Okay," I said, bracing myself.

"You broke down her defences. You drew her out from a very dark place – from a place the rest of us couldn't reach. She opened up to you, showed you her grief, gave you her heart. So don't you dare abandon her."

"I won't ... I wouldn't," I said. But I couldn't look at her. "I love her, Morag ... more than you know ... but—"

"But you can't handle that she has other things going on in her life that don't necessarily involve you."

"No! It's not like that. I get that she's independent, that she's her own person. I don't have a problem with that." I made myself look her in the eye. I could see she didn't believe me. I didn't blame her. After all I *was* lying to her *and* to myself.

"Really?"

"She's the one who went away. I asked her to marry me, but she said no and she went away."

"You proposed?" Morag couldn't hide her surprise.

"Yes, I did. So you see it's not me who doesn't want to commit."

"Oh, for heaven's sake! Rachel couldn't be more committed to you. But she didn't exactly have a good experience of marriage first time around."

I knew Morag was right. I wanted to assure her that things weren't over between Rachel and me, and that I hadn't given up, and that once Rachel was home I'd sort things out. But I couldn't even assure myself about any of it. I didn't know what to say. All I did know was I wanted to end this scrutiny of my shortcomings as a partner. I glanced at my watch, reached for the car door.

"I'm sorry, Jack. I know you want to get on the road and I do wish you all the best with this job. But please, if you *are* going to end things with Rachel, come back and do it face-to-face. She deserves that at least." Then she surprised me by opening her arms and hugging me. And I found myself hugging her back. "I'm sorry," she said, as she let me go. She looked as if she might be about to cry. "I know I'm an interfering old bag, but you're the best thing that's happened to Rachel in a long time. And I had to speak up. She's my best friend and I care about her."

"So do I, Morag. I care about her very much," I said, as I got into the car. I found myself smiling at her. "And, yes, you may be an interfering old bag – but Rachel's lucky to have you on her side. And I promise I will come back."

# Chapter Thirty Six

*Jack*

On my first evening in Edinburgh, Bridget cooked us dinner. Before we sat down at the table in the flat's large kitchen she poured us both a glass of wine.

"Cheers," she said, as she handed me my glass, and came to join me as I stood looking out of the window at the street below.

"Thanks," I said, as I clinked my glass against hers. She was looking great as always. She'd changed out of the immaculately tailored suit she'd worn to work, and was now wearing a low-cut, tight-fitting, black dress that showed off her slender body and long slim legs. Her long blonde hair was pinned up with just a few loose tendrils left skimming her neck. In her high heels she was as tall as me, and she was standing close enough for me to pick up the exotic scent of her, no doubt, expensive perfume

She took a sip of wine and then ran her tongue along her freshly lipsticked lips. "This is like old times," she said.

"Not quite," I replied as we took our seats at the table. "You're here because you needed somewhere to stay. That's all. And—"

"Oh, Jack, lighten up. All I meant was—"

"I know what you meant. And it's not going to happen. I'm here to work. I will *not* be going to bed with you."

Ours had been a no commitment relationship. I'd known from the start Bridget was married. But she'd told me the marriage was an open one. She'd also made it clear to me that she and her husband intended to stay married, which suited me fine. But now it seemed the marriage was over and I was wary of her intentions.

Bridget gave a little nod of her head as she smiled. "Whatever you say," she said.

"I mean it," I said. But even as I spoke I found myself remembering the good times we'd enjoyed during our years together.

"I miss you," she said. "That's all. It's good to have you back, to be able to spend some time with you. You used to enjoy my company, didn't you? It wasn't just sex, was it?"

"No, no it wasn't just the sex. But whatever it was, it's over."

"So it's all good on your island, all good with farmer Rachel?"

"Yes, yes it is." I tried to keep my expression neutral. I didn't want Bridget to guess how things actually were. But that didn't stop her questions.

"And she doesn't mind you being away? Doesn't mind you being here with me?"

"No ... no she doesn't."

"Right ... and she didn't want to accompany you?"

"She's away working too. She's away until August as it happens, back in Israel."

"That's where she'd got back from when I came to visit you last year, wasn't it?"

"Yes," I said. I cringed as I recalled Bridget's surprise visit to Skye, recalled how she'd come to beg me to come back to Edinburgh, back to our affair, and how I'd sent her packing. I also remembered that she'd told Rachel she was welcome to me and that I had a history of infidelity and couldn't be trusted. But I didn't want to talk about any of that. "Any joy finding your own place?"

Bridget shook her head and laughed. "Clunky change of subject, even for you, Jack," she said. "But, no I haven't. I've been so busy with work – and then there are all the divorce negotiations." She stood up and cleared our plates away. Back at the table she picked up the bottle of red wine and refilled our glasses. "There's no rush is there?" she said. "Unless, that is, all is not perfect at your Highland hideaway and you're thinking of moving back permanently?" Bridget rested her chin on her hands and her gaze was intense.

"Not at all," I lied, and then, clunky or not, I changed the subject again. "So, Ailsa told me about Harry Gray's situation and about the appeal. Which way's your boss going to jump do you think?"

"Christ, Jack. Lighten up, will you. I can't tell you anything anyway. The decision's been made and will be announced soon. But for now can we relax?" She reached across the table and put her hand on mine, her foot brushed against my shin.

I sat back, pulled my hand away from under hers. But she just smiled and stood up. Picking up the wine bottle and her glass, she said, "Come on. Bring your drink and grab us another bottle from the rack and we'll go through. We'll be comfier on the sofa."

"That's all right," I said. "You go on. I'll load the dishwasher and make us some coffee."

She frowned at me.

I suspected that the suggestion of being 'comfier on the sofa' was a loaded one and I knew she understood my avoidance tactic. But she'd so obviously disregarded my assertion that I would not be having sex with her I hoped my actions would be more effective than my words. So I said, "I insist. You cooked – so the least I can do is clear up."

When I did eventually join her in the living-room, she'd drawn the curtains and put on the lamps. There was also a CD playing – one of these compilations of popular operatic arias. Yes, the scene was set. Bridget was on a mission.

I sat in one of the armchairs. We drank our coffee. The conversation was pleasant enough and an hour or so later we went to bed – alone – Bridget to the space and comfort of the double bedroom and me to the single bed in the small, back bedroom.

I hoped Bridget had got the message.

# Chapter Thirty Seven

*Jack*

It was weird walking into the Fettes building on my second full day back in the city. The multi-storey block had once been the HQ for the former Lothian and Borders police force, before Police Scotland came into being and policing went national rather than regional. Over the years, I'd attended many meetings, several interviews, and been on the wrong end of more than a few bollockings within its glass and concrete walls. Nowadays it was home to a local police station and lots of admin and office space.

Ailsa met me at reception, a folder and a tablet computer in hand. "Jack," she said, smiling as she approached. "Good to see you."

"And you. You're looking well," I said, returning her smile. And I meant it. She was looking great. Ailsa had always been striking in appearance. She was tall, almost as tall as me, and she'd retained her slim but athletic build. Her short dark hair was now, like mine, streaked with grey, but she suited it and she looked younger than her fifty-seven years.

"Thank you," she said. "Don't get as much time as I'd like on the golf course, but I still go running most days. It's a great antidote to the stresses of the job."

As we headed up stairs and along corridors on our way to the meeting room, we spoke a bit about Maddie and about our grandchildren. And, as we walked and talked, I was reminded how grateful I was that Ailsa didn't seem to hold any animosity towards me. God knows she'd have been justified if she had. I'd been a terrible husband, unfaithful more than once when we were married. She'd given me more than just a second chance, but in the end she'd had enough. It was seventeen years since our divorce, and she'd flourished ever since.

When we got to the meeting room, Ailsa took the seat at the head of the large table in the middle of the room. She indicated that I should sit in one of the seats closest to her. "The others will join us soon for the meeting proper, but I have some preliminaries I wanted to discuss with you first."

There was the usual new job paperwork to check over, complete and sign. When Ailsa said she assumed I'd be living at my flat while in the city, I confirmed that was the case. And when I also told her I was sharing the flat with Bridget and why, her reaction gave little away.

Once we'd got the forms out of the way, Ailsa said, "Thank you for accepting the job and welcome back."

"Thank you for the offer. It's come at the right time for me."

"Good. So – to recap the brief – this is a twelve-week contract and there are two separate areas we'd like your input on. There's working with Detective Chief Inspector Ian Wilkie at Historic Crimes, filling in blanks, giving your insights into any still open cases you were involved in. It will be a great help to them in setting their priorities for the next year or so. But, perhaps even more pressing, there's the contribution you can make to the work being done to bring down the Gray gang and for that you'll be working with Chief Superintendent Maureen Thomson from Organised Crime."

"I'm looking forward to getting started," I said. "And I hear the decision's been made about Gray's appeal for release."

"How did you—ah, Bridget told you." Ailsa raised her eyebrows.

"Only that the decision's been made. She didn't tell what's been decided."

"You'll know very soon," Ailsa said, as there was a knock at the door and we were joined by the two senior officers for whom I'd be working.

And so my briefing began. I would split my time between the two divisions and I'd also be part of their joint work on the Gray gang. DCS Thomson explained that there was an intensive operation about to get underway to finally put a stop to the gang's activities. She outlined the crimes they were currently suspected of. "Buying and selling illegal firearms, prostitution, drugs and money laundering for starters," she said. "Then there's the suspected shooting of the member of a rival gang, the abduction and torture of another member of that gang—"

"And Tommy Gray's definitely the gang leader nowadays?" I said.

"Definitely." DCS Thomson nodded. "He took over when Harry was convicted, began expanding the gang and its activities, set about getting rid of any rivals for the position of the capital's most powerful and feared gangster."

"So, why now?" I asked. "The Gray gang has been in business for some time, but apart from when ... when Harry Gray ... when he shot Mike McRae ... we've never been able to get them on anything major. They've never slipped up."

It was Ailsa who explained the thinking behind Operation Endgame. "It's the main reason I'm here today. I have overall responsibility for this initiative and I wanted to be here when it was explained to you. As you yourself guessed, Jack," she said, "now that Harry's death is imminent, we suspect that with him gone, Tommy will get even more ambitious. Harry was relatively old-school as far as the type of crime he and the gang engaged in, and Tommy seems to have gone along with that up to a point. But all the intelligence we've got on Tommy suggests he's been biding his time and that with his father gone the gang will diversify and expand even more."

"And how long has Endgame been running so far?" I said.

"Just started," DCS Thomson said. "We've got them under

intensive surveillance, but we don't want to rush it. We'll need solid evidence before we do anything, and Tommy's very good at covering his tracks. However, we can't go on indefinitely. There are the usual manpower and budget constraints to consider. So anything extra you can tell us – stuff that's not necessarily in the records – impressions, ideas or insights you have about contacts, former associates, previous activities, could be very helpful and might speed things up."

"Bring it on," I said.

"So now would seem like a good time to let you all know the result of Gray's appeal," Ailsa said. We all turned to look at her. "The Justice Secretary has agreed to it. Harry Gray is being transferred to a hospice as we speak. The press and other news media have been informed. The Chief Constable and the Justice Secretary will be doing a joint press conference later."

It was Ian Wilkie who broke the silence that momentarily greeted Ailsa's announcement. "Great, so a murdering bastard who showed no mercy and shot one of our own gets to die a peaceful, merciful death. Christ knows what you must be thinking, Jack. This is very close to home for you."

Unable to speak, I raised my hands and shook my head. My main emotion was anger and my thought processes seemed to have crashed.

"What kind of bloody message does that send out?" said DCS Thomson.

"Look, I know it's not the decision anyone in this room would have wanted," Ailsa said. "But the official line is Police Scotland approves this decision. It's being presented as ethically and morally correct to show mercy – and it's a way of saying we don't stoop to the criminal level of an eye for an eye."

"So if anyone asks?" said Wilkie.

"You make the customary response in such circumstances, i.e. no comment." Ailsa replied. "And I suggest you all channel your strong feelings into bringing the whole Gray gang to justice." She stood up. "And now," she said, "I'll leave the three of you to plan how you'll work together on that."

# Chapter Thirty Eight

*Jack*

I quickly settled into a pattern of working three days a week with Historic Crimes and two days with Organised Crime. And even though I wasn't on active duty and the work mainly entailed sifting through large amounts of paperwork and making notes as I went along, I enjoyed being back in the work environment. Both teams made me feel welcome. There was all the usual banter and camaraderie and they seemed to find my opinions and suggestions helpful.

From time to time I met and worked with both teams simultaneously. The Organised Crime team would update us all on Operation Endgame and me and the Historic Crime officers would chip in with anything we considered helpful.

I didn't find it as difficult to revisit all the Gray-related stuff as I'd feared it might be. It's true that when the news of his move to the hospice first broke, I found it difficult. But I coped by focussing on building a case against Tommy and the others. And perhaps it was because I felt there was a real possibility of bringing the whole gang down that I was able to control all the Mike-related anxiety and guilt.

I spent most of my weekends with Maddie and the family. Sometimes I'd take Poppy out for the day, sometimes I was even brave enough to take William as well. My evenings were spent mainly at the flat – although I occasionally went to the cinema or out for a drink with colleagues. Bridget and I got along okay. She sometimes teased me about taking our relationship beyond the boundaries I'd set, but for the most part she seemed fine with how things were between us. And I have to admit I did still enjoy her company.

And Rachel? I'd be lying if I said I didn't think about her or miss her, but I tried not to go there. Sometimes I'd catch myself, phone in hand, my finger hovering over her number, but I never went through with it and actually called her. I couldn't. It was too painful.

So, yes, the job definitely came along at the right time. I was away from Skye and all its associations with Rachel, and my troubled mind was constructively occupied.

It wasn't until my tenth week in Edinburgh that Harry Gray died. I was at work and Ailsa came to tell me in person. Because he'd ended up lingering on for two months rather than the predicted two weeks there'd been an ongoing thread of controversy about his release. And, as a result, there was to be another press conference. Ailsa told me the Chief Constable would once again be taking questions – and then she hit me with it. "They've asked if you could be part of the panel and make a statement about how you view it all," she said.

"Me? Why?"

"You know the media. They want the human interest side of things, want to speak to someone directly impacted by the … by Mike's murder and by Gray's release. And they reckon you're just the person."

"And the Chief's okay with that, is he?"

"Yes, he reckons it would be good to remind the public what Gray did and for them to hear it first-hand as it were. It's a way of getting our condemnation of the man and his actions across, but without seeming to gloat or appearing unprofessional."

"God, how do you do it?" I said.

"Do what?"

"All the PR, the politicking and pandering to press and public. Don't you find it sickening?"

"Sometimes, yes. But in this case I actually think it's the right thing to do. Hearing your take on things – I think it would be a good way of respecting Mike's memory – of taking the limelight away from Gray."

"Hmm, I suppose so," I said.

"So you'll do it?" Ailsa looked surprised.

She wasn't the only one. I surprised myself by agreeing to do it. But it felt right and it felt like it was another way of kicking my demons into touch.

I was briefed beforehand by a police PR person. I was assured that I'd be introduced as DI Baxter, with no reference made to the fact I'd retired or that I'd since returned to work. I was given the official Police Scotland take on Gray's passing, but I was also told I should be honest and say what I thought.

And so that's what I did.

At the start as I sat, flanked by the Chief and the Deputy Chief Constable, and facing a room full of journalists and cameras I felt nervous – nervous enough to consider walking away. But, as I was about to begin speaking, I spotted Ailsa slipping in at the back of the room. She looked right at me and gave me the thumbs-up. It was enough for me to be able to get a grip and go through with it.

I began by saying I supported the decision to allow Gray to die in the hospice as it showed our society's capacity for mercy. But I didn't hide the fact his release had made me angry at first. I paid tribute to Mike and I said that justice had been served by Gray's incarceration. And I finished by saying that my thoughts were with the victims of his many crimes and that I hoped that their loved ones would draw some comfort from the fact he wouldn't hurt anyone ever again.

Ailsa came up to me as I was preparing to leave the HQ conference room. "Well done," she said. "I'd say your statement was perfectly judged."

"That's good," I said. My voice had gone a bit weak. I was aware I was shaking, could feel a cold sweat trickling down my back. Please no, I thought – not now. I fought to keep it down, but a full-blown anxiety attack was definitely threatening.

Ailsa put her hand on my arm. "You all right?" she said, frowning.

"I will be," I said, wiping at the sweat on my forehead.

"Come on," she said. "Come with me."

Once we were seated in her office, Ailsa with a coffee and me with a glass of iced water, Ailsa said, "You're sure you're okay. It's not your heart, is it?"

"No, no," I said. "Nothing like that, just the after effects of stage fright. I'll be fine, honestly."

"As long as you're sure. It looked as if—"

She was interrupted by her PA who'd come to remind her she was due at a meeting. I immediately stood up to leave.

"Before you go," Ailsa said, "I keep meaning to ask. Would you like to come for dinner one evening?"

It was a surprise but not an unpleasant one and without thinking about it I said yes.

"Great," Ailsa said. Tonight, my place, seven-thirty, see you then."

# Chapter Thirty Nine

*Jack*

"That was a lovely meal, thank you," I said, when I'd finished my second slice of raspberry cheesecake.

"You're welcome," Ailsa said, as she topped up my wine. "But I'm afraid the fish pie was Marks and Spencer, and the cheesecake was Waitrose, so I can't take the credit." She stood up. "But I intend to make the coffee myself."

I smiled at her, appreciative once more of how amiable my ex-wife was. I'd meant it when I said it had been a lovely meal – okay so it wasn't home-cooked – that wasn't the point. It had been lovely because of the relaxed atmosphere, because of the chat about our grandchildren and our reminiscences of when Maddie was little.

While Ailsa made coffee, I remained sitting at the table. It was positioned in the bay window of the Georgian flat's kitchen. It was a beautiful July evening and I was able to look out over the sweep of the New Town street below.

"I meant it," Ailsa said once we were settled in her beautiful and expansive living-room. It contained two of the largest sofas I'd ever seen and we took one each. "You did a great job at the press conference. It was dignified and professional."

"Doesn't bring Mike back though does it?" I said, speaking more sharply than I meant to.

"No, it doesn't but—"

"Why? Why did he do it? Gray – the bastard – why did he shoot? Mike was unarmed. Gray must have known it was pointless. He must have known there was no escape. He'd worked out Mike was police, so he must also have known we had enough evidence to charge him. Shooting Mike was only going to make things worse for him."

"Who knows what he was thinking? Angry at getting caught, a need for revenge, feeling he had nothing more to lose? It's pointless to speculate."

"Yeah, you're right. It's just—"

"You did take the counselling didn't you – after what happened – after Mike?"

"Yes, I did," I said, skipping over the fact I'd only attended one session and then given up. "I'm fine … really I am."

Ailsa didn't look convinced. "You've nothing to feel guilty about. Mike's death wasn't your fault. And if it's any comfort, Jane doesn't hold you responsible."

"Jane? You mean Jane McRae – Mike's widow?"

Ailsa nodded. "She's been amazing. Had her dark times of course, but she told me recently she was coming to terms with what happened to Mike and she blames nobody but Gray."

"Right," I said. "So you're in touch with her, are you?"

"Yeah, she's a DCI now in the Aberdeen and North East section of Serious Crimes division, so we've got to know each other that way. And she's a golfer too. We've played together in police matches, socialised afterwards."

"Sounds like she's got her life back on track."

"She certainly has. Her boys are both at university and she's getting on with her life. She's even set up a memorial foundation in Mike's name. It helps disadvantaged young people get access to advice and support about education courses and other opportunities. The aim is to divert them from crime, show them other options."

"Impressive – setting all that up must have taken a hell of a lot of work."

"It did – lots of fundraisers and lots of help from friends and family, and her police colleagues too."

"Good for her," I said.

"And you Jack? What about you? Is your life back on track?"

"Good question."

"You're happy on Skye, aren't you?" Ailsa seemed genuinely concerned. "And unless there's something you're not telling me, you seem fit and healthy again."

"Yeah, yeah I'm fine health-wise, no worries on that score," I said. But I could hear my own lack of conviction as I added, "And Skye's a great place to live. I'm looking forward to getting back."

"And you're happy … with Rachel?"

I hesitated before answering that one. I couldn't face telling it how it actually was, couldn't say it was most likely over – especially to my ex-wife. So I went with, "She's away at the moment, working in the Middle East."

"That wasn't what I asked," Ailsa said, her expression sympathetic. "But, it's fine, and you're right it's none of my business."

"No, no I didn't mean you were—"

"Prying? I suppose I was. But it was out of genuine interest, not to score points. For what it's worth though, from what Maddie's told me, you'd be a fool to mess this relationship up."

"You're not the first person to say that," I said. "And thanks."

"For what?"

"For giving a toss about me. I don't deserve it. Not from you. I wasn't sure how it would be … working with you … but it's been good. And so has this – I've enjoyed it."

"The past is the past, Jack. It's been seventeen years since our disaster of a marriage ended. But we loved each other once, and we still have Maddie and our grandchildren. They'll always be a link between us. And I'll always care how you are."

"Again, thanks. I certainly don't deserve your concern."

"No, you probably don't. The way you behaved, the affairs – it was horrible at the time. But it happened. I let go of it all a long time ago."

"I couldn't have been so forgiving."

"It's not about forgiveness, Jack. It's about acceptance and moving on. Regrets, bitterness, negativity, they just sap the spirit."

"Wow," I said.

"What?"

"I don't know. You sound very ... very wise I suppose ... very sorted."

"I don't know about wise but yes, I'd say I'm sorted. We should be at our age. It's good to find a sort of peace, reach a realistic accommodation with how things are. But I suspect you're maybe still trying to do that?"

"Me?" I said. "Oh, I'll reach an accommodation with life once Tommy Gray and his associates are behind bars." I knew that wasn't quite what Ailsa was referring to. And she probably knew that I knew – but she let it pass.

"That prospect's looking increasingly likely," she said. "It won't be long now until Operation Endgame can close them down for good. And it's due in no small part to your recent contributions – especially your suspicions that Tommy has long-established links overseas – and that he might be about to use them."

"Seemed obvious. When Harry was in charge he was adamant they were an Edinburgh based firm. They had this city to themselves and they didn't encroach on the territory of other gangs, not in Glasgow, not anywhere. But Tommy was always more ambitious. It makes sense, now he's in charge, that he's keen to move beyond Edinburgh, beyond the UK. Major crime's gone global just like other big businesses."

"Yes, well, it was only obvious because of your valuable knowledge. It was an excellent move getting you in as a consultant. And not only for the Gray case, I hear from Ian Wilkie that you've been instrumental in progressing a couple of cold cases too."

"Is it likely there'll be more consultancy work in future?" I asked. "I don't necessarily mean for me. But there must be a lot of expertise out there among my fellow retired cops."

"There could be. Especially since our first choice for such a post has worked out so well." Ailsa smiled.

"First choice, eh?"

"Yep, it was you and your old boss Lawrie McDade who were top of the list for the former Lothian and Borders area."

"Ah, yes, poor Lawrie. He wouldn't be able to offer much help nowadays."

"I was so sorry to hear about it. Vascular dementia following a stroke, wasn't it? Such a shame. Only what ... sixty-five or sixty-six ... he hardly got to enjoy any of his retirement. Tough on his wife too, I'm sure. How's he doing?"

"We haven't been in touch recently. I've been meaning to call, find out how he is ... but ... you know ... didn't get round to it."

"Yes, well it can be hard keeping in touch. We all put these things off more than we should. Justify it to ourselves because we're busy."

"No excuse," I said, realising how wrapped up in myself I'd been lately and feeling ashamed.

Lawrie, or 'The Law' as he was known in our division, had been my DCI. We'd been colleagues for years and we'd retired around the same time. It was he who'd been in overall charge of the Harry Gray investigation. As with all our operations, it was his job to do all the budgeting and planning and to put the arising proposals to our superiors for authorisation. It was also his job to keep those same superiors onside when in their opinion costs were outweighing benefits. These were all tasks that had put me off going for promotion to Chief Inspector. The fact Lawrie did them so competently and still remained a first-rate detective meant my respect for him was enormous. He was a friend as well as my boss – especially after Mike's death. And now I felt I'd fallen short in returning his friendship.

"Don't beat yourself up," Ailsa said, as if she knew the guilt I was feeling. "I'm sure you can arrange to visit while you're still here in the city."

"Yeah," I said. "I think I will."

"Good – and be sure and pass on my regards when you do."

"And so what about you, Ailsa?" I said. "How are things with you? You seeing anyone?"

"Me?" Ailsa laughed. "No, not seeing anyone – not seriously – not in the way you mean. I have good friends – a couple of them are even male and single and not police. We do dinner, theatre, stuff like that – even went on a walking holiday with one of them last year. But I'm afraid I'm living the cliché of being married to the job."

"Happily married?"

"Yes, most of the time."

"And not lonely?"

"Not as lonely as I was when I was married, no."

"Touché," I said.

"Just being honest. As I said, I have friends, holidays, fit in some golf. I have a great relationship with our daughter and spend time with her and the kids whenever I can. And I do actually enjoy my own company. I also enjoy being in charge of my own life. It would take someone exceptional to make me want to compromise, to make me want to make the space and time to work at a serious relationship. Unlike you Jack, I can see past romance, see it for the illusion it is, and happily live without it."

# Chapter Forty

*Jack*

I called Lawrie's wife, Margaret, the morning after my dinner with Ailsa and arranged to visit a couple of days later on Saturday morning.

Margaret made me very welcome when I arrived. She explained to me that Lawrie seemed to like seeing old friends – even if he wasn't entirely sure who they were. She reckoned seeing someone he'd liked in the past stirred up positive emotions for him. True recognition and putting a name to the face didn't seem to matter.

It was a sunny morning and Lawrie was sitting in the conservatory at the back of their house when I arrived. Margaret told me that he liked watching the birds on the feeders and could still name some of the species he saw.

I'd been concerned about what Lawrie and I would find to talk about, but I needn't have worried. Lawrie took the lead and, as Margaret had suggested, I went along with what he said.

Lawrie's face lit up when he first saw me. "Hallo you," he said. "Long time, no see. You not working today then?"

"No, not working. How are you?"

"I'm grand. Not working today either – on leave at the moment."

"That's nice," I said.

"Yes and this hotel's good. You been here before?"

"A couple of times," I said.

Lawrie looked over at Margaret. "I'll get the lassie to bring us a cuppa," he said. And when he laughed it was almost as if he knew he was making a joke.

Margaret smiled at me. "He's not wrong there. He does treat this place like a hotel."

After she brought us our tea, Margaret left me and Lawrie to have a chat. But she checked on us from time to time, made sure Lawrie was okay in lots of small ways. It was humbling to spend time with them. Margaret appeared to cope easily with Lawrie's frequent mood swings. He would be good-humoured one minute and then get angry and frustrated the next.

"It's hard for him," Margaret said. "And it's so unfair. He was looking forward to his retirement. He even had plans to set up a youth club, somewhere for youngsters who might otherwise get up to no good could go, do car maintenance or get help with school work or advice about jobs. But then he had the stroke." She paused for a moment, obviously struggling with her emotions. "It must be so frustrating and frightening for him at times. I just try to help him make sense of things."

"But it must be hard for you too," I said. "I don't think I could do it."

"If you had to, you would. That's what marriage is about. We've been together more than forty years and there's been ups and downs all the way through, but we promised to be there for each other, for better or worse. Besides, Lawrie is my best friend and I'm not ready to give up on him yet."

Like I say, it was humbling. It also made me realise I was actually very lucky to have choices – choices about my retirement and where and how I would spend it.

I spent the rest of that weekend at Maddie's. I went straight there from Lawrie's and arrived in time for lunch.

"So, Dad, one more week of work left," Maddie said as we all tucked into our pizza and salad. "You heading home to Skye next weekend?"

"Yeah, that's the plan," I said.

"Are you excited, Grandpa?" Poppy asked.

"Excited about what?" I said.

"About seeing Grandma Rachel – when you go back to Skye?"

"Oh ... yes ... I am," I said. "It will be good to see her."

"Have you missed her lots?" Poppy said.

"Eh, yes ... yes I have."

"And have you called her and done lots of Facetimes like I do with Grandma Ailsa?"

"Mm ... we've spoken to each other a little bit," I said. "But Rachel has been away from Skye too, so we've both been a bit busy."

"That's a shame," Poppy said, frowning. But then she smiled. "So when you and Grandma Rachel do see each other you're going to be so happy, and you'll give each other the biggest hug ever."

"I hope so," I said.

"You will, Grandpa, you will."

Poppy may have been convinced that Rachel and I were in for a happy reunion, but, like me, her mother wasn't so sure. We were at the park with the children. Poppy was playing on the swings and her father was doing circuits of the park trying to get William to sleep in his buggy. Maddie and I were sitting on one of the park benches watching Poppy and enjoying the afternoon sun.

"You've not kept in touch with Rachel, have you, Dad?" she said. "While you and she have been apart?"

"We ... we were in touch at the start," I said.

"Uh-huh, and then?"

"And then we weren't."

"Okay, and why was that?"

"She ... I ... oh, for heaven's sake, Maddie! Why do you even care?" I got to my feet, ready to walk away.

But Maddie stood up too. She caught hold of my arm. "Dad, dad," she said. "I'm sorry. Please ... come and sit down. None of my business. I'm sorry."

I turned to look at her. "No, I'm sorry," I said as I hugged her. "I shouldn't have snapped at you. I'm lucky you can be bothered to care. I'm annoyed at myself – not at you."

"Oh, why?"

"I told her to stop calling me," I said when we were back sitting on the bench.

"What?" Maddie looked baffled.

"Yeah, I know it must sound ridiculous, but that's what I did." I went on to tell Maddie about the last conversation I'd had with Rachel.

"Nice one, Dad," she said when I'd finished.

"I'm not proud of it," I said. "But at the time it felt easier. She'd said she didn't want to get married – and then she'd gone away to do stuff that was so obviously more exciting than being with me. I suppose I was scared it was over. I suppose I felt rejected."

"Rachel didn't reject you. She rejected your romantic notions. You need more staying power, Dad. Long-term relationships can be a bit of a slog at times. Yes, getting married and all the lovey-dovey stuff is great – but it's not what gets you through. Rachel knows that. But you don't get it."

I was about to try to defend myself, but Maddie was in the zone and nothing was going to stop her.

"In the past," she went on, "when the going's got tough, you've always gone off and got someone new and started the whole romantic thing all over again. That's what I mean about staying power. In a proper loving long-term partnership, you stick around. You accept the worst of each other as well as enjoying the best. You bicker about emptying the dishwasher, argue about mess and money. You say horrible things to each other, but in the end, it comes down to still caring for each other in spite of all that."

"And breathe," I said, smiling at her when she'd finished.

"Sorry," she said. "It's just I want to see you settled … you know?"

"I know," I said, putting my arm round her shoulders and kissing the top of her head. "It's like you're the parent here."

"Yeah, that's how it feels sometimes." She rested her head on my shoulder for a moment and then turned to look at me. "Promise me you'll try to put things right with Rachel."

"I promise," I said.

"Good," Maddie said. "Show her you're not fickle, that you'll go at her pace." She gave my arm a little punch. "And like I said before, be supportive."

"Okay, okay. She's due back about the same time as me so I'll be seeing her very soon."

"And what about the panic attacks? How have they been? Have you done anything about getting some help?"

"No need," I said. "They seem to have gone. I reckon Harry Gray's death and me being able to contribute to the rest of the gang's imminent arrest has put an end to all that."

"I hope so, Dad," she said, giving me a sad sort of half smile.

"Oh, come here," I said, as I pulled her into a hug. "Don't worry about me. I'll be fine."

"I'm going to miss having you close by," Maddie said. "But you need to be back on Skye and you need to be with Rachel."

# Chapter Forty One

### *Jack*

As my final week in Edinburgh began, I was feeling more positive than I had in quite some time. My time away from Skye had undoubtedly been good for me.

As I'd said to Maddie it seemed like I'd put the Gray thing behind me. But it wasn't only that.

Talking with Ailsa and Maddie, and seeing Margaret's devotion to Lawrie, and even my pep talk from Morag before I left, they'd all given me a bit of much-needed perspective. I could now see I needed to think less about me, and I needed to work to fix the cracks in my relationship with Rachel.

But quite apart from all of that I was keen to get home to Skye. Even if the worst happened and Rachel told me to get lost, I didn't want to leave the island. I wanted to live and work there. I was looking forward to the photography work and I even had the seed of an idea for something else I could work on. It had appeared when I'd heard from Ailsa about Jane McRae's work in memory of Mike, and it had taken root when Margaret McDade told me of Lawrie's thwarted plans. Perhaps I could develop something similar on Skye.

On the Wednesday morning of that last week, before we both left for work, Bridget said she'd like to take me out to dinner that evening. She said it was both to say goodbye before I went back up north and to say thank you for letting her stay at the flat.

"Great," I said, trying to show some enthusiasm. All I really wanted to do was relax with a beer or two and watch some mindless television. I also hoped this wasn't Bridget making a last-ditch attempt to rekindle our relationship.

So I was surprised to find I enjoyed the evening. Bridget was looking good – her hair, dress, make-up and jewellery – everything perfectly judged. She also seemed happy and relaxed. She was easy to be with and, as we sat opposite each other in the restaurant, I was reminded of why I'd been attracted to her in the first place.

She'd got us a table at a recently opened restaurant in the New Town which, she told me, the foodies were raving about already. The food was indeed excellent as was the wine. Bridget chatted away about work and filled me in on some gossip about mutual acquaintances.

It was as we laughed at the latest in a series of disastrous romantic liaisons entered into by a senior member of the judiciary that Bridget reached across the table and put her hand on mine. "This is good, isn't it, Jack?"

"Hmm, yes," I said, looking round, pretending to misunderstand. "This place is as good as you said it would be."

"You know that's not what I meant," she said, withdrawing her hand.

"No?" I said, knowing full well it wasn't.

"No. I meant you and me. We're comfortable again with each other. I'm glad."

"Yes," I said, nervous about where this might be leading.

Bridget laughed. "Your face," she said. "Don't worry, I'm not planning to seduce you, but I *am* enjoying your company."

"Good," I said. "That's good."

"And what of you and your shepherdess?" she said. "You know I'd still be willing to share you

"That's not—"

"No, let me finish," she said. "I'd still be willing to share you, but I know that's not going to happen. However, if I'm right in my suspicions that your relationship isn't as idyllic as it was, and if things don't work out between you – you know where I am."

In the end I told her exactly how it was between Rachel and me. I told her the problems were down to me and I wanted to put them right.

I also told her that while I'd always be grateful for what she and I had shared in the past, we had no future as lovers. To which she replied that I should fuck off, stop fannying about, and sort things out with Rachel who, she said, was welcome to me.

All in all I thought we ended things amicably. Except it wasn't quite the end.

We'd just got back to the flat when Lawrie's son, David, called me. He told me his father had died earlier that day having apparently suffered a sudden and catastrophic stroke. He went on to say that the funeral would most likely be early the following week and he'd let me know when the day and time were confirmed. I was shocked by the news and found it hard to speak as I passed on my condolences. David also mentioned that his mother had told him how much Lawrie had enjoyed my recent visit. And when he said that Margaret would like me to say a few words at the funeral, I told him I'd be honoured.

My return to Skye was going to have to be postponed.

Six days later, I drove to the crematorium. Lawrie's funeral would be taking place at noon. I'd arranged to meet Bridget there. She'd be accompanying her boss as the Scottish Justice Department wanted to pay their respects to someone who'd been such a senior and highly regarded police officer.

Ailsa would also be attending and, as I walked from the crematorium car park to the chapel, I saw her and the chief constable getting out of an official car. We gave each other a nod of acknowledgement.

The turnout was large, reflecting the liking and respect that so many people felt for Lawrie, and I spotted many familiar faces from my time in the force as I looked around.

It was a theme I picked up on in my own speech about Lawrie. I alluded to the fact that Lawrie's strengths were things I admired but could only aspire to, things like his talents as a detective and manager, but also as a husband and as a man.

After the service was over, the mourners congregated in little groups outside the chapel. I made a point of speaking to Lawrie's wife and son. They thanked me for what I'd said about Lawrie and were very understanding when I explained I'd not be attending the post-funeral lunch as I needed to get organised for my return up north the following day. Yes, it was a feeble excuse, but for some reason I couldn't face the wake.

I spoke briefly with some ex-colleagues and then Bridget found me. She said she had to get back to the office for an hour or two, so we arranged to meet back at the flat later in the afternoon. She also suggested another 'one last time' dinner and said she'd book us a table.

It was as I was about to leave that Ailsa approached me. "I can't stop," she said. "I have to get back to work. But I just wanted to say well done with the eulogy. It was spot on."

"Thanks," I said. "I was glad to be able to do it."

"And I also wanted to let you know," Ailsa said, lowering her voice as she spoke, "Operation Endgame is about to take action. They've got everything they need and they're confident of arrests and successful prosecution."

"Right," I said. "Good."

I was still contemplating the significance of what she'd said, still letting the real prospect of an end to Gray and his associates sink in, when she said," Sorry, must go, safe journey home tomorrow."

As it was a pleasant, sunny day I decided to leave the car in the crematorium car park and to go for a head-clearing walk in the nearby Royal Botanical Gardens before going back to the flat.

I probably should have been more aware of my surroundings, more alert to who was around, should probably have noticed the white Transit van that left the car park and followed me out of the crematorium grounds. But I was no longer in the habit of being wary. So I didn't see any of it coming. I didn't see *them* coming.

It was all over quite quickly. There were two of them. One of them punched me in the kidneys a couple of times and while I was doubled over they dragged and pushed me towards the Transit. The van's rear doors were open and I was shoved in the back. I did put up a fight, tried to hit back, tried to resist, but it was no use. I was tied up, a hood placed over my head and I was hit again several times. By the time the van got moving I was on the verge of passing out.

"He's waking up," a voice said. "Now the fun can really begin." The voice was male, an Edinburgh accent, and I recognised it right away. Thomas Gray.

# Chapter Forty Two

*Jack*

I'd questioned him enough in the past to be able to instantly recognise his voice. Adrenalin and fear flooded through my body. I tried to move, which was a mistake. The pain in my head and from my, presumably, broken ribs was excruciating and I thought I would pass out again. Attempting to move was pointless anyway as I was tied down. The hood was still in place and my wrists and ankles were secured to what I assumed was a bed frame.

"You can leave him to me now." Gray's voice again.

"Okay boss. Enjoy yersel." The speaker of those words laughed as he walked away and then I heard the sound of a door closing.

"Just you and me now, DI Baxter." I could hear the smirk in Gray's voice. "Although I think we know each other well enough for me to call you Jack." He pulled the hood off and I had to screw up my eyes even though the room was only dimly lit. Gray's face was close to mine and I could smell the mix of garlic and cigarette smoke on his breath. He undid my shackles and pulled me to my feet. The mixture of pain and fear induced a terrible nausea and I threw up.

Gray laughed as he sidestepped the pool of vomit and shoved me towards a chair in the middle of the room. "Now that's no way for a guest to behave," he said, and hit me hard across the face with the back of his hand, before pushing me onto the chair.

"Tommy, what do—"

Another blow to my head made me gasp and fight back yet more nausea. "Tut, tut, Jack. Some respect please. I'm Mr Gray to you." He pulled my arms round the back of the chair and I felt the handcuffs as he slid them shut on my wrists.

"What do you want?" My voice was a whisper.

Another blow caught me on the temple. "You're not to speak unless I say so." He leaned in towards me, close enough that I could smell his rancid breath again. "I know you'll be wondering why you're here, and I *will* tell you," he said. "But right now I've got other stuff to attend to." He stood up. "You'll have to be patient. Oh, and don't even think of trying to escape. I know about your island hideaway – and better still I know where the redhead lives. So, you disappear and it will be bad for her."

I tried to process what he'd just said as he reached into his pocket and took out a mobile phone.

He jabbed at the screen before turning it to show me. "See," he said. He swiped through a series of photos – photos taken outside Halladale village hall on Sophie's wedding day – photos of me and Rachel.

I struggled not to be sick again as I remembered – the guy we thought was a badly-behaved tourist hanging about near the hall and taking pictures of us.

Gray continued to run through the photos. "And here's some taken near your house," he said. "And your lady-friend's place too. She's a good-looking woman, Jack. What's she called again? Rachel is it?" This time the grin was more of a leer. "And I also know where you and the blonde are shacked up in town too – same threat applies to her."

All attempts at logical thought failed. All there was, was terror.

"Two good-looking women you have there, Jack. You're a lucky man – or you were – your luck, has now run out."

"Wait, I don't understand—"

The punch was hard, up under my ribs. Gray wagged a finger

at me as my upper body crumpled in agony. He punched me a few more times, blows to my face, head and body.

When he'd finished, he tutted. "You're not permitted to speak, remember?" He turned to go, started to walk away, but then he stopped and came back to me. "In view of your poor memory, a little something to focus your mind." He unlocked the handcuffs, took hold of my right arm, pulled it back and twisted. There was a sickening crack as my arm not only broke, but my shoulder also dislocated. I assumed the yell I heard was mine but all I could be sure of in that moment was the excruciating pain, a pain that tore through my whole body.

I don't know how long I was unconscious for, but when I came to I was alone, gagged and handcuffed. There was still daylight coming in through a window in the far wall, and I guessed it must be late afternoon or early evening. I tried to take in my surroundings, but it was difficult as I only seemed to be able to open one eye. I guessed the other one must be swollen shut after one of Gray's punches. I appeared to be in an old-fashioned kitchen. The walls were bare stone and the ceiling was low. I guessed I was in some ancient and isolated cottage.

My head ached, I was in agony from the injuries to my arm and my ribs, and my mouth was parched. The sound of a tap dripping into a sink only added to my torment.

My fear and nausea levels ramped up as I remembered what Gray had said about knowing where I lived, and about knowing of Bridget and Rachel. The thought that he, or some associate of his, had tracked me down and been watching us was beyond chilling. I assumed his plan was to see me suffer and then kill me. I pulled at my restraints with my good arm but it was futile. The pain not only limited my movements, but I was considerably weakened too. Besides, if Gray was serious, and I'd no reason to believe he wasn't, then me escaping would only put others in danger.

I had never felt so hopeless, so impotent, so humiliated. But after a while a sort of peace came over me. I saw Rachel. She was smiling at me, telling me she loved me. The pain receded and I drifted in the blackness, whispering her name.

# Chapter Forty Three

*Jack*

"Wakey, wakey, Jack," a voice spoke close to my ear. I was being shaken back to consciousness. The hand on my injured shoulder caused new agony. I could still only open one eye, but I could see it was now dark outside and a lamp had been switched on in the corner of the room.

I turned my head, smelt the rank breath, saw Gray leering at me. I looked away but Gray grabbed my chin, pulled my head back round, then jabbed at my wrecked shoulder. "Come on now. Sit up. You and I have some talking to do."

I couldn't help flinching as he lifted his hands. "Oh dear, you are jumpy," he said, laughing as he removed the gag from my mouth.

He dragged a chair into place and sat down facing me, hands behind his head, legs stretched out in front. "So, anything you'd like to say before we get started?"

I looked at him.

He laughed again. "Oh, sorry, should have said, you're free to speak."

"Why?" I said, my voice weak.

"Sorry?" Gray said. "You'll have to speak up a bit, DI Baxter." He grinned a hideous grin.

"Why?" I said again as loudly as I could manage.

"Why did I come looking for you? Why are you here? Why now?"

"Yes," I said. "Why?"

"When my dad got sick back in the spring, when the doctors said it was terminal, I knew then I'd have to find you. Dad was going to die in prison and it was down to you – and so you'd have to pay."

"I didn't put him in prison. He murdered a policeman – that's why he ended up in prison – that and his other crimes."

"Ah, but you never let up, did you? It was personal for you, wasn't it, Jack? You were determined to get him – you and McDade and that lying bastard, McRae."

"Harry broke the law. We were doing our job." My voice was now so weak that talking seemed to require almost all my remaining energy. I paused before continuing. "It wasn't personal."

Gray shook his head. "Your job was to catch scum – the murderers, thieves and perverts. The Gray gang, we provide a service. We're not out on the streets troubling the good folks of the city. Our customers come to us. You don't mess with us, we don't mess with you."

"Drug dealing and people trafficking are not a service. Your father committed crimes. He was caught, tried and sentenced. That's how the system works."

"You must have loved it that he got cancer and was left to rot."

"I didn't love it. It didn't affect me one way or the other," I said. "And he wasn't left to rot. He was released. He was shown mercy."

Gray laughed, but it was a bitter, mirthless laugh. "Yeah, I saw you spouting on the telly after he died – being all reasonable and gracious about his release. It turned my stomach. It was down to you – you and your two sidekicks that my dad was put away to get sick and die – and there you were acting like it was you – you that had shown mercy."

"It wasn't my fault he got cancer."

"Irrelevant, Jack. That was just the final straw – or the catalyst if you prefer. I'd been waiting for the right time to do it – to deal out justice. Dad's diagnosis – it focussed my mind. The time had come to kill you."

"Killing me isn't justice."

"We'll have to agree to differ on that one. The way I see it – Dad dealt with McRae. McDade did the decent thing and died – couldn't quite believe my luck there – especially as his funeral meant I knew exactly where you'd be and when." Gray sniggered. "So that just leaves you."

"How did you ... how did you find me?" I was finding breathing difficult and it was increasingly difficult to speak.

"In the end it was quite easy. I heard you'd retired and that you'd left Edinburgh and it didn't take my contacts long to find out where you'd gone. I sent one of my crew to check that the information I'd been given was correct, and besides finding out a bit more about your situation, he also took the photos – so I could verify it was you. Finding out about lovely Rachel and where she lives was a bonus."

I struggled to swallow the visceral bile that rose in my throat when he mentioned Rachel. "So why ... why didn't you have me killed then and there ... on Skye?"

"Good question, Jack. It didn't happen then because I'd preparations to make. But although it would have been trickier, I'd have done it up there if necessary – when the time was right. But then another bit of luck – you moved back down here."

In the small part of my brain that was still able to think I knew that the longer I could keep Gray talking, the greater the chance was I'd be found before he killed me. I could see he loved talking about himself, so I needed to keep the questions coming. So, in spite of the pain and the effort involved I persisted.

"And did you figure out why I was back in Edinburgh?" I said.

"Didn't take much working out. My man, who was keeping tabs on you up north, followed you back to the city and then tracked you when you reported for duty. Then I was informed you were back to dig up long-dead cases, to help your old colleagues catch the bad guys who thought they'd got away with whatever they'd been up to."

I grasped that it would have been possible to follow me from the flat to work, but as to how Gray could have found out the type of work I was doing – that I couldn't work out. Maybe that was a lucky guess on Gray's part. After all, logically it was the most likely reason a retired cop would be asked back.

Gray's mocking laugh interrupted my speculation. "Ah, Jack," he said, "I can see you're a bit puzzled there. You're wondering how I could know the nature of your work. And no, it wasn't a guess. Insider information, it's an essential part of the Gray firm's operation, helps us plan, helps us keep at least one step ahead."

I reckoned it would be pointless to ask who the insider was. I was wrong.

"I wouldn't normally reveal my sources," Gray said. "But since you're not going to be in a position to tell anyone, I'll tell you." There was the hideous grin again. "Canteen worker at Fettes, his son owed us a bit of cash, he was repaying the debt. Listened in to conversations in passing, snippets here and there, soon had it figured out."

"Right," I said. I could see how it would be possible to work out I was back to work on Historic Crimes – an ex-colleague, surprised to see me, greets me in the lunchtime queue asks what I'm doing there. I tell him. Canteen worker confirms Gray's speculation as to why I'm back.

But I was almost certain that in the case of Operation Endgame, no employee at the station – other than those in the covert operation team – would have heard anything about it. Gray certainly didn't seem to have a clue about the surveillance he and his associates were under. So, even if I didn't survive, my colleagues had already built a strong case against Tommy and his sickening trade would soon be over. I took some comfort from that.

"So why now?" I asked. "You said you didn't have me killed when I was still on Skye because you had preparations to make. But that was months ago, why the delay?"

"Because, DI Baxter, apart from the plan to kill you, I have other plans, big plans, plans that couldn't be carried out till my dad was gone."

"And now you're all set?"

"Yep, I've said my goodbyes to Dad, and once I've settled the score with you on his behalf, then it's all about the future."

"Your future's going to be just like your father's. One day you'll be caught and sent to prison. It's only a matter of time – especially if you kill me."

"I don't think so. You see that's where I'm smarter than my dad. I tried telling him, told him we should leave but he wouldn't listen. But now I'm the boss and I'm moving on. I'm not staying where the cops know where to find me." Gray sat back again, hands behind his head and smiled. "My future's actually looking good. It's all set. Me and the business, we're adapting, diversifying and we're relocating, leaving the UK, off somewhere sunny, somewhere more relaxed."

"What about Danny? Are you taking him with you?"

"Ah, wee brother, Danny." Gray sighed and shook his head. "I offered him the chance to come with me, but he turned it down. Said he wants to finish college, get what he calls a proper job. He's probably right. He's way too soft for the work I do – mummy's boy – he always was. Good luck to him – ungrateful wee bastard. Can't say I'll miss him."

I was relieved that Danny would be free of his brother, but the possibility that Tommy might actually get away was unthinkable. All I could do was hope – hope that Endgame would live up to its name and terminate Gray, his gang and everything associated with them. I also was able to reflect that taking the job had been a good decision. For one thing, since I was going to die anyway it was good that I'd got the chance to help with my killer's future capture and conviction. And for another, by coming to the city, I'd protected Rachel from possible danger. I closed my eyes for a moment and thought of her, could feel myself drifting.

A slap across my face brought me back to reality. "Hey now,

stay with me. I need you wide awake and aware – aware the end is near." Gray looked at his watch. "On the countdown now. My car's all packed and ready, boat's waiting for me at Queensferry, my new life awaits."

"You really believe," I had to pause, get my breath, "you won't get caught?"

"Yes, I do. Oh, I know you're thinking if you keep me talking, then there's a good chance your colleagues will find you, but that's not the case." He raised his arms and looked around. "You see nobody knows this place exists."

"Really," I said. "Doesn't matter – my phone can be tracked. It—"

"What phone? That was dumped down a drain in the street where you were picked up. And I haven't got one either. I'll activate a brand new one when I'm well clear of here – but for now, I'm untraceable."

I took a minute to process what he'd said, my feeling of hopelessness increasing. "Where … where are we? What is this place?"

"Shepherd's cottage – belonged to my great-granddad – farm owner gave him it when he came back from World War One – a thank you for serving King and country. Farm's long gone and this place is officially derelict now – off grid – no electricity, no mains water – but it has served me and Dad well as a hideout over the years."

"How far … from … from the city?" My need to know, to cling to the tiniest hope of rescue, only narrowly outweighed my need to give in to unconsciousness.

Gray cackled. "Dear, dear, you're struggling a bit, aren't you," he said. "We're in the Pentland Hills, so not far, but far enough. Good place to dispose of a body too, and," he said as he stood up. "Your grave's all ready for you."

He came towards me, undid the handcuffs, and dragged me to my feet. He pulled me across the floor. The beating he gave me was so bad, I was almost glad to see the gun. But the instinct for self-preservation was still there and I kept on fighting to stay conscious. I even attempted a lunge, which was really just a stagger, and I hit out with the arm that I could still use. There was a shout and then a bang.

It was over.

# Chapter Forty Four

*Rachel*

I suppose it was natural to have mixed feelings as I prepared to return home to Skye. I'd enjoyed my time in Israel. I'd loved being with Jonathan and his family and it had been good to see Hana again. I'd found the work challenging and rewarding and I'd met some amazing people.

And, yes, it had been good spending time with Eitan. We'd become close friends. I knew he'd like us to be more than that but he seemed to accept that I didn't.

I suppose, too, that it could be seen as strange that I felt less personally conflicted in such an otherwise conflicted environment. I missed Jack, but I didn't have the time or energy to wonder what was going on with him. I had a job to do - a job with a goal and a time limit to concentrate my mind. And, although there was a lot that was challenging and upsetting in what I witnessed and experienced during my time away, I was inspired by how the people I'd met dealt with it all.

It would have been understandable if people like Hana, or those who ran my niece and nephew's school, or the ex-soldiers of *Breaking the Silence* gave up their fight to improve the lives of all who lived in the region. They could so easily be daunted and overwhelmed as individuals or small groups fighting a state and trying to change the thinking of a nation, but they believed in what they were doing. They believed in truth, justice and reconciliation and they viewed all human lives equally. They were not prepared to be responsible for evil succeeding and they believed in taking small steps to reach their aim.

They so deserved to be heard. The world needed to hear more from brave souls like them. Oh yes, I was inspired.

So, although I was sad to leave, I also couldn't wait to get started on putting the book together. I had a productive meeting with Lana and the publishers after I flew back into Glasgow and before I headed north. There were positive comments about the pictures and video clips and the suitability of my material for both the YouTube channel and for a possible TED talk. Everyone seemed happy that I didn't want the book to be overtly political or preachy. The stories we'd be publishing would speak for themselves. They would be personal and from people with differing perspectives and opinions.

After our meeting, I went back with Lana to her place. I was staying over with her before driving north the next day.

"Your car's fine by the way," she said, as we sat at her kitchen table eating our Thai takeaway. "I've driven it from time to time as per your instructions. And I've checked the tyres and filled up the tank. So, don't worry it'll get you home to Jack no bother." Lana sipped her wine and gave me a look.

"Good. Thanks. And it's wee Miriam I can't wait to see."

"Ah, right," said Lana. "I see, sorry."

"No need to apologise." I took a gulp of wine, as I tried and failed to ignore the sadness and the hurt that was now pushing through whenever Jack crept into my thoughts. It had been easier to suppress these feelings when I was away and busy but now...

"So, things no better between you?" Lana spoke gently.

"No better, no worse ... we haven't spoken ... no change." I shrugged.

"What? You've not been in touch – not talked while you've been away?"

"No," I said. I told her what Jack had said and that at his request we'd had no contact since.

"But you *will* talk? When you get back? You must, surely?"

"I don't know, Lana. I don't know if he'll want to. I don't know why he didn't want to when I was away."

"He's a bloke. He's in the huff. Though I thought better of Jack."

"Me too. It was the proposal and me refusing, and then me going away. He found it hard, I know he did, but—"

"But he couldn't come out and say it – talk about it! God, men! So it's down to you, my girl. You have to take the lead in this."

"Yes, but why should I? I've done nothing wrong. I wanted to be with Jack. I just didn't want to get married. And my work – work that excites me and that means a lot to me – took me away for a while. Neither of these should have meant he couldn't talk to me or – or meant the end of things between us." I sighed. "I couldn't bear that ... couldn't bear it if things were over between us. I *did* miss him when I was away. But it was his choice, not mine, that we didn't keep in touch, and now what if ..." I couldn't go on. My voice caught, tears formed.

Lana leant across the table and squeezed my hand. "Jack's a good man. He loves you – that's obvious to anyone. He's good for you and I reckon what you two have is worth working at. Don't give up."

I had to laugh. "Says the woman who's so good at long-term relationships."

"As I *say*, not as I *do*." Lana laughed too. "But I meant it – it's down to you to ask him. You deserve an explanation if nothing else."

# Chapter Forty Five

*Rachel*

I arrived home in Halladale in the middle of the afternoon. Once I'd unpacked the car and put away the grocery shopping I'd picked up on my way north, I took a little time to walk round the house. With Sophie and the family having recently moved into their new home, I knew it was going to be strange living at Burnside on my own again.

Sophie had texted me to let me know that they were all in Portree. She and Miriam were at the Friday mother and toddler group, and Steven was fetching supplies for both humans and animals. She said they'd be back just after five and would call in to see me then.

So, I walked from room to room, stopping to look out the windows at the loch or up towards the hill. I smiled to myself as I picked up an abandoned teddy bear and gave it a cuddle in the absence of my much-missed granddaughter. I smiled even more when I went into my bedroom and found a vase of fresh flowers and a card. They were from Sophie and Steven to welcome me home. I admit that for a moment I'd hoped they might be from Jack, and, for a moment I was disappointed they weren't – very disappointed.

But my spirits lifted again when I went outside. It was a lovely afternoon. White clouds, pushed by a good breeze, moved briskly across the blue sky. I watched the ferry leaving the harbour at

Uig on its way to the Western Isles, and I listened to the bleating of the sheep and the call of gannets as they skimmed the clifftops. I breathed it all in. It was good to be home.

I decided to seize the moment and go and see Jack. I wanted to see him face to face, ask if he would talk, and if it wasn't convenient right now, then I would get him to commit to seeing me some time soon.

My plan fell apart when I discovered Jack wasn't at home. So I decided to go and see Morag.

Her welcome was warm. For the first few moments we stood and hugged each other, both of us with tears in our eyes. "It's so good to have you home. I've missed you so much," Morag said, as she released her grip on me. She looked me up and down and said, "You look well, if a bit on the skinny side."

"I'll take that as a compliment," I said, laughing and already feeling better for being with her.

I felt even better once we were sitting in her kitchen where, over a cup of tea and some cherry cake, Morag updated me on all the local gossip. Then I told her a bit about my trip and promised to show her my pictures as soon as I'd got them into some sort of order.

Then, inevitably, the conversation turned to Jack. It was me who mentioned him first. "Do you have any idea where Jack is today?" I asked, trying to sound casual. "I knocked on his door earlier, but he wasn't in."

Morag gave me a strange look, somewhere between confused and surprised. "Of course he wasn't in," she said. "He *was* due back this weekend, but he has the funeral to go to so he won't be home till Wednesday. Did you forget?"

"I didn't know he was away," I said.

Morag looked even more baffled. "He's been away for three months – nearly the whole time you've been away. You know he's back at work, working for the police in Edinburgh?" Morag paused.

I couldn't answer. I shook my head. It was my turn to be baffled.

"Okay," Morag said, frowning, before she went on to explain about Jack's job and his former boss's recent death. "And that's all I know," she said when she'd finished. "Alasdair knows more of the details. Apparently there was some other stuff Jack told him in confidence that Alasdair's not prepared to share with me." Morag raised an eyebrow at me as if to say I might know what that other stuff might be.

I shook my head and shrugged, still trying to grasp the fact I'd known nothing about what Jack was doing while I was away, never mind any secrets he'd shared with Alasdair. "I've no idea what's going on with him," I said, before going on to explain how things were between Jack and me.

Like Lana, Morag was on my side. "Silly man," she said. "I can't believe he didn't keep in touch with you. But he hasn't given up on you and him, and he *is* coming back. He promised me."

"He promised *you*?"

Morag looked shifty. "Oops," she said, putting her hand to her mouth. "I didn't mean to say that."

"Tell me," I said.

"I spoke to him – had a word before he left for Edinburgh. Like I said, I don't know the full story behind him going, but I had my suspicions he might not be planning on coming back. So..." Morag hesitated.

"So ... what did you do?"

"I warned him he better not let you down. I reminded him how he was able to reach you when none of the rest of us could, how he'd forced you out of yourself, and that he couldn't now abandon you."

"You said that?" I wasn't sure if I was angry, touched or impressed.

"I did and I meant it. He told me he'd asked you to marry him and —"

"And that I'd turned him down," I said, feeling sure I'd now be in for a lecture on why I'd been mad to say no.

But Morag waved her hand at me. "I know you'll have had your reasons. I told him that too, and I said that you not wanting to marry him was neither here nor there. In short I told him to get over himself."

I found I was smiling at her. "You're something else," I said. "I'm lucky to have such a loyal friend."

"Mmm, that's similar to what Jack said – although he also agreed I was an interfering old bag. But he still loves you – he told me that – and he promised he'd be back."

"Oh, Morag," I said. "I had no idea. Why didn't you mention any of this to me when I was away?"

"I didn't think I needed to. I thought you two would be in touch with each other." She frowned at me. "And talking of not mentioning things – why didn't you tell me you and him weren't communicating?"

"Yes ... well ... it was easier while I was away to put it out of mind."

"Hmm," Morag shook her head. "You two really need to sort yourselves out. And don't you go hiding away in that shell of yours," she said. "When he gets back, *you* must go to him. You must get him to talk, tell him he's being an idiot and that he's bloody lucky to have you, and he can't always have things his own way."

I laughed again.

"Why are you laughing?" she asked.

"Because of you, Morag, because you've always got my back, and you always make me feel better."

# Chapter Forty Six

*Rachel*

It was only five days. Five days and Jack would be home. Yes, I was disappointed that I'd have to wait to see him, but I took comfort from the positivity and encouragement I'd received from Lana and Morag. And, once I'd got over my surprise about Jack being back at work, I also saw the positive side to it. After all if he was going away from the island to work, he'd surely be more understanding that I sometimes had to do the same. I also just about managed to convince myself that his work was the reason he didn't want to keep in touch. Just about.

I was more successful in convincing myself that it was best not to contact him by phone or message. I wanted our reunion to be face-to-face. There was too much risk of misunderstanding when using other methods of communication.

So – five days – I could wait.

On the Saturday morning I got my official tour of Sophie and Steven's new house. The plot I'd signed over to them was on the same side of the track as Burnside but was further down the croft and nearer the loch. It was beautiful outside and in, clad in larch, a long one-storey building with a back wall that was almost entirely glass. It was not only eco-friendly with its solar panels, windmill and ground-source heat pump, but it was also perfectly adapted for Steven's needs as an amputee. They'd only been in it for a fortnight but already they seemed completely at home.

After I'd been shown round I spent a wonderful hour sitting on the floor with Miriam and her current favourite toy – a plastic bucket full of bricks which she would empty and meticulously refill one brick at a time. Now almost nine months old, she was more delightful than ever, babbling and giggling as she and I played together.

Then, while Sophie made us all some lunch, Steven walked me round the croft. He smiled broadly when I told him how I impressed I was with how good it was all looking. "Phew," he said. "I hoped you'd say that. And I must say it's good to have you back and on hand for when I've got questions."

"So I'm not redundant then?" I said.

"Far from it." Steven laughed. "You're back on the rota as from next week."

In the afternoon Sophie and I went for a walk – just her and me. We drove into Dunvegan and went to Coral Beach. As we strolled along the shingle she told me about some freelance work she'd been doing while I was away. She'd been commissioned by her former boss at BBC Scotland to do some research for a couple of radio programmes he was producing. "It's ideal because I do all the work here at home and fit it in around Miriam," she said. "It's interesting too – all about the recent wave of refugees into Scotland. Oh, that reminds me would you mind if I took a look through Grandma's diaries and other papers and stuff?"

"Of course not," I said. "They're in a box in the loft – along with the little case and the doll she brought with her from Germany. They're not an easy read, but they are interesting – especially as she never talked about her experiences."

"Thanks, it's just with what I've been working on, I've been thinking a lot about her and what it must have been like being an unaccompanied child refugee."

We went on to talk a bit about how I'd got on in Israel and the material I'd got for the book. But then, she too asked about Jack.

And yet again I had to tell the whole sorry story. When I

finished, she said, "I'm so sorry, Mum. You should have told me before now."

"Yeah, I probably should, but I didn't want to talk about it."

"I assumed you knew he was away and I assumed you two were in touch."

"Did you see him – before he left – did he speak to you?" I said.

"Not to me, but he met Steven before he went and he told him about the job."

"Seems like I'm the only one who didn't know," I said.

"I suppose he had his reasons but I can't think what they could possibly be. And as for him not wanting to keep in touch while you were away – I don't get that. He surely wasn't sulking, was he – about you not wanting to get married?"

"Maybe, partly, I don't know," I said.

"I feel bad now that I didn't ask you about him," Sophie said.

"Don't feel bad," I said. "If I'd wanted to talk about it I would have."

"Well don't back off, Mum. Don't accept this. Tell him how you feel. Get him to listen, make him explain, make him talk to you."

I couldn't help but smile.

Sophie looked puzzled. "I'm glad I've made you smile, but I'm not sure I get why," she said.

"I'm smiling partly because you seem to be channelling Lana and Morag, but mostly because I love you, love that you're on my side."

"Yes ... we ... we can all see what you and Jack mean to each other. And I *am* on your side." Sophie got up and hugged me again. "Don't let things with Jack get like they got between us," she said as she let me go. "Promise me?"

"I promise," I said.

I felt better after speaking to Sophie. I knew she was right. She and I had been through our own estrangement after Finlay died. It had gone on for far too long and I'd let it happen. When things had gone wrong between us, I didn't speak up for myself. But we had fixed things. It hadn't been easy, we'd both had to be honest, to make ourselves vulnerable, but it had been worth it. Of course it had.

And now I had to do the same with Jack. My former default reaction to relationship difficulties – that of quiet withdrawal and acceptance – was no longer an option I was comfortable with.

So my decision was made. As soon as Jack got back from the funeral, we'd talk. I loved him and I wasn't going to lose him. We'd sort things out and we'd be together.

In the meantime I had plenty to occupy me. Over the next three days I made a start on sorting out all the material I'd gathered for the book. I played with Miriam and took her out to visit the hens and sheep, and I even made an effort to get my unpacking and laundry done.

On the Monday, I had a business meeting with Steven and Sophie about how things were going on the croft and their plans for its development – including the purchase of a couple of cows. Steven was also keen to get more sheep and I was so pleased that under their stewardship the croft would soon be back to how it was in my dad's day.

So, by the Tuesday evening I was feeling positive and excited. Jack was due back the following day and I was hopeful we'd work things out.

# Chapter Forty Seven

*Rachel*

Maddie phoned me around ten-thirty that evening. I'd been watching television and was about to take Bonnie out for a quick walk before bed. I was puzzled when I saw her name on the house phone's caller display. It was late and she presumably knew Jack was in Edinburgh.

And just as I was wondering why she might be calling, Sophie appeared, adding to my puzzlement. She picked up the phone and said, "Yes, I'm with her." She glanced at me, her expression concerned. "Sit down, Mum," she said. Only once we were side by side on the sofa did she pass me the phone.

Nothing could have prepared me for what Maddie told me. Memories of hearing of my son's death came and went as I struggled to take in what she said, struggled against the nausea and the waves of shock. Sophie held my hand and I gripped hers hard. At some point Morag arrived. At some point the call with Maddie ended.

Jack had been shot – kidnapped, beaten and shot. As far as I understood it, he'd been targeted by some criminal with a grudge. He was in hospital and he was in a critical condition. Sophie said Maddie had phoned her first, explained the situation, asked her to be with me when she called. On her way to me, Sophie had phoned Morag.

After a while, as the initial shock receded, I got to my feet and began pacing. "I need to go. I need to go now. Be with Jack."

"No," Morag and Sophie spoke together.

"No, Mum," Sophie said, she caught hold of my hand and guided me back to the sofa. I sat between my daughter and my friend.

"Tomorrow," Morag said. "Alasdair and I will take you to Edinburgh."

"And I'll stay with you tonight," Sophie said.

I did actually manage to sleep that night, but it was a restless, shallow sleep filled with bizarre disjointed dreams – dreams of Finlay standing proud in his uniform; of Jack's kind face in the darkness as he hauled me from the river. In the morning I couldn't focus, couldn't eat breakfast. All I wanted was to be on my way to Jack. Sophie helped me pack a bag before she went home taking Bonnie with her.

Alasdair drove. I sat in the back of the car with Morag. She was unusually quiet, seeming to sense I couldn't cope with talking. Sometimes she held my hand and at other times she put her arm around me and I managed to sleep for a bit with my head on her shoulder. Alasdair was his usual discreet self. He had the radio or music playing for most of the way – and I actually found both to be a bearable distraction.

I got a couple of texts from Maddie but all they said was that there was no change. Jack was still critical and unconscious. She said she'd see me at the hospital and that I was welcome to stay with her and Brian at their house.

As we neared Edinburgh's Royal Infirmary, Morag explained that she and Alasdair were going to a hotel for the night and would return home to Skye the following day. We arrived in the hospital car park, at around five o'clock.

Alasdair fetched my bag from the boot. "If you need anything, anything at all, you just ask and I'll be back down the road," he said. I could hear the emotion in his voice. He cleared his throat. "And tell Jack to hurry up and get better," he said, as he hugged me.

"I will – and thank you – both of you." I turned to Morag and we embraced. We looked at each other, no words necessary.

"In you go," she said. "Jack needs you."

As I made my way to the Intensive Care Unit, I was filled with a mixture of dread and anticipation. I was buzzed in and a nurse showed me to the door of Jack's room. I said I was Jack's partner when she sought to ascertain if I was close family, and I surprised myself with how comfortable I felt saying it. It didn't feel at all like a lie.

Before taking me to his room, the nurse took me into the relatives' room and told me to sit down while she explained Jack's condition. "He's had an operation to remove a bullet from his upper chest," she said. "His other injuries are as a result of him being badly beaten. He has broken ribs. His skull is fractured and he has some swelling in his brain. He also has a spleen injury that we're monitoring." She paused and glanced at the clipboard she was holding. "His right arm's broken and in a temporary cast and his shoulder was dislocated." She laid the notes down. "Don't be alarmed when you see him," she said. "He's lost a lot of blood so we've got him on a couple of drips and his face is quite badly bruised. He's sedated and we'll keep him that way for a few days, but it's all right to touch him and to talk to him."

At first, I was speechless, struggling to process the horror of what I'd just heard.

The nurse spoke gently. "Is there anything you'd like to ask me before you go in?"

"His heart?" I said. "He has a heart condition. Is it okay after … after …"

"We're monitoring it – and so far so good. He's almost through the first twenty-four hours and there's been no regression in his condition. He's critical, but he's stable." Her smile was kind. "It's good for him that you're here."

The nurse explained who I was to the young police officer who was standing outside Jack's room. He checked his notebook and indicated it was all right for me to go in.

Maddie stood up as I entered the room. Even in the low level lighting I could see she was tired. Her face was pale and her expression strained. But she managed to smile as she came to meet me at the foot of Jack's bed. She gave me a quick hug. "I'm so glad to see you," she said. "Dad would be too if he ... if he ..." She turned to look at her father and then turned back to me, shaking her head, too upset to speak.

I looked at Jack. A sheet covered the lower half of his body. His chest was bare apart from a post-operative dressing and the several small sensor pads that linked him to an ECG machine. He had two intravenous drips attached to his arm and his face was covered by an oxygen mask that didn't quite conceal the bruising. It was weird and unreal to see him so still, dependent and vulnerable. In the background the monitor flashed and beeped and I struggled to take it all in.

"Come and sit," Maddie said, as she blew her nose and wiped away her tears. She indicated two chairs by the side of the bed.

Before I sat down, I leaned over and kissed Jack on the forehead. "Hello, my love," I whispered as I stroked his hair and gave his hand a little squeeze. There was no reaction from him, but his chest rose and fell as he breathed, and his skin felt warm. I took some reassurance from that.

"Have you been here all day?" I said, as I sat down beside Maddie.

"Pretty much. I took over from Bridget. She's was here all night. I sent her home to sleep."

"Bridget?" I said.

"Yeah, she's been amazing actually – and she helped save Dad's life."

"What – how?" I asked, baffled as to how Bridget could be involved, and trying to ignore the feelings of unease and jealousy merely hearing her name seemed to be inducing.

"Ah, you don't know, do you?" said Maddie.

"Know what?" I said, feeling like my whole world was about to sink away from me.

# Chapter Forty Eight

*Rachel*

Maddie told me about Bridget lodging at Jack's flat since the end of her marriage. I was still letting this sink in, wondering about the times they must have been together there over the summer when she said, "Don't worry. He's not seeing her. They're not together – you know – as a couple."

"Right," I said, my voice sounding shaky.

"Rachel, it's you he loves – even if he doesn't always get it right."

I nodded. Now wasn't the time to get into how things had been left between Jack and me.

"But like I say, Bridget helped save Dad. She raised the alarm when he didn't turn up as arranged. The police weren't too bothered at first. Said it had only been a few hours. But she made sure my colleagues at the local station knew who Dad was, that it was out of character for him not to turn up, and that he probably had several enemies amongst Edinburgh's criminal population. And while she was there, she also made sure they heard her contacting Mum. Then she threatened them with her boss, the Justice Secretary, too."

"How did they find him?" I asked.

"Based on what Bridget told them, and him being last seen at the funeral, they checked the crematorium car park. They found Dad's car still there, which was odd enough to convince them to take her concerns seriously. It was Mum who made the possible connection with that bastard ..." Maddie flinched, closed her eyes and put her hand over her mouth. She took a deep breath before continuing. "Mum guessed, correctly, that it was a gangster called Tommy Gray who'd taken Dad. Did Dad ever mention Gray or his father to you?"

"No, he's never really talked to me about his work – other than very general stuff," I said.

"It's a long story for another time," Maddie said. "But the short version is Dad has history with the Gray gang. So officers were sent to the Gray family home. Tommy Gray wasn't there, but his younger brother Danny was. And, amazing as it sounds, it was Danny who told them where he reckoned Tommy might be."

"Right," I said, taking a deep breath as a mix of visceral fear and unbearable anxiety threatened to overwhelm me. "And I take it this Danny's information turned out to be correct."

"Yes, and he insisted on going with the armed response team – said they'd struggle to find the place without him. They got there with seconds to spare. Gray shot Dad as they burst in. But at almost the same moment they shot Gray, killed him outright." Maddie reached for her father's hand, tears now running freely down her face.

I put my arm round her shoulder and we sat there leaning into one another, both looking at Jack. After a while Maddie sat back. She wiped her eyes and let out a long sigh.

I glanced at the wall clock. It was just after six. "You should go home," I said. "See the little ones, be there for bedtime. I'll stay here."

"I don't know," Maddie said. "Brian and Mum are at home. They'll put the kids to bed."

"I'm sure they will. But you need a break. You've been here for hours."

"She's right. You should go home."

Maddie and I both turned. Bridget stood at the door. "Go on. Rachel and I can take it from here."

Jealousy, annoyance, gratitude, those were only some of the emotions that ran through me as I stared at Bridget.

"I ... if you're sure," Maddie said looking from me to Bridget. "Oh wait ... Rachel ... how will you get to my place?"

"I've got your address. I can get a taxi."

"Rachel can stay at the flat," said Bridget. "It's nearer the hospital and, no offence, but it will be quieter there and much more convenient all round."

Maddie looked at me, unsure.

I could see what Bridget was suggesting made sense. It would be one less thing for Maddie to think about if she didn't have me as a house guest. And it would be easier for me if I could come and go as I pleased without having to take Maddie's family's needs into account. But I'd be staying with Bridget, and not only that, I'd be at the flat she'd shared – on who knew what basis – with Jack.

However, now was not the time to be petty and I got a grip on the animosity that I felt towards Bridget. I turned to her. "Thank you. You're right. Staying at the flat does make sense."

"Yes," said Maddie. "I suppose it does. It also means I don't have to explain anything to Poppy just yet." She did try to hide it, but I'm sure I could see relief on her face.

"Good," said Bridget. "Now, you, young lady, get home, see to your family, get some sleep, come back in the morning."

"I could stay at a hotel," I said after Maddie had gone.

Bridget was still on her feet, standing now at Jack's bedside looking at him. "Nonsense," she said turning to me. "There's a bedroom all made up for you – Jack's room. And we can take it in turns to be here, so we won't have to spend too much time together."

"Okay, thank you," I said.

She handed me a key-ring and a piece of paper. "Keys and address," she said.

# Chapter Forty Nine

*Rachel*

We got into a bit of a routine – me, Bridget, Maddie and Ailsa – over the next few days. One of us was always with Jack while the others ate, caught up on sleep or went for a walk.

I did the longest shifts. I was the only one of the four of us with nowhere else I had to be and, besides that, it was where I *had* to be. I did go to the flat to shower and change. But as for sleeping, what little I did get was mostly done in the chair at Jack's bedside or on the sofa in the relatives' room.

When I was alone with him I would sit close holding his hand, sometimes whispering, sometimes talking to him. I talked about all sorts of things, but mostly I just said his name, asked him not to leave me and told him I loved him.

Sometimes there'd be two of us keeping vigil. I didn't mind at all when Maddie was with me. We knew each other reasonably well. We liked and trusted each other. Sometimes we talked or tried to read but mostly we sat at Jack's bedside in companionable silence. During one of our conversations, Maddie told me a bit about what Jack was like as a father especially during her teenage years after her parents' divorce. Some of her stories made us smile, but others brought us both close to tears.

Bridget was as good as her word and kept our time together to a minimum, but inevitably some of our times at the hospital did coincide. However, I was surprised to find we actually managed to be civil to each other. In fact it was Bridget who filled in most of the gaps for me.

It was on my second day at the hospital and she and I were in the hospital cafe having a quick coffee while the doctors were with Jack. We sat at a small circular table by the window. I watched a blackbird hopping about on the grass outside. I tried to block the thoughts of Jack and his injuries, of what he'd been through, of whether he'd survive. But it was no use.

"I still can't get my head round how all this happened," I said. "Until a few days ago I didn't even know Jack was back at work."

If Bridget was surprised by this admission, she didn't show it. Instead, she told me calmly and in more detail than I'd heard up to now, about the sort of work Jack had been doing and about his history with the Grays. She also told me about the murder of Jack's colleague and showed me the TV news clip of Jack saying how he felt about Gray senior's release from prison. She said that only Jack could tell us what lay behind Tommy Gray's desire to kill him and why Gray had waited until now. But she guessed it was to do with Harry Gray's death.

I took a minute or two to process what she'd told me before I said, "But why did Gray have to beat him like that, have to … to torture him? If he was going to kill him, why didn't he go ahead and shoot him right away?" I scrabbled in my bag for a tissue, not wanting to cry in front of Bridget, but unable to help myself.

Bridget put down her coffee cup and looked at me. "Because Tommy Gray was a sadist, because he wanted to see Jack afraid and suffering." She took a sip of coffee before continuing. "But in a twisted sort of a way, it's as well he didn't shoot Jack immediately. Holding him captive, doing … what he did to him … it bought his rescuers time."

An involuntary shudder, somewhere between a deep sigh and a sob, prevented me from speaking for a moment.

But the horror of what had happened gradually gave way to relief and gratitude. This wasn't like it had been with Finlay. Jack was alive. He had a chance of survival. When I could speak I said, "Thank you. Thank you for what you did – helping to save him." My voice faded. I covered my face with my hands, felt the tears.

"I know how hard this must be for you," Bridget said. "Jack means a lot to me too."

I sat up, looked her in the eye, dreading what she might be about to add.

But Bridget just gave a small shake of her head and smiled. And it was in no way a triumphant smile. Her expression was part conciliatory, part rueful. "We've been sharing a flat, but not a bed – in spite of my best efforts. His heart belongs to you. He's made that very clear."

"Really?" I said. "He hasn't ... that is ... lately ... he hasn't made it clear to me."

"If that's the case then he's a fool. And I'll tell him so when he comes round."

I surprised both of us by smiling at her.

"What is it?" she said.

"I don't know exactly," I said. "Gratitude I think."

"For what?"

"For your honesty," I said. "I appreciate it."

I'd also been apprehensive about spending time at Jack's bedside with Ailsa. This was Jack's ex-wife after all. They'd been married for around twenty years, and I felt sure, as far as Ailsa was concerned, I'd simply be the latest addition to the long list of women Jack had been involved with.

But like Bridget, she surprised me. She was friendly and warm towards me and certainly didn't make me feel I'd no right to be there. It was Saturday, my fourth morning at the hospital. The medics had decided Jack no longer needed the oxygen mask and that it was time to reduce his sedation and let him wake up. Ailsa and I were sitting side by side at Jack's bedside, watching and waiting, when she said, "You're right for him, you know."

I glanced at her, unsure what to say, then turned back to Jack.

"He's told me a bit about you – and so has Maddie," she continued. "You're not his usual type at all – and that's good."

I managed to look at her, but responding still seemed too difficult.

"Tell Ailsa to mind her own business." Jack's voice was weak and only just audible as he opened his eyes and turned towards us.

# Chapter Fifty

*Rachel*

"Jack," I said, putting my hand on his arm. "You're awake." My voice sounded almost as weak as Jack's.

He looked at me. "It seems so," he said, his voice even quieter now. He winced as he tried to move.

"Careful," I said, pulling my chair as close as I could to the bed and taking hold of his hand. "No sudden movements."

"Good to have you back," Ailsa said. She was standing behind me, her hand on my shoulder, looking at Jack. She then turned to me and said, "I'll go and let the staff know he's awake."

After Ailsa had gone, Jack's grip on my hand tightened. "Gray?" he said. "What happened to Gray? And you – are you safe?" It was the first time I'd ever seen Jack look afraid.

"Me?" I said. "Of course *I'm* safe. And you are too. Gray's dead – shot by your colleagues – right after he shot you. He can't hurt you anymore."

Jack sighed. "Good. That's good," he said. "I thought *I* was a dead man."

"You came close," I said, fighting to keep my voice even, but it was a pointless struggle. I felt the tears start. "But you're going to be okay."

"Am I?"

"You bloody well better be."

"You're crying," he said. "That's not good." He tried to move his right arm towards me, but winced again.

"Keep still," I said. "Your arm's broken and your shoulder's damaged. And I'm not crying, not really. It's just the relief – that you're alive and awake and I—"

The door to Jack's room swung open and the nurse who'd met me on my first visit, and who'd kept me updated since then, came in. "Mr Baxter," she said. "Good to see you're back with us. I'm Nurse Maxwell and this is Mrs Wilson." She stood aside as a tall elegant, silver-haired woman entered. "She's the consultant in charge of your care."

"Good to meet you properly Mr Baxter," Mrs Wilson said as she approached the bed. "And you too, Mrs Baxter. Sorry I've not met with you before now but I know my colleagues have been keeping you informed."

"Oh, I'm ... that is ..."

But Mrs Wilson had already turned away and picked up Jack's chart. As I stood up to make room at the bedside, she said, "Good idea, Mrs Baxter, you go and get a coffee while we see to Mr Baxter."

I didn't dare look at Jack. I knew I'd have to tell her at some point that I wasn't actually married to him, but ...

It was the last I saw of Jack that day. I'd been about to go back into his room, but was met at the door by Nurse Maxwell and two CID officers and was asked to wait outside while Jack was interviewed. While they were in with Jack, Maddie arrived and it seemed only fair for her and her mother to go in when CID left. Nurse Maxwell told them not to stay long and that Jack should be allowed to rest. She also ordered me to take a break and told me to go home. I did as I was told.

Jonathan called me while I was in the taxi on my way back to flat. We'd exchanged a few texts while I'd been at the hospital but he said he wanted to hear my voice and to check I was as okay as I said I was. I couldn't help smiling at that. He knew me so well.

Once at the flat, I must have fallen asleep in the chair the moment I sat down. My phone woke me and it took me a moment to work out where I was as I fumbled to find it in my bag. It was Lana.

"I hope this isn't a bad time, but I wanted to check how things are," she said. "Are you at the hospital? How's Jack? How are you?"

"No, no, not a bad time. I'm at the flat. Jack's awake but needing to rest so I've been sent back here to do the same."

"Good – that's good – for you both. And Jack's okay?"

"He will be," I said. "I'm sure he ..." My breath caught as I spoke, more tears threatened.

"Are you on your own?"

"Yes, Bridget's away for the weekend."

"Right, I'm coming to Edinburgh. Text me the address and I'll be with you soon."

While I waited for Lana to arrive, I called both Morag and Sophie.

Morag was pleased to hear the latest news about Jack and she even offered to come down to keep me company. But I'd refused her offer, knowing what a busy time of year it was for her. She told me to look after myself and that she hoped I'd be home soon. I sensed she had more to say, but for once, Morag kept her own counsel.

Sophie, too, had been delighted with the good news about Jack, but she was bolder than Morag when she mentioned me coming home. "How long do you think you'll be in Edinburgh?" she asked. "I mean I get it that you wanted to be with Jack, when ... when things looked bad for him. But now if he's making a recovery and it's just a matter of time ... you could probably come home quite soon?"

"I suppose so," I said. "But there's no rush, is there? Do you need me?"

"No, no there's no rush. It would be nice to have you back and there are some more croft things we need to discuss with you. But it's more *your* welfare I'm concerned about."

"I'm fine Sophie. I am. But I ... I want to be here for Jack, to support him."

"I get that. But, Mum, you and he ... you're not ... you know ..."

"I know, but I can't just walk away."

"It wouldn't be walking away – not really. But now Jack's out of danger, maybe ... maybe for your own sake ... with the way things are ... you need to take a step back for now?"

"Perhaps you're right. Of course you're right. But it ... it hurts. It hurts to think of him so injured, to think of not being there for him. I don't know if I *can* leave him."

"You wouldn't be leaving him – not in any final sense. But you'd be giving him space to recover ... and giving you both some emotional space. Anyway, it's none of my business, Mum. I'm just concerned for you. Now hang up and I'll go and fetch Miriam for you two to have some Face-Time."

# Chapter Fifty One

*Rachel*

Lana arrived with an overnight bag. "God, you look awful," she said as she came through the door. "And, yes, I'm here till tomorrow whether you like it or not."

"I do like it," I said.

She put her bag down as she looked at me," Oh dear, you need a hug, don't you?" And without waiting for an answer she wrapped her arms around me. As she let me go, she said, "Now show me where the coffee is. You look like you could do with a strong cup."

"Yes, good idea," I said, smiling at her. Glancing at my watch, I was surprised to see it was nearly four o'clock. "I seem to have missed lunch."

"Good job I brought cake then," she said. "And after we've had coffee and cake and you've filled me in on how Jack's doing, I'm taking you out for a drink and a meal. And then it's an early night for you."

I didn't think I could be bothered going out, but I knew resistance would be pointless. I also knew it was exactly what I needed.

So by early evening we'd had a couple of cocktails in one of George Street's trendy bars and had moved on to eat at a small Italian restaurant at the top of Leith Walk. We kept off the subject of my relationship with Jack and all things serious, but the conversation was good and, as always with Lana, I found myself enjoying a good laugh.

"It's good to see you relaxing," she said as we waited for our food. "You actually look as if you might be enjoying yourself."

"I am. Thank you, Lana, it's what I needed."

"I know it is." She smiled. "And forgive the shop talk, but we do need to discuss the book. The publishers have been in touch and they'd like another planning meeting sometime soon. They need to discuss timescales and how the content's coming along."

"I haven't forgotten about the book," I said. "I'd begun sifting through all my material before … before all this with Jack."

"And how was it going?"

"It was good. I had lots of ideas about presentation." I was aware how flat my voice sounded. "Not than I can remember most of them at the moment. It feels like ages ago since I looked at it all."

"Look, don't worry about it. I gave them an edited version of your situation – sick relative in hospital – and they weren't unsympathetic, but they will need to see you fairly soon."

I only partially stifled a sigh and made a pathetic attempt at a smile and a nod.

Lana reached over and patted the back of my hand, before topping up our wine glasses. We sipped our drinks in companionable silence and she let the subject of work lie until we were eating our pasta. "It could be good for you, you know," she said.

"What could?"

"Getting on with the book, going home, getting back to work – take your mind off Jack. I mean, from what you've said he's going to survive, but he does have a fairly lengthy recovery ahead. Perhaps a bit of space – in view of how things are between you?"

"That's what Sophie said." I pushed my plate away and sighed.

"But you don't want to leave him, do you?" said Lana.

"Not really, no."

In the end, though, it wasn't up to me.

# Chapter Fifty Two

*Rachel*

The next day, after Lana left, I went to visit Jack. It was mid-afternoon when I arrived and Maddie was just leaving. She had Poppy with her and we met outside Jack's room.

"Rachel!" said Poppy, launching herself at me and throwing her arms around my waist. "Have you come to see Grandpa too?" She looked up at me, smiling.

"Yes, I have," I said.

"He's not well. He fell and broke his arm and he hurt his head and his chest and his tummy. I told him he was very silly. When I fall I only hurt my knees."

I glanced at Maddie. "Poppy was missing her grandpa," she said. "She was wondering why he didn't visit this weekend. So I had to tell her about him *falling over* and having to go to hospital."

"I see," I said, nodding.

"And once she knew he was in hospital, she had to see him," said Maddie.

"Yes, I drew a picture for him and I wanted to give it to him," said Poppy. "You're in the picture too."

"Am I?" I said. "That's nice."

"Yes, it's a picture of you and Grandpa after he's better, and you're with Bonnie and the hens and the sheep, and you're best friends forever and you're both very happy."

"Oh," I said, jolted by the yearning Poppy's words had provoked. "That sounds ... it sounds lovely."

"Right," said Maddie, "It's time we went home. Daddy's taking you swimming, remember." She mouthed 'sorry' at me and I could see sympathy in her eyes, as she took Poppy's hand.

They headed off down the corridor and I took a deep breath as I waved to them. For now all that mattered was that Jack was alive – everything else would have to wait.

He was sitting propped up against the pillows when I went in. He had a piece of paper in his hand which he laid face down on the blanket as he smiled at me.

"Hello, you," I said, kissing his cheek and rubbing his arm. I pulled the visitor's chair a little closer to the bed, before sitting down and taking hold of his hand. "It's good to have you back," I said.

"It's good to be back," Jack said. His voice was still weak and he remained hooked up to the monitors, his injuries still obvious. And although it was hard seeing him like that, I tried to keep my own distress hidden and to concentrate on offering support.

He tilted his head back and looked at the ceiling. "I thought ..." He closed his eyes for a moment before turning back to look at me. "I thought it was all over ... that Gray ... the guy who—"

"Shh," I said, desperate to ease Jack's obvious distress as he recalled what had happened. "It's no wonder you thought you wouldn't survive, but you did. And it's okay, I know all about Gray and about you being back at work and how it all ... how it all happened." I squeezed his hand and he nodded.

"So," I said, "how are you doing?"

"Better than I was, by all accounts."

"That's good," I said.

"But I've got a bit of a way to go yet according to the consultant."

"What did she say?"

"I've got to have an operation on my arm and shoulder

tomorrow and then I'll need intensive physio. And they also want to be sure the other wounds are healing as they should before they even think about letting me out of here."

"Quite right too. You'll have to do as you're told and be a patient patient."

Jack smiled."You're as bossy as Mrs Wilson. Oh, she said to apologise to you on her behalf."

"What for?"

"The Mrs Baxter thing ... I told her you aren't my wife."

"Ah."

"She said she hadn't looked properly at the next of kin information and had made a wrong assumption."

"Right," I said.

"The strange thing was that Nurse Maxwell assured her it wasn't that big a mistake as you were my partner."

"Ah," I said again.

Jack looked at me, obviously waiting for an explanation.

"It's what I told them. I had to say something like that, otherwise they wouldn't have let me see you."

"At least Poppy knows the score." Jack turned over the paper he was holding."She knows we're just good friends."

I made myself look at the picture. And there we were – Jack and I framed by a heart – and labelled *Grandma Rachel and Grandpa, Best Friends Forever*. But I couldn't look at Jack and I held back the threatening tears. Much as I wanted to talk about how things were between us, I knew now wasn't the time.

He reached out his hand to me. "Don't look so sad," he said. "I get it, and you were right about the marriage thing. Us, as a couple, it was unlikely to have worked. Friends is probably the best arrangement."

I nodded, scared to say anything, scared that if I started I wouldn't be able to stop.

For a moment we held each other's gaze. Jack frowned slightly at first, as if he was working something out and then his expression changed – changed to I'm not sure what – perhaps relief. He was still holding my hand in his when he said, "You've been great, Rachel. Dropping everything, being here for me these last few days, but you should go home now—"

"No, I—"

"Yes, I mean it. I feel guilty enough that you've had to be here at all. You must have stuff you need to be doing at home – your work and everything. And, like I said, it's going to be weeks yet before I'm home."

"But—"

"Please, Rachel!" I jumped. Jack's voice was suddenly loud. He let go of my hand. "I'm sorry," he said. "But please, listen to me. You've done your bit. You've been a good friend. But now you need to get back to your life and I need … I need to concentrate on getting well and getting back to mine."

"Fine," I said, standing up. "Fine, if that's what you want. I'll go, leave you in peace."

Jack said something as I left, but I didn't stop to hear what it was. I just about held myself together until I was out of the hospital building, but once in the back of the taxi I wept all the way back to the flat.

# Chapter Fifty Three

*Rachel*

Alasdair picked me up from the bus stop in Portree the next day. He'd wanted to drive down and fetch me, but I'd said no. I wanted some time on my own on the journey north. So, as soon as I got back to the flat from the hospital, I booked my seat on the coach, called Alasdair and texted Bridget.

"Thanks for this," I said, as Alasdair put my bag in the boot. "No, Morag?"

"Oh, she'd have liked to be here, believe me. But I persuaded her that I should be the one to collect you and she should stay and welcome the folks due at the holiday cottage any time now."

"Right," I said, as we got in the car.

"I hope it *was* right – me coming – and not Morag," Alasdair said as we drove off. "I guessed from yesterday's conversation – and the fact you called *my* phone and not Morag's – that you don't want to talk about Jack or anything else at the moment?"

"You guessed right."

"Doesn't mean Morag won't be over to see you at the first opportunity, mind," Alasdair said.

We both continued to look at the road ahead, but I could hear the smile in his voice.

Morag came round that evening and Sophie was over to see me early the next morning. They were concerned about Jack and pleased to hear he was recovering, but both seemed even more concerned about me.

"God, Mum, I bet Jack looks better than you do right now," Sophie said, when she walked into the kitchen. She took the kettle I'd been about to fill out of my hands. "You sit down and I'll get us some tea."

And, as I had the previous evening with Morag, I told my daughter as best I could how things were now between Jack and me. But like Morag, Sophie seemed to think it would all be fine once Jack was fully recovered and back on Skye, that he and I would talk and we would get back to how things had been in the spring, back to being a couple. I didn't have the strength or the heart to disillusion them and it was comforting, at least in the short term, to go along with their optimism.

Being busy helped. I enjoyed working on the book, sifting through all the material I'd gathered and making decisions about what to use and how to use it. I thought deeply about the people and issues I'd encountered during my time in Israel as I sought to crystallise the message I wanted the book to convey. I also found myself thinking about Finlay and my mother. At first I wondered what their message about life and humanity would be. And then an idea seeded itself in my mind. I began considering using the book as a starting point for some sort of ongoing project in their honour, but I wasn't sure what or how.

Sophie was the first person I mentioned this latest idea to. I'd been back on Skye for a couple of weeks and we were sitting at her kitchen table. Miriam was on my knee, happily playing with her trusty bucket of bricks on the table top.

Sophie, Steven and I had finished our overdue croft meeting and Steven had gone back out to check on the newly acquired Highland cattle. They'd got a yearling heifer and a young cow with her first calf, and I'd been impressed with their account of how it was going with these latest additions to croft life.

"Thanks for approving the barn extension," Sophie said. "Steven was nervous about asking, but we're definitely going to need it for our winter feed storage and other cow-related paraphernalia."

"No need to thank me. Even taking into account that you hope to grow your own hay next year, you'll probably still need to buy feed in if you expand to a full fold."

Sophie smiled. "I remember Seanair talking about his fold of cows. I got quite a ticking off for calling it a herd."

I smiled back at her as I thought of my father. He'd loved it that she and Finlay used the name Seanair, the Gaelic for grandfather, to refer to him – and it was good to hear it again. And besides that, I also recalled how Sophie and he had always had a special bond. "He'd be proud of you," I said. "Of what you and Steven are doing here on the croft – it's what he'd have wanted – and I'm proud of you too."

"Aw, that's nice." Sophie reached over and touched my hand. "I wish Seanair could have met Steven. He loves it so much here."

"He's certainly taken to crofting life," I said. "I enjoy it too, but I was never as committed as Steven is. Don't get me wrong, I'm more than happy to be back on the croft rota, but I like having my other work too."

"Hmm, I do worry if maybe he's taking on too much. He's talking of doing a land management course in order to know more about producing our own feed, and he can't wait to expand the sheep numbers even more, but we can't afford any hired help yet. And although he never complains, I know he suffers a fair bit of pain in his legs despite his prostheses being state of the art."

"That's not so good," I said. "He's a hard worker, there's no doubt about that. Maybe the work – even though it can be physically painful, maybe it's therapeutic mentally. You know – helps him cope with his loss."

"Yeah, I'm sure you're right. And I do my bit, but there's Miriam, and like you, I want to do other things too – other professional things."

"Apart from your freelance stuff, you mean?"

"Yeah, I've got a bit of an idea actually. It involves Grandma."

"Oh?"

"I had a look through her papers and stuff – like we talked about. Her diaries are amazing. Reading them – the stuff she says about her family losing their home in Berlin and ... and the rest of it ... it made me think that maybe I should ..." Sophie hesitated.

"Should what?"

"The thing is – I'd only do it if you approved."

"Do what?"

"Tell Grandma's story – maybe mention it to my contacts at the BBC – propose a further series of programmes on refugees who recently arrived in Scotland – but specifically those who arrived as children – prefaced by what happened to Grandma and maybe some of the other Kindertransport children. I don't know exactly how I'd do it ... but I think it's worth exploring."

"I don't know," I said, unsure how I felt.

"I know Grandma didn't talk about it, but she did write it all down, her experience as a child refugee, the impact of the Holocaust on her and her family. For all she buried her Jewish heritage and history, I think she needed to share what had happened to her, but she didn't know how."

"She wanted to be seen as a native of her adopted country. Seanair told me more about Grandma's childhood than she ever did. And she got so anxious and cross at the mention of Germany or Judaism, I avoided it all too."

"Nowadays she'd be diagnosed with PTSD and offered therapy and counselling."

"Hmm, but would she have accepted it?" I said, recalling my mother's stubborn stoicism.

"Probably not. But I think writing it all down helped her to cope."

"But would she have wanted others to read what she wrote? She couldn't even share it with those closest to her."

"I think deep down that's exactly what she wanted. There's

a message in her writing – a message for everyone about the importance of tolerance and compassion, about being vigilant against hatred and injustice."

I looked at my daughter's face, at the passion I saw there, and I felt such love and pride. "Then I think you should pursue your idea," I said. "Tell your grandmother's story."

"Really? Oh, Mum, that's great." Sophie stood up and came round to my side of the table. She hugged me and lifted Miriam off my lap. "Come through to the living-room," she said. "This one can play with her toys until lunch-time and we can talk some more."

And we certainly talked. I told her more of what I'd seen and heard in Israel and about the wonderful people I'd met there. We talked about the parallels between what happened in Nazi Germany and what was still happening all over the world – ordinary, decent people mistreated, displaced and killed simply for being seen as 'other'. We spoke about war and about Finlay, and I shared my desire to do some sort of long-term project in memory of my mother and Finlay – something that would be a force for good.

"Go for it, Mum," Sophie said. "I've no doubt you'll come up with something amazing."

And so, gradually, as the weeks passed, I settled back into life on Skye and got used to having Burnside to myself again. I divided my working day between the book and the croft. In my spare time I walked with Bonnie, met up with Morag and other friends, and took my daughter out for a belated birthday lunch. I was welcomed back into my local book group and into the Portree Gaelic choir. And I spent time with my granddaughter whenever I could.

I made good progress with the book and continued to think about my memorial project idea. I had an online meeting with Lana and Communicado and everyone seemed pleased with what I'd done so far as dates and deadlines were confirmed.

The publishers of the children's book were also in touch and I felt excited as we discussed plans for the November launch. I was looking forward to seeing Jason going out into the world.

I also had a lovely, but almost overwhelming, surprise when a parcel arrived from Eitan. It was his Sea of Galilee painting, the one I'd admired when I'd seen it at his house. After I'd unwrapped it, I sank down into a chair with it lying across my lap. For a while I sat and gazed at it and enjoyed again the beauty and calmness of its blues and greens. The card that came with it said,

*'For Rachel, who, like the sea, whether calm or troubled, is always beautiful. My love always. Eitan.'*

After I'd cried, I called him. He said he didn't need to be thanked but that having heard from Jonathan about what had been going on, he did need to know I was all right. We talked, or rather I talked and he listened. And after we'd spoken, I marvelled again at Eitan's capacity for warmth, generosity and steadfast friendship.

In amongst all the good stuff however, there was Jack – or rather there was his absence. And my longing for him was intense.

While I'd been away, I'd convinced myself that all we needed was to talk, that once I was home we'd fix things. And then during my time at his bedside, once it became apparent that he would recover from his terrible injuries, my hope persisted.

But now it seemed I had to accept that for Jack our love affair was over. He not only believed I'd been right not to want to get married, but he also thought our relationship had run its course.

For me though it was far from over. Thinking about him and what he meant to me was torture, but not thinking about him was impossible. I clung to the hope that he'd honour his promise to Morag, that he'd come back to Skye and that we'd talk. Because the truth was I loved him more than ever.

# Chapter Fifty Four

*Jack*

My physiotherapist was Lauren. She was young, small and blonde, with a nice smile. And she was completely without mercy.

It was never going to be easy coming back from the kind of injuries Gray had inflicted on me. I've never known pain like it, not even when I had the heart attack. There were the operations to recover from, the fractures to my skull and ribs needed to heal, and then I had to regain the use of my right arm.

I had three weeks of daily physio with Lauren while I was still in hospital, followed by a further three weeks – every other day– after I was discharged and living at the flat. Lauren was relentless. I'd master one set of exercises, and see a bit of progress, and then she'd come at me with a new more demanding set. But I was glad the going was tough, glad I had to concentrate, glad it left me exhausted. That way I had little energy to think about anything else – to think about what had happened to me, or about the future, or about Rachel. Don't get me wrong, I was grateful to be alive, but if I'd been unsure where my future lay before the kidnap, I was even more uncertain now.

A day at a time was all I could manage. While I was in hospital, my world narrowed down to the routines of the ward and to small daily triumphs such as being able to lift my arm to waist height.

I appreciated visits from former colleagues who brought with them glimpses of the outside world and who promised to take me out for a beer or two when I was better. But by far my main visitors were Ailsa, Maddie and Bridget, all of whom were absolute stalwarts, both while I was still in hospital and afterwards.

And I did have one unexpected visitor. It was my second last day in hospital. By this time, any threat to my safety was deemed to have passed and I no longer had a police guard at my door. I was sitting in my bedside chair reading when he arrived. I looked up when I heard his knock, and saw Danny Gray standing in the doorway looking hesitant and uncertain.

I was both shocked and pleased to see him. "Danny!" I said in a way I hoped sounded welcoming. "Good to see you. Come in, have a seat." I pointed at one of the visitor chairs.

"Is it?" he said, as he sat down. "Good to see me, I mean."

"Of course, it is. I've been told you played a key part in saving my life. And now you're here I can thank you."

Danny was hunched forward, looking at the floor and twisting his clasped hands. "I wasn't sure ... you know ... about coming? I thought maybe you'd never want to see any of my family again." He paused, took a deep breath and sat up. He looked right at me as he continued. "But I wanted to apologise ... for what they did ... my father and then Tommy. I am so sorry."

"There's no need for you to apologise. As you said it was your father and then your brother who tried to kill me, not you."

"But—"

"But nothing. You're a good man, Danny, in spite of the odds. You did the right thing on both occasions. You didn't get involved when your father shot my colleague, and you gave vital information when I was taken by your brother – even if it must have felt you were betraying your family."

"They ... they've never felt like family. That life, their life, it was never what I wanted. And you ... you DI Baxter ... you gave me a chance to break free of them when you spoke up for me at the trial. I'm at college now, got a part-time job, and a place to live. It was you who got me a second chance, even though Dad had killed your friend. I owed you. I had to stop him ... stop Tommy."

"Right," I said. My voice was hoarse as I took in Danny's words. I felt both proud and humble but also sad at the life Danny had been forced to endure. And these were just some of the emotions that threatened to ambush me as I continued to speak. "I don't know about me being responsible but that's ... that's great you're at college."

"Yeah, I'm doing a catering course – want to maybe be a chef some day. Maybe cook you a meal, you never know." Danny smiled shyly.

I smiled back at him, then swallowed and cleared my throat before replying. "I'd like that," I said.

For a moment or two neither of us spoke. Danny looked awkward. And I realised if I was finding the conversation hard, how much more difficult it must be for Danny. But he needed to tell his story and I needed to hear it.

"So," I said. "Did you know what Tommy was up to that day ... the day he ... he kidnapped me?"

"Not exactly, no," Danny replied. "The day before he took you, he'd told me he was leaving – moving abroad – wanted me to go with him. He said he had plans for the business and wanted me to be involved. Said some rubbish about brotherly love and blood ties, how now both our parents were gone, we only had each other and should stick together." Danny wiped his hand across his forehead. He looked down at the floor again.

"But you didn't want to go?" I said.

Danny shook his head. "When I said no, he got angry. The brotherly love vanished. It was back to the real Tommy. He was just like Dad. He said I was a loser, a coward, and ... and a whole lot of other stuff. He finished up by knocking me about a bit, warned me not to talk to anyone about him leaving or he'd have me killed. Said he'd be gone the next day once he'd tied up some loose ends – and I'd never see him again."

"And you – you realised later when the police came round – I was one of those loose ends?"

"Yes." Danny nodded.

I could see the emotional turmoil on the young man's face, see what all this had cost him. He seemed lost and alone and I desperately wanted to offer him some comfort. "I'll never be able to thank you enough for what you did," I said. "I admire you Danny."

"*You* admire *me*?"

"Yes, I do. You stood up for yourself and you've risen above the circumstances you grew up in."

"My mum – she wanted better for us. She was trapped with him – with my dad – but she wanted *us* – me and Tommy – to get out. She tried to help me, but she was scared of him – of Dad – and then after one too many beatings, she got ill and died. But I promised her ..." Danny was now obviously struggling.

I had to do something; something to comfort this young man who'd so courageously helped me in a way I'd never be able to repay. It also occurred to me that him coming to see me was also a brave thing to do. So I leaned forward in my chair and put my hand on his arm, gave his shoulder a bit of a squeeze. "It's okay, lad," I said. "I can see how difficult this is for you. And I appreciate the effort you've made to come here."

Danny looked at me and nodded.

"So," I continued, "you promised your mum you'd get out; you'd not follow your father?"

"Yeah, but sometimes I wished I hadn't. Sometimes I couldn't see the point ... just wanted to give up."

"But you didn't give up, Danny, and you've certainly kept your promise."

"Yes ... sort of ... I suppose ..."

"You have. Look where you are now – at college, got a job, your own place," I smiled at him.

He managed to smile back. "It's only a student flat, and the job's in a call centre, but it's a start."

"Exactly," I said. "And presumably the house – the family house – it'll come to you now." I remembered the Grays' place – a big Victorian villa on Edinburgh's south side – bought with the untraceable proceeds of unproven crimes.

"Hmm, yeah, Dad's solicitor was in touch about that. I've told him to sell it. I don't want it, but I'm hoping to put the money to some good use."

"Oh, in what way?"

"Don't know yet exactly – but something good – something that might give other folk like me a chance of a better life."

"Wow," I said. "That's pretty amazing."

Danny nodded, his expression thoughtful. "Thanks, DI Baxter. It means a lot that you think so."

The buzzer announcing the end of visiting time sounded before either of us could say any more. Danny glanced at the wall clock and got to his feet. "It's time I was going anyway," he said. "I'm glad I came and got the chance to talk to you."

"I'm glad too," I said. I reached over to the locker and got my phone. "Before you go," I said, "Put your number in here – if you don't mind that is. I'd like to keep in touch."

"Course I don't mind," he said, taking the phone from me.

"I'll text you mine," I said, as he handed me back the phone. "And if there's ever anything that you think I can help you with, you get in touch, okay?"

"Okay," he said. "Thanks, DI Baxter."

"And Danny," I said.

"Yes?"

"Call me Jack."

# Chapter Fifty Five

*Jack*

By the time I was discharged from hospital in early September, Bridget had moved to her new place. And although my arm was out of the cast, it remained pretty useless, and I still had to wear a sling to support it. So I'd have found it quite difficult to cope once I was back at the flat if it hadn't been for the trusty trio.

Ailsa looked in every morning on her way to work, and Bridget every evening. And I spent the weekends at Maddie's. They all helped me with dressing, shopping and other chores and, if they were available, they'd drive me to physio and to check-up appointments. If not, I took taxis.

It was strange spending so much time with my ex-wife, but despite the circumstances I found I enjoyed her company. It was Ailsa who told me Tommy Gray's funeral had taken place. She also told me they had seven of the gang members in custody.

"You did a great job, Jack," she said. It was a couple of weeks after I'd got out of hospital and she was driving me back from physio.

"I take it you don't mean in surviving my latest session with Lauren?" I said.

"No, not that," Ailsa said. "I mean your input to Operation Endgame. Your insights and hunches into how the Grays operated, along with the months of surveillance, means it looks as if we have a strong case. The Gray gang is history."

"That's good."

"I'm just so sorry we didn't get Tommy before ... you know ... before—"

"Before he nearly killed me."

"Yes, that," Ailsa said."It wasn't part of the plan to put you in any danger."

"You didn't," I said. "You didn't put me in danger. Tommy was determined to get me whether I was working for the police or not."

"I'm glad you see it like that – makes it easier to ask you something."

"Oh yes?" I said, sensing what was coming next.

"I was wondering if you'd like to continue working with Historic Crimes – after you're better – on a consultancy basis like before – it wouldn't be active duty." We'd pulled up at traffic lights as she spoke, and she turned to look at me.

I glanced back at her before returning my gaze to the road ahead. "I don't know, Ailsa." And I honestly didn't. All I did know was I wasn't sure what I wanted.

"It's fine," Ailsa said. "Wait till you're fully recovered and at least think about it."

Bridget also asked me about the future. It was early evening and we were sharing a takeaway. I'd been out of hospital for three weeks and I'd had my last session with Lauren that day. Bridget had suggested an Indian meal at the flat as a celebration.

"So, I imagine you're keen to get back to Skye soon?" she said, as we sat at the table eating.

"I don't know. Perhaps ... probably."

"Right." Bridget smiled. "Not sure if that was a yes or a no."

"Obviously I need to go back, check on the house and so on."

"That implies it would just be a visit and then you'd be back down here."

"I suppose it does."

"But you and Rachel—"

"No!" The force I spoke with surprised me as much as it appeared to shock Bridget. "Please, don't." I pushed my plate away and stood up. "I ... I can't ... I don't want to talk about it."

Bridget held up her hands. "Okay, okay," she said. "Sorry. I wasn't prying, honestly. I assumed—"

"Well don't. Don't assume." I was aware I was pacing.

Bridget raised her eyebrows and topped up her wine as she spoke. "Okay, message received."

I flopped down on the sofa, wishing I was off the painkillers and could have a much needed whisky.

Bridget came and sat beside me. "I really am sorry. I didn't mean to upset you."

"No, I'm sorry. You weren't to know. I know I said she went back home because she had to get back to work, but the truth is ... the truth is we ... that is I ... I decided it would be better if we stopped seeing each other."

"Right."

I could see Bridget was surprised, could see she wanted to say something.

"What?" I asked.

"No, you said you don't want to talk about it."

"I've changed my mind."

"Right ... well ... and I can't believe I'm saying this – there was a time, as you know, when I would have been delighted to hear you were no longer with Rachel—"

"But now you're happy on your own?"

"I've been on my own for a long time, Jack – in the sense of not being in an exclusive relationship. But if you mean living on my own, then yes, I am quite happy actually."

"And in terms of relationships – you're not looking for anyone new?"

"Not for the moment, no. That's not to say I'm not having sex. There's a rather fit young guy started recently in the press department at Holyrood that I didn't say no to." Bridget smiled her beguiling smile and put her hand on mine. "And you know

*Settlement*

I'd never say no to you." She tilted her head, smiled and fluttered her eyelashes whilst flapping an imaginary fan.

"Oh, very Jane Austen," I said, smiling as I removed my hand from hers. "Don't think I can compete with fit young guy, but thanks for the flattery."

"It's not flattery, Jack. You know how I feel about you. That hasn't changed. I'd go to bed with you anytime. But what I was going to say was – about you, about Rachel – are you sure it's over?"

"Oh yes, I'm sure."

"Hmm, I find that hard to believe."

"Why?"

"You mean apart from how right you seem together, apart from how much in love you are with her, and she with you."

I sighed and shook my head.

"She may not be into marriage," Bridget said, "but the Rachel I saw at the hospital – she was distraught. She practically lived in that room with you while you were unconscious. And she even said—"

"What, what did she say?"

"It was on the second or third day, I bumped into her in the doorway to your room. I'd just arrived to visit and she was coming out. She was in tears – in quite a bad way actually. I thought ... for a minute ... I thought you'd—"

"Died?"

"Yeah, or at the very least that you'd deteriorated. Anyway, I sat with her on the chairs outside your door and waited with her till she got herself under control. She assured me there'd been no change in your condition, but that she was scared. She said she'd only just survived losing her son, but to lose you too would be too much. She said she loved you very much."

"Right," I said. I wasn't sure what to think at first. I felt a spark of hope, but then I got a grip, remembered why I felt I had to send Rachel away. "It was probably shock making her upset. She was perfectly calm when I saw her, and she didn't put up much of a fight when I told her to go home."

"Yeah, but that was after, after you were conscious, after we knew you were going to be okay. No, I know what I saw, Jack. Whatever you think the state of play is with your relationship, for Rachel, it ain't over."

I couldn't face discussing my reasons for telling Rachel to go and for ending our relationship. And I certainly didn't want to admit it wasn't what I wanted. "Can we change the subject?" I said.

Bridget smiled. It was a patronising, if-you-say-so-but-I-know-I'm-right, sort of smile. "Okay," she said. "Forget I mentioned it."

# Chapter Fifty Six

*Jack*

Maddie didn't let me off so lightly.

"Let's take these through to the conservatory," she said, picking up the mugs of tea she'd made for us. I was at hers for the weekend. We'd just finished clearing up after lunch and, as William was down for his post-lunch nap, and Brian had taken Poppy swimming, we had the house to ourselves.

The autumn sun had made the conservatory pleasantly warm and I felt relaxed as I sat opposite my daughter and sipped my tea.

"It's good to see you're not using your sling so much," Maddie said. "Your arm's obviously getting stronger."

"Yep, I'm gradually building up my out-of-sling time ... can't manage a whole day yet though."

"And how are you coping without the painkillers?"

"Okay, mostly. The shoulder can still give me trouble and the ribs and the chest wound still make themselves felt. But it's getting easier."

"You seem to be handling it well. Not only the physical recovery, but mentally ... especially with you ... you know ... already suffering with the panic attacks and stuff. Hasn't what happened made all that worse?"

"No, no I'm fine as far as all that stuff goes," I said. "Gray's dead. I survived. It's over."

I didn't like lying to my daughter, but I didn't want her worrying about me any more than she already was. So I didn't tell her. I didn't tell her about how I'd recently been waking in the night, sweating and scared, after the nightmares. I didn't tell her about the couple of daytime flashbacks I'd had in the past week, episodes that left me a trembling, whimpering wreck.

"That's a pretty amazing attitude, Dad," Maddie said. She put her hand to her mouth and closed her eyes for a second. When she opened them, I saw tears escape and run down her cheeks. She looked as if she was about to speak, but then she shook her head and bit her lip.

"Maddie?" I said. "What is it? What's wrong?"

"Oh, Dad," she said, wiping the tears with the back of her hand.

I got to my feet and held out my good arm. "Come here," I said.

She came to me and I hugged her as best I could as she wept.

"Sorry," she said eventually, looking up at me. "I wish I could be as stoical as you about what happened but when I think how Gray ... what he did ... how you could have..." A sob stopped her speaking.

"Hey," I said. "Hey now, it's okay." I kissed the top of her head. "Come on. Come and sit down." I led her back to the sofa and sat beside her. "Don't upset yourself," I said. "It's over and I'm still here."

We sat side by side in silence for a little while, and I held Maddie's hand while she composed herself.

"Love you, Dad," she said eventually and kissed my cheek.

"And I love you too, Maddie. Now stop worrying. Like I said, I survived. I'm still here."

"Hmm, about that," Maddie said. But now she was smiling.

"About what?"

"You still being *here* – as in Edinburgh. When are you thinking of going home to Skye?"

"Ah," I said.

"Ah?"

"Before all this – the shooting and everything – I was ready to go back. But now, I don't know that Skye is home anymore."

Maddie frowned. "Sorry? You can't mean that. You love it there – the house, the stars, the photography. And what about that photography job? What about Rachel? You're not sulking because she had to get back to work, are you? And please tell me you haven't accepted Mum's job offer. You haven't, have you?"

"Eh, which question would you like me to answer first?" I asked when she paused for breath. I smiled at her, but I also felt uncomfortable. If I answered any of her questions honestly, Maddie wasn't going to like what she heard.

She smiled back at me, but then she narrowed her eyes as she looked at me suspiciously. "You're squirming. You're going to confirm my worst suspicions, aren't you?"

"That's some interrogation technique you've got there. I guess it works well with suspects in the interview room."

"Yep, you bet it does. Bombard the dodgy characters with questions I know are near the mark, gauge how close I've got by the level of discomfort caused." She sat back, her gaze still fixed on me.

"Smug doesn't suit you," I said.

Maddie raised an eyebrow as she shook her head. "Don't bother trying to deflect me. Just answer the questions."

"You know me too well," I said. I took a deep breath. "I do love Skye. And I've spoken to Richard Macdonald, the guy who offered me the photography job. *He* got in touch with me actually. He'd seen the news story about what happened, and he wanted me to know the offer still stood, and to take all the time I needed before starting."

"So, why are you hesitating? Is it because of Rachel and you? Because if it is that would be daft. From what I saw at the hospital she loves you more than ever. She only left your bedside because she had work—"

"She left because I sent her away. If I'm honest, I could see she didn't want to go, but I sent her away anyway."

"What? Why?"

"I had to. To protect her."

"Protect her?"

"Look, Maddie, the kidnap, the shooting – Gray had it all carefully planned. He'd done his research, tracked me down. He told me he knew about Rachel. He'd have used her to get to me if necessary. Being with me put her at risk. That is unforgiveable. So it's only right that I ended it."

Maddie shook her head. "Sounds like an excuse to me. Yes, it must have been horrible to have her threatened like that. But there's no threat now."

"Maybe not, but … I don't know … it feels like everything's changed. Before all this happened I was looking forward to getting back to Skye. The Gray gang would soon be arrested. I'd done a good job. I was ready to talk – really talk to Rachel. It was all going to be fine. But I'm not sure about anything anymore."

"And you told Rachel all this? Told her your reasons and how you were feeling?"

"Not exactly, no. I just said she was right not to want a serious relationship with me, that she'd done her duty as a friend by visiting me in hospital, but that she should go and get on with her life."

Maddie shook her head again. "Done her duty? Dad, you're impossible. You love Skye. You love Rachel. You've been through a horrible ordeal, but it's over. Now you need to look ahead. Seems like you've got a lot of thinking to do."

"Yeah," I said. "You're probably right."

# Chapter Fifty Seven

*Jack*

And Maddie didn't let the matter lie. She called me at the flat a few days later.

"So, have you given it any more thought?" she said.

She didn't have to explain what *it* was. "Yes, I've thought of little else."

"And?"

"And nothing. I'm no further forward."

I heard her sigh. I knew she was right to be exasperated, but I seemed to be incapable of making any decisions. I was so tired – tired of my thoughts going round in circles, tired of the nightmares, tired of being sabotaged by flashbacks of the kidnap.

"Okay, here's what I think. I think you need to get back to Skye – sooner rather than later. You need to remind yourself what you love about the place. And you need to talk properly with Rachel."

"Yes, yes I know you're right but—"

"But nothing – no excuses, Dad."

"No, I know no excuses. But there's a good reason I can't go right now. I'm not allowed to drive yet."

"That's not a problem. Alasdair's coming to get you."

"What?"

"I spoke to him yesterday and he's travelling down on the bus today. That way he can drive your car back up to Skye so you'll have it there for when you can drive."

"Today?"

"Yes, he said he'll stay the night with a friend of his, a former colleague that lives in Edinburgh now apparently – someone he's been meaning to catch up with for ages."

"So it's all sorted," I said.

"Yep." And don't worry about the flat. I'll make sure it's all tidied up and organised."

"Seems like you've thought of everything."

"Someone had to. I know this is right for you, Dad. Please don't say no."

I took a breath, feeling suddenly queasy. I knew she was right, but so soon?

"Dad? Are you okay?"

"Yes," I said, "I'm fine."

"Then you'll go back?"

"It would be a bit unfair on Alasdair if I didn't."

I heard Maddie's sigh of relief.

"Good," she said, and I detected the break in her voice, "thanks, Dad. I know none of this is easy for you, but I know you need to do this. The time is right."

I had to swallow away the lump in my throat before I could reply. "Thank you, Maddie. I love how you keep me right. So, when should I expect Alasdair?"

"Tomorrow morning, he'll pick you up at ten."

I didn't have a lot of time to prepare for my departure, but I did let the hospital know I was going back up north, and they said they'd get in touch with my GP. I also let Bridget and Ailsa know I was leaving, and both sent me back supportive messages.

And when the door buzzer sounded at ten on the dot the next morning, I was packed and ready. Or rather I was as ready as I would ever be.

It was good to see Alasdair. And being Alasdair, he judged

things exactly right as far as our in-car conversation went. He kept the chat light-hearted. He filled me in on local gossip, told me some amusing stories about townie visitors to the holiday cottage, and about his recent bird-watching walks. And we chatted a bit about our grandchildren.

The talk was interspersed with listening to the radio or to music. It was all very companionable and relaxed. I managed not to think too much about anything, about any of the stuff that had happened since I'd left Skye, or about my imminent arrival back there. I even dozed off a couple of times.

I was actually snoozing when we pulled up outside Dunhalla. Alasdair had to nudge me awake. "You're home, Inspector Baxter," he said. I looked out at the house and the loch and, for a moment as I got out of the car I wondered, *was* I home?

When I told Alasdair how grateful I was to him for coming all that way to get me, and especially for coming down on the bus, he just laughed.

"That's all right. Being on the bus, it was a day of peace and quiet. A day to myself, to read, listen to music, and snooze whenever I felt like it. Aye, the bus is a bit of a sanctuary, if you know what I mean." He nodded in the direction of his own house back down the track and grinned at me. "Besides, I got to drive this beauty," he said, patting the soft top of my car.

"Aye," I said, surprising myself by laughing. That was a sound I realised I hadn't heard in a while. "It's a privilege granted to very few."

Alasdair retrieved my bags from the boot and said, "Right, let's get you inside and settled." He waited in the kitchen while I had a look round the place.

The first thing I noticed was the smell. The house smelt clean and some of the windows were open, so the scent of polish mingled with the loch's salty vapour. The bed had fresh linen and there was a small pile of towels, which still smelled of having been dried outside, sitting on the chest of drawers. Everywhere was clean and tidy and definitely not how I'd left it. When I returned to the kitchen I noticed a vase of flowers in the middle of the table.

"That was Rachel," Alasdair said. "The flowers are from her garden. She cleaned up for you coming back and stocked up the fridge and freezer for you. Morag's contributed some cooked meals too. There's soup, lasagne, other stuff too."

"Right," I said. "Please say thank you to Morag, and Rachel too if you see her."

"Will do. Though you'll be able to thank Rachel yourself. She said she'd leave you in peace today, but I think she's planning to call in tomorrow."

# Chapter Fifty Eight

*Jack*

I didn't sleep well during my first night back on Skye. It wasn't that I didn't need to sleep. In spite of the naps I'd had in the car, I was exhausted by the journey and by the cumulative effect of so many bad nights. But the sleep I did get was as troubled as it had been in Edinburgh. And then there was the anticipation of seeing Rachel. It had hurt like hell sending her away and saying what I did, even though I'd thought I was doing it for the right reasons. But now, after talking to Maddie, I could see maybe I'd been wrong, but I hadn't a clue what to do about it.

Fed up with the torture of thinking, I took my breakfast coffee outside and sat on the bench. The early October sunshine was just warm enough in this sheltered spot and I closed my eyes and turned my face up to enjoy it. For now I just needed to get used to being back.

The sound of approaching footsteps made me open my eyes. I looked round and there she was.

"Hello, Jack," she said.

At first I could only look at her. She looked great, dressed in jeans, fleece and wellies and her hair clipped up. It felt so good to see her.

"Okay if I sit down?" she said and I noticed her cheeks were slightly flushed and she seemed a bit awkward.

"Yes, sorry." I shuffled along to make room for her.

"How are you?" she said. "You look tired."

"Yeah, didn't sleep too well – but I'm okay thanks. You?"

"I'm fine."

We both stared straight ahead.

Then we both spoke at once. "It's good to see you," I said.

"I missed you," she said.

We were now looking at each other. "You missed me?" I said.

Rachel frowned. "Don't sound so surprised. Of course I did. I wanted to stay longer while you were so ... while you were recovering."

"I'd no right to expect that. You have your own life to attend to."

"Yes, but I ..." Rachel gave a small shake of her head, her expression a mixture of exasperation and sadness. "No matter what you think, Jack, I *have* missed you. I was wondering if you'd like to come to Burnside later – for dinner. It would be good to catch up and besides, Bonnie's desperate to see you."

I couldn't help but smile. "Oh, she is, is she?"

"Yes, so you better turn up – six o'clock, okay?" She stood up.

"Okay," I said, still smiling as I watched her walk away.

I spent the rest of the morning and the early afternoon unpacking and doing some laundry. My injured arm remained weak and its range of movement was still limited. That, along with the fact my ribs resented most movement, meant it was a slow, tiring and painful process. But I kept going and I also made a start on the mail, and the bills, and all the other stuff that had accumulated in my absence.

When I'd had enough of all that, I went back outside to the garden for a proper look round. It was very tidy considering how long I'd been gone, and I guessed this was another debt I owed Alasdair. After I'd reacquainted myself with the full panorama of the view of the loch and the hills, I sat again for a while on the bench.

It was around four when I went back indoors. I stoked up the woodburner, poured myself a drink and sat watching the flames as I drank.

I don't remember exactly when I fell asleep. I remember finishing my whisky, and the room starting to get dark as I lay back on the sofa. Then I was back there, back in that filthy shack, alone, tied up and in pain. It was the same dream as before. A rat watched me from a corner. I struggled to free myself. It hurt. The rat came over to me and began gnawing at my arm. A figure loomed over me, laughing as he released more rats from his sleeves. They crawled all over me, biting and ripping at my flesh. I yelled in agony.

I felt a hand on my shoulder. This was it. I swiped at the hand, pushed it away. "No, no!" I shouted.

Then the hand was back, on my arm this time. "Jack, Jack, wake up."

I opened my eyes and looked into Rachel's. She'd put the lamp on and was kneeling on the floor beside me, one hand on my shoulder, the other stroking my hair. "Shh, now," she said. "You're okay. You were dreaming. It's okay."

At first all I could do was lie there, feeling Rachel's gentle touch and listening to her soft, reassuring voice. Eventually I sat up and Rachel came and sat beside me. I let her take me in her arms, aware I was now sobbing like a child.

She held me tight, rocking me slightly, stroking my back and whispering to me, "It's okay, Jack. You're safe. It's over. You're safe."

Gradually, the sobbing stopped. Rachel continued to hold me and I relaxed in her arms. Her chin rested on my shoulder and I felt the softness of her cheek against mine, smelt the faint lemon of her shampoo and the unique scent of her.

I don't know how long we stayed like that. Rachel pulled away first. I glanced at the clock. It was quarter-to-seven. She saw me looking. "Yeah," she said. "When you didn't arrive or answer your phone I decided to come and look for you."

She put her hand to my face, and wiped at my tears. Her

expression was full of care and concern. "Does that happen often?" she said. "The dreams and the shouting."

"Every time I fall asleep," I said.

"So you avoid going to sleep. No wonder you're so tired."

"I think I'm beyond tired," I said, leaning forward and putting my head in my hands. "I'm actually a bit of a mess to be honest."

"No, you're not," she said, smiling a soft sympathetic smile. "You're actually a complete mess."

I shivered. The stove's flames had died down and the room had got colder, but I don't think it was the fall in temperature that caused the shiver.

"Right," said Rachel, standing up. "Grab whatever you need for overnight, then get your jacket. You're staying at mine tonight."

I didn't need any persuading.

"Told you," Rachel said as we walked into her kitchen and Bonnie greeted me with much tail-wagging, circling and yelping.

I looked around as I made a big fuss of the ecstatic dog. It was beyond good to be back at Burnside. The kitchen was warm and there was a lovely smell coming from the Aga oven. Rachel told me to take a seat at the table while she took my bag upstairs. It felt so good to be there and to be about to share a meal with Rachel. I tried not to let myself think back or to look beyond those feel good moments.

Dinner was a delicious and hearty beef bourguignon casserole and there was an equally delicious and hearty bottle of red wine to go with it.

At first we ate and exchanged family news. And, as Rachel asked questions about Poppy, I was reminded of how much it meant to me that she and my granddaughter had formed such a strong bond. I appreciated it that she didn't ask anything about the kidnap or its aftermath as if she sensed that for me, now wasn't the time. And the more we talked, the more I was reminded of how much I loved her.

And, like earlier, I tried to focus only on the present and to savour it.

When we finished eating, my offer to help with the clearing up was rebuffed. So I remained in my seat at the table and distracted myself from staring at Rachel by fussing over Bonnie.

"Bonnie and I would like it if you'd join us on our evening walk," Rachel said, as she closed the dishwasher door.

I looked up to see her smiling at me. "Sounds good," I said.

When she saw me struggling to put my jacket on, she didn't fuss. She just gently supported my right arm and guided it into the sleeve without comment. My initial urge was to try to resist, but if she noticed she didn't react, and I was surprised as my reluctance quickly evaporated and I accepted her help.

It was a typical October night, already frosty, the sky clear of cloud and filled with stars. Rachel shone the torch to light our way and Bonnie walked on along the track ahead of us.

We hadn't gone very far when Rachel said, "I was at Morag's star party last weekend. Do you remember going to last year's one?" She glanced up at me and then looked away.

"Yes," I said, looking straight ahead. I did indeed. It was an annual event hosted by Morag and Alasdair to welcome back the darker nights complete with a bonfire and a ceilidh. It was after last year's party that Rachel and I had gone to bed together for the first time – and she'd been the instigator.

She slipped her hand in mine. "It was ... it was a good night wasn't it?"

I squeezed her hand. "It was," I said. "And you, do you remember?"

"Remember what?"

I stopped walking, and pointed at the sky. "Them," I said. "Do you remember the names of the constellations?"

"Oh," Rachel said, as she too looked up. She pointed and said, "Em, I think that's the Plough and ... and is that single star across from it, is that ... is that Polaris?"

"Right so far," I said. "What about that cluster of five just to the right?"

"Oh ... em ... no, can't remember, sorry."

"Cassiopeia," I said. With my good arm I gently turned her to face in the opposite direction and stood close behind her with my hand on her shoulder. "What about that square formation of four?"

She shook her head. "No."

I shook my head too. "Oh dear," I said laughing. "That's Pegasus. I can see we have some work to do."

She also laughed as she turned and reached for my hand once more. "I look forward to more lessons," she said as we walked on.

I smiled in the darkness, and for a brief moment I let myself hope.

# Chapter Fifty Nine

*Jack*

When we got back to Burnside, Rachel made us both some tea. We drank it sitting side by side on the sofa, Bonnie snoozing at our feet. It was almost like it had been before. Almost. But I knew I had to be realistic. I sighed with frustration.

"Tired?" Rachel said, as she stood up. "You go on up. I put you in the bigger of the spare rooms – thought you'd prefer the one with the double bed."

I stood up too. "I should go home," I said. "This has been great – the meal and everything. It was very kind of you. But there's no need for me to stay. I—"

"There's every need. I don't think you should be on your own at the moment, Jack. "

"I'll be fine, honestly I—"

"Please, Jack, let me do this." Rachel put her hands on my arms. "Let me look after you. No agenda ... one friend helping another."

Her eyes looked into mine and her expression was so tender, I couldn't help but put my hand to her face. "Okay," I said, my voice only just managing. I cleared my throat. "Okay, thank you. I'll stay."

As had become usual, I fought sleep at first. But exhaustion won and it wasn't long before the dreams started. The rats, the pain and the fear were all there and this time they were accompanied by a man who lurked in the corner and whose face I couldn't see. He laughed before coming towards me and pointing a gun at my head. I struggled to break free of the ropes tying me down. I shouted at him not to shoot. I felt his hand on me and struggled to move away.

I heard a voice, "It's just a dream. You're okay. Jack, you're okay. You're safe." Again I felt a hand, but its touch was gentle as it stroked my face and my hair. I opened my eyes. Rachel was leaning over me. She switched on the bedside lamp before climbing onto the bed and lying beside me. She lay on top of the duvet and continued to stroke my hair and to whisper that I was safe.

It was getting light when I next woke. Rachel was asleep beside me, still on top of the duvet but covered by a blanket. She lay on her side facing me, one arm outstretched protectively across my chest. To say I was moved doesn't begin to describe how I felt as I looked her. I was flooded with love for my beautiful, loyal, strong Rachel. Except she wasn't mine – not anymore – and that was all down to me.

I was about to give myself a hard time when Rachel woke up. She looked at me and smiled. "How are you?" she asked. "Did you get some sleep?"

"I'm all right," I said. "And yes, I did sleep – thanks to you."

"Good," she said, as she threw back the blanket and got up. "I'm on sheep checking duties this morning and I've got the hens to feed. So you relax and I'll get us breakfast when I get back."

But I couldn't relax. My arm was stiff and sore as was usual first thing and my ribs ached too. However it wasn't only physical pain that I was suffering from. I could feel my anxiety building, and this, along with the turmoil of my feelings for Rachel, meant I had to get moving, had to distract myself.

So as soon as I heard Rachel calling Bonnie and the back door closing behind them I got up. Showering and dressing were still a slow process but I got there eventually. I resisted the urge

*Settlement*

to take any painkillers, but I did put my arm in the sling.

When I got down to the kitchen I decided to make a start on breakfast. Progress was slow with only one functioning arm but by the time Rachel and Bonnie returned, the teapot was ready to be filled, the bread was in the toaster and the eggs just needed to be put in the boiling water.

"Oh my," Rachel said as she came into the kitchen and saw what I'd been up to. "This is a nice surprise."

"Take a seat," I said. "It'll only be a few minutes."

"Sure you don't need any help?" Rachel asked.

"No, I'm fine," I said, hoping I sounded convincing. The truth was I was struggling a bit with the pain, but I didn't want Rachel to think I was completely helpless physically, as well as being an emotional wreck. I didn't look at her as I got on with the food, but I was acutely aware of her presence as she sat at the table.

It wasn't long before everything was ready. I'd managed to get it all to the table without groaning out loud, but as I sat down my damaged ribs complained so forcefully that I couldn't help gasping.

Rachel immediately got to her feet. "Are you okay?" she said, as she reached her hand out to me, her expression as full of tenderness and concern as it had been the night before. And I couldn't handle it.

"It's nothing!" I snapped. "Sit down. Get your breakfast." I knew I'd spoken sharply, knew she didn't deserve to be the recipient of my bad temper. And I hated seeing her hurt look as she backed off.

"Sorry," she said.

"No, I'm sorry," I said, looking at her across the table, my gut a foul mix of guilt, shame and self-pity. "You didn't deserve that. You've been nothing but kind to me, and believe it or not I am grateful."

Rachel bit her lip. Then I was horrified to see tears in her eyes.

"Christ, Rachel. Don't, please don't. I'm not worth it."

"But that's the point. To me you are worth it," she said, tears now running freely down her face. She wiped at the tears with the back of her hand and frowned at me for a moment, looked at me as if she was weighing something up. Then her expression cleared. "It's actually quite simple," she said. "So here's what we're going to do. We're going to eat this lovely breakfast and then we're going to talk. Okay?"

"Do I have a choice?" I asked.

"No, you don't. Now eat up."

# Chapter Sixty

*Jack*

"Would you like to go for a walk?" Rachel said, as she finished clearing the breakfast things.

"That would be good," I replied, thinking it might be less intense if we did that, and there would be distractions along the way if the talking got too difficult.

"So long as you don't think you can use the walk to avoid talking," Rachel said with a knowing smile and a raised eyebrow.

"Ah, you read my mind there," I said. I couldn't help laughing, but I gave a little gasp as my ribs objected.

"You sure you're up to walking?" Rachel said.

"Absolutely. The pain is lessening overall, but first thing in the morning's still bad. Walking will ease it off."

It was a relatively mild day for October despite the frost of the night before. The wind was light, and the sky was clear with only the odd patch of high cloud. Bonnie walked ahead us as we headed for Halladale beach. We followed the path down past the edge of the dunes to the beach's grassy border. We walked in silence, but it was an easy silence, and I began to wonder if Rachel had changed her mind about us having a serious talk. She hadn't.

We'd made our way onto the shingle. Bonnie made straight for the sea and ran in and out of the small waves as they made their way ashore.

Rachel and I also headed towards the sea, and as we walked along close to the water's edge, she said, "How did we come to be here, Jack?"

"Here?" I said, knowing perfectly well she wasn't referring to the beach, but unsure how to respond to the question's true meaning.

"Yes, here, where even our friendship seems to be in doubt."

"Is it? Is that what you think?"

"What else am I supposed to think? You sent me away from the hospital, dismissed me like I was some well-meaning acquaintance who'd done their duty by visiting you, but was no longer needed or wanted."

"No, no, that wasn't it. That wasn't it at all. I didn't want you to go ... not really ... it hurt like hell sending you away like that. When you said you'd go and leave me in peace, I called after you, said I didn't think I'd ever be at peace again – but it was how it had to be. Part of me ... the irrational part ... hoped you'd turn back."

"Yeah, I knew you said something, but I didn't hear what it was. I was so upset, I had to keep walking, had to get away."

"Sorry, but I believed it was for the best."

"Why? Had you come to dislike me so much?"

"What? No! It was because of the guilt ... the guilt I felt for putting you in danger."

"In danger?"

"Gray – the guy who – who tried to kill me. He threatened you."

Rachel stopped abruptly, bringing me to a halt too. "Threatened me? How?"

So, as we walked on, and with Bonnie now running in circles around us, I explained. I explained about Gray tracking me down, having me watched, and about the photos that had been taken on the day of Sophie's wedding. I told her how Gray had made it clear he would have used her to get to me if necessary, and that he'd also used his knowledge of her and Bridget's existence and whereabouts as a deterrent to me trying to escape. I felt quite sick as I recalled the fear Gray's threats had induced in me.

Rachel listened without interrupting and she kept a firm grip on my hand while I spoke. When I finished, she said, "Oh, Jack, how awful for you. And I get why you felt guilty – but it was misplaced. Gray was the bad guy, not you." She looked at me, must have seen the sweat on my forehead, and felt me shaking. "Come on," she said, "That's enough for now. Time we went back." She whistled for Bonnie to join us as we turned around.

Rachel did most of the talking on the walk back. She updated me on what had been happening on the croft, told me about the newly acquired cows and about Steven and Sophie's plans to develop things further. She also mentioned Sophie's plans to put forward her ideas for a radio series about refugees that would incorporate Rachel's mother's story. And simply listening to her voice, the soft tones and the rhythm of her accent, combined with her obvious enthusiasm for what she was telling me was enough to restore my equilibrium.

By the time we got back to Burnside, Rachel had moved on to tell me about the coming launch of *Jason Jumps Over the Moon*. And, as soon as we got into the kitchen she put the kettle on and said, "I've just received a couple of copies. We could take our coffee through to the study and I'll show you them if you like."

"Impressive," I said, when I'd finished reading. Rachel had cleared the old armchair in the corner for me to sit on. She sat at her cluttered desk and had swung the office chair round so she was facing me. "I thought Seamus was quite a character, but he's got nothing on Jason," I said, smiling at her. "I think he's my new favourite."

She laughed.

"What's funny?" I said.

"That's exactly what someone else said, someone whose tastes are obviously similar to yours." Her smile had a sly edge to it.

"Who was that?"

"Eitan," she said, her smile now a mix of mischief and teasing. "I showed him an earlier proof when he was here. He said the same as you."

"Ah," I said. "I see." I managed to smile. The old jealousy was still there, but for some reason, it wasn't so strong. I looked around, searching for a way to change the subject, and I spotted a painting propped against the far wall. "That's nice," I said, pointing at it. "The colour's great. Is it one of the Skye lochs?"

Rachel laughed again, and her smile was now positively gleeful with a bit of wicked mixed in.

"No," I said as I realised. "Please, don't tell me—"

"Eitan painted it," she said, not even trying to hide her amusement. "It's just back from the framer. It's the Sea of Galilee. He sent me it as a gift."

"That was generous of him," I said.

"Yes, he remembered I'd admired it when I saw it at his house, said it … it was like …" Her smile was gone now, replaced by a look of embarrassment.

"Like what?" I said.

She moved stuff around on her desk, looking for something. "Here," she said, passing me a card. "Here's what he said."

I read it, read how the beautiful sea reminded Eitan of Rachel, and how he'd always love her. I stared at it, not trusting myself to speak, horrified to realise I was close to tears.

"He sums you up perfectly," I stuttered. "And he says he loves you." I let the card drop and pressed my fingers to my eyes.

Rachel was beside me in an instant. She knelt down and gently took hold of my hands. "Oh, Jack," she said. "I'm sorry. I didn't show you the card to upset you. It was just I was too embarrassed to quote the nice things he said out loud. I thought you'd laugh, have some witty put down for me and for him."

"Yeah, I seem to be all out of wit. Besides, what he said about you is true … and I can't blame the guy for loving you."

"It's not … he doesn't—"

"You don't need to explain," I said, as I freed my hands from hers and stood up. She got to her feet too. She was standing very close to me. I breathed in the scent of her, the mix of fresh air and soap and *her*. I touched her face for a brief tortured moment, noticed that yet again I'd made her sad. "But now I should go," I said. "I've taken up enough of your time and I know you have work to do."

"Please, don't go." Rachel reached for my hand, but I moved away.

"You don't owe me anything, Rachel, not your time or your loyalty. It was me who messed us up and I have to live with that. You deserve better ... someone like Eitan who appreciates you."

"But I don't want—"

"I'm going home. This is all ... being with you ... it's too hard. I need some time alone. I'll call you."

# Chapter Sixty One

*Jack*

I knew I was being an idiot. In the past, whenever things got difficult in my personal life, I'd always run away. But this was Rachel. Rachel, who in spite of everything, still wanted to be friends. Rachel who believed we could sort everything out by talking. Rachel who I loved so very much. Why couldn't I stay and fix things between us?

I didn't have an answer other than the fact I was an idiot. That and the feeling that I was completely and utterly broken and didn't know how to even begin to put myself back together again. I'd been lying, not only to Maddie and the others who'd asked, but also to myself. Tommy Gray's death had not sorted out my mental health problems. Far from it. My body may have been healing, but my mind was in a bad way.

So I put up the barricades – physical and emotional. I locked the door, I didn't go out and I ignored my phone.

I did, however, open the door to Alasdair. It was the day after I'd come back from Burnside. I was in the kitchen and saw him approaching. I knew he'd seen me too, but I hoped that when he tried the door and found it locked, he'd go. But this was Alasdair and his knock was loud and persistent.

"Not going to invite me in?" he said as he stood on the doorstep.

"No," I said. "I don't feel like talking."

"Fair enough. Been speaking to Rachel. She told me about your nightmares and some of the other stuff you're going through. She's worried about you. So am I."

"No need," I said.

"I disagree, but I respect your right to privacy, so I'll go." He turned to leave, but then turned back. "But only on one condition. You text me every day before lunch-time and you let me know you're okay. If I don't hear from you I reserve the right to break down your door and call whatever emergency service may be required. Agreed?"

"Agreed," I said. I was touched by his concern, and I reckoned I could manage a daily text if that was all it took to be left alone.

"And if you need anything – anything at all you call me," he said. "Understood?"

"Understood," I said.

At first, most of my days and nights were spent sitting on the sofa, the TV on in the background. I was terrified of sleep, knowing there would be the inevitable night terrors that would reduce me to a screaming weeping wreck.

And the only thing worse than the nightly episodes were the daytime flashbacks. These took the form of hallucinations where I was either back with Gray in that stinking shack – or worse still – he'd appear to be in the room with me at home in Dunhalla. They caught me unawares, breaking through without warning or any specific trigger, but I noticed it was mostly when my mind wasn't engaged in any other activity.

I ate when I could be bothered, relying almost completely on the stock of cooked food Rachel and Morag had provided, especially after the fresh stuff ran out. And I couldn't see the point in taking a shower. Oh yes, I was in a bad way.

It was Steven who successfully broke through my defences. It must have been about a week since I'd gone into hiding. I'd summoned up the energy to take some rubbish out to the bin, and I'd forgotten to lock the back door when I came back inside. It was early afternoon. I was in the living-room, adrift in a light sleep on the sofa when Steven did that Skye thing of knocking and walking in. The sudden sound of the knock triggered my panic. And, for the second time, Steven witnessed me having a meltdown.

His voice quiet, calm and steady, reached me through the terror and dizziness. His hands were on my shoulders. At first I tried to push him away, but then his words got through to me. "Breathe, Jack, in through your nose, out through your mouth, long slow breaths. Go with me, follow the count. In for five, out for five." Gradually my heart stopped racing and my breath steadied. "Good," Steven said as he sat down on one of the armchairs. "So, things not going so well?"

"Not really, no," I said. "I thought I'd kicked all this nonsense into touch. I was free of it for a while there but—"

"But after everything you've recently been through it's back with a vengeance."

I nodded.

"What did you think was happening – just now – when I came in?" Again Steven's voice was calm and steady.

"I don't know ... not exactly ... a gunshot ... danger?"

"And what actually happened?"

"You came in and I lost it."

"So, no threat, no actual danger."

"Yeah."

"Like I said to you that time in the barn, I'm no therapist, but that's the kind of thing you should maybe start doing. Start retraining your brain to stop associating every unexpected noise with danger."

"You sound like a therapist," I said, managing a smile. "How much do you charge?"

Steven smiled back. "You know what I'm going to say – you do need to see a real one. Didn't the medics in Edinburgh suggest it – or your GP even?"

"No, they didn't. But that would be because I assured the doctors down south I was fine – and I haven't been to my GP since I got back, though they have left a couple of messages on the landline."

Steven raised his eyebrows. "I know it's hard – believe me I do. Admitting that you're hurting, that you're troubled by shame or guilt or fear, it *is* hard but it's not a sign of weakness."

"No?" I said.

"No, weakness is not handling it, not doing something about it. The way Sophie described it to me is that letting others see you as vulnerable, see you warts and all, that's what's truly brave."

It was my turn to raise an eyebrow.

"I know," he said. "Easier said than done. Look, why don't you take the first step while I go and make us a coffee. Phone the GP, fix up an appointment." He passed me my phone and left the room.

I did as I was told. It was easier than arguing. Steven had experience and credibility, there was no getting round it. Besides, I knew he was right.

"No milk, I'm afraid," Steven said, when he returned with our coffee. "And you've no clean mugs left. I had to wash these two."

"Right, thanks," I said.

"Things *have* been getting on top of you, haven't they?"

"You think?" I said.

"So, doctor's appointment made?"

"Yes, tomorrow morning."

"I'm happy to drive you," Steven said. "Could take you to the Co-op too – get you stocked up with some groceries."

"Thanks, but I've already phoned Alasdair. He's going to give me a lift."

"Good," Steven said. "Appointment made and asking for help, that's two significant steps taken already."

"You sure you're not some kind of counsellor?" I said.

Steven shook his head and smiled. "Just been there myself."

"Well, thank you. Thanks for coming round and for ... for

what you said. Mind you, you were lucky you got in. I've been keeping the door locked."

"Yeah, I was surprised when I was able to walk in. Alasdair had warned me to knock loudly and keep at it. But I thought I'd give the door a try anyway."

"Ah, Alasdair," I said. "Was he behind this – you coming here today?"

"Not exactly, but he heard I was planning to visit and gave me the advice about gaining entry." Steven grinned. "Oh, that reminds me – the reason I came round – or at least the pretext." He picked something up off the floor, something I assume he'd discarded when he was helping me get a grip. "Rachel gave me this. She was keen for you to send it to Poppy." He passed me a copy of *Jason Jumps Over the Moon*.

As well as signing the book, Rachel had also written a message to my granddaughter. It said,

*To Poppy, Jason and I hope you enjoy this book and that like Jason you too never stop chasing your dreams. With all my love Rachel xxx*

It was too much, too kind, and so typically Rachel, that I had to blink hard to hold back the tears.

"She's worried sick about you, Jack," Steven said. "She's finding it hard that you don't want to see her, but she's doing her best to respect your wishes."

"It's not ... it's not that I don't *want* to see her. It's just ... it's just—"

"You feel daunted merely thinking about where to start putting things right. And even if you did feel up to it, you don't reckon you're worthy of her, you feel she's had enough suffering in her life without you adding to it. But apart from all that you still love her and seeing her simply hurts too much. Am I close?"

"Yeah, that about sums it up," I said. "The last thing she needs is some needy, hopeless case. Someone who can't keep himself or those close to him safe, someone as messed up as me."

"Give her some credit, Jack. Rachel knows what it's like to

have to recover from trauma. It was the third anniversary of Finlay's death last week and she was amazing, offering support to Sophie even though she must have been suffering so much herself. But I know she's had to work hard to get to where she is now emotionally."

"I didn't know about the anniversary," I said. "Sort of confirms how useless I am to her."

"She doesn't need you to be strong on her behalf, she doesn't need some manly protector. What she needs from you is honesty, honesty about your vulnerability and how you truly feel. She needs her friend and lover back."

"Even if that's true. I don't know where to start."

"Start small. Maybe take a shower." Steven smiled.

"Ouch," I said. "That bad, is it?"

"Only just noticeable. But seriously, begin by starting to sort yourself out. Slow and steady is the way to go."

"Yeah, I'm not ready to see her yet."

"You couldn't even if you wanted to. She's away for the next couple of weeks. Book launches for *Jason* in Edinburgh, Glasgow, Aberdeen and Inverness – to name just some of the places."

"I didn't know about that either," I said.

"Don't look so gutted. Use her absence to begin your recovery. You can start by getting out of this place for a wee while. Come and have dinner with us this evening – after you've had that shower, of course."

# Chapter Sixty Two

*Jack*

Steven's visit finally gave me the kick up the backside I needed. I began following his advice immediately and had that much needed shower. I also had a shave – and then I texted Morag.

She appeared in the kitchen within ten minutes of receiving my message. "Hello, you," she said, holding her arms out towards me. We hugged each other. "How are you?" she said, as she let me go.

"I think, thanks to Steven, I might have turned a corner," I said.

"We hoped he'd get through to you."

"Oh, you did, did you? And who exactly is *we*?"

"All of us – your friends, the people who care about you – me, Alasdair, Steven, Sophie, the other residents of Halladale – Rachel." She looked me in the eye as she said Rachel's name.

"Right, I see."

"This is Skye, Jack. We do community support, we look out for our neighbours."

"I know – and it's a good thing, just difficult for a privacy obsessed townie like me to get used to."

Morag frowned. "Privacy?" she said. She shook her head. "No, no idea what that means." She grinned at me and then reached into her pocket. She took out a set of hair clippers. "So, take a seat and we'll get started," she said.

"I hope you didn't mind me texting – asking you to do this," I said, as she began to give my hair a much-needed trim. "Long hair looks good on Steven, but I look like Wurzel Gummidge's older, uglier brother. And I remembered Alasdair saying you cut his hair."

Morag laughed. "I can't do much about the old and ugly, but I can at least make you look tidy. And no, I don't mind at all."

To her credit, Morag kept the conversation light as she worked on making me presentable. She asked after Poppy and told me a bit about her own grandchildren. It was only as she was preparing to leave that she ventured into more serious matters. "I'm so sorry about all the horrible things that happened to you and I'm delighted you're starting to move forward, because believe it or not, you ugly old wurzel, I care about you."

I didn't bother hiding the tears in my eyes. "And I care about you too, you interfering old bag."

Morag tried and failed to look outraged, then, as she laughed and hugged me again she said, "Yes, and you'd do well to remember that this interfering old bag will be watching."

"Message received," I said, hugging her back.

My evening with Steven, Sophie and Miriam was a tonic. I was given a tour of the new house and then I played with Miriam while her parents cooked our meal. I soon had the wee one giggling as I played peek-a-boo with her. She also enjoyed my reading of a picture book version of *Old Macdonald Had a Farm* complete with my version of the animal noises. In fact her parents declared themselves so impressed with my child-minding skills that they now knew where to come if they ever needed a nanny.

Over dinner I heard more about the developments on Burnside croft and Sophie told me about the progress she was making with her ideas for her refugee series. It was strange to be there without Rachel – and I felt her absence keenly. But Sophie and Steven made me feel so welcome that I managed to keep my focus on the here and now, and I even managed to relax and, yes, enjoy myself.

I also got a few uninterrupted hours of sleep that night. And even although it was only a few hours and I did have one bad episode, it was an improvement.

Alasdair arrived promptly the next morning. He displayed his usual empathy and wisdom and seemed to sense how nervous I was feeling about seeing the doctor. So it was Cuillin FM on the car radio, and only minimal chat as he drove me to the surgery.

Afterwards however, when I returned to the car, he did venture to ask how it had gone.

"It was actually okay," I said. "Nice young guy, Dr Matheson, not met him before, seems to know his stuff."

"Oh aye, he's new, local lad though, so bound to be good," Alasdair said, smiling as we drove away from the medical centre and headed for the Co-op. "So he's sorted you out then?"

"Yep. He's happy with how everything's healing. He seemed impressed with the strength and movement I've regained in my arm and shoulder and the ribs seem to be doing okay too. Not allowed to drive just yet though."

"And the other stuff?"

"Ah, yes, the other stuff," I said.

"You told him?"

"He asked me directly if I was having any symptoms – you know – of emotional or mental stress as a result of the assault. So I told him – told him it all – all the bad stuff to do with the shooting of my colleague, and then the more recent stuff."

"And?"

"And he surprised me."

"In what way?"

"With his approach. He listened to what I was saying about not wanting to lie on some psychiatrist's couch and not wanting to take mind-altering drugs – and then he put me straight."

"He did, did he?" Alasdair laughed. "And how did he do that?"

"He asked me if I'd felt the same reluctance to accept the recommended treatment when I had my heart operation, or when I had the operations to remove the bullet from my chest and to fix my arm, or when I was referred to physiotherapy. And when I said I hadn't, the way was clear for him to win his argument."

"And what was his argument?"

"That I'd presumably viewed those other treatments as life-saving or improving my quality of life. I agreed I had. So he then said that what he was going to recommend would also improve my quality of life and will prevent my symptoms becoming worse or maybe even life-threatening."

"Life-threatening?"

"Yes, it seems not only do I have PTSD, but I'm also displaying some signs of mild depression. And he pointed out that untreated mild depression could all too easily become severe and yes, life-threatening."

"So what has he prescribed?" Alasdair asked as we approached the supermarket car park.

"Anti-depressants, ones that are good for anxiety symptoms, but just a low dose and for the short term, on condition I agree to see the Community Psychiatric Nurse for ten weekly sessions of something called Cognitive Behavioural Therapy."

"And you agreed?"

"Dr Matheson is very persuasive," I said. "He assured me it will help me cope with the flashbacks and the panic attacks, should sort out the nightmares too. But he also said it will help me come to terms with the guilt I've been feeling."

"So, no-brainer, then," Alasdair said as we drew up into a parking space.

"And he gave me this," I said taking a leaflet from my pocket. I handed it to Alasdair.

"*Walk the Talk with Colin Crichton*," Alasdair said, reading from the cover of the leaflet.

"Yeah, it's a new venture based here on Skye. It's a guy Dr Matheson knows, he's ex-military but he's retrained as a psychotherapist and has now set up a practice. But the doc says it's therapy with a difference and there isn't a couch in sight."

"So I see," Alasdair said. "Sounds like your sort of thing." He read some more. "*Enjoy the outdoors, therapeutic walks from 5K to all-day treks. One-to-one guided walks with Colin. Talk while you walk. Improve your mental health and wellbeing while on the move.*"

"The doctor said he'd refer me if I wanted. It's private, not NHS, but the fees seem reasonable. And you're right it does sound like my kind of thing."

"So are you going for it?"

"I reckon it's worth a try," I said.

"Good for you. I admire you, you know."

"No, I didn't know, and I can't think why."

"You're a brave man. Not only for being a policeman and putting yourself in harm's way because of that, but also for coming through heart surgery and having the guts to retire afterwards and make a fresh start here. I considered moving from Skye in the past, even if only to have a few years living somewhere else, but I was always too scared to leave home."

"I don't believe you've stayed out of fear. I reckon it's more you know you'll not find anywhere better than here. But thanks for your kind words ... means a lot."

"Well, I'm glad you finally accept Skye's the best place to be and I hope that means you're staying." Alasdair looked at me, eyebrows raised.

"Looks like it," I said.

"But what I said, Jack, it wasn't just empty words. I value our friendship, and I mean it, I do admire you. Coming back from your injuries, admitting you need help to get fully better – makes you a hero in my book."

"Blimey," I said, grinning at him. "Don't know what to say. I think I prefer it when you're nagging me. Now are we going to the shop or not?"

# Chapter Sixty Three

*Jack*

When Alasdair dropped me back home, I tried to thank him, not just for the lift but for all his support. But he wasn't having any of it.

"No need for thanks. Just get better. I need my beer buddy back," he said.

I smiled at him. "I'll keep that in mind if my motivation flags," I said.

"And remember if you need anything, lifts or whatever, call on Team Jack."

"Team Jack?" I said.

"Aye, good isn't it?" Alasdair beamed. "Rachel gave us the name – me, Morag, Steven and Sophie. After you told her you didn't want her help, she asked us to intervene."

After I'd put the shopping away, I decided it was about time I looked at the unread texts that had arrived on my phone over the previous week. There were all the ones from Alasdair acknowledging my daily check-ins, there was one from Steven saying not to hesitate if I'd like to talk, and there were several from Maddie pleading with me to get in touch. She'd also left a couple of voicemails too.

And there was one text from Rachel. It said,
*I miss you. Please get in touch when you're ready.*

I reread it several times – and had to fight back the tears.

When I'd recovered a bit of control, I called Maddie. She let me apologise to the point of grovelling before she started laughing.

"You can stop now," she said. "It's great to hear from you at last. How are you? How did you get on with the doctor?"

"Eh, how did you know I'd been to see the doctor?"

"Rachel let me know."

"Rachel? How did she—"

"When I couldn't get hold of you, I contacted Rachel. She told me how things were – told me about the Team Jack plan – and then when Steven reported back to her, she let me know."

For a moment I was speechless as feelings of surprise, annoyance, gratitude and humility all passed through me.

"You still there, Dad?"

"Yeah, still here. Just trying to figure out how I feel about all the subterfuge and this Team Jack thing."

"It's only because we care about you – even if you don't deserve it." I could hear the smile in her voice as she said this.

But her amusement changed to shock when I admitted the extent to which I'd been suffering. And she was more than a little cross that I hadn't been honest with her before. But she did seem pleasantly surprised – and maybe even a bit impressed – when I told her about the treatment plan I'd agreed to.

I also apologised to her for missing Poppy's recent seventh birthday and promised I'd make it up to her.

"Don't worry about it," she said. "I guessed you wouldn't be thinking about shopping so I took the liberty of getting her more Lego – allegedly from you – which she loved. And she happily accepted that there was no card from you because, obviously, you can't write with your broken arm. You can thank me now and pay me back later." Again I could hear Maddie smiling.

"Thank you," I said. "That was … that was good of you." I cleared my throat, emotion starting to get the better of me once more as I thought how I didn't deserve such a wonderful daughter. "I did manage to post something off to Poppy today though," I said, and I went on to explain about the copy of Rachel's new book.

"That's lovely," Maddie said. "We'll be seeing Rachel next week actually – on a couple of occasions."

"Oh, how's that?"

"She invited us along to a book launch event she's doing in a bookshop in Edinburgh on Saturday. Poppy was so excited she took the invitation into school to show to her class, and her teacher asked her if she thought Rachel might be able to come and do a talk at the school. So Poppy called Rachel and she agreed. She'll be visiting Primary Three next week and the parents are invited along too."

Yet again, I was moved by Rachel's amazing thoughtfulness and by the strength of the bond she had with my granddaughter.

It was later that evening that I finally psyched myself up to text Rachel. I couldn't think of what to say. Everything I came up with sounded either needy or forced. So in the end I just wrote,

*Team Jack?* and added a smiley face.

It was a very long thirty minutes before her reply came.

*Rumbled! Guilty as charged. It was me who set up the team. Done with the best intentions.* She also added a smiley face.

I replied immediately,

*Thank you.* This time I added three kisses.

A couple of minutes later my phone rang. It was Rachel.

A powerful mix of hope, anticipation and dread made my heart hammer and my hands shake as I answered. "Rachel," I said.

"Hello, you," she said.

"It's good to hear you."

"Is it?" she asked. I didn't detect any sarcasm in her voice. She sounded more surprised than anything.

"It is. It's very good," I said. "How are you? Where are you? I mean I know you're doing a book tour, but I'm not sure of the itinerary." I was aware I was speaking too fast and that I sounded nervous.

"I'm fine, thanks," she said. "Yesterday I was in Ullapool, and today and tomorrow I'm in Inverness and Morayshire, then it's three days each in the Aberdeen area, followed by Edinburgh along with the Lothians and Borders, and finally Glasgow."

"Sounds busy," I said.

"It is, but I enjoy it – and I get the two Sundays off."

"Right," I said. "I hope it all goes well. And thanks for the book you gave Poppy, and for inviting her to one of your events, and for agreeing to visit her school. I … I really appreciate it and … and how much of an effort you make on her behalf."

"It doesn't require much effort. She's a lovely wee girl and I'm very fond of her."

"Good … that's good," I said. "So, I … that is I … I wanted to … to say…" I stopped. There was so much to say, I didn't know where to start.

"It's okay, Jack," she said. "There are things we both still need to say, but let's keep all that for when I get back. We can talk then. If you'd like to, that is."

"I'd like to," I said, allowing myself a smile and a sigh of relief.

"Great," she said, and I think I detected relief on her part too. "So, I hear you've been to the doctor and you're going to be getting some help."

"Team Jack reported back did they?" I was smiling even more now and hoped she'd know that.

She laughed. "They did," she said.

"Well, you were correctly informed. I've been to the doctor and I am getting help with … with everything."

"I'm glad to hear it and I look forward to hearing more about it when I see you," she said. "Until then, keep in touch, just by text if that's easier. But now I better go. And, Jack?"

"Yes?"

"Thanks for contacting me. I wasn't at all sure you would."

# Chapter Sixty Four

*Jack*

The fact I was now impatient to see Rachel was itself a sign of the progress I'd made in the couple of days since I'd seen Steven. But I wasn't under any illusions. I knew I had a long way to go until I was fully recovered. And, despite my impatience, I was also glad I still had a couple of weeks to prepare for Rachel's return.

It was two weeks I was determined to put to good use. I tidied up the house and tried to get myself into some sort of routine. It was hard having to rely on other people for lifts, but the desire to get my independence back acted as an excellent motivator for me to apply myself to my recovery.

I kept up with my physio exercises, and I also got into a routine of taking a daily walk. Sometimes I borrowed Bonnie – if she wasn't on sheepdog duties with Steven – and having her with me gave me a much-needed link to Rachel.

I even got the camera out and took some photos including some night sky ones. This prompted me to contact Richard Macdonald and update him on my progress. He was as supportive as he'd been all along. He shared with me that he had suffered from depression in the past, and he assured me he was happy to wait until I was ready before beginning to work with him. We pencilled in a date in January for a two-night shoot which he said he'd cover if I was unable to.

An additional benefit of my daily walks, over and above

getting me mobile and out of the house, was that I met many of my neighbours, people I'd mainly only known by sight before. They all stopped to chat and said how awful it was what had happened to me, and how they wished me well. That was touching enough, but I also got used to finding all sorts of thoughtful gifts left on my doorstep. Gifts that included biscuits, a pot plant, flowers, a book on local history and even a bottle of whisky. Then when I knocked on these gift givers' doors to thank them, I was more often than not invited in for a cup of tea.

One day when the number of flowers I'd been given was greater than the capacity of my one vase, I asked Alasdair to do me yet another favour. He was happy to oblige and drove me to the cemetery near the north end of Waternish where Rachel's son was buried. I laid my surplus flowers on Finlay's grave and took a minute to pay my respects. I also apologised to him for not being there for his mother on his recent anniversary – and I promised him I was going to try to be a better friend to her.

And most significantly, I started my weekly sessions with Penny Macdougall, the Community Psychiatric Nurse, or CPN as she referred to herself. And I also did my first *Walk the Talk* outing with Colin Crichton.

Penny reminded me of Lauren the physiotherapist. She was older than Lauren, probably in her fifties, but she had the same high expectations of success, and she commanded my respect and, mostly, willing co-operation. She was direct but compassionate, and her calm professional approach was exactly what I needed.

As Morag drove me to the medical centre for the first appointment, I'd been so nervous I'd almost asked her to turn back. But I was probably more nervous of issuing such a request to Morag so I went through with it. I was glad I did. I quickly trusted Penny, and I soon found myself saying things I'd never said to anyone, things I hadn't even said to myself, things about my personal life as well as what I'd been through with the Grays. I felt ridiculously pleased when she praised me for my honesty, and after only two sessions, I found I was already following her suggested ways of coping when any of my PTSD symptoms occurred.

I was similarly impressed by Colin. When he called me to arrange our first walk, and I told him I wasn't allowed to drive yet, he said he'd come to me. So walk one was on Halladale beach and then on inland through the local forestry plantation. The way was relatively easy and was ideal for a first, getting-to-know-you session.

There was no jargon or gimmicks from Colin. And though he was ex-military there was no macho posturing either, and he came across as both easy-going, but also astute. On the surface, because we were walking, the talking appeared less intense and the questions less probing than with Penny. But even though it was my first time out, I found myself opening up as I talked with him. He'd got some background in the referral letter from my doctor, but he wanted me to tell him in my own words why I'd asked to be referred and what I was hoping to get out of our walks.

He was similar to Penny in the way he responded to what I told him about the difficult emotions and terrifying episodes I'd been experiencing. He didn't appear shocked and he offered calm and reasonable insights and advice. But unlike with Penny it wasn't all talk.

We walked and part of the time, yes, we talked – but some of the time, the talking stopped and Colin gave me time to think as we progressed along our route.

We also took time to stand and stare, whether it was to watch a flock of gannets following a fishing boat, or observe a hen-harrier hovering above a field, or simply to take in the view – and this gave me further time for reflection. And after that first outing, I found I was definitely looking forward to more.

I knew I wasn't going to be instantly cured and, during those two weeks, I still experienced episodes of crippling anxiety, and bouts of taunting guilt and shame. But I did notice I was beginning to deal with them better. My sleep also improved a little. I had made a start.

I received photos from Maddie of Rachel's Edinburgh bookshop event, and some that had been taken at the visit to Poppy's school too. I printed out my favourite and put it on the fridge door. It showed Rachel and Poppy holding a copy of the new book between them and both of them smiling broadly while giving the thumbs-up sign. I also heard from Poppy – via a video phone call – that both events had been brilliant.

And, I kept in contact with Rachel. We sent each other regular texts. There was nothing deep, just updates on what we planned to be doing on a particular day – or how our day had gone. But we were in touch. Another start had been made.

# Chapter Sixty Five

*Jack*

When I woke on that Friday morning, my first thought was that this was the day Rachel would be coming home. My second thought was that I mustn't expect too much. After all I might not even see her that day. She'd be tired after the drive from Glasgow and her first priority would be to see her family. And my third thought was it was good I had plenty to keep me occupied throughout the day.

Colin arrived at nine o'clock as arranged, and we drove south to Glen Brittle. We needed our walking boots and waterproofs as squally showers were forecast. But although it did rain during our two-hour trek it didn't spoil my enjoyment. We followed the path that runs the length of Loch Brittle and made for its southern end at Loch Aird. It wasn't a route I'd walked before so I was especially impressed by what we saw. The ground either side of the cliff-top path was covered in heather and ferns. Lots of little birds which Colin informed me were wheatears flitted around us and black-headed gulls sat on the rocks far below us. I was glad I'd brought my camera as, after climbing steadily for some time, we gained a view over to the west of the islands of Rhum and Canna. I also managed to get a shot of a kestrel that we inadvertently startled as we walked by.

Of course it wasn't all about the walk. There was talk too, but as on the first occasion, I found I was comfortable with Colin's approach. I even coped when, as Penny had done, he asked me how I handled stress in my personal life. I told him I handled it badly and he suggested that on a future walk we explore that a bit more. I amazed myself by agreeing.

Colin dropped me back at Dunhalla at about twelve-thirty. After I'd had some lunch I decided I'd put together a chicken casserole. I admit I'd now gone from trying to be realistic in my expectations to hoping Rachel would join me for dinner.

I'd just put all the prepared ingredients into the casserole dish when Steven called. He sounded unusually flustered as he spoke. "Sorry to bother you, Jack, but we need a favour," he said.

"Not a bother. What do you need?" I asked.

"It's Sophie. She was chopping vegetables – sliced her finger – it's a very deep cut. I phoned the medical centre. They said, if I can, I should drive her down to the hospital in Broadford to get the wound stitched."

"Oh no, poor Sophie," I said. "How can I help?"

"Thing is – Miriam – she's having a nap. She's got a bit of a cold and has been a bit grizzly, so I don't want to wake her and besides that I don't think—"

"And besides that you've got enough to worry about getting Sophie down to hospital. No problem – I'll look after the wee one. On my way."

When I got to Burnside Steven said Morag had taken Bonnie for the afternoon and could be called on to help me if necessary. I assured him I'd be fine.

Naturally Miriam woke up almost as soon as her parents left. And it's fair to say she wasn't best pleased to see it was me – and not her mum or dad – who responded to her cries. I lifted her from her cot and walked the bedroom floor with her as I explained what had happened. She wasn't interested, but fortunately, she stopped crying just as my right arm decided it had had enough heavy lifting. I managed a nappy change before taking her downstairs, and even got a giggle out of her by pulling some faces while I did so.

At first she was happy to sit on the floor with her toys, then when she got fed up with that I read one of her picture books to her. Every now and then she'd give me a quizzical look, but as long as I made a face or a funny noise, or both, her frown would disappear and she'd smile.

When book reading was no longer of interest and I was running out of ideas, I remembered that William was currently into drumming using the age-old equipment of saucepan and wooden spoon. I fetched both items from the kitchen. Then I got down on the floor facing Miriam and gave a demonstration. This was an instant hit and she made her demands clear. I handed over the spoon and she was off.

And when the enchantment of drumming inevitably wore off, we played peek-a-boo. She laughed so much she gave herself hiccups and, when I mimicked her hiccups, she laughed even more. After a while she also incorporated simultaneous drumming into our game, which had me laughing too.

It wasn't surprising that neither of us heard Rachel coming into the house. And, as I had my back to the door, I don't know how long she watched us from the living-room doorway before she spoke. "You two sound like you're having a good time," she said.

Maybe it was because of the softness of her voice, maybe it was because it was Rachel's voice, or maybe it was because I was anticipating seeing her at some point that day, but her sudden interruption didn't cause me any fear or panic. On the contrary what I did feel as I turned to look at her was a sort of tentative joy. I had butterflies in my stomach and felt quite shaky. It reminded me of how it was when I was a teenager and would meet up with a girl I fancied. Then there was also the feeling of mild embarrassment at being observed in baby-entertaining mode.

"Hello," I said as I clambered to my feet, using my left arm and the sofa to steady myself. I winced as my ribs complained. "Probably shouldn't have sat on the floor," I said, managing to smile. "I had planned a slightly more dignified way of greeting you."

"Dignified is over-rated," she said. "Seeing you two having fun together like that, it was the perfect greeting." Her voice shook a little as she spoke and she looked away for a second.

I hesitated – unsure what to do or say. It was Miriam who broke the tension. "Ga-ga, ga-ga," she said, bouncing on her bottom with arms outstretched towards Rachel.

"Hello, my darling," Rachel said, going over to her granddaughter and picking her up. "Have you been a good girl for Jack?"

"She's been a wee star," I said.

"I think it's you who's been a star – stepping into the breach." Rachel's smile was warm. "Steven sent me a text about what happened. I read it when I got home and thought I better come and rescue you. But then when I got here, it didn't look to me like you needed rescuing."

"I was happy to help out. God knows Sophie and Steven have been very good to me. But I must admit I was coming to the end of my baby-entertaining repertoire."

"From what I saw, it's a most excellent repertoire. I'm sure you could have rerun it."

"Yeah – about that – how much of it did you see?" I asked, raising an eyebrow.

"I arrived during the drumming lesson. What of it?"

I couldn't help laughing at Rachel's look of mock defiance. "And you didn't have any qualms about spying on us?" I said, trying and failing to sound serious.

Rachel shrugged as she smiled. "No, not really – anyway, it wasn't spying. You two were so in the zone with what you were doing, I wanted to enjoy watching you both." She turned to Miriam. "And I enjoyed it very much," she said, before kissing her on the cheek.

As she turned back to look at me I found myself swaying a little. I put my hand on the arm of the sofa to steady myself, before sitting down. Rachel's smile disappeared. Her look now one of concern. "Jack, are you okay?" She put Miriam down on the floor with her toys and came to sit beside me.

"Yeah, yeah, I'm fine," I said. "I think it's just my day catching up with me. It's been my busiest in a while."

"You do look tired," she said, putting her hand on mine. "You should go home, get some rest. I can take over here."

She was right I was tired, but I was also reluctant to part company with her so soon. "I can wait with you till they're back," I said. "You must be tired yourself, after the drive and your busy time away."

"Don't worry about me. Anyway, they'll be back soon. Steven's follow-up text said the cut was all stitched and bandaged and they were about to leave the hospital. He probably messaged you too, but you'll have been too busy to check your phone." She stood up and held out her hand to me. I took it and got up. "Go home, Jack," she said – her voice tender as she let go of my hand.

"Yeah ... okay, I will," I said. I ran my hand through my hair. "It's just ... it's just ... I made a chicken casserole. I was going to ask you dinner. I want to spend time with you. I need to ... to ..." I closed my eyes, swallowed hard and sighed. "Sorry," I said.

Rachel touched a hand to my face."I want to be with you too," she said. "Chicken casserole sounds great. I'll come round at six. Now go home and rest."

# Chapter Sixty Six

*Rachel*

If I'd had any doubts about my love for Jack before seeing him playing with Miriam, they'd have disappeared as I watched the two of them together. But I was already sure of my love for him, and what I saw only highlighted my feelings. I was watching a good and kind man, a man who'd saved me from a very dark place, and whose love and friendship had changed my life for the better. And now it was him who was damaged and hurting, I was determined to be there for him. And I wanted more than anything to fix things between us. I could only hope he did too.

So, it's fair to say I was nervous as I prepared for the evening ahead. I was unsure whether to dress up or down. In the end I decided to aim for somewhere in the middle. When I'd been in Glasgow, during time off from book launch business, I'd visited some of my favourite shops and I'd treated myself to a pair of very smart and very expensive new jeans – definitely not ones for wearing on the croft – and a cashmere sweater. I put them on and liked what I saw when I checked in the mirror. The sweater felt so soft and, with its deep green colour and wide rolled neck, it definitely suited me. I put my hair up, and took care applying my make-up. Then a spray of perfume and I was good to go.

I called Bonnie and we set off.

"Wow," Jack said, as I slipped off my jacket. "You look nice."

"Thank you," I said, delighted with his appreciative look. I handed him the bottle of wine I'd brought and looked him up and down as I did so. He was wearing chinos rather than his usual jeans, and an open-necked, deep blue shirt with the sleeves rolled up. "You're not so bad yourself," I said.

After I'd assured him that Sophie was fine, Jack bent down to greet Bonnie who was making it known she wanted some attention too.

"I hope you don't mind me bringing her," I said. "But I'd only just collected her from Morag and it seemed a shame to walk out and leave her."

"Of course I don't mind," Jack said, as he made a fuss of her. "She's my pal, aren't you Bonnie." He straightened up and looked at me. "I'm always pleased to see her." For a second or two we held each other's gaze before he continued. "Dinner's in the oven, keeping warm, it's ready when we are. You go through." He pointed in the direction of the living-room. "I'll get us a glass of wine."

I was standing with my back to the wood-burner, Bonnie curled up on the rug at my feet, and both of us enjoying the warmth, when Jack joined me.

"I've missed this," I said, as he handed me my wine.

"Wine?" he said.

"No, being here. Sharing a meal. Being with you."

"Ah, right," he said, looking unsure as he cleared his throat. "That's ... that's good."

"Actually, I was just remembering the first time you made me dinner, and I arrived early. You were in the shower and met me in the hall wearing only a towel." I hoped this memory would help him relax. It seemed to – as for a moment at least – he smiled.

But then his smile faded. He gulped some wine. "A lot's happened since then – and not all of it good."

"Indeed," I said. "But you and me ... a lot of that, what we had ... it was *very* good ... or at least it was for me."

"Was it?" Jack's tone was as sharp as the look he gave me. "Really? You've no regrets?"

"Regrets? No, definitely not. You saved me Jack, saved me from myself, from ... from all the sadness and doubt and guilt ... all that ... that shit I was going through. And I hope ... I hope I can do the same for you. If you'll let me, that is." I stopped as my voice faltered. Emotion was getting the better of me. My plan to keep things reasonably light while also having a heart-to-heart seemed to have evaporated. It was my turn to gulp down some wine.

Jack put his glass down on the coffee table and raised his hands in a gesture of apology. "I'm sorry," he said. "I don't know if I can do this. I thought I could but ..." He looked down at the floor, one hand behind his neck.

Without stopping to think, I put down my drink and walked over to him. I put my hands on his shoulders as I let my tears fall. "I love you, Jack. Do you hear me? I love you ... and I want to be with you." I shook him, trying to get him to look at me. "Don't you dare shut me out," I said, shaking him again.

He raised his head and looked at me. "What did you say?" he said.

"I said, don't shut me out – please – don't."

"No before that. What did you say?"

"I said, I ... I want to be with you. I love you. I love you ... you ..." My sobs were now robbing me of my ability to speak so I took to shaking him again.

"Please," he said, taking hold of my hands. "Please, my shoulder can't take any more shaking."

"Oh God, I'm sorry," I said. "I forgot. How could I forget? Oh, God—"

"No, Rachel, no, it's okay. I was teasing you." He let go of my hands and stroked my face, wiping at my tears with his thumbs.

We stood there looking at each other, his hands now either side of my face. "Tell me again," he said, his voice soft now.

"I love you," I said. "I love you – and I can't bear the thought of losing you."

And then we were in each other's arms, kissing, then stopping to look at each other, and then kissing some more. I was unbuttoning his shirt when I said, "Will dinner be okay in the oven for another wee while?"

"Oh yes," Jack breathed in my ear as he kissed my neck. "It'll be just fine."

"Good," I said, leaning back to look at him. "Bed?"

"Bed," he murmured, slipping his hands under my sweater.

# Chapter Sixty Seven

*Jack*

Going to bed with Rachel was the one outcome I hadn't even dared to hope for when I'd anticipated our evening together, and I couldn't quite believe what was happening as I followed her into the bedroom.

We resumed kissing and undressing each other immediately, and I confess, as we fell together onto the bed, I was shaking as much with nerves as with desire. I was so scared of getting it wrong. Rachel stopped kissing me and put her hands on my chest as we lay on our sides facing each other. "You're trembling," she said. "Are you okay?"

She looked so concerned that I decided not to fob her off with reassurances that I was fine, and decided on the truth instead."Not really," I said. "I mean I want to do this ... but it seems so ... so significant ... and I'm not in great shape either."

"Oh, Jack," she said. "Relax, it'll be fine. Allow me." She resumed kissing me as she pushed me onto my back. She kissed my mouth and neck and moved down to my chest. She paused there a moment to run her finger along the scar left by the removal of the bullet. She looked at me as she did so, tears in her eyes again as she said, "Oh, my darling." Then her kisses and caresses resumed and it wasn't long before my anxieties disappeared and were replaced by a level of desire that I don't think I've ever experienced before. It went beyond even our first time together. I let Rachel continue to take the lead. She was gentle and careful and brought things to a natural and incredibly satisfying conclusion.

However, we'd barely got our breath back when I wanted more. "My turn," I said, as I took her in my arms. I ignored the twinging and complaints from my shoulder, arm and ribs. And instead, I enjoyed the sound of her moans and gasps. I became lost in the scent and sensation of her body until, once more, we rolled apart sated and exhausted.

"That was amazing," I said, as she curled up beside me.

"Yeah, it was quite nice," she said grinning at me.

"Nice?" I said. "Nice? Is that the best you can do?" I smiled as I stroked her face.

Her look was stern but then there was a smile too. "When I'm this hungry, yes." She rolled away from me and got out of bed. "Come on," she said, as she started getting dressed. "I came here for my dinner and it's high time you delivered."

We sat facing other at the table by the window in the living-room. It was dark outside and all we could see as we looked out were the lights of Uig harbour across the loch. Inside the only light came from the flames in the woodburner and the candles on the table.

"Before we start," I said, after I'd served up the casserole and filled our wine glasses.

"There's something I need to say to you."

"Okay," Rachel said.

I paused before replying, listening to the crackling of the logs and Bonnie's gentle snoring as I took a moment. "My love for you, Rachel ... it never went away. Through it all ... whatever *it* all was ... whatever stupid things I've said and done ... that has never changed. I love you, and I want you back in my life."

She reached across the table and put her hand on mine. "That's what I want too," she said.

"I ... I sent you a text – when you were away in Israel. I said to remember that whatever happened I loved you."

"Yes, I got it. I ... I've looked at it many times since then," she said as she stroked my wrist with her thumb. "It seems you meant it."

I nodded, too emotional to speak.

Rachel squeezed my hand and smiled her beautiful smile before sitting back. "And now," she said, "can we please eat?"

So we did – and I allowed myself to relax. I even found myself laughing as I reflected on her complete lack of dinner table conversation.

"What's so funny?" she asked.

"I'd almost forgotten how much you enjoy your food," I said. She was eating quickly and with obvious relish judging by the appreciative sounds she made every now and then.

"Sorry," she said. "It's probably not pretty. But I was starving and this is so good – the chicken, the mash, the gravy – and do I detect a hint of chilli?"

"You do," I said. "And there's no need to apologise. You're a rewarding person to cook for."

"Well," she said, as she scraped the last remnants onto her fork, "you're a great chef and you can cook for me anytime. That was delicious."

My feeling of relaxation continued as we had our dessert. It was simple, a scoop each of vanilla, chocolate and salted caramel ice-cream, but it was Rachel's favourite and she assured me I definitely got extra points for remembering that.

It was nearly nine o'clock by the time I'd loaded the dishwasher and we'd settled side by side on the sofa. We stared into the flames behind the stove's glass as we sipped our coffee. Bonnie had managed to drag herself over, stupefied by the heat as she was, and resettle herself at my feet.

I asked Rachel about how the book launch tour had gone. And I enjoyed listening to her enthusiastic account of the talks and signings she'd done.

"It was good of you to fit in the visit to Poppy's school," I said. "She was so excited about it and very impressed with how it went."

"It was a pleasure. I was treated like a celebrity – and Poppy was amazing. She introduced me to the school assembly and then she was part of a team of interviewers from all the classes who did a Q and A with me."

I put my hand on her face and stroked her cheek. "It's one of the many things that made me fall in love with you, you know."

"What's that?" she said, leaning into my hand.

"Your bond with Poppy. It ... it seems so strong."

"It is. And ditto that. Seeing you with Miriam, it meant so much to me seeing how you cared for her. It ... it sort of melted my heart."

"That's good to hear," I said. "That I can still touch your heart."

"Not only touch it," Rachel said. "You've sort of taken up residence there."

# Chapter Sixty Eight

*Rachel*

After we'd finished our coffee we took Bonnie out for a walk. It was a cloudy night so there was no stargazing to slow us down, and the cold wind and drizzly rain also meant there was no incentive to linger. But it wasn't just a desire to get indoors that made Jack's suggestion we head back so welcome, it was the fact he wanted us to go back together to his place rather than me going home.

When we got in, he fed the stove with more logs and we resettled ourselves on the sofa. At first we sat quietly, me with my legs curled underneath me and Jack hunched forwards, both of us watching the flames as they stretched and leapt around the new fuel.

It was Jack who broke the silence. "I'd like to begin ... to try and tell you the whole sorry story," he said, still staring straight ahead.

"Okay," I said, with a mixture of relief and trepidation. Yes, I wanted him to open up, wanted to understand what had happened to him – and to us – but I realised it wasn't going to be easy to hear. And it would probably be even harder for Jack to tell it.

Although I knew a bit about the shooting of Jack's colleague, and about Gray's motives for wanting to kill him, it was still shocking to hear it from Jack himself.

I was even more shocked when he told me the full extent of the symptoms he'd been suffering since the beginning of the year. And, when he admitted it was a fear of falling asleep – and having the nightmares and their aftermath in front of me – that had made him reluctant to sleep with me, I was devastated.

"Why didn't you tell me?" I said.

"I know ... I should have ... but I couldn't. I told Alasdair and I told Maddie, and that was hard enough, and they both said I should tell you—"

"How could you tell them and not tell me?" I couldn't keep the hurt I felt out of my voice. "I thought we were close, that we had the kind of relationship where we could tell each other anything."

"I ... I was ashamed."

"Ashamed? You shouldn't have been—"

"I know ... but I was. And it wasn't only that I was ashamed of the panic attacks and everything, but I was also ashamed of the cause. There was the awful shame and crucifying guilt over what had happened to Mike. I felt responsible ... and it was hard to admit, even to myself." Jack leaned forward, his head in his hands. "It all caught me unawares. I thought I was okay with it, but it turns out I was merely distracted. It was just waiting till I let my guard down."

I moved closer to him, stroked his arm as he paused for a moment.

"And I also couldn't tell you because of what you'd been through yourself," he said, continuing to look at the floor. "You'd been so strong and you'd recovered. And there was me ... being pathetic and needy. You were looking forward, focussed on new things, and I was ... I was all over the place. Then on top of all that I got jealous, couldn't handle you going back to Israel or seeing Eitan. And then the icing on the cake ... my stupid proposal." He sighed.

"Oh, Jack," I said.

He sat back and looked at me. "It was like the more I tried

to put things right, the worse it got. I couldn't even see you off properly when you left for Israel. And then it seemed only fair to back off. It ... it seemed easier somehow. You had your work to do. I had the job in Edinburgh. I convinced myself it wasn't a big deal. But..."

"But what?" I said, desperate for him to continue.

"But I was gutted. I missed you so much. Couldn't believe how stupid I'd been, but couldn't see a way back to you."

"I thought ...when you didn't want to keep in touch ... I thought you wanted to end it," I said.

"It was never that. I'd got myself into a hole that I didn't know how to get out of. Then, ironically, as it turns out, taking the police job helped me. I enjoyed the work. It felt good to be on Gray's tail and to have helped build a case against him. The guilt about Mike lessened because of that and the bad dreams stopped. I felt more positive about everything, about me, about us. I'd made up my mind to come back and sort things out. But then ... then Gray got me, and I realised I'd put you in danger and then he..." Jack covered his face with his hands and curled forwards again in a defensive pose. I put my hand on his arm and could feel him trembling.

"Jack," I said, moving even closer to him. "Jack, look at me."

He turned and I put my arms round him. "That's enough for now," I said, as I stroked his back. "You need to rest. Let's leave it there for the moment. You should get to bed, get some sleep."

He moved to look at me. He tried to smile but he looked both tired and strained. "Yeah, you're probably right," he said. "But there's more I want to say, and ... and besides that I don't want this time together to be over."

I smiled at him. "It won't be over. I'm not going anywhere ... except up to bed with you."

# Chapter Sixty Nine

*Jack*

It was a strange mixture of normal and weird to have spent the night with Rachel. And making love and then falling asleep beside her felt as good – if not better – as it had always done. I did have a bit of an episode during the night, but, as she'd done before, Rachel woke me gently from the torture of my dream and calmly helped me come back to reality.

Then, after breakfast Rachel suggested we go for a walk – something I was happy to agree to.

"Great," she said. "I'm going home to shower and change. Call for me in an hour – and wrap up well – waterproofs, scarf, the lot."

I did as I was told. "So, where are we heading?" I asked, as Rachel drove out onto the track.

"Neist Point, if you're up for it. It's quite a hard climb on the return leg, but worth the effort."

"Oh, I'm up for it," I said.

The descent to Skye's most westerly point was steep. We followed the sloping path and the flight of steps that took us from the car park to a wide grassy area below. Bonnie scampered on ahead – but never so far that she couldn't keep an eye on us. We walked hand-in-hand, skirting the edge of a hill before coming to the imposing lighthouse and the keepers' former living quarters.

And I felt so at ease in Rachel's company that I had to remind myself not to take anything for granted.

We passed by the foghorn on its concrete block and paused to take in the spectacular wide-open view of the sea. Gannets circled overhead and a brisk, nippy wind blew in our faces as the waters of the Minch churned below us.

It was bracing, but refreshing, standing there – and I breathed deeply, enjoying the feeling of wellbeing this place had induced in me. I had a sense of being buffeted but also of being firmly grounded. I became aware of Rachel watching me and turned to look at her.

"You look as if this place is speaking to you," she said. "What's it saying to you?"

I laughed. "You sound like you're channelling Colin," I said.

"Colin?"

"Colin Crichton – the *Walk the Talk* guy I've been doing the therapy walks with."

"I'd like to hear more about that – and your other therapy sessions – when you're ready, that is."

I nodded. "I reckon I'm about ready."

"No rush," she said. "For now, let's walk."

We walked back towards the hill and then, with Bonnie on the lead, we branched off along a sheep track which took us past a flock of grazing sheep and on out to the cliff edge. Here the view of the nearby headland and its distinctive cliffs was even more spectacular than the earlier one. And, again, we stood and stared as the sea swirled and crashed far below us and all sorts of seabirds swooped, landed and took off again.

"You weren't lying," I gasped, as I paused to get my breath when we were half-way up the steps on the way back to the car.

Rachel, who was beginning to stride ahead, stopped and turned to look at me. "Wimp," she said, laughing.

"It didn't seem that bad on the way down. But it's damn near vertical," I said, leaning on the handrail. I managed a smile. "It's fine, don't wait for me, you go on."

She came towards me with her arms outstretched. "I'll wait for you as long as it takes," she said, before kissing me. Then she took my hand and said, "Hold on to me and I'll pull you back up."

"Would you like to come in for some lunch?" Rachel said, as she let Bonnie out of the back of the Land Rover. We'd just got back from our walk and were standing on the driveway at Burnside. "Although I'd completely understand if you'd like a bit of time to yourself."

I shook my head and smiled at her. "You're amazing," I said.

She frowned. "You mean in a good way?"

"Oh yes, a very good way. To be honest, I was thinking that – that I'd like a bit of time on my own. But I didn't want to offend you by saying so."

"I'd never be offended by that, Jack. We all need time to ourselves ... even the closest of couples."

That she referred to us a couple brought a huge smile to my face. And I could tell by the smile that came back to me that Rachel realised what she'd said too.

"I'm sorry," I said. "I just need a little time to ... you know. I was worried you'd think I was shutting you out again."

"I understand, Jack. You've been through so much. You need time to process, to gather yourself. And I do too. Giving one another space is healthy. It's not the same as shutting someone out ... or being shut out." She gave me a meaningful smile.

"You should run a relationship academy," I said.

"I feel like I am." She came up to me and put her arms round my neck. "But don't worry, you're proving to be a star pupil."

"I'm doing my best," I said, before kissing her.

Then, as she stepped away from me she turned and said, "And if you want to call round later, please do. You're welcome to join me for dinner – but no pressure."

It had been pretty intense since Rachel and I'd got together the day before and I did need some down time, as Rachel rightly said, to process and gather myself, but within a couple of hours I was missing her. At first I tried to give my brain a break by distracting myself. I emptied the dishwasher, tidied up the kitchen, cleaned out and reset the stove, and made the bed. Although that last activity didn't exactly help to keep my mind off Rachel. I sat on the bed with the bedsheet in my hands – hands that no longer trembled. I could smell her unique scent, and sitting there in the peace and quiet, the room bright with sunshine, her smell alone felt so calming. A tear rolled down my cheek. We were a couple. Rachel had made that clear. She was good for me, there was no doubt about that. And I wanted so much to be good for her.

Yes, it had been difficult opening up to her and letting her in, letting her see how broken I was, but it had also been a release. It was similar to how it had been opening up to Penny, but the fact that Rachel was listening out of love – a love I still wasn't quite convinced I deserved – made me feel both humble and grateful. It also made me impatient to tell her the rest of what I'd been going through.

So by mid-afternoon I was back at Burnside. I knocked and went in. Bonnie was snoozing in her basket by the Aga. She lifted her head and wagged her tail, but made only a half-hearted attempt to get up. I gave her a quick pat and told her she was a good girl.

"I'm in the study. Come through," Rachel called, in response to my shout of hallo.

She was sitting working at her desk when I went in. "Sorry," I said, feeling suddenly nervous. "You're busy. I should have phoned first."

"Not all," she said. "I'm glad you've come. I wasn't sure you would." And the warmth of her smile helped steady my nerves.

"I ... I wanted to ... to talk to you some more," I said. "If you can bear it."

"Hmm, a cup of tea and a comfy seat," she said, getting to her feet, "and I reckon I'll cope."

I was instructed to go and put more coal on the living-room fire while Rachel made the tea. And soon we were sitting beside each other on the sofa. And, as the coal crackled and the clock ticked, I prepared myself to tell I Rachel everything I still needed to tell her.

"It was terrifying," I said, as I began. "Being kidnapped and held captive – I've never been so scared."

Rachel slid closer and took my hand. "Take your time," she said.

And so I told her. I told her about the beatings, and the pain, about the stuff Gray had said and how he planned to kill me. And I told her of the sickening, visceral fear and how when I heard the gunshot, I'd thought my life was over. This led me on to talking about the return of my PTSD symptoms, along with all the feelings of guilt and shame – and then the depression.

As always Rachel quietly listened. Although she said very little, she would occasionally nod or put her hand on my arm, and at all times conveyed nothing but attentiveness and sympathy. She was so open, so receptive, and so supportive towards me that I was able to be more honest with her than I'd been with anyone – including the medics.

"Even when you weren't actually with me, you saved me," I said. "When Gray was doing his worst – it was thoughts of you that gave me comfort. And when the beatings and the pain got too much ... I took refuge in you."

"Oh, my love," she whispered. She stroked my face, tears in her eyes as she looked at me. "But it's over now and you're recovering."

I nodded, not hiding my own tears.

"So tell me about the help you're getting," she said.

It felt good to move on to the positive stuff. I told her about Dr Matheson and Penny and a bit more about Colin, and about the treatment they were giving me. And I admitted that in spite of my initial reluctance and scepticism, I felt that the medication and the therapies were already helping.

"Thank you, Jack," she said when I'd finished.

"What for?"

"For your honesty, for opening up, for trusting me. I appreciate it – and it makes me love you all the more."

Unable to hold her gaze, I looked away, rubbed at the tension in my forehead with my fingertips. "It's me who should be grateful," I said. "I don't feel like ... like I deserve your love."

# Chapter Seventy

*Rachel*

"It's not a case of you *deserving* my love," I said, as I stroked Jack's arm. "I loved you before all of this, and I loved you during it, and I still love you now. And it's because, through it all, you remained you – the man I fell in love with the night we met."

Jack ran his hands through his hair and I sensed he needed a minute, so I got up to put more coal on the fire. It was almost dark outside and I switched on the table lamps. I glanced at the clock. It was nearly half-past-five. When I looked back at Jack he was sitting back with his eyes closed.

I went through to the kitchen and fed Bonnie. I also put the cottage pie I'd prepared earlier into the Aga to heat. And as soon as Bonnie had finished eating I sent her through to Jack while I tidied up and set the table.

When I went back through to the living-room Bonnie was sitting at Jack's feet and he was talking softly to her as he stroked her.

"I thought you might enjoy each other's company," I said, as I sat down beside him.

Jack smiled at me. "She's as good a listener as you," he said.

"Yeah, and she never interrupts," I said. "But if she could talk I reckon she'd ask you to stay for dinner," I said.

"And I would accept her invitation," Jack said.

"Good," I said. "I was hoping you'd say that."

Jack nodded, but he looked serious and slightly uncomfortable.

"What's wrong?" I said, sitting down beside him.

"There's something I want to say ... something I should have said before now."

"Oh," I said, my heart thumping with fear that he was going to say something I didn't want to hear.

"I'm so sorry," he said.

"Right ... what for exactly?"

"For the way I treated you. I'm sorry I wasn't honest with you when I first started having the nightmares and the panic attacks. And I'm sorry I was less than supportive of you going back to Israel, and sorry I behaved like a jealous prick, that I didn't keep in touch, that I proposed, and that I sent you away from the hospital. For all of it. I'm sorry."

My heart rate returned to normal as relief took over. "I appreciate you apologising, but don't give yourself a hard time. Grief, guilt and shame are a toxic combination. Believe me I know. I completely lost my way after Finlay died. I withdrew from everything and everyone, pushed away anyone who tried to help me. I blamed myself for his death, for not stopping him from joining the Marines, I was ashamed that I'd failed as a mother, ashamed I'd become estranged from Sophie, but couldn't see how to fix it. You know what a mess I was."

"Yes but—"

"But nothing, Jack. I knew ... deep down I knew ... that the way you were behaving, it wasn't something personal against me. But I didn't know how to ask you about it, how to reach you – and I probably should have tried harder. But what I do know is I never stopped loving you. I'm also extremely grateful. Grateful to that young lad Danny, to the police, the medics ... and yes, even to Bridget, that your life was saved and that we've been given a second chance."

Jack hesitated before he spoke. He seemed to be struggling with various emotions. "I'll ... I'll let Bridget know," he said.

"No need," I said. "I already did."

"Ah," Jack said.

"Yeah, we'll never be best friends, her and me, but Bridget's all right."

"She has an equally grudging respect for you," Jack said, smiling properly now.

"Okay enough about her," I said. "But I'd like to hear more about Danny, why he helped the police, and about him visiting you in hospital." I stood up. "So come through and you can tell me over dinner."

"He sounds like a remarkable young man," I said, when we'd finished eating and Jack had finished telling me Danny's story. "And it seems you two have a bit of a bond."

"I like to think so," Jack said. "In fact Danny's situation has got me thinking ... about some work I'd like to do ... when I'm ...when I'm better."

"Oh?" I said.

"Yeah, there's the photography job I told you about and I'm looking forward to that. But I want to do something more, something *worthwhile* with my time. I miss work, miss having a challenge and a sense of achievement."

I got up, began clearing the table, not sure what he was leading up to, not sure if I wanted to hear what he was considering. But I needed to know. "What sort of work?" I said, my mouth suddenly dry.

"Not sure exactly – at the moment it's just ideas I'd like to explore. I'd like it to be a ... a sort of tribute to Mike and Lawrie. Maybe set up a mentoring and opportunities scheme for young folk at risk of offending, youngsters like Danny."

I put my hands over my mouth as relief ran through me. "So not police work, then?" I said. "You're not going back to Historic Crimes or ... or anything?"

"What? No ... no, I'm not..." He got to his feet and came over to me. "Are you okay?" he said putting his hands on my shoulders.

"Yes, yes I'm fine," I said, looking up at him, at the concern in his expression. "I was afraid you were going to go back to the police, that you'd be putting yourself at risk again. And, yes, I know that's hypocritical. After all, I expect you to support my work choices and … and I would support you if it was what you wanted to do … I would … but I'm so glad you don't." I blinked hard. "Sorry," I said."They're tears of relief."

"Hey, hey now," Jack said, putting his hands either side of my face, before kissing me. "Here, you sit down. I'll make us some coffee to take through."

I did as I was told.

"I know you would support me … it seems you would no matter what," Jack said, as he spooned coffee into the percolator. "And Ailsa did offer me more work, and I said I'd consider it. But the way I feel just now – I think I'll probably pass."

"Good," I said. "But I think your idea of supporting vulnerable young people is great. I'd love to explore the possibilities with you … if you'd like me to."

"I'd like that very much," Jack said. Then, as he poured the coffee he said, "Another thing I'd like very much is if you'd show me some of what you're working on now – the stuff for the peace book."

"You would?" I said. "You're really interested?" I clasped my hands together, unable to hide my surprise and delight.

Jack grinned at me. "I'm really interested."

I got up from the table. "Come on then," I said. "Bring the coffee through to the study and I'll show you some of it right now."

# Chapter Seventy One

*Jack*

To say I was impressed by what Rachel showed me would be an understatement. The sketches she'd done were brilliant. There were some incredible photos too. And the video clips of the discussions and interviews she'd taken part in were amazing. And I don't only mean in a technical context. I could see the photographer was a skilled professional – but what impressed me more was the content. Rachel too, was a skilled professional, and she was also passionate and committed. I could have listened to her talking about her time away, and about her ideas and experiences all night. And I told her so.

"And I could talk about it all night," she said. "But I think two hours is more than enough for now."

"Yeah, I suppose you're right," I said, reluctant to bring the evening to an end. I looked at my watch. It was just after nine. We both got up from the desk. "I should probably—"

"Yes," Rachel said. "You should probably come with me and Bonnie for her evening walk and then you should probably come back here for the night."

I laughed. "Hmm, I probably should."


"I've actually been thinking about something similar to you," Rachel said as we set out along the track. "Being back in the Middle East and working on the peace book ... it got me thinking

... I'd like to do something in Finlay's memory ... something of my own besides the book ... for peace, for a ... a better world."

"What sort of thing?" I asked.

"I don't know yet, not exactly, but something that would bring people together, get them communicating, accepting – even if not necessarily agreeing with – each other's point of view. Nothing large scale ... or trying to change the world overnight, but something that would lead to small, individual actions for peace and understanding, even if it it's just at a local level."

"Sounds like a brilliant idea," I said.

"Thanks, I was hoping you'd say that." Rachel slipped her arm through mine. "And I'm hoping maybe we can share ideas for both our projects, maybe there's even some common ground."

"That sounds like a brilliant idea too," I said.

"Oh, and another thank you," she said. "I only remembered when I was showing you all the photos and stuff. Gideon – I owe you a thank you on his behalf."

"What for?"

"For the encouragement you gave him regarding his photography. It meant a lot to him. But it meant even more to me. I was so touched when he told me. So thank you." She squeezed my arm.

"A pleasure," I said.

"It's good isn't it?" she said.

"What is?"

"How we're involved with each other's families – me with Poppy, and you with Miriam and Gideon."

"Yeah, it is good," I said, smiling in the darkness.

We paused at the end of the track, looked out across the loch and then up at the stars. And the sigh I let out was one of contentment, gratitude and yes, peace. I knew I had some way to go before I'd be fully recovered, but I also knew I would put in the work – and I would recover. I put my arm round Rachel's shoulders and, when she looked up at me, I pulled her to me and kissed her.

"So where do we go from here?" I said, as I held her.

"We move on. One step at a time, we move on."

"As a couple?" I said.

"As two people who love and care for each other, who give each other space, and who are honest with one another."

"Right," I said.

"I want to be with you, Jack. Whether we live as a conventional couple or not, I want you as my friend, my lover, and my partner for as long as we're both still breathing."

I let her words sink in. I let myself believe them. I let myself punch the air – with my good arm. "Yes!" I shouted making Rachel laugh and Bonnie bark and wag her tail as she ran in circles round us.

"So that's settled?" she said.

"Settled," I said, before kissing her again for a very long time.

## THE END

Anne Stormont writes contemporary, compassionate and thoughtful fiction. Her stories are for readers who enjoy a good romantic story, but who also like romance that is laced with realism and where the main characters may be older but not necessarily wiser.

Anne can be found on Facebook and Twitter and you can also find out more about her on her blog and on her website.

Facebook: www.facebook.com/annestormontauthor
Twitter: www.twitter.com/writeanne
Blog at https://putitinwriting.me
Website at www.annestormont.co.uk

# Also by
# Anne Stormont

## *Displacement*

First book in the series of the Rachel and Jack novels.

*It's never too late to fall in love, but the past can get in the way of a happy future.*

From the Scottish Hebrides to the Middle-East, *Displacement* is an intense love story where romance and realism, and the personal and the political meet head on.

Divorce, the death of her soldier son and estrangement from her daughter, leave Hebridean crofter, Rachel Campbell, grief stricken, lonely and lost.

Forced retirement due to a heart condition leaves former Edinburgh policeman Jack Baxter needing to take stock and find a new direction for his life.

After the two of them meet in dramatic circumstances on a wild winter's night on the island of Skye, a tentative friendship develops between them, despite their very different personalities. Gradually, however, their feelings for each other go beyond friendship.

But Rachel is about to go to Israel-Palestine where she plans to explore her Jewish heritage and to learn more about this contested land. And Jack is already in what is, for him, the ideal relationship – one where no commitment or fidelity is required.

Will they be able to overcome the obstacles that lie in the way of their deepening love?

Will Rachel find a way forward and let herself love again?

Can Jack trust himself not to hurt her?

For readers who enjoy a mature, romantic, and thought-provoking story.

# *Change of Life*

*A tale of life. A poignant mix of sadness, hope and love.*

Be careful what you wish for…

Wife to Tom and mother to four adolescent children, Rosie feels taken for granted as she juggles family life and her work as a teacher. She longs for a change.

When she hits a teenage boy with her car, her life veers into unpredictable and uncharted territory. The boy is Robbie - and Rosie discovers he is part of a terrible secret that Tom has kept from her for seventeen years. Then Rosie is diagnosed with breast cancer.

Rosie leaves home and begins the fight for her life. Meanwhile heart surgeon, Tom, learns what it means to be a husband and father. He struggles to keep his family together and strives to get his wife back.

*'A good convincing voice that had me identifying with the characters from the outset.' David Wishart, Novelist*

*'It's a real emotional roller-coaster of a read. I was completely involved in the characters and their lives.' Romantic Novelists' Association.*

Lightning Source UK Ltd.
Milton Keynes UK
UKHW01f2204170918
329067UK00001BA/3/P